THE
LAST
PARTY

THE
LAST
PARTY

SB GAMBLE

The Good Fight
Publishing

FIRST EDITION
10 9 8 7 6 5 4 3 2 1

Names: SB Gamble, 1984-
Title: The Last Party / by SB Gamble.
First Edition: Chicago, Illinois 2016.

ISBN 978-0-9973869-0-5 (paperback)

Cover photo by Shironosov
Cover design by Marlon Joshua Namoro
Book layout by Michelle Lange | Whack Publications
Author's photo by Annalise Freytag

ACKNOWLEDGEMENTS

Thanks, mom (of course) for always allowing me to be who I am and giving me the strength to believe in the good in the world. And my sister, Sheena, my first reader—my stories would never exist without you. I love you both so much. Thanks to the rest of my family who taught me how laugh and love.

To my brilliant partner Philip Taylor, I don't know how you manage to love a writer, but I'm glad you do. My homeys, Annalise Freytag and Tahif Attiek aka Nunca Duerma, thanks for always pushing me to greatness and all the drinks, shots and wild night in these streets. To my co-conspirator Michelle Lange, you are so smart, patient and the by far the coolest person I know. Also Casey Coker, you are light in darkness and the best writing partner I could ask for.

Um and every friend, co-worker and roommate I've ever cornered and talked into the ground about my book, thank you all.

This is for those first perilous nights in the city, when anything could happen, when we were all so young, reckless and beautiful... for those first few nights when we were utterly invincible...

R ussell Cowell tossed back a whiskey and soda and worked his way through the bar. He glanced over the bar through his fellow denizens and shoved past them. Around him, they offered up their voices to the raucous yelling, thumping music, and howling sirens. It was another night at Broken Jaw, a tight, dark bar in Logan Square. The place was nearing its maximum capacity. Over heads and through the mass, at the far wall, he saw Ava. Her face was tight and her arms were locked across her chest. All night she had been putting on a brave front for him. He wanted to appreciate her efforts, but he'd had enough of her wincing at the loud music, the compact space, and the sticky floor below.

She'd insisted on coming out to this bar with Russell and his roommates, and now here she was, tense and wedged tightly in her misery. Ava was beautiful, small and slender, perched along the wall with her designer heels and short dress. He swayed in his own inebriation and assessed the lithe of her body in slim-fitting floral. The sight of her, glancing at him through the discordance, stirred him. Her short hair left the delicate smooth skin of her neck exposed. He knew from experience that delicate skin ran over every surface of her body, and how, if he could save this evening, she would willingly open herself and give way to his massive bulk. But trying to turn this evening into something she would enjoy dried up in those two shots of tequila and three drinks.

Now all he saw was how ill-suited Ava was against the black night. Her cocktail dress clashed with the women in ripped jeans and heavy work boots. While people let go, she wound herself tighter. Russell stood locked in her gaze on the fractured, filthy linoleum, surrounded by a rising swell of drunkenness inside a seedy bar that seemed to consume its sordid patrons. She remained guileless while Russell was a tenant to this warm, familiar drunkenness. He was a keen apparition of Broken Jaw and so many other bars like it.

When he made his way over, he gave her a feeble smile.

"Are you having a good time?" she asked under her strained pretext.

"I'm fine," he said, getting close to her ear to be heard over the music. "You want something at the bar?"

"No," she said. "The glasses here are kind of dirty."

"Really?"

"Just joking," she said quickly. Unconvincingly.

Before he could ask more, fingers tapped his shoulder from behind. Russell turned to face a beautiful black woman staring at him with a coy smile. She balanced two drinks— one clear, one copper—in one hand, extended the other, and slightly bowed. Russell raised his eyebrows and chuckled.

"You're Russell Cowell," she said.

"Yeah, and you are?"

"Isabelle Boldwyn." She flashed a quick smile at Ava and offered her hand.

Ava sneered and limply shook it. "Ava Von Hoffman, Russell's girlfriend."

"You're just lovely," Isabelle said, unshaken, turning her attention back to Russell. "Look, I'm sure this probably isn't the time, but how do I put this?"

Isabelle shifted her heels and offered Russell a glass. "You drink whiskey, right?"

Russell accepted, sipped the drink, and turned to Ava, whose frown deepened. He shrugged helplessly and focused on Isabelle, who was pulling at a loose curl hanging from her afro. Russell soon found himself as nervous as she had become. Clearly, the woman wanted something and was searching for the words.

"Thanks for the whiskey," Russell said. He grabbed Ava's arm and moved through the crowd in search of his roommates.

"Does that sort of thing happen often?" Ava asked, her body stiff with tension.

"What?" Russell asked, reaching for something like innocence.

"Strange women buying you drinks."

Russell set the drink on a nearby table and glanced down haplessly. "I don't even know who she is."

Ava waved him off. "Can I get some fresh air?"

Russell sighed and his shoulders went slack as they waded through the people outside onto the street. Weary patrons milled around Broken Jaw and the nearby bars that shape the point where Milwaukee and California avenues cross. The people—a boorish assemblage of piercings, gauged ears, tattoos, flannel shirts, and tight skirts—carried the party in their steps and on their shoulders to the street. Most of them were cold and beaten by the night. Brothers in this shared set of circumstances, they made fast and fleeting friendships, too drunk to exercise caution. Seldom breaking from the steady oscillation of traffic moving bar to bar, they stumbled upon cracked concrete, chain link fences, and brick walls that opened into deep, black chasmal alleys. Their lips carried cigarette smoke and laughter, and somewhere close, Russell could smell the sharp musk of burning weed.

Russell and Ava stepped over flattened cigarette butts and crushed paper cups toward the curb. Closing his arms around her small waist, Russell bent to kiss her. She raked her tiny hands through the coarse bristle of his beard gracefully, forgetting the tension between them. Eclipsed in red by a nearby stoplight, Ava's face glowed crimson and softened.

"I'm sorry you're having such a terrible time," Russell said.

"It's just everyone here is so …"

"I know it's not your scene."

Ava Von Hoffman was the daughter of the high-grossing investment banker, Hayes Von Hoffman, of Midstate Regional Bank. Her father was also Russell's colleague—a fact that weighed on him. Russell spent his days as a lowly personal banker. A fluke job, a necessary evil, a means to pay the bills. He was a simpleton amongst a quandary of sales goals, federal banking regulations, profit margins, and revenues, which constructed his weekly existence in one of Chicago's most lucrative banks. His girlfriend's father, on the other hand, dealt with high-powered clients, tripled company earnings, and garnered huge bonuses. Von Hoffman's God-like success landed him on the pages of business magazines. Russell, meanwhile, was dating the daughter of Midstate Regional Bank's shiniest knight, bringing her to the darkest, grimmest corners of the city.

Nearby, a guy lurched forward to spew vomit. A few people laughed and Ava went pale with disgust, a voyeur who had seen too much. Russell's jaw clenched as an aching suspicion realized itself, and Russell found himself wanting to apologize over and over. He had been drawn to her for the very reason he wanted to apologize. This party world was his, but she shouldn't be out here, this late at night, on these streets, with their prolonged threats of dealers, homeless men, and muggings. She could no longer conceal how out of place she was, and it was almost embarrassing.

She should be home, safe in her penthouse apartment.

"Let me get you out of here," he breathed in her ear.

"Come with me," she said, stretching her arm up to his shoulders.

"Ava, I'm gonna stay with my roommates."

"Are you sure?"

"They're drunk. Gotta get them home, too. I'll get you a cab."

Her expression deflated and her arms dropped to her side. She nodded, then said, "No man left behind."

"Nothing so noble," Russell said with playful smile. "I just need them to pay half the rent."

They both knew that was a lie. His loyalty to them ran deep.

Russell inched into the street, sticking his hand out, waving toward the small cab a block back. He reached back, pulling Ava toward him as the cab stopped alongside them. He pulled a twenty-dollar bill from his wallet and kissed her again, guiding her into the cab.

"Good night," she said. Russell watched her cab roll east through the neighborhood and out of sight, then stepped back on the curb. He stuck a cigarette in his mouth and patted his pocket for a lighter. Isabelle appeared from the street, weaving past a couple to approach him and fishing a lighter from her purse. He lit his cigarette and handed it back to her.

"Do you want a smoke?" he offered, opening his pack.

"I quit smoking cigarettes," she said. "I just like having a lighter."

Russell cocked his head at her. She was bolder, a bit more drunk than earlier.

"Look, I was trying to talk to you," she began.

"I have a girlfriend," Russell said.

She lurched back, barking with laughter with her hand on her throat. "Oh no. Oh, God, no. That's not what I want."

Russell flushed and turned away, taking a drag on his cigarette. "Then what do you need?"

"I opened an art gallery," she said, pointing down the stirring night street. "Just around the corner."

"Good for you," Russell said, sharp with contempt.

"Well, I remembered your artwork and wanted to know if you have anything you were working on," she rushed on, pulling at her curls until Russell's glare smashed whatever confidence led her out here to find him.

"I don't paint anymore," Russell said with shifting guts. "Everyone knows that."

"No," she said. "Everyone knows how good you used to be."

Russell snorted and tossed his cigarette into the street. He couldn't believe this woman's audacity. He wanted to salvage at least some of this night, and talking about his would-be art career meant irreparable damage to that plan. He cleared his throat and headed through the stream of people on the sidewalk toward the entrance of the bar. He'd met gallery owners looking for his work before, but normally it was through an email exchange or voicemail he could delete. Most of them were looking to stir up publicity or scandal, trying to get recluse artists in their galleries. But none had been as brazen as Isabelle, and the thought of putting himself through that type of scrutiny again brought a burning bile to his throat.

Isabelle's footfalls rushed up behind him. "I've never seen art as real as yours. And I've seen a lot of art, digital, installations—I've seen art made from literal shit. Like, someone's *shit* shit, but nothing as moving as your pieces."

Russell stopped and she slammed into his back, nearly falling to the ground. He whipped around to glare at her. "Did you compare my art to shit?"

"No! Oh, dammit." Isabelle threw her head into her hands. "I'm normally so much better at this."

"Hard to believe," Russell said, then continued toward the bar.

"That critic was wrong about your work, Russell," she called after him, halting him midstride.

Russell blinked hard and stared up into the black sky, through the glare of the streetlights. He couldn't make out the stars above him, just the slow red blink of a plane. He hadn't felt this vulnerable since he stepped away from his easel and traded it for a smooth desk in an office. He bit back his lips and said, "I'm not an artist anymore. Go find someone else."

He turned his gaze down, passed the doorman and into the frantic movement of Broken Jaw. He stepped back inside, ignoring the last of Isabelle's pleas.

2

Russell was off balance and lumbered forward as he pushed

through the people. The night had grown sour, and not just for him. Near the bar, he saw one of his roommates with her phone pressed to one ear and her finger plugged hard in the other. Katherine Davalos's dark eyes flickered with provocation under the shroud of thick bangs cut sharply across her face. The beautiful Puerto Rican woman appeared poised even though her slumped stance over the bar showed signs of drunkenness. Kat wore a sheer black blouse showing off a red bra underneath. She spotted Russell and strolled on long legs softly in her miniskirt. Her long black hair swung with her movement at the middle of her back.

"Your boyfriend's not coming," Russell said to her.

"No, he's not even answering the phone," she said, flinging her phone into her small purse.

"Let's get Leslie and go," Russell said. "It's four a.m."

Kat peered across the bar and pointed to a table in the rear, where Leslie Graham scowled and jabbed his finger like a weapon toward a thin man in front of him. From this distance and over the roar of music, they couldn't make out what was being said, but it captured sneers and laughter from the people nearby. Russell had seen his roommate angry like this before and knew it would take hours before Leslie was calm again. Russell rubbed the back of his neck and glanced at Kat.

"He's arguing with his boyfriend again," Russell said. "I'm not breaking that up."

Kat pursed her lips and gripped Russell's arm. "Come on."

She crossed the room with Russell in tow, elbowing through the small group gathered to watch the show. As Russell looked at Leslie, a pang of embarrassment twisted in his chest.

Despite many polar differences that separated him from

his friend, Leslie was like family. Russell towered above Leslie standing at six feet and five inches. His muscular bulk feeling as though it would barely pass through most doorways. Russell felt like a giant stumbling through a toy world, whereas Leslie was a slender black man who stood only five feet and ten inches. Leslie's sharp features lay kindly on his brown skin, regularly assigning him one of the most beautiful men in the room, contrary to Russell whose round childlike features hid themselves in his pale cherubic face and a thick, groomed dark beard. The beard itself had been a suggestion by Leslie, which indeed served to give him a rakish quality, after Russell's fervent complaints about his boyish appearance. It had also been Leslie that had pointed Russell in the direction of a decent barber, where Russell's tuft of curly brown hair was styled with precision.

Russell stepped in front of Kat and worked his way between Leslie and his boyfriend.

"Hey, what's going on?" Russell said, his height forcing the two to look up.

"Nothing," Leslie said with his hands tight at his sides.

Russell glanced over at Leslie's boyfriend, a gaunt Hispanic man named Isaac. His eyes shifted from Russell to Leslie and he threw up his hands in defeat.

"You bring in your guard dog?" Isaac said, gesturing toward Russell.

"And you wonder why I didn't want you to come out," Leslie said.

"You're the one making a fucking scene."

"And you're the one in a bar three weeks out of rehab."

Russell bit down to suppress his gasp. He glanced at Kat for help, who stood silent, gaping back at him. Russell shook his head and narrowed his eyes at Leslie.

"Maybe we should go home now," he said in a soft voice.

"That's a real fucking good idea," Isaac said. He turned on his heel and launched through the bar toward the door.

Leslie's shoulders dropped and his eyes glassed over. He opened and closed his mouth and gestured wordlessly for a moment until Kat took him by the arm. Together, they left the bar. Russell led the progression down the street, the path lit by the harsh glow of a nearby bodega. Out of his sight, he heard the rhythmic clicks of Kat's stilettos and the scuffling of Leslie's combat boots fall into cadence. Russell's gait fell into concert with their steps. After several years accompanying the two through myriad of band openings, deejay shows, bars, and every other excuse to get drunk, it proved difficult not to fall in line. This well-honed reciprocity started long ago and eventually led to renting out the other half of a duplex a few blocks off the Damen stop on Chicago's Blue Line.

They walked in a heavy silence and climbed the stairs to the train platform. Quiet hung over Russell as he processed the liquor and overall failure of the night. He stepped into the train and surveyed his roommates as the CTA carried them home. All three bore the same exhaustion, jostling in time with the dank train car. After two stops, they stepped onto the warped, wooden platforms adorned in garish billboards and minor vandalism. They moved through metal gates rotating like meat grinders with each passing rider. The sky was fading into pink in the east over Wicker Park.

Russell pulled out a cigarette, realized he was again without a lighter, and let it hang limply in his mouth. He would have asked for one, but the silence had become soothing. "Leslie, I told you it was a bad idea to bring Isaac."

Russell winced, knowing Kat would cost them a peaceful morning.

"Kat, are you trying to lecture me?" Leslie's voice went shrill as they stepped onto their quiet, dark street.

"I'm not lecturing you," she said as they crossed the block toward home.

"Kat, don't," Russell pleaded while he ascended the stairs of the narrow brick brownstone. He pulled open a rusty grated storm door and fumbled with the keys. The roar of a nearby train swallowed the propagating clash between Leslie and Kat. Turning the lock, he pushed open the door and ushered them inside. They stammered past him, voices rising in conflict. Russell tucked his cigarette into his pocket, passed through the door, and locked it behind him.

"Oh, come on, Russell," Kat continued, kicking off her heels only to suddenly drop down six inches. "You know bringing Isaac to the bar was an awful idea."

"Well," Russell said, nodding at her words but quickly silenced by Leslie's admonishing glare, "I... don't know..."

Russell ambled into the living room, taking in the aberrant tapestry of its occupants. The living room let in light from four wide windows draped in heavy purple velvet, directly across from Kat's punctilious exhibition of black-and-white photos. The adjacent wall leading into the kitchen displayed Russell's tribute to the first *Star Wars* trilogy, including framed collectible posters. Most of the apartment furnishings were products of secondhand stores and Goodwill trips, bought together with no relation and causing a violent collage of clashing colors. Leslie loved to joke that the collective décor looked like the set of an '80s porno. Russell retired on the lumpy, square, pea soup green couch. On a chipped white-lacquered wood entertainment stand sat a flat screen TV—one of the few appliances everyone agreed to spend money on. A nearby bookshelf held the record player Kat found in the garbage on a drunken binge two summers ago. Kat, teetering in platform heels as her thin arms strained to carry the cumbersome player, presented it to Leslie and Russell with a fatuous smile, as if she'd found the cure for all of life's ailments.

Russell had taken it from her, placed the device on the coffee table, and examined its parts to see if it could, in fact, function. Leslie disappeared into the back of the apartment and came back brandishing a Tina Turner record. Russell swiftly hooked the record player into the stereo system and with deft hands placed the needle on the record. The explosive sound of the crackling record turned Kat into a pile of giggling, flailing arms. Leslie managed to capture one, despite her paroxysm, and spun Kat around to the throaty howl of Tina Turner. Russell, quaking in laughter, had watched as they ascended in buoyant choreography.

Now the two were pitted in treacherous combat.

"Look," Kat began, clearing her throat and tilting up her chin with deference otherwise reserved for a jury, "I'm your roommate, your friend, your family, okay? I'm not the one with a coke problem." She paced the room, making thoughtful gestures. "I mean, for Christ's sake, Leslie, your boyfriend has been out of rehab for three weeks and you take him out to a bar? Aren't you shit broke because you're the one who has been paying for his rehab?"

Leslie's scowl deepened. "He didn't do anything."

"I'm just saying, taking Isaac around the same crowd that got him into this shit may not be the best idea."

"And you have the 'best' judgment with men?"

Kat recoiled. "I'm just trying to help."

"No, you're just pissed because you were stood up again." Leslie eyes narrowed as he positioned for attack. "Is this the fourth or fifth time?"

Russell shoulders slumped and he dropped his face into his hands.

At this early in the morning, after copious amounts of liquor, they had devolved, like macabre children poking sticks at rotting roadkill.

Russell was certain if sustained this would go on for another half hour. He hauled himself off the couch and between them, hoping his stature would serve as a sufficient barrier.

Kat leaned forward on tiptoes, scowling over Russell's shoulders. "I wasn't stood up, asshole."

Leslie sneered, successful in his assault. "Really? How many voicemails did you leave on Jacob's phone?"

Russell's muscles tensed as his roommates, vaulted on their toes, bickered over him. Edging to anger himself, he put his hand on Kat's arm and ushered her to the couch, her eyes livid. He pivoted quickly, rounding a brawny arm over Leslie's shoulders. "Let's go out for a smoke."

This adroit breach in combat left his roommates nonplussed. Russell passed through the door and led Leslie to the alley behind the duplex. There, in the narrow space shared by a concourse of black trash bins aligned in militarized formation against brick walls, underneath a yellow cone of light dropping from a nearby streetlamp, Leslie lit a cigarette. Smoke curled from his lips, adding itself to the dense smell of garbage rot in the April air.

Moments passed before he spoke. "I don't know what I'm doing."

Russell raised a speculative eyebrow and Leslie half smiled. "I don't know what I'm doing with Isaac."

"I don't know what to say, man. Give it time? Truth is, I don't know. Shit got bad."

"I thought once he got out of rehab..."

"That things would go back to normal?" Russell offered.

"Yeah." Leslie breathed in his cigarette, then he abruptly shook his head as if trying to dislodge from the maudlin heaviness. "I'm sorry we ruined your night."

"Don't worry about it."

"Fine, let me be honest—sorry we ruined your chances to get laid."

Russell snorted and smiled, giving Leslie's shoulder a playful punch.

"Don't worry about it."

"I should go apologize to Kat, huh?"

"Yeah."

"You think she was right?"

"She often is."

"I hate that," Leslie said.

Russell, with nothing witty to say this early in the morning, nodded at his friend and watched wind swell into the alley. This spring breeze, a chilly echo of a hard winter survived, remodeled scraps of debris into fluttering critters rushing toward the street. The sky was no longer pink but a balmy blue. The first twinges of exhaustion felt heavy in Russell's knees. As if Leslie sensed this, he stamped out this cigarette and they climbed the steps into the apartment.

Kat, on the couch underneath an afghan, had stripped off her makeup, twisted her hair into a bun, and hidden the shape of her body in a battered sweatshirt. She was now one of the boys. She glanced up at them, her brow knit with remorse.

"I'm sorry," she said.

"No, I'm sorry." Leslie rushed to her side and took her hands. Kat offered him a smile as he kicked of his shoes, then joined her underneath the afghan.

Russell chuckled at Leslie's sweeping gesture and once more at the frivolity of his friends. He took the remaining edge of the couch and turned to the illumination of the TV.

"What are you watching?" he asked.

"Some foreign movie," she replied, resting her head on Russell's massive shoulder.

Russell stretched, his arm span overtaking the top of the couch. He felt his roommates nestle into him. He was too fatigued to fight them, and besides, they were warm; he had been cold all night.

Silently, they waned off to sleep, settled upon each other on the couch, an odd makeshift family, much like the apartment décor. In that moment, Russell was impervious in their solitary to the urban depravity, the mounting suffering, and the jobs that drove him a like a cog in a stolid machine. All Russell could see from the blackened edges of his consciousness was the gallery owner determined to acquire his artwork, even though he had long ago left that world.

3

Kat awoke with a dull throb at the front of her skull. She grimaced, lips smacking, from an acrid coating thick in her mouth. She quietly promised herself she'd never drink again—a promise that would be short-lived, of course. She opened her eyes, only to plummet into vertigo. She found herself on the couch, curled tight in Russell's heavy arms. Leslie had abandoned them while she slept, leaving her on the couch with Russell. His hold on her seemed to wrap around her twice. Her body undulated with his breathing and the meter of his heartbeat thumping in his wide chest. His grip around her felt primal and base, not so much in a way of perversion, but in the sense that this was where she was supposed be. His arms held her on the side of her body and his hand rested at her hip with possessiveness. There, deep in sleep, his face motionless, he was virile and possibly handsome. Kat considered closing her eyes and conceding to the warmth of him.

But then again, this was Russell, the closest thing life had allotted her as a brother. He had been the guy she'd lived with for years now; a guy who had victimized her with merciless pranks; a guy blind to innumerable pleas to put the toilet seat down. And if the toilet seat *was* down, it most likely had urine droplets along the rim. She'd endured barbarous displays between Leslie and Russell in the form of farting and burping contests, all of which Russell retained his title as victor. Then there was his defiance against the house cleaning. He was unable to pick up a broom or help in the effort against crusted dishes, grimy glasses, and greasy pans. Lying snug in this man's arms, despite how good it felt, was just too strange. Even if he didn't have some little suburban girlfriend, this would undoubtedly lead to an onslaught of pubescent taunts. Kat had to be the first to strike.

She withdrew her arm and wrenched back, curled her fist, and drove it directly into his chest.

"Jesus!" Russell screamed, only to clutch Kat closer.

His face was no longer a statuesque exposé of masculinity, but rounded with alarm.

"Let me go, jackass!" Kat said, squirming to unearth herself from his grasp.

"Did you hit me?" Russell asked, his eyes bright. His arms tighten playfully.

"Are you trying to kill me?" Kat began to kick against him, shaking free her hip from his hand.

"Maybe," Russell said, not yielding in his grip.

"Russell, your breath smells like a dog took a shit in your mouth!"

"And then the dog took a shit in your hair."

Leslie emerged from the back of the apartment, fully dressed and preened. He glanced down at them with feigned malediction. "Really—sex in the living room?"

Kat and Russell dove on opposite sides of the couch like Leslie had thrown a match at them. He crossed his arms and smiled, pleased. "Come on, let's do brunch. There's a new breakfast place on Kedzie."

"Fine," Russell said, standing up, "I call dibs on the bathroom."

"Bastard," Kat shot as he retreated toward the rear of the apartment. "You better not use all the hot water."

Leslie squatted down next to her on the couch.

"Sorry about being a bitch," she said.

"No, you were right."

"Well, I wish I wasn't," Kat said, pulling at her knotted mess of hair. "I wish Isaac could go out with us like nothing happened. But you're a nurse; you know how these things are."

"I work at retirement home. So, no, I don't know."

Kat let herself fall forward into Leslie's lap with counterfeit distress. "Help me, I think I might die."

Leslie smirked, placing a hand on Kat's head. "I don't think there's any treatment for skank."

Kat twisted to face him. "Then how'd you cure yourself?"

Leslie and Kat roared with laughter. Her face grew solemn in Leslie's lap, and she reached for his nearest free hand. She squeezed it and said, "It's gonna be okay. We're here, Leslie."

Leslie kissed her forehead. "Love you, girl."

"Love you, too."

Kat was always warmed by Leslie and sat there while he stroked her messy hair. She closed her eyes and tried to pretend everything was normal. It definitely appeared to be and she could almost convince herself it was. She was simply suffering from a hangover and mending things with her friend. Kat could almost forget that her period was more than two weeks late.

The bathroom door opened and footfalls rushed over the creaking floorboards.

She rose from the couch. Russell's bedroom door closed. "That was quick—how much you wanna bet he still smells like ass?"

Leslie cackled as Kat headed into the bathroom. Kat was aware that she would have, at most, twenty minutes to complete her transformation before her roommates started to protest. She pulled back the ratty Chicago Bulls shower curtain, the one Russell had insisted on in spite of Kat's and Leslie's shared expressions of chagrin. Inside the old claw-foot tub was a dingy grey ring of dirt. Irritation prickled her spine, and she silently counted the reasons she chose to live with two men who, in their mid-twenties, still behaved like brutish children.

Children... She couldn't possibly be pregnant. She used condoms. She used birth control. Although, there were times when she'd been too busy, or out, or forgot to take a pill here and there, but surely not often enough to get pregnant.

After a shower made short by the quick dissipation of warm water, Kat ran a hair dryer through her hair, ignoring Russell's playful catcalls. With a quick application of foundation and lip gloss, Kat was dressed, and together they exited the apartment into the temperate afternoon.

Early April meant the threat of rain, and the air was dense with moisture and the smell of soil. After winter's icy thrashing, Kat's thin body was a bundle of knotted muscles and aches, and she welcomed this alleviation into warmer weather. She and her roommates traveled the same path that took them home hours before, Russell leading the way to the train. The businesses occupying the brown brick buildings stirred in blithe activity. The streets channeled moderate Sunday traffic. The route appeared benign in the late afternoon. The alleys were no longer black pools carrying menacing unknowns.

An Asian woman in wide, dark sunglasses came toward them, leisurely pushing a stroller through the narrow parking lot. The woman's head was turned toward the sun as light footsteps carried her forward. Kat's heart fluttered as she strained not to look into the stroller. As the woman passed, Kat's eyes betrayed her and she peered down at a small, doughy face. The pace of the world slowed to a crawl as the toddler stared back at her with dark, pristine eyes. His black hair trembled with the steady breeze and his tiny fingers rested in his mouth. In that moment, Kat entertained how the boy's smile could stretch across his portly face and how tears could roll off his plump cheeks. Maybe he was the type of child who ran with arms open to his mother. Maybe he was prone to toddler's tantrums. Kat imagined how she would reach down and comfort him. She saw the mother gaping into his eyes, cooing and laughing until the child smiled.

Kat felt hot terror pierce the muscles in her back.

And there, passing through the sphere of subdued time, Kat heard the hushed mutter of his voice. A cheerful hum made of capricious melodies. This tiny refrain was barely audible against the traffic. It was pieces of nursery rhymes scattered together in some familiar carol. This child played with the volume of his voice through this little euphony.

Kat's heart again shuddered, and she suppressed a scream as the sound of the child faded from earshot. Time returned to normal. Her feet could move again. She noticed Leslie watching her as they hiked the stairs to the 'L' platform.

Her neck grew hot and her face was flushed. "Cute kid."

Leslie gave her an uneasy look. "You still drunk?"

Kat shrugged at him with a sheepish smile as the train came to a jarring halt before them on the platform. They boarded it and it carried them westward, deeper into Logan Square. After the next stop, the roommates emerged onto the street. They ambled a few blocks toward a restaurant called By Land and By Sea, a cozy restaurant with a short wait. Soon they were seated and served.

Now that the matter of brunch had been resolved— and Kat had successfully reassured herself her period would come—only the day's agenda was left to attend to. Forking down twelve-dollar waffles and bacon, Kat nonchalantly made a suggestion that Russell seconded, sputtering his approval through a mouthful of crab omelet. Deliberating with an upturned chin and waiting for all eyes to fall on him, like a king stilling the crowd to bestow a decree, Leslie consented. At six that evening, they'd head deep into Ukrainian Village to see a band Kat was friendly with at a show that promised free beer. There had been no need for persuasion.

For more than two years, Kat had worked as a part-time bartender for Stratosphere Bar in Wicker Park, an effete establishment consistently determined to be "hip" by those writing the reviews.

This, in conjunction with a shrewdly timed flirt, made

her privy to shows, deejay sets, and a throng of admirers who, elated, invited her anywhere if it meant a few moments of undivided attention. She was a deity, gliding in circles from patron to patron, pouring vodka in glasses, one hand concussing a shaker and the other grabbing a credit card. She dazzled, imbued in the bar's black lights, behind glowing bottles of liquor and her movements abstractly in time with the thump of Stratosphere's trance or house music. Those lucky few positioned at the bar became a benefactor of her sudden quips and amiable smile. Outside the bar, she spent her days as a freelance photographer for Belle Journee Studios, which stationed her in a frenzy of local eccentrics and their art exhibitions, gallery openings, and infrequent fashion shows. Kat's resume suggested a horribly glamorous life, much more-so than it actually was.

In truth, this tawdry exertion at glamour was a thin veil that concealed a woman who grew up in foster homes and often wondered how she would make her monthly student loan payments. Most nights at Stratosphere were saturated with boozy idiots passing out crude sexual advances. "What can I get you?" answered with "A *blowjob!*" If not them, then the broke misanthropes who would coerce their way up to her bar and doggedly inquire about the drink specials, squinting at the drink menus, acutely studying prices only to buy several drinks and not tip. On hard nights, Kat put on the guise of an alluring bartender. Her vexed feet floundered in viscous slime made of dirt and spilled liquor. She moved at a manic pace and occasionally jammed herself into tight corners so the barback could reach for dirty glasses and return with clean ones. This culmination of hysteria constructed a drunken assembly line featuring different characters each night. There, suppurating in the dim bar, pressed upon each other, dissonant in dark lights, would be the young woman with questionable self-esteem and a skirt that hiked north with each cosmo; the blundering meathead enveloped in rash posturing, making foolish bids at women; the venereal new lovers grinding hard on each other to the music; the inebriated girl teetering in knock-off designer shoes, spilling her drink on passing victims. Smiling at her regulars through the smashed pieces of her sanity, Kat rang up tabs and counted down the hours on the cash register's digital screen.

The next morning, after a few hours of fitful sleep, she would jump in a cab and rush downtown, following vague directions to a photoshoot for Belle Journee. Barreling through the streets, clinging tightly to her camera bag and assorted folders, Kat would try to make sense of the walls of skyscrapers surrounding her. A desultory homeless man would wave his cardboard sign and scream about the impending wrath of God. The chorus of honking cars would reach apex as the 'L' train squealed overhead. Drudging through the profusion, Kat would somehow find her way to the random office building and spend the next long hours placating to the hubris and narcissism of that day's older photographer. She'd gratefully offer creative input when possible, but spend most of her time shifting lights and backdrops with photo assistants. At the end of the day, she would collect all the cameras and memory cards and upload the day's take to the computer back in the studio. Between cropping and color-correction, moments of glamour were few and fleeting.

Kat was always trapped in a vice grip of stress—certainly enough to stall her period from time to time.

As for now, those connections served Kat and her roommates well, and she was content to control the group's social calendar.

Russell looked up from the remaining omelet bits, a hopeful smile stretched across his lips, and over the ting of forks and bluster of conversation said, "I have something to tell you guys."

"You leaked a sex tape?" Kat said.

"You're gonna pay me the twenty dollars you borrowed last night?" Leslie asked.

Russell's face tightened, and he glared at them. "I'm serious."

Russell straightened in his chair and removed from his jacket pocket a small black jewelry box. Kat's ears started to tingle with heat. Russell flipped opened the box, revealing a curved cut diamond that drew in the dim light of the restaurant only to eject tiny spears of white as if lit from within. The center diamond was cradled in an aureate platinum band encircled with smaller brilliant diamonds. This ring, which radiated a small rainbow like a peacock's expanding feathers, was overwrought and theatrical. The declaration of illuminate stones and platinum in Russell's hand seemed disconnected. Kat felt her stomach constrict looking over the engagement ring's lustrous diffusion. She turned down to her waffles and bacon, and at that moment, they were no longer suitable for consumption. The food had shaped into cold bits of mire.

"I'm going to ask Ava to marry me," said Russell, whose eyes mirrored the ring's brilliance.

"Are you giving that ring to a rapper?" Leslie asked, squinting suspiciously at the ring. "You can buy that but can't give me back my twenty dollars?"

Russell scowled at Leslie, then turned to Kat, pleading.

"It's great," Kat said flatly, as her stomach lurched again. Vomit seemed certain, or at least possible, if the ring stayed in her sight. Her face was florid as heat moved from her ears to her neck. This was worse than her delayed period.

"Wow, guys." Russell breathed, his face lulled with disappointment. He snapped the box closed and tucked the ring back into his coat.

Leslie glanced at Kat for help, but she could only swallow and breathe, desperate to regain equilibrium. She was more bewildered by her reaction than the ring itself. This sense of repulsion had overtaken her and left her speechless.

The waiter soon came with the checks, drawing them into an uneasy silence.

4

"I don't get it," said Kat, sipping a vodka concoction from a red plastic cup in the corner of an apartment beat down by excessive partying. She absently wondered how long the party hosts could keep inviting bands to play here, considering this place was, at best guess, a year away from total dilapidation. Spilled liquor warped the floorboards underneath them, and the only room with any charm was the small cell of a bathroom that held a murky toilet, a dirt-speckled mirror, and a handwritten sign: "NO SHITTING!" In the kitchen, every chipped countertop and rusty stove surface became a depository for cheap beer. The overall bareness gave the apartment liberty to house a growing mass of people. Over unintelligible conversations and a saccharine moan rising from the three-piece band, Leslie and Kat hissed fervent whispers with Russell safely out of earshot.

It was the first time they had to talk about Russell's big announcement. After brunch, the three roommates had gone home and retreated to their rooms. The cab ride to the party was quiet with tension. Leslie's menial small talk hadn't been enough to pull them back to normalcy, and soon after ascending the rusty fire escape up to the party, Russell had fled deep into the congestion to the front of the apartment, where the band was playing.

Kat and Leslie circled each other with somber faces appearing more like a cabal than close friends.

"He hasn't even been dating Ava that long," Leslie said.

"And she's his coworker's daughter," Kat said.

"That family *is* the one percent."

"A suburban princess who always looks uncomfortable."

"So, I'm not the only one who notices her scared-of-black-people look?"

Kat giggled. "You *are* a scary black man."

"That whole college-educated, tax-paying thing I do is *so* threatening. Bitch better clutch her purse."

"I've tried so hard to like her."

Leslie raised an eyebrow. "You hate every girl Russell dates."

"So, Isaac isn't coming?"

Leslie suppressed a scowl with a swallow of beer, noting Kat's curt subject change. "No, Isaac isn't coming. You know that."

Leslie felt irritation slowly rising at the mere mention of Isaac, whom he hadn't spoken to since last night.

"Leslie, talk to him," Kat said. "He loves you."

Even though Leslie never admitted it, Isaac Ortiz was the most handsome man he knew. This wasn't some mawkish symptom of affection; Isaac's magnetism was evident. There were times Leslie despised Isaac for meeting his glare with a stately smile or drawing Leslie closer with a persuading collection of words. Seduced by a smooth, tan face that faintly whispered of some long-lost Native American genealogy, Leslie would forgive and then try to forget the disagreement. This reverent submission had taken over their relationship for a few years, until night after night, Isaac's nose would end up full of coke. That same submission quickly descended into horror as Leslie helplessly paid witness to Isaac's destruction. No amount of self-delusion could shroud the tyrannical mood swings, the stretches of time he'd disappear, persistent calls from debt collectors, and finally Isaac's termination at *Chicago Sun-Times* for failing meet his deadlines.

This man's blitz toward annihilation left Leslie in a state of frantic desperation. In a wave of terrorism, he bombarded their apartment with late night phone calls and early morning visits. His roommates didn't say much, only awkward gaping and exasperated sighs. Then one night, after another manic sojourn, Isaac left, covertly stuffing Kat's tip money into his pocket. He'd stolen the money from a coffee can she kept in her room, before she'd been able to make a trip to the bank. This caused an eruption among the roommates. Thinking back, Leslie couldn't recall much of what happened or what was said in hostility, but the sharp feeling of dismay remained buried deep in his chest.

After that, Isaac was exiled from their apartment. He presented a feeble apology. In the wake of that offense, Leslie acknowledged that Isaac became a faint echo of a man. His gaunt face could no longer pacify with a smile. The only thing that remained was an emaciated shadow, stalking around a few weeks from eviction. With no place to go, Isaac reluctantly agreed to Leslie's offer to pay for rehab.

"Last night," Leslie now said, "seeing him at the bar, talking to the same people who got him into this mess, I freaked out."

"His old friends are still snorting away," Kat agreed, "and maybe they can handle it, but God knows Isaac can't."

"I'm not going through that again."

Kat looked directly into Leslie's face. "Tell him."

The two drank from their cups in resolution, and Leslie said, "So, honestly, what's the deal with you and Russell?"

Kat responded with a harsh glower and a short humorless chuckle. "Let's join the party," she said, turned away, and walked into the crowd. Leslie rolled his eyes and followed her into the tangled horde.

The air was dense with the smells of sweat, liquor, and marijuana. The band roared, led by a guitar screech. The crowd reciprocated with an exuberant bellow. Drinks were lifted and spilled in the fracas. The music pulsed over them causing the mutilated walls to quake and the contorted floorboards to groan. Russell towered near the band, thrusting his hand in the air. His face was overtaken by a giddy smile.

Leslie leaned over to Kat. "We have to be happy for him."

Kat's face darkened.

"Look, I know we normally don't do the whole happy-people thing," Leslie continued, "but we have to."

Kat's entire body convulsed as she exhaled a deep sigh. "Fine. But my goodwill stops at bridal showers."

Leslie nodded in concurrence. He took Kat's hand as they forced their way to Russell's side.

He raised his drink and nudged Kat to follow suit. "To Russell and Ava!"

Russell's smile, already dominating most of his face, managed to extend even further until his eyes were pressed into slits. Clearly, this was an achievement capable only by the drunk. He stretched his arms around Leslie and Kat, lifting them off the floor a few inches. Leslie, stunned, managed not to spill his drink while Kat's toppled onto the trampling feet below.

When her feet returned to the ground, Kat adjusted her top, which now showed a visible strain. Hiding her indifference, she offered, "Yeah, we're happy for you."

"Thanks, guys," Russell said.

"We're your family," Leslie said back.

The music came to an abrupt stop and conversation soon followed. There, within a hushed quiet of the crowd, someone shouted, "Five-O!"

This heralded a rising panic in the crowd. Leslie and Russell were at first stunned, and then turned their contempt toward Kat. They gathered near the cracked window, colored by pulsing blue and red lights from nearby squad cars. Leslie pictured himself handcuffed, escorted by the police to a small jail cell, and barked, "What the fuck, Kat?" They followed the crowd streaming toward the front door. "You know they arrest the black guy first."

"Hey, how was I supposed to know the cops would come?"

"We need to get out," Russell said, as he grabbed Leslie's arm. "Not through the front."

Russell took Kat's hand and turned the hull of his body against the flow of the crowd. He propelled forward, pulling Leslie and Kat with him. Despite a protest here and there, the people before him had no choice but to give in, encouraged by a well-placed elbow or sudden shove. He led them back to the fire escape and heaved the window open. Kat dismounted first, followed by Leslie, then Russell.

They plunged into the night, scampering through the alleys. Leslie was hysterical with movement, launching farther into the darkness. His heartbeat backfired in his ears. His breathing heaved out with each step. Kat ran alongside him, heels in hand, while her nylons split on the concrete. Russell floundered up ahead, looking back with every few steps and demanding they stay together, while nearly tripping on a sewage drain.

After several blocks, they slowed to a stop. Leslie leaned forward with his hands on his knees, gasping for air. He saw Kat leaning against the brick wall, surveying the damage to her stockings. Russell paced, pulling in ragged breaths.

"We are too old for this shit!" Leslie said. "I have a 401(k)!"

Russell and Kat stared at Leslie, then at one another. Laughter thundered between the three. They joined Kat on the wall and then collectively reached for cigarettes.

"Look at me!" Kat said, slipping on her shoes. "I look like I've been hate-crimed."

Russell put his hand to his chin and thought out loud. "It probably was just a noise violation."

"Hey, I'm not trying to risk calling in to work because I got arrested," Leslie said.

"Yeah, what would Ava think?" Kat said, and Leslie flashed her a glare.

Oblivious, Russell gathered his friends in his arms and migrated them back to the street. He'd gotten their tacit approval on Ava and didn't consider its sincerity.

Leslie broke apart from his roommates. "You guys go on."

"Really?" Russell asked, his drunken smile returned. His arm was still around Kat, but this time it appeared his was leaning on her to stay upright. The commotion did nothing to sober him up, and now safe, he submitted to his drunkenness.

"I'll take him home," Kat said. "Leslie, go handle your business."

Determined, Kat hauled forward with Russell's cluster of dead weight, more parody than reality.

Other party escapees giggled as they passed them on the sidewalk, and Leslie heard Kat's obscene scoffing in the distance.

Leslie laughed as he journeyed a few more blocks toward the main street. There, on Damen Avenue, he hailed a cab.

He gave the driver his destination and settled into the musty leather seat. He sat in dense contemplation as the city stretched ahead. Yellow streetlights punctuated the night, and illuminated the slip into municipal degradation. Streets, already martyrs from an existing economic divide, lay helpless under the recent recession. Waiting at a stoplight miles away from the glimmer of downtown, Leslie eyed a block overtaken by abandoned brick buildings. Windows shattered and planked over like eyes unwilling to see, the building also housed a bundled figure huddled in the doorway. Splits in the concrete were havens for stubborn weeds. Windblown debris filled the nearby gutters in indiscernible clumps. Here, on the main street, was a simple interlude, a primer to the actual suffering. The side streets led to the last remaining projects.

The light turned green and the cab pushed forward. They were relatively safe here on the main road where the police cars patrolled. There was still palpable tension along that street. Every figure, passing in the distance, still rendered a possible threat. No amount of streetlights could banish the jeopardy from the shadows. And here Leslie was fine, almost camouflaged.

The cab arrived at Leslie's destination. He stood before a stout, three-story brick building. This structure, posed under the facade of a motel, was more commonly used as a halfway house. The motel was a battle-worn soldier with rusty wire bars and grates over the windows. The light over a dented thick steel door blinked and Leslie heard the buzz of electricity pop through the filament. In the closest window to the door, a vacancy sign yellowed from sun exposure. Leslie swallowed, readying himself, as he pried opened the heavy door. The inside lobby was a dimly lit space paneled with imitation wood. He nodded as he passed the balding, apathetic clerk, whose desk was encased in thick, possibly bulletproof, glass, and climbed the narrow stairs. Carpeting so filthy the original color couldn't be determined led up the stairs and through the hallways. Cigarette smoke, fried food, and trace body odors saturated the air. Leslie made his way to the second floor, counting the doors along the way. He gathered his inner focus, trying not to hear the lingering sounds of life within the rooms. He didn't want to hear some man arguing, some baby crying, or some people screwing. He didn't want their tragedy to weigh on his—the tragedy of this slightly drunk black gay guy visiting his addict boyfriend, in a building barely suited for habitation on the edge of one of the city's most dangerous neighborhoods.

Leslie knocked on the door and heard stirring from within. Several clicks later, Isaac's head edged out. His weary face lightened when he saw Leslie. He gestured him in and Leslie stepped into the small room. The muscles tightened in Leslie's back as Isaac retired on the full-size mattress on the floor. His eyes stung. Leslie blinked and rubbed them, but it did nothing to change this abrupt condition.

He resisted the urge to flee down the stairs and into the street, flailing his arms in panic until a cab rescued him. Instead, he squatted down on the mattress next to Isaac.

"I didn't think you were coming."

Leslie took Isaac in his arms and adjusted to the small room. The ugly carpet, browned with grime, displayed an assortment of items. Empty soda bottles transformed one corner of the room to a home for a small gnat cloud. A half-eaten bag of chips had spilled nearby, and a few of the chips had fallen victim to careless footsteps, their entrails ground deep into the carpet fibers. Ripped, bent, and dated magazines were scattered around a mound of dirty clothes that smelled sour as Leslie had passed. He assumed that if any ill-fated object touched this carpet, the result was permanent abandonment.

A small picture taped to the wall showed the two of them, locked in an embrace at Millennium Park, on a summer day two years ago. It was the only effort to make this dwelling hospitable. The picture, a faded vestige of sapid summer nights and a devout courtship, now resembled no one in the room. Isaac had been healthy and beaming with his enchanting charm turned toward the camera. Leslie's smiling gaze was fixed on Isaac.

On the mattress, Isaac wore nothing but gym shorts and looked thinner than Leslie remembered. His ribs were clearly visible through his tan skin. His face was stony and hard, and his wiry body pulsed with the blinking light pouring from the barred window. The lines on Isaac's face betrayed him. He appeared older than his true age. This veteran of rehab and addiction stared at the empty wall with sad eyes.

"I'm sorry about going to the bar last night."

"I shouldn't have overreacted," Leslie said, trying to beat back the growing sting in his eyes. "I mean, yelling at you in public is how stupid people solve problems."

Isaac grunted a short laugh. "I love you," he whispered.

Leslie vision blurred. He put his hands to his eyes only to draw back wet fingers. He wiped his tears quickly, hoping Isaac wouldn't notice.

5

Russell spent most of the morning encumbered by the general misery of Mondays at his office and his hangover's anguish, produced by too many beers and sleep deprivation. He contended through his pain with gallons of burnt coffee in a mug stamped with Midstate Regional Bank's spiraling logo. When a moment of solitude presented itself in his confined office, he placed his head in his hands and breathed steadily with his eyes closed. He vowed as soon as the workday concluded he would shrink into his apartment. The whole of his day was filled with the desire to loosen his tie, go home, and liberate himself from this constricting suit. He would then rummage for beer in the refrigerator. Then, just before succumbing to the comfort of his ugly couch, he would excavate a blunt from a shoebox hidden deep in his closet and share with whomever was home. A well-rehearsed routine that dissipated any hardship. Russell needed to distance himself from the conducts of businessmen who were plaguing more and more of his time and himself.

But those desires had to wait. In the mere twelve minutes from the cramped train to his home, his phone glowed with a kind text message from Ava, reminding him of the dinner reservations they had at Cibo e Amore. Earlier in the last week, Russell had agreed to dine with Ava and her father as part of Ava's spirited campaign to ensure that Russell was, at the very least, accepted by Hayes Von Hoffman.

Russell climbed out of the cab with unsteady steps

onto the streets of the financial district. He tugged at the collar of his cheap navy suit. On the street, moving through the current of people discharged from the nearby office buildings, Russell pushed his way up to the glass doors of Cibo e Amore. The five-star Italian restaurant would require more dining etiquette than he felt capable of rousing. He wondered if anyone else in the restaurant's hushed semblance had a blunt waiting at home.

Russell gave his tie an adjustment before he approached the maître d', and followed her to the rear of the restaurant, mimicking her careful footsteps upon the blush-colored limestone. He moved through the restaurant, a throng of luxury and excess. The walls dripped with exotic foliage along the opulent interior architecture. Arched windows unveiled the city streets starting to shimmer with the onset of dusk. Urban aristocrats populated the restaurant, and they ate with repose. Russell was a pilgrim in this bizarre decadence.

He was escorted to a far table raised on a cement platform bordered by thick pillars embellished with potted roses and orchids. Hayes Von Hoffman sat alone, sipping coolly from a wine glass. He nodded to Russell, who quickly ascended the platform and gathered himself in a chair across from the man.

The timber of Von Hoffman's voice reached across the table and rattled Russell's ribcage. "I arrived a bit early."

The man before him was no different in his ease than anyone else in the restaurant. He was in his mid-fifties, outfitted in a double-breasted suit. At a glance, he was another indistinguishable businessman stalking the streets of the financial district, but when he spoke, one could discern this man's prominence. Words emitted from his mouth with concise authority, and Russell was transfixed in his piercing gaze.

"Ava will be here shortly. You know how she can be with time," Von Hoffman said. He held up his wine glass to survey it. "Do you like wine?"

Russell shifted in his seat, unsure of how to respond.

"I'm a simple man. I enjoy simple wine. Nothing foreign. Preferably from Napa. Nothing too expensive or too complicated, you understand. A perfectly aged Sauvignon Blanc. I like to know what I'm getting," he continued, moving his eyes from the glass to Russell. "Your performance at Midstate Regional is impressive."

"Thank you, sir."

Russell was a banker capable of handling basic accounts, loans, and mortgages. At work, he sat erect in his swivel chair behind a wooden desk, appearing earnest and knowledgeable. Within the fluorescent glow of the office, he was a competent sales associate, an enviable young man who garnered the respect of his colleagues. He wasn't the guy who had hidden in the bathroom earlier that morning, battling the urge to vomit. Nor was he the guy heaved from a cab and into his apartment by his pint-sized female roommate. Those colleagues could safely argue that this morning, he hadn't woken up on the floor, in his underwear, with creases in his face from the hardwood paneling.

In their eyes, Russell Cowell was a decorous banker and a sensible businessman.

Years hidden in this pretense pushed him steadily away from the truth. Russell, the banker, wasn't Russell, the failed artist. College years spent heaving acrylic paints on thick canvases had ultimately ended in defeat. Series of crushing reviews and general misinterpretations had sent him retreating to something practical. Against his misgivings, he landed with a business degree.

Days spent in air-conditioned cells of the bank's offices didn't quiet the stacked rows of half-finished paintings that wept from the corners of his bedroom. Wild strokes of color converged into the shapes of faces on canvas. Lines and textures entwined into expressive human forms. Their colors waned with time and dust on the paint drew into a thick grey sediment. There in his room, thriving in the wake of his art's death, was anger. It clung at his ankles and suspended itself above him.

"If you maintain your numbers, you'll be very successful," Von Hoffman continued.

"Thank you."

Von Hoffman nodded again. Russell swallowed at this gesture of consent, understanding he'd achieved one of his hardest sales yet. At that moment, it didn't matter about the failed artist canvases that he kept hidden or the mounting discontentment of his day job. He sat before this man with an invitation to a world of fifty-dollar entrées and three-hundred-dollar bottles of domestic wine.

"Ava really cares about you," Von Hoffman said, drinking from his glass.

"I care about her, too."

"Good."

As Von Hoffman turned toward the restaurant door, Russell followed his gaze. Ava headed toward the table with a balletic stride. She joined them, her face full of satisfaction. Thoughts of blunts and faded paintings vanished from Russell's mind.

6

After dinner, Ava sat before empty plates and bloated

stomachs. The bill was paid, the town car called, and they gathered in front of the restaurant, where the financial district was all but empty, save a few harried office workers frantically hailing cabs to get to wherever they called home.

Russell had been sweet to meet them out, and Ava had sent him the text message with the full knowledge that he had forgotten. He made quite the valiant display for her, eating more delicately that she thought he was capable of, though he still rested his elbows on the table and spoke with his mouth full. Ava had eyed Von Hoffman, feeling vindicated by his visible strain. She almost giggled when her father winced, and for a little over an hour, the three struggled through forced smiles.

When the black town car pulled up, Russell insisted he take a cab rather than a ride. "Give you some father-daughter time." He smiled, extending his hand to Von Hoffman.

Von Hoffman didn't insist, simply took his hand and exchanged farewells. Russell kissed Ava on the cheek and walked down the street to find a ride in the madness.

Ava stepped inside the town car while her father relayed the address of her Gold Coast apartment to the driver. In the backseat, Von Hoffman's shoulders slumped as he turned to his daughter, his face wounded with frustration.

"Him?" he finally said.

Ava turned to the window and considered not saying anything at all. Everything with her father was a quid pro quo. There was no conversation had between the two, only business deals and cold negotiations. She wasn't exactly okay with this, but after being a spectator of Von Hoffman for enough years, she had come to resentful acceptance. His nature ruined two marriages, the first being her mother. Memories of a kind mother were overridden by a tight-lipped woman who had, after getting the raw end of too many deals, decided to concede to the alimony without custody of Ava. Von Hoffman paid her handsomely to stay far away, off in the warm hills of San Francisco. Ava's childhood hope was that the warmth there would thaw her mother's heart.

Ava eventually stopped waiting and her cavernous childhood home in Winnetka grew less empty. Women tried to woo her father and make it their home, eager to placate Ava and seduce Von Hoffman. One of these women even made it as far as the church, the altar, and into the house. But after costly attempts to remodel the home around the hard-edged businessman and his daughter, she—like the wife prior—was paid to go away, this time to the humid tropics of Florida. The second wife had left the house roaring in tears with her hands in her hair as if she was fleeing a maniac with a butcher knife. Von Hoffman and then twelve-year-old Ava could do nothing but look back at her in silent contempt.

Von Hoffman's current wife, Mrs. Von Hoffman III, made sure she was well-insulated with alcohol. Although she had endured the longest, Ava couldn't help but wonder when the woman would finally reach her limit, and what coast she would seek for asylum. This woman's drunkenness was an adequate buffer between the warring conglomerates Ava and Von Hoffman became over the years. Their trades were made from the emotional currency of Von Hoffman's guilt and Ava's ceaseless anger.

As of late, Von Hoffman's opinion had been inconsequential concerning the men she should date. He originally sought out men for his lovely Ava, an undertaking more problematic than he anticipated because these men, like Von Hoffman himself, were handsome, well connected, driven, and ruthless. Not only had this been disappointing, it came with catastrophic results. Von Hoffman received an early morning call from the hospital, in which Ava's anger reached an all-time peak. She was seated in an examining room barely able to her hold the phone to her split face while gingerly touching the cluster of lumps and bruises—gifts from one of the men her father set her up with.

Once Von Hoffman's wide-eyed terror subsided and Ava's faded from black-and-blue to yellow, he began the lengthy process of compensation. He opened up a platinum card for Ava with virtually no end to its credit. He paid for a furnished apartment in Gold Coast and granted her control over her trust fund. Ava felt he was trying to drown out the memories of her broken face. The harder he tried, the less his opinion mattered to her. Eventually, his disapproval was met with stone-faced dismissal.

In fact, any man who emulated her father sickened her. Ava surprised herself when she realized that she was taken with Russell even though he was in the financial industry. Then again, Russell had a gentle face and she hadn't known a man to look gentle in her life. The more time she spent with him, the more she truly realized this was sincere.

Ava turned to her father as the town car made its way toward her apartment.

"You seemed to like him," she said.

"He does a notable job at Midwest," Von Hoffman said.

"He might be your future son-in-law," Ava said.

The rest of the ride was reserved in silence.

If her father taught her anything, it was that every deal has a cost. Yes, Russell was clumsy and at dinner spoke with a full mouth. Yes, she found it peculiar and sometimes alarming that his best friends were a black homosexual and a crude, badly dressed Latin girl—honestly, Ava didn't know what her ethnicity was. And yes, Russell was from a trailer park in southern Illinois and spent at least part of his life as an artist...

Frankly, the list of his cons could wrap around Chicago, but most importantly, she knew with startling certainty he would never hurt her. He would never pelt her with closed fists. He would never put his hands around her throat until she blacked out. She would never feel that type of fear from him. This was enough to overlook his drunk, high, and gay friends. And she was certain she could outlast them and convince Russell he didn't need them in his life.

The car stopped in front of a series of luxury high-rise apartments that stretched up into the night. Ava opened the door and placed one foot on the sidewalk. Her father grabbed her arm.

"But he's nobody. You know that," he said.

"He's somebody to me."

Ava slipped from his grasp. The doorman posted at the lobby desk buzzed open the entrance and she stepped inside.

7

Kat bought a pregnancy test before her shift at Stratosphere. Today's missing period meant she was closer to three weeks late than two. She could no longer attribute this to stress. Kat shifted back and forth on beaten feet. She scrubbed the bar with a damp rag, watching a husky bouncer shepherding the few remaining drunks toward Stratosphere's doors. The music ended and the lights were raised. The floor was set to be swept and mopped. The emptiness was a welcomed precursor to a much-needed rest. When she got home, she planned to take the test that sat concealed deeply in her purse.

Kat pulled the tip money from a tin near the register

and began to count the night's gains. She barely detected the movement of shadows over the bar. Without looking up, she said, "We're closed."

"That means I can take you with me?"

Heat swelled within her from the sudden recognition of the husky voice. Jacob's silver eyes scanned over her. He dropped a hundred-dollar bill from the inside pocket of his suit jacket into her tip pile. "That's for standing you up this weekend."

The slender thirty-two-year-old man reached out to tuck a loose strand of hair behind Kat's ear. His face's Machiavellian features upturned to a toothy grin. He leaned over the bar, kissing Kat softly. She was rigid at first but quickly yielded to the gentle coaxing of his lips.

He pulled back, whispering, "I have a room tonight— when can you leave?"

Kat's eyes dropped from his face back to the pile of money with the hundred-dollar bill addition. She knew she should have resisted him. She should have screamed at him and commanded that he leave. Maybe she could have the bouncer throw him onto the pavement outside. Kat planted her achy feet on sticky floor below and faced him. She opened her mouth to speak, only to have his playful smile overthrow her bravado.

His fingertips crawled over the surface of her forearm. Kat shivered with the hopes he hadn't noticed.

"Give me ten minutes," she said.

"I'll be outside," he replied, and then backtracked the way he entered.

Kat finished adding up her tips and dividing them with the barback. She expedited her closing duties and, with a passing nod to the manager, rushed outside.

Jacob was harbored from the misting rain underneath a nearby coffee shop's awning. His hands were tucked in his pockets. He stood firm, braced against the brisk breeze with a cigarette bobbing from his lips. Kat quickly hopped down the sidewalk beside him, shielding the rain in futility with her hands. She yanked the cigarette from his mouth and drew in smoke.

"Hey, baby," he said.

Kat blew smoke back at him with flagrant disregard. Jacob closed his eyes and chuckled while a plume of smoke careened across the arcs of his face.

"Don't ever stand me up again," Kat said, crushing the cigarette underneath her shoe.

The surrounding storefronts and bars were vacant mausoleums in the placid two o'clock hour. A lone siren mewled off in the distance. The rain had driven lingering insomniacs to shelters unknown. The quiet, stormy street in Wicker Park belonged to them.

He hooked her in his arm and pressed his lips against hers. Kat inhaled hints of burnt tobacco and sugary pomade. His mouth was piquant with cigarettes and gin. Kat's mutual kisses grew ravenous. She pulled at his suit jacket, desperate to prolong the moment.

"Come on," Jacob said, severing from her, swallowing his words as he made an attempt to collect his breath.

The air felt colder now, away from his arms.

He stepped off the curb and stuck his arm out onto the street. He turned back to her with a timid smile as his dark hair was flattened from the sheets of rain. His suit's shoulders sagged with moisture. A cab shortly rolled to a stop before him.

As they scrambled into the cab, Jacob called out, "Take

us to the Grant Park Hotel."

Jacob enclosed Kat in his arms. They were saturated with rainwater and keeping close for heat. Kat eyed the cab driver, a Nigerian man spiritedly speaking into his headpiece in a foreign tongue. The air permeated with the driver's rising and falling rhythmic syllables. When she was assured that the driver's focus was devoted to the road ahead, she leaned into Jacob. A soft peck was shared between them.

Kat studied Jacob's lips before she kissed him again. Streetlight scattered by beads of water and the steamy windows cavorted across his face. She wished she had her camera in hopes of capturing the image. They kissed once more while Jacob's hand slid between her thighs. Kat closed them tighter, seizing his hand in their warmth. She exhaled a euphoric sigh.

This was quickly ended by a dry crackling of the driver clearing his throat in objection.

"No sex," he said in a thick accent.

Kat and Jacob exchanged sheepish smiles and private glances with one another, until the cab arrived in front of the Grant Park Hotel. Jacob gave the driver several bills in appreciation.

He took Kat's hand and they charged past the rain into the narrow lobby. Kat had grown to know this hotel through the many nights they had together. The gilded suites with their Rembrandt prints in brass frames and the alleged affluence of artificial flowers. The dated baroque touches and Persian rugs left the rooms overwrought. Kat struggled against a pang of familiarity.

A mirrored elevator led them to the seventh floor. The elevator walls' reflective surfaces reverted and multiplied their images until the small space was populated by thousands of hands sliding past clothing and thousands of lips nibbling at shivering flesh.

They entered a wide hotel room. Jacob shed his shirt and suit jacket. His stalwart arms gathered Kat, and with two long strides, they dropped into the bed at the room's center. Kat arched her back while Jacob peeled her shirt over her head. He released her breasts from her bra.

His mouth tasted the surface of her neck, then collarbone. His warm breath stretched across her bare skin. An ascension was brought about while her legs parted for him. He mounted her softly and a moan sounded from Kat. She was almost high enough to ignore that her bag held a pregnancy test and that his left hand that had slipped off her underwear bore a simple gold wedding band. And almost high enough to allude that his kisses and touches were stolen. His affection wasn't a gift, just a sordid misdeed expressing itself between them like an ugly compulsion.

And soon after riding the crests and heat of him, he would leave her. She would spend the rest of the night alone in the hotel room accompanied only by the solemn discord of raindrops.

8

Leslie stepped through his apartment door to greet his roommates with a grunt. His head edged into pain. The week had labored by in excruciating slowness. The days were spent underneath a dome of malevolent storm clouds. When Thursday evening finally arrived, the weather, coupled with the tight train ride home, Leslie's mood had soured sharply.

He wasted no time separating his body from his scrubs. He'd spent the day in disputes with pharmacies and fighting for a refill for an elderly woman with poor insurance coverage. Ultimately, his efforts had been fruitless. His silver-haired patient would have to choose between which medications were vital and which could be missed. The next weeks could be filled with prolonged misery if Leslie couldn't come up with a solution.

Leslie tossed his backpack down and collapsed on the couch next to his roommates. Russell looked at him with lulled eyes, and between his fingers was a bowl stuffed with marijuana. Russell offered it to Leslie, who lit the bowl, sucked slowly, and exhaled. The pungent stench of weed added to the smoke spires left by burning incense sticks. Leslie ached from a sudden release of tension in his muscles. Russell and Kat were sprawled out like marionettes with cut strings on the other end of the couch. A '90s sitcom flickered on the TV screen followed by an intermittent laugh track.

"You got mail," Russell said. He threw his head in the direction of envelopes on the coffee table as if he suffered from paralysis.

Leslie had to rally to collect the envelopes. He scanned over them: a credit card offer, a coupon screaming the urgency of a spring clothing sale, and a crisp letter from Chicago Rehabilitation Institute of Hope. Next to the name was an embossed heart with a cross. The envelope felt dense, and he resisted a chuckle rising in him. The irony of stoned fingers battling around a pen to write a check for rehab was too much to process. Giggles pressed past his lips.

"What is it?" Kat asked, shifting listlessly toward him.

"A bill for Isaac's rehab."

Underneath the bill was a certified letter. Leslie frowned when he saw his father's return address, ripped open the envelope, and found a small notice and a check. He stumbled forward, reaching for a wall to lean on. Russell, on the couch, made a joke that Leslie didn't hear. He was too busy repeatedly reading the notice until the black words blurred into a featureless line. The letter came with a check written for forty thousand dollars.

The floor veered underneath him and his knees bowed. Tears blinded the sight of Kat and Russell, and there wasn't enough air to fill Leslie's lungs. He heard himself gasp wildly.

"My mother's dead."

Kat vaulted from the couch and was at his side. He handed her the letter and gave in to gravity, sliding down the wall, unable to swallow. Russell scooped up Leslie's backpack and emptied it, searching for his phone. He knelt down and handed Leslie the phone.

"Call your dad," he said.

Kat read the letter and began to pace. "Wait, this letter said she died two months ago."

Leslie glanced up, wiping tears from his face. "I don't understand."

Russell reached up for the letter and scanned it. "The check is part of the settlement. There's probably going to be more coming to you."

"Why is he now just telling you?" Kat asked.

A heaviness fell over Leslie. He stared at his phone and tried to recall the last time he spoke to his parents. It had been so long that he wondered if his parents had the same phone number, though that thought was irrational. The last time he had been to Novi, Michigan, was when he graduated. Those dizzying months applying to school, under the harsh glare of his parents. During that time, they had been more concerned with why he wasn't dating. Every conversation invariably turned to why he hadn't brought a young woman around.

And now, as he sat with his phone trembling in hand, feeling the grief turning sour within him, his mother's face replayed incessantly in his mind. All he could see was her repulsion as her awkward eighteen-year-old skinny boy admitted that he was gay, followed by his father's anger erupting in an onslaught of vicious slurs that after all these years still stung fresh. Years had hardened the bitterness between them, but his mother's death made the distance insurmountable.

Leslie could feel the bitterness digging deeper into him, feeding on his entrails. He was being hollowed out, leaving a leaden numbness.

Russell and Kat both joined Leslie on the floor. Their faces were fraught with concern, but Leslie felt like they were sucking out the air around him. He became aware of the heat they were giving off and began to sweat himself. He closed his eyes and made a desperate attempt to breathe.

"Call your dad," Russell said. "There has to be some sort of mistake."

"There is no mistake," Leslie said, clutching his head. "I was cut off."

Leslie hauled himself up from the floor and walked to his bedroom. He closed the door behind him. Tremors overtook him and he teetered before falling onto his bed. He dialed his parent's home and listened to the answering machine. On the machine, he heard his mother's rich voice, "Hello..."

"Mom?" he asked, heart jolting in his chest. It could've been a mistake.

"You've reached the Graham residence, sorry we're not available. If you leave a message, we'll be sure to get back to you. Have a blessed day."

The machine let out a sharp beep. Hot tears dropped

from Leslie eyes. Dismayed, he paused, realizing he hadn't thought about what he'd say if someone answered, or what kind of message to leave. He almost hung up. If his mother's death didn't warrant a phone call, a message wouldn't do much in return. But he cleared his throat.

"Dad, it's me. I got your letter, please call me."

He hung up the phone and recalled the letter he'd read:

Dear Leslie,

Your mother passed away on February 26. Enclosed is an early check from the settlement I expect to receive. I expect more and will forward you the additional checks according to her will.

The words were callous, as if they weren't about death, but those clipped sentences opened up so many questions. Leslie couldn't possibly be expected to believe any of this. This had to be an act of spite against his homosexuality. He understood that his parents loathed him, but shouldn't death end this feud? His mother died nearly two months ago in Michigan, and he'd been living his life in Chicago as if nothing happened.

As fresh tears came, Leslie laid back on his bed, waiting for a phone call he knew wouldn't come.

9

Russell didn't quite know what to do with himself in the apartment. Kat had already left for her shift at Stratosphere and Leslie hadn't come out of his room since he'd learned of his mother's death. Russell knocked a few times to check on him, but Leslie insisted his was fine. This left Russell all the more awkward and unable to figure out what to do.

He slipped on his leather jacket, left the apartment, and was strolling in the direction of Stratosphere when his phone buzzed. He glanced down at his screen, which notified him of an invitation to Playnight.

Playnight was an annual party that inspired myths. Attendees learned details of the event through a labyrinth of social networks, text messages, and blog posts, and select VIPs were rumored to receive gift baskets of Moët and flowers. The guest list boasted deejays, painters, performers, models, and even a few celebrities. No one on the outside knew how to get on the list or identify the ingenious artisans behind the actual party. Whoever it was had enough financial backing to rent out buildings and close down streets without any corporate sponsorship. The anonymous party planners were the center of many urban legends, which connected them to the mob, prohibition, and even a cult dedicated to heinous rituals.

Playnight traditionally took place on Chicago's north side, at a location revealed on the night of the party. Passwords were sent through a wave of emails and text messages, and those who weren't well-connected followed instructions from a protected website and expected to withstand long lines to get inside. Those who knew the right people move past the line with ease, and this rigorous process maintained the party's exclusivity.

At his first Playnight, Russell spent forty minutes alone in line until he met Kat and Leslie, who cracked jokes with him and passed around a flask, forever cementing their friendship. In the past few years, he'd met the right people and now breezed by the lines populated with eager newcomers and those unfortunate enough to lack social capital.

This most recent clandestine notification announced that the party was a month away.

At the bar, Russell nodded to Kat, who made her way over to him.

"So we're going to Playnight?" Kat asked, leaning from behind the bar with someone's credit card in her hand. She spoke at an elevated level over pulsing trance music.

"I mean, yeah," Russell said. "It's tradition."

"A religious holiday," Kat said with a smile.

From the end of the bar, a guy wearing sunglasses called out, "Hey, girl. Can you close my tab already?"

Russell smirked as a tiny line creased between Kat's eyebrows. She spun around and fabricated a smile, before blurring away to heed the crowd's thirsty cries.

It was Friday night and Stratosphere was starting to fill up. Russell came early enough to secure stools at the bar, but elbow room was growing scarce. In the matter of a half hour, a small line would form just outside the door.

Kat came back with a whiskey and coke and slid it across the bar to Russell.

"Have you talked to Leslie?"

"He's not really talking," Russell said. "I don't know what to do."

"God, his dad is a fucking prick," Kat said, then she glanced past Russell.

He turned to follow her gaze and saw Leslie amble through the door. Face dark, pace slow, he made his way to his friends. Surprised, Russell wrapped his arm around Leslie and gave him a rough squeeze. Kat reached over the bar and grabbed Leslie's hand.

"How are you?" they asked simultaneously.

Leslie gave them a thin smile. "You guys are freaking me out."

Russell and Kat pulled back and offered smiles.

"Sorry," Russell said sheepishly.

"I really just don't want to talk about it," Leslie said.

"We're worried about you," Kat said, "and if you need anything—"

"Anything at all," Russell said.

"Just let us know," Kat finished.

Leslie smirked. "Okay, okay... just please stop finishing each other's sentences."

Kat placed a glass in front of Leslie and with quick hands added gin, lemon juice, and simple syrup. Leslie nodded and took the glass.

"I love you so much right now," Leslie said. "So, I got the invite."

"You want to go?" Russell said.

"It's our Christmas," Leslie said.

"This will this be the fourth Playnight we've been to," Russell said.

"Fifth," Leslie corrected, sipping the gin gimlet.

"So you think we'll have to wait in line this year?" Russell asked, turning his whiskey and coke into his mouth.

"I'm a fucking nurse and you're a lowly banker," Leslie said. "We're lucky to even get the invites."

Despite their mundane vocations, they were fixtures in a constellation of cliques and partiers, these same groups that fed parties like Playnight. Russell had witnessed many meltdowns, fistfights, hookups, and exiles. His social standing was merely a by-product of staying power and enough foresight to avoid conflict.

Kat went to the other end of the bar to refill glasses and returned as quickly as she had left. Her hands popped lids off beer bottles.

"There's an art show tomorrow in West Loop, and you have to come," she said, then vanished toward the end of the bar.

Russell frowned. "I don't think so."

Leslie angled his head toward him. "So you're an artist who won't support art?"

"I'm not an artist," Russell said matter-of-factly.

His mind flashed to the canvases concealed in his room and he felt the shame of one trying to bury a decomposing corpse before the investigators came with questions.

"Not this shit again," Leslie muttered. "You had one bad year as an artist and flash-forward you're Mister Banker."

"If you and Kat want to pay my part of the rent, I'll go back to my... what did that critic call it?"

"It doesn't matter," Leslie said.

Russell tossed back his drink to aid in the recall. "'An exercise in contrivance.'"

Leslie gave him a repentant glance. Russell's voice sounded terse played back in his ears. His face was florid with embarrassment. He tugged at his collar.

"Sorry, man," he said.

Kat emerged. "Sorry for what?"

"He went crazy-white-boy over that art critic again," Leslie reported.

Kat poured liquor into a glass full of ice and topped it with squirt of Coke. She slammed it in front of Russell. She leaned forward, inches separating them. A lock of dark hair fell from behind her ear as she softly reached out. Kat's hand was impossibly small on his large shoulder. Tiny fingers extended over the muscle. Her bright red lips arranged into a smile while black lights dyed her skin an artificial neon blue. An array of liquor bottles glowed from the shelves behind her, casting a halo of light around her face. In that moment, she paralleled all the Virgin Mary paintings Russell had seen growing up. She stared back with that same pious tenderness.

Holy rays of divinity were replaced by strobe lights. A saint consecrated in the commerce of vodka, whiskey, and gin.

"You're a real artist, stupid," she said, "regardless of what you think."

He blushed suddenly at the words of his profane Mary.

Kat's hand slipped away as she dipped back out to attend to her thirsty mob.

"Oh, so you don't cuss her out," Leslie snorted.

"Shut up," Russell said with a playful grin.

"Because she's pretty, right?"

Russell stammered for a retort. There was none. He silently sipped his drink because Leslie may have been right.

10

Leslie drained three gin gimlets before feeling the first tingle of intoxication. In the last few hours, he'd quipped back and forth with Russell, their jest periodically interrupted by Kat's wistful commentary. Stratosphere's crowd was comprised of the usual, cool faces. The night had pushed on and dispositions gave way to baser conduct. The drunken coterie, heaped upon itself, was an unbridled exertion of laughter and crude conversation. Bodies swayed together with lecherous ferocity to the thump of trip-hop.

While Russell's eyes shimmered with concern, Leslie felt the urge to hit him. He could almost believe this night was normal if it hadn't been for the look in Russell's eyes. No matter what they talked about, the result was the same. His mother had died and he was denied the opportunity to grieve and attend her funeral. He still didn't know how she died and was afraid to find out. He had called off work and stared at the screen of his MacBook, afraid to even Google her name.

What good could come from the details? Even in death she didn't want anything to do with him.

Russell slurped his drink and said, "I think you should invest the money your mom left you."

Leslie sucked his teeth. "I don't want to talk about it."

The money had been a surprise. His best guess was that the will was drawn up before he had come out to his parents.

"I know, but I really think you need to talk to a financial adviser," Russell said.

"Wow, you really aren't an artist anymore."

Russell winced and swallowed his drink. "Fine. Never mind."

"Sorry," Leslie said. "I didn't mean that."

"It's okay."

"And I already decided what I'm going to do with the money," Leslie said. "I'm going to pay for Isaac's rehab."

"But that's nearly all of your money."

Leslie sighed and felt the sting of tears. "Let's talk about anything else. Did you get Ava's dad's permission to propose yet?"

"Not yet," Russell replied.

"You'd better do it before the ring starts collecting dust," Leslie said.

"Dinner went well," Russell said. "I think he likes me."

"Well, I guess he's not as smart as we thought," Leslie said.

Russell chuckled.

"Yo, boys!" a voice shrilled in their direction.

Leslie jerked, startled. Russell's eyes rolled and he tensed with annoyance. Leslie spun in the direction of the voice.

"Shit," he muttered.

"When the fuck did he get back in town?"

Beck Ashby approached them with open arms and exaggerated cheerfulness. He snaked forward, his inflated movements forcing nearby bodies out of his advance. His bleached-blond hair stood up in stiff spikes, and even in the dark bar, his skin glowed the sickly copper of too many spray-on tans. Behind him trolled a small posse with duplicate pomposity.

"Hey," Leslie and Russell said in unison.

"It's so good to see you, man," Beck said, his dilated pupils leaving his irises barely visible. His face was slightly slacked.

His company included two young women with pinched faces and a muscular Asian guy with harsh tattoos and enough facial piercings to resemble a decorative pin cushion. They shoved up to the bar around Russell and Leslie and usurped any remaining personal space. Leslie turned to Russell, who had grimaced as he constricted his body to make room for the willowy women. Beck was too high to care about the invasion on Leslie and Russell.

"Isaac's outta rehab?" Beck asked.

"Yeah, he's out," Leslie said between clinched teeth.

"I would've seen him, but I had business in Madrid."

Leslie noticed whitish powder smeared at the tip of Beck's nose.

"How is he?" Beck asked.

"As good as anyone getting out of rehab can be," Leslie said. "He wondered why you didn't visit."

Beck forced a guffaw. Leslie thought about lunging at him. The thought of his fist cracking over Beck's orange face warmed him.

"I love the guy, but I don't do rehab," Beck said, and his cohorts laughed as if on cue.

The pitch of the cackle was coarse against the smooth tones of trip-hop, and Leslie's muscles tightened with indignation.

Styled to precision and armed with a supposed trust fund, Beck Ashby was a career party boy. He surrounded himself with those of equal beauty, with the same nonchalance one would choose new shoes or a trendy shirt. He was notorious in several social circles. His past exploits followed him like stagnant funk.

Leslie witnessed Beck dragging people into the delirium of parties that thumped into the early morning hours. In his presence, there were endless amounts of top-shelf liquor, and in bathroom stalls, dark alleys, and hotel rooms he shared handfuls of pills and lines of coke. A genteel connoisseur in cocaine consumption, Beck only snorted it through hundred-dollar bills. There were talks of after-parties so hedonistic they bled into orgies. Rumor of Beck's sexual ambiguity was confirmed when he slept with anyone willing to pay him attention.

Urged by Isaac, Leslie ventured out at Beck's invitation a few times. Isaac, for some baffling reason, graciously took his station as one of Beck's disciples, following him to spacious lofts and luxury downtown apartments. Isaac had been giddy in his consumption of liquor and mysterious little pills.

Leslie had, too, been taken in by Beck's charms. But a young woman near overdose mixed with physical assaults exploding between a few high partygoers had acquainted him with a propriety he thought he'd lost.

Isaac claimed Beck was one of his best friends. He never wavered in his conviction even though Beck hadn't visited him or answered any of his phone calls.

The party had to roll on.

"Look, tell him I said hi," Beck said. "And if he needs a place to stay, he's more than welcome to stay with me."

Beck was handed a tall, red drink from the decorative pin cushion lieutenant. He and the invaders withdrew into the crowd.

Kat reappeared, her face pensive. "What did he want?"

"Nothing worth a damn," Leslie said darkly.

11

Beck Ashby's body was euphoric and weighted down by exhaustion all at the same time. He drank warm vodka from a glass as he lay in his bed. Restless, bloodshot eyes took in the first hints of morning light, slicing wisps of clouds coloring the withering shadows in his bedroom purple. The light bounced off the small mirror on his nightstand covered in a powdery residue from the lines he snorted earlier. In bed with him, a female companion sprawled out bare and exposed. Her large breasts slid off to her sides, pointing her nipples in different directions. Alongside her was another friend who had, hours before, eagerly stripped down to her G-string and shared the bed with them in exchange for Beck's pretty lines of coke.

This first woman, Marcie, turned to stripping after a successful dance career with a Chicago ballet company. Rumor said too many drugs and an unplanned pregnancy with her thuggish on-again, off-again boyfriend changed her life course.

Marcie's friend rested on the edge of the bed in a spot made damp by spilled bodily fluids and sweat. Her head was propped up, eyes barely opened and mouth slack, too high to care. Lost in a narcosis, she was grateful for the pills offered to her.

Across the room, past piles of clothes, scattered Oxy, and a broken bottle of Grey Goose, was Marcie's boyfriend. His face was tight with slumber, exposing the jagged scar that ran from his chin through his beard to his closed eyes. Drugs and chemicals had gotten the better of this massive man, now slouched over an armchair with his pants around his ankles. He'd settled on watching before passing out.

Beck had hoped vodka would bring him down enough to get a few hours of sleep, but nearly a glass later he was still wired and dead tired. His stomach twisted with hunger. His bladder ached. He slipped on his robe and he walked through his bedroom, careful to avoid the broken glass. In the living room, the TV flickered upon the wall, sending a steady pulse of light over the demolition. More broken glass was scattered on the kitchen floor, the smell of vomit hung in the air, and muddy footprints flecked the carpet. Cigarette butts floated like logs in half empty beer bottles littered all over the countertops.

Beck's dehydrated posse lay disposed on the couch, his lieutenant engulfed in the two women. With the promise of a good time financed by Beck, they followed him anywhere, but looking at them curled up on his couch, so grateful to be occupants in his kingdom, he felt disgust rise from his feet. *Sucker fish attached to a shark,* he thought, *waiting for the scraps.*

Despite his annoyance with his comrades, he accepted them. They would never offer any profound commentary or opinion to conflict his. They watched his movements desperately and did all they could to stay in his favor, always afraid the good time would end. Arguably, this was a small price to pay for the sucker fish, ravenous for any stray bones or bloody flesh left over by the shark. The only purpose they served was keeping Beck's treacherous loneliness away. His loneliness could be so profound in moments when things were still. When Beck was sober, it was as if the world had completely discarded him.

His posse, simple and vapid, was an adequate barrier. Spewing their humorous nonsense, they kept him far from the sinkhole that found him in their absence.

Beck stepped over the legs of another of Marcie's friends, snoring in a corner. Her legs were stretched out open and her mini shirt hiked up around her waist, exposing herself. Beck grumbled and placed a nearby throw pillow over her midsection.

He walked into his bathroom where another guy with all the trappings of a musician from an indie rock group slept. Curled next to the toilet, the rocker's face was pressed against the bathroom's tiled floor. The smell of vomit was more pronounced in the air and the muscles tightened along Beck's chest as he fought off the urge to heave. In the toilet, chunks and spackle made a swampy substance within the bowl. He flushed and began to relieve himself, and the force of his urine stream caused a mist to fall on the rocker's stirring body.

"You're pissing on me!" the rocker said as he opened his eyes.

Beck glowered down at him and even showed his teeth in a snarl.

"Sorry, man," the rocker whimpered, moving away from the urine cloud and lying back down.

Beck walked back through his spacious Wicker Park apartment. The cleaning service would return its harshness of chrome, glass tables, and black leather couches. Any softness or warmth the space possessed was in a large collection of art pieces produced by neighborhood artists in appreciation for a party he had invited them to or drugs he had managed to score for them.

In the open space of the kitchen, he opened his refrigerator. After a brief scan of its sparse contents, he settled on leftover chicken shawarma. He sniffed it cautiously before he brought it to his mouth. Past his counter, bodies stretched out like corpses before him. He had announced an after-party for the last few remnants as Stratosphere closed. A couple of cab rides later, his apartment was crammed with nearly twenty people consuming thousands in coke and pills, kept lively by loud music pounding throughout the night. Until the morning, he successfully managed not to end up alone.

Beck returned to his room and his glass of warm vodka. The woman in the G-string was staring blankly at the ceiling, humming softly. He opened the window, lit a cigarette, and watched the morning life below him on Damen. There was the runner clad in athletic gear jaunting down the sidewalk, dodging poles and chained up bikes, and the early dog walker tugged along by a black, midsize canine. There was a pair of happy lovers walking close, coffees in their free hands. He had seen the two frequent Stratosphere, where they were drunk, lusting in public and practically simulating the sex they would have. Sober now, the horny lovers were completely different. They were in their late twenties, healthy, and happy. The type of people who were exemplary in their normalcy, dressed well but not too sharp. The woman was beautiful in that painfully ordinary girl-next-door sort of way. The man appeared well-to-do with plastic rim glasses, probably a guy with a comfortable job, making comfortable money. In the morning, the lovers were so harshly pedestrian Beck wanted to heave his glass out the window at them.

Those lovers, happy and together, have some audacity walking past his apartment, marring his view with their obvious uncomplicated love for each other.

Beck felt the chill of his own hollowness that deepened with every monthly deposit made from his dwindling annuity. This money was contingent on him never returning to Boston to bring embarrassment to the Ashby name. No one had the patience to understand his recklessness or eccentricities. The Ashby Legacy, established now over four generations, had one chief purpose: maintain appearance, even at the cost of exiling wayward members.

The brazen faces of his parents looked back at him from the front seat of their car as they drove away from the police station on a morning much like this. Posting bail had been their final act of compassion before they cut him a check and—at the behest of the rest of the Ashby clan—changed the locks. He received the occasional Christmas card and obligatory phone call, where he was forced to ignore their disgust and mask his own elevating contempt.

Beck heard stirring behind him. On wobbly legs, the woman he'd been calling G-string nearly crashed into the doorframe of his bedroom. Marcie sat up and gestured Beck to her, a craving smile on her face. He downed the last of his vodka and tossed off his robe. He joined Marcie in bed, and she straddled him. She found a condom in his nightstand and placed it on him, her hands were swift in the well-rehearsed act. She then dropped on him, angling him into her. She plowed forward onto him and Beck's eyes closed. Time fell away and he became aware only of the sound of flesh on flesh. And when he opened his eyes, he saw Marcie's maniacal grin turned toward her scarred boyfriend, who had begun fondling himself.

Warmth sparked in Beck as he reached his climax under the gaze of them.

For a moment, his hollow loneliness vanished. Exhaustion finally descended upon him. After everyone finished, Beck curled into a comforting blackness. Again, his grasp on time loosened. Down in sleep's dark pit he heard the sound of his apartment slowly emptying out. He imaged the rocker's face pale, reeking of vomit and Beck's piss, with the throw pillow flasher and G-string staggering out like zombies to whatever their lives were. They were probably keen to wash away their sins and stains while nursing hangovers. An hour, or maybe minutes, elapsed when he heard Marcie at the edge of the bed wiggling into her tight clothes. Her high heel steps were a series of combustions as she made her way out of the apartment, taking her scarred, voyeuristic Peeping Tom with her.

With the last of them gone, leaving only his trio, he returned to his living room. His lieutenant was in front of the TV, clicking between sports channels. Beck heard playful splashing from the bathroom as his female companions shared the shower. He considered joining them until he heard thumping on the door. *The cleaning ladies must have come early.*

Hazy from coming down, Beck nodded at his lieutenant, who set down the remote, walked to the door, and kneeled to retrieve a folded piece of paper.

"Hey, Beck," he said, scanning it. "You might want to check this out."

Beck stopped in his progression to the shower. He rolled his eyes, making his way to the door, snatching the paper. His sucker fish moved past him and back to the couch.

He stared over the paper. His mouth fell open as Beck slowly reread the words to himself.

"DUE TO EXCESSIVE NOISE VIOLATIONS AND A PAST DUE RENT WITH A BALANCE OF $11,250, TENANT(S) HAS FIFTEEN DAYS FROM THIS DATE TO VACATE THE PREMISES."

Beck heard a popping crunch and then felt wetness dripping around his foot. He peered down, passed the paper to his heel, which had settled on shards of broken glass. Sudden pain from severed skin ignited Beck's leg. He drew back his foot.

The pain began to fade and that familiar dreadful loneliness gripped him as blood seeped from the cut, adding to the wreckage around him.

12

Like most obligations planned far ahead in advance, this was innocent enough, nothing to anticipate with any great excitement. Months had separated Russell from this impending threat, but with the steady passage of time, the event slowly ensued its ominousness. Ava brought a small cardstock square with her a few weeks ago. She shoved aside the massive collection of chip-clip magnets and crude innuendoes spelled out in magnetic poetry so she could fasten the cardstock to his refrigerator with a magnetic bottle-opener. The card was fortified with pink ribbons and lace and inscribed with a thin, curling script. Since its placement, the card survived injuries caused by trampling feet when the refrigerator was closed too quickly and the magnet's strength succumbed to the weighty paper. Even mauled, the cardstock became a vehicle of stress. Without waver, this wedding invitation proclaimed the union of one of the Von Hoffmans' random family friends.

Ava practically mandated Russell's attendance.

She had been swift in returning her RSVP. She wrote out Russell's name in legible lettering on the response card, grieving that misspelled names on place cards was a cataclysmic faux pas. Ava rattled on about the dangers of April weddings and the risk of rainstorms. It's not good luck if it rains on your wedding day, she opined, but merely a matter of poor planning. Her zeal left Russell confused and silent.

A dank bouquet of marijuana and patchouli hung over his apartment. Orange light broke through the purple curtains onto the floor where Kat sat cross-legged. Her laptop rested on her knees while she mindlessly modified photos. Without smoking, she passed a blunt to Leslie, still in his work scrubs and near comatose on the couch.

Like most Wednesday nights, they locked the doors, shut the windows, and laid out a contemptible spread of pizza, weed, and loosely scripted reality television.

"This old woman I've been taking care of is going to die," Leslie said, spewing smoke and gawking at the ceiling. "She has no insurance, barely any money, and no one to give two shits about her."

Kat grumbled in response.

Leslie lifted himself from the couch and peered into the kitchen. "Are you going to stare at the wedding invitation all day or are you gonna bring me a beer?"

Russell turned from the refrigerator, his awareness hampered from a few hard hits off the blunt. He placed two beers on the counter and took down the beer-opener magnet and invitation. He considered it for a moment. The wedding was this weekend and there was no avoiding it. He would soon be outnumbered by Ava's family and friends.

He set the invitation on the counter and walked back

to the couch, where he forced Leslie up and made space for himself. He handed Leslie a beer and the opener.

"Anything else, diva?" Russell laughed.

"How about service with a smile?"

On the counter, the invitation was subjected to more torture than a prisoner being held for questioning. The paper absorbed grease from a nearby pizza box, which stained it in circular splotches. The rosy pink discolored to a sickly yellow. A vehement discussion in which Leslie tried to prove the importance of reality TV left the invitation wilting in an aggressive tide of toppled beer. No effort was made to resuscitate the invite, though it was mopped dry and placed back on the refrigerator, lettering still vibrant on the bubbled and mangled cardstock.

13

The day began with Kat missing her train to downtown. In a panic, she floundered on the steps up to the train's elevated platform. Her foot slipped and the jagged edges of stairs surged toward her. She quickly cradled her camera as her body absorbed the impact with a sharp slap. She ignored the stares of others and watched the doors slide shut and the train glide away. Her heart sank.

She struggled to her feet and up the remaining stairs. Her body was wracked with pain. She was certain grisly bruises would later brand her forearms and shins. Kat was ten minutes late when she reached downtown. She dashed through the sidewalks. Adrenaline ricocheted off the walls of her chest by the time she made it to a glass office building. She pushed through the doors, stepped into the elevator, and steadied her breath in a bid to rid herself of dread.

The elevator opened and Kat was standing on the eighteenth floor of Gil Malv Designs. She moved on plush carpet through the hallway. At the end of the hallway, a desk separated a network of offices. A wan receptionist peeked from behind her computer screen. Disdain mounted on her face at the sight of Kat.

"Hi, I'm here for the Belle Journee photo shoot," she said.

The receptionist turned to her screen dismissively. "You're late."

"I know," Kat said. "I'm so sorry."

"Well, it doesn't matter anyway." The receptionist began typing. "The shoot was cancelled."

"Cancelled?"

The receptionist stopped typing to focus solely on glaring at Kat. "You didn't get the memo?"

Kat sighed and anger prickled her voice. "Obviously not." Her voice seethed with sarcasm. "Thank you for your time."

She plodded back to the elevator and pressed the console. She could feel the receptionist's glare chafe at her. Kat held her breath as she shrank within herself, pushing the elevator button and feeling her moment of defeat prolonged, serenaded by a merry electronic chime as the elevator made its slow ascent. Her earlier injuries began to bite at her in nauseating swells. Kat deserted her life for this horrid realm of purgatory, where the receptionist reigned as her tormentor. Sobs crawled up her throat. Before they could assert themselves, the elevator doors opened.

She nearly dove in and turned to see the door close on the receptionist's sneer.

Once on the street, she scrolled through her phone with

an urge to hear a friendly voice. She placed the phone to her ear, listening to the dial tone's soft drum punctuated by a rapid scuffling.

"What are you doing calling me?" a panicked voice breathed.

"Jacob, I..."

She was silenced by the muffled intonation of a woman's voice. She could pick up the soft, measured muttering lifting at the end to pose a question.

"It's just work asking about the MacIntyre project," Jacob said.

His voice was replaced by a muffled wrestling of movement, most likely Jacob passing through rooms. Kat envisioned him passing through the condo she'd never been to, distancing himself from a wife she couldn't picture. She imagined this woman as a featureless silhouette moving through fog, not an actual construct of reality. This wife could only be a ghostly figure in her mind. Anything else would cripple her with a searing guilt.

"What do you want?" his asked in a hissing whisper.

A weight was dropped on Kat's chest as she came to a standstill in the middle of the sidewalk. People nudged past her. Under knocks of shoulders and bags, she was wreckage tossed by the rapids. Faces blurred past and altered into a varying shade of flesh. She was engulfed in the current.

"I just... wanted to talk," she whispered.

An exasperated sigh blew back into her ear. "I'll call you later."

There was an acute click. Discomfited, Kat returned her phone to her bag and turned up to the chilly streets before her. She stepped forward, milling into the activity ebbing between the mountainous walls of concrete and glass. Her aimless feet scuffled down into the subway, through glossy tiled walls and onto the platform. The air around her was still and dank. With her gaze pointed directly at her feet and her peripheral obstructed by a panel of black hair, she almost convinced herself she was alone. She pretended that at Jacob's dissent the concrete mouth of the city swallowed her up.

She hadn't sought out be intertwined with a married man. He hadn't worn his wedding ring at the photoshoot where they met, a Belle Journee assignment to take corporate headshots of an advertising agency. She spent hours coaxing the rigid human resources team to appear less like corpses. Kat's nerves were crackling at their ends when a handsome, tailored man settled into the small box of her camera lens. He lent himself generously to her direction. He then introduced himself and stared into her face, past the camera, making it increasingly difficult for her to take the picture.

He had asked her out for dinner. He presented his simple request as if he was doing her the favor. She pretended to hesitate but had been drawn in almost immediately. His words worked over her thoroughly while they picked coolly at nearby French cuisine. The man was cunning, brushing hair from her face and hinting about her beauty.

She willingly slept with Jacob that night and was now wondering if she was pregnant with his child. A married man's child.

The air within the subway station stirred and Kat was pulled out of her reverie into the present. Grinding metal gears squealed as the train came to a standstill. Kat boarded and sat next to a window. The glass looked out at the black curved walls of the tunnel, dotted with small yellow lamps. With a jolt, the train propelled forward and the wall surged by. The lamps became a long wavering line of light.

She rocked with movement as the train barreled underneath the city. She felt something akin to relief in the dense inactivity of the train car. Her eyes moved along the narrow space from passenger to passenger—an elderly man with a face besieged by thin winkles, a lean man dressed sharply in a charcoal suit, and a middle school girl bobbing her headphones in rhythm to her music. A bald man faced away from Kat, braced by one hand on a train pole. Kat was ready to resign herself to this arrangement when the man turned in her direction. There, snug against his chest, dangled a baby in a sling. Using his free hand, the father supported the child, stroking the baby assuredly. The infant's fleshy limbs hung and kicked absently. Tiny hands naturally curled into fists, and the baby's blushed face was lax in contentment. The child had that eerie uncomplicated newness that extended into something primal and beautiful.

The scene siphoned air from Kat's lungs. A deep ached worked along the length of her spine. Wetness glistened in her eyes as she clutched her stomach with empty arms.

14

Beck moved calmly through the night. He stepped through shadowy, unmarked alleys. Cool drops of water fell from the gutters and fire escapes onto his forehead. His light footsteps hopped over puddles, and he charged toward a rusted door. He carefully coiled his fingers around the door handle and pushed. The door lurched opened and sounds of rusting iron upon iron cried high through the alley.

Beck took a set of metal stairs deeper into a basement where the familiar blast of hip-hop grumbled along the small hall. A few strays lingered, trying to angle a way into the party. A woman dressed in black leather stood guard, busy with her iPhone, her tiny, pale features lit by its screen. She roosted in front of the double doors like a bird on a stoop.

Beck stepped past her, through the double doors and into a darker space. Cigarette smoke and burning marijuana made a harsh, grey atmosphere in this small industrial basement. Exposed ventilation ducts hung overhead, and a portable floodlight lit a makeshift stage. Beck ebbed through the heavy crowd to a dim corner with a roped-off booth.

At the table sat his clique, his minions, giving a valiant performance. His lieutenant slouched a bit too much, his arms draped over the two women who were poised as if under the glare of an audience. Instead of alluring, their beautiful faces seemed sullen and their arched backs looked like a contrived attempt at sexiness. Across from them, Marcie the stripper sat pressed up against her scarred boyfriend's mass. In the center of the table sat two bottles of champagne.

Beck wondered who had the gall to order bottle service. He knew, like always, the tab would be left in his hands. Tightness gripped his gut. If his money was going to be used, they could have, at the very least, waited for him.

One of the thin women extended her bony hands around a nearby champagne flute. She brought it to her mouth and Beck's jaw clenched.

He reached deep down into his pocket and his fingers pried open a small plastic bag. He quickly gathered one of the Oxy pills and elbowed a path to the bathroom. Once inside the small room, he made an attempt to secure the door. The door handle was rusted, so to secure the door he used his foot. He twisted to grab a paper towel from the nearby dispenser, wrapped the pill in it, and placed it on the sink. Using the edge of his phone, he pounded on the pill under the paper towel and it crumbled underneath the blows.

He pulled a hundred-dollar bill from his money clip and rolled it tightly. Beck brought his face to the crushed pill, stuffed the bill in his right nostril, and pulled back a heavy snort. The pill shot through this canal and Beck winced, eyes filled with tears.

He threw his head back and felt a rise. The tightness in his gut simmered to a soft warm tickle. He sniffed, massaged his nose, and lumbered though the crowd, shoving his way into the booth. Everyone shuffled abruptly, stiffening almost fearfully at his presence. The woman struggling with her champagne flute stumbled to keep from falling. Settled in the booth, Beck reached out for her flute and snatched it from her.

She frowned and stood there awkwardly, moving her hand from her hips to crossed over her chest. The rest of the table, grateful to not be the subject of his anger, greeted Beck. Beck ignored them, swimming in the warmth of his high. He sniffed again, ensuring no leftover residue was in his nasal cavity.

He took at long swig of the flute and stared at its original owner. She gave him a beautiful, apologetic pout. He smiled at her, his eyes gazing past her as the chemicals settled deeper into him. He settled into a buoyancy that was like being lifted into the warmth of the summer sun.

Talk turned to the underground hip-hop artists who would cram onto the rickety stage and excite the air with profane rhymes. Beck mumbled and nodded when the conversation came his way. Finally tired of punishing his minion, he gestured toward his de-fluted female friend and let her sit on his lap.

Beck eyed the crowd until he saw Kat, Leslie, and Russell

moving through the basement. Behind them was a nervous blonde woman. They were laughing as Russell danced over expressively, grinning at the blonde. His large limbs almost swatted some near bystanders. Kat pulled back his arm and said something to one of them, most likely an apology. Leslie shook his head, said something, and they all laughed again.

Beck recognized the effects of the Oxy; the threesome was so beautiful they glowed. If he squinted, he could see the waves of their friendship curling off them like heat. He could feel it from where he sat in the booth. He smiled secretly as he felt their warmth tickle his skin. They seemed so cheerful, laughing and nudging each other.

If his lap hadn't been occupied, he would've joined them. He wanted to know the joke. He wanted to laugh at Russell's goofy dancing. He wanted to feel something real. Beck turned back to the table. He felt no warmth there. He felt nothing from the attractive, slender figures sipping the champagne he would he pay for. He looked at their vacant faces and their mouths spilling cold words.

15

Russell took Ava's hand and led her through the crowd to the dim bar in the wide basement. Once at the bar, he turned back to her.

"What do you want?"

"Is it... sanitary to drink anything from here?" she asked, her expression tight, straining to manage her anxiety.

Russell swallowed his irritation. "I don't think you'll die from anything behind the bar."

Ava had called him hours earlier, after work. He had been in the living room and naturally answered his phone.

When he told her of the night's plans to see a small concert, she casually asked if she could join in. Stammering, with his roommates simultaneously mouthing "no" in panic and waving their arms as if they were on fire, he gave his roommates a regretful smile and extended the invitation to Ava.

Leslie mock fainted and collapsed on the couch.

"Seriously, guys," Russell said.

Leslie opened one eye and propped himself up. "I'm joking. Kind of..."

"Weren't you the ones who said I should invite Ava out more?"

"Yes, you should," Kat said, "but not tonight. We're going to cheer up Leslie tonight."

Leslie smiled. "I'm fine, really. But Kat is right."

"Why?"

"Because we're going to a grimy ass back alley basement bar to listen to rap," Leslie said. "This is gonna scare the hell out of Ava."

"She'll be fine," Russell said.

"Are you sure?" Kat continued. "Half the room will be brown folks."

"What does that mean?" Russell said, sweat tickling down his neck. "She's not racist."

Kat grunted in skepticism.

Leslie rolled his eyes and said, "We know. Kat's not saying that. Look, it just might be a bit much for your future wife to deal with."

"She'll be fine."

"I don't want to babysit the rich white girl all night," Kat said.

"Kat, come on," Russell said, frustration rising.

"Yeah, Kat, chill," Leslie said. "Russell said she'll be fine—so, she'll be fine."

Russell nodded, and a few hours later, Ava joined them at their apartment. After a few celebratory shots, they gathered into a cab and took it east into the city. The taxi took them to the edge of South Loop, a few blocks from Chinatown, to a series of new rehabilitated high-rises and an abandoned warehouse.

They stepped on the street and walked a few blocks into the alleys behind the high-rises and warehouses. Ava had stopped talking and Russell sensed fear creeping over her. She barely made it through the door—Kat had to sweet-talk the vampire-looking hostess, whom she knew from prior parties.

"I'll have what you're having," Ava said now, wrapping her arms around herself. She flashed him a nervous, toothy smile.

Russell handed Ava a shot of Jameson and a canned beer. She held them out for inspection. Russell quickly swallowed his shot before the regret of inviting her began to settle. He watched her take the shot, coughing and wincing.

Russell felt his heart sink a bit as she took a napkin from her purse and wiped the edges of the beer can. He quickly looked around to see if his roommates had seen this. Kat and Leslie were gathered in the center basement, talking and unaware.

Russell sighed, but his relief was short-lived. He locked eyes with a skinny blond guy, hair twisted in knotty dreadlocks and light glinting off his silver septum piercing.

"Russell!" the skinny guy said as he trapped him in a hard, friendly hug.

"Curtis," Russell replied, quickly worming away from Curtis Newman's hold.

Borrowing a trick from Ava, Russell hid his disgust with a forced smile.

Curtis offered his hand to Ava, which she reluctantly shook as they introduced themselves.

"How do you two know each other?" Ava asked, shifting her gaze between the two.

"Friends from art school," Russell said.

"Are you kidding?" Curtis upturned with laughter. "This guy was my arch nemesis."

"Really?" Ava said, glancing at Russell.

"Yeah, we were the best students in class and every art contest we entered ended up being between him and me," Curtis said, and snickered.

Russell remembered the few years before he ended his art career. Intervals away from the highs of layering canvas with oil and acrylic were filled with icy glares between Curtis and himself. They would glare across classrooms, parties, and art shows, and when they did talk, their conversations were laced with backhanded compliments.

Curtis was more skilled with people. He'd pile on witty anecdotes for art professors and gallery owners. He'd spit out his winded philosophy on striving to find art in everything he did. He grew dreadlocks and began to fashion art more pleasing than provocative. Through it, Curtis became more of a caricature than a true artist.

Then again, Russell gave up art completely. With one disastrous art show and a damning review, Curtis finally won their longstanding rivalry, despite his numerous compromises.

Curtis playfully inspected the room, drew in closer, and lowered his voice. "Seriously, I don't know a better artist than Russell. I mean, besides myself."

"Yeah, thanks," Russell said flatly as his anger spiked.

"Huh. Wow," Ava said.

"You've seen his work, right?" Curtis asked.

Ava shook her head.

"Are you still painting?"

"No," Russell said.

It pained him so much he didn't have the stomach to acknowledge it. His hand hadn't touched paint in so long. He recalled the old toolboxes stuffed in the back of his closet with aging acrylic and oil paints. Hidden in shoe boxes, his brushes grew brittle from inactivity.

"You should check out his art," Curtis said. "Oh, and I told Kat about my art show. You should come."

"You're the art show in West Loop?"

Curtis slapped Russell on the back, stinging his skin. "See you there."

With that, he swung his dreadlocks and strolled back through the crowd.

Russell reached to scratch his own back. Ava grimaced while she sipped her beer. A group of black men moved toward them at the bar. Wide-eyed, Ava moved closer to Russell, gripping her purse.

She turned to Russell with a shaky smile. "When does the concert start?"

Russell stifled his disgust and shrugged.

16

Speakers, suspended on chains from the low-hanging ceiling, boomed over the stage. There, two men took their places. One stepped behind a computer and the other took the lone microphone. As he began to chant with the music, the crowd turned to the stage. Kat and Leslie wedged closer to the stage as deep bass rumbled over them.

Kat and Leslie exchanged smiles as the chorus started.

"Where is Russell?" Kat called into Leslie's ear. "He loves this guy."

Leslie frowned and pointed to the bar where Russell stood sullenly sipping beer and Ava clutched his arm, her face twisted with distress.

"Why doesn't he listen to me?" Kat asked.

"We know," Leslie said over the bass. "You're always right."

"I am," Kat said, crossing her arms in indignation.

"What do we do about her?" Leslie asked.

"We'll babysit in shifts," Kat said. "You go first."

"Why me?"

"I'll let you order drinks on my tab."

Leslie stroked his chin and pretended to consider Kat's offer.

"You know I have top-shelf taste."

"We're in a basement that probably has asbestos in the walls—I'm sure I can afford it."

Leslie pursed his lips and narrowed his eyes. "I feel like you're challenging me."

Kat playfully shoved him in the direction of the bar. Leslie faked an injury as he toiled his way to get drinks. Kat watched him negotiate with Russell. When the first song ended, Russell hauled his way up to the stage. His face was screwed in a grimace when he arrived at Kat's side. Kat turned to Leslie, standing next to Ava at the bar, most likely searching for the most expensive liquor he could find.

"What's wrong?" Kat asked.

"Please don't act like you don't know," Russell said as the band shifted into another set.

Kat shook her head and grinned.

She watched Russell slowly rock his head to the blast of bass. As the music began to surge, the rap artist's voice reached a wild recklessness and Russell's long, thick limbs unlocked. He bounced up and down with the crowd, stretching out so his fingertips brushed the ceiling. Kat moved alongside him, reaching her hands up next to his, almost rushing to reach the outpour with him. They jumped and yelled along. The small space grew humid with body heat.

Russell's face was swollen with a drunken smile. He peeled off his sweatshirt, revealing a barrel chest in his T-shirt, and swung it over his head like a flag of surrender. His curls were plastered on his sweaty forehead. He was unbridled and massive, carving a small harbor in swell that Kat danced in. His body gave off a familiar sweetness, and she was so close to his heat it caused pinpoints of sweat over her skin.

The song ended, and for a brief moment they were still. Kat was pressed to the front of Russell. His breath blew over her and stirred her hair. She turned to him. Russell's smile faded under his beard, and in the darkness, his eyes shimmered as he locked her gaze. His chest rose and fell in count with her breathing. He was all she could see, expanding over her vision. He was all she could feel, this wall of muscle solid around her. His dense legs in denim and his torso in a white T-shirt, now almost transparent from his sweat, exposing dark swirling hair.

Kat tried to move back, her breath starting to flutter.

Russell smiled and Kat blushed. Bass erupted from the speaker, rattling the air, and the crowd began to move. Russell focused on the stage while Kat gasped for relief.

Kat was almost convinced it was them alone in that cramped cove, breathing in sync and sweating in the darkness.

17

"Another gin gimlet," Leslie said, stretching over at the bar.

"Another one?"

They stood near the bar on the edge of the crowd where there was slightly more space, but not much more. Ava's arms were wound tightly around her chest, and she stood rigid next to Leslie, refusing to move.

"Yeah, sweetie, I'm grown," Leslie said, collecting his drink from the bartender. "Maybe if your ass had a few more drinks, you'd loosen up."

"What?"

"Nothing."

Ava palmed her ears as the music climaxed. Leslie rolled his eyes and swallowed his drink, which sated his desire to mock her.

"Are you okay?" Leslie asked and Ava responded with a pained smile. "You don't have to stay if you're not having a good time."

Ava took her hands from her ears.

"It's really okay," Leslie said.

"Can we step outside for a moment?" Ava said. "Just with the smoke and how hot it is in here..."

Leslie nodded and led the way through the mass, out through the double doors, and up the steps. Outside, low-hanging storm clouds were golden with city light. The air was cool and the narrow alley gave them some shelter from the light mist.

Ava closed her eyes and turned upward, fanning her neck with her hand. She breathed in deeply and Leslie noticed the sweat on her face. Cool now and with sudden awareness, she glanced around the alley.

"We're safe here," Leslie said. "I got you."

She shook her head. "I must look like an idiot."

"Have you seen the crowd in there? You're far from the worst."

She crossed her arms over herself again. "Russell told me about your mother."

Leslie pursed his lips and sucked in a deep breath.

"Don't be mad at him," Ava said. "I just wanted to say that I'm sorry. I know this is a hard time for you. And I just... I'm not saying this right."

"No, you aren't."

"Sometimes people you love do crazy things that you don't like," she said. "Like what your dad did..."

"Or go to a rap concert on Thursday night," Leslie said.

"Yeah," Ava said with a smile. "Although, I'm probably going to be deaf before it's over."

"You seriously need to have another drink."

"I'd rather not," she said. "Let's go back."

"You go on ahead," he said. "I'll be there in a minute."

Ava nodded and made her way back through the door and past the cynical door woman. Leslie lit a cigarette and pulled out his phone. There hadn't been any calls from his father since he left the message. He puffed slowly from his cigarette, biting the inside of his mouth to keep the tears at bay. He desperately needed to hear from his father—even if it was to curse at Leslie or yell at him some more. He was stuck in this stasis, unable to truly believe what happened to her, swinging from denial to being on the brink of tears. If his father wanted to torture him, make him pay penance for being gay, he had certainly done it.

Leslie heard the crack of bass shoot through the alley and he jumped. He laughed at himself, but the quaking muscles in his sides and bark of his own surprise diverted into sobs.

He clasped his hand over his mouth, sidestepping the door and into the shadows of the alley.

He called his parents' home again. It was already late, and an hour later in Michigan, but he didn't care. A part of him hoped he was disrupting his father's sleep—hoped he caused a small measure of discomfort. The phone rang and rang. Leslie was afraid he'd hear his mother's voice again, daggering itself into his chest. He heard a click, then silence.

"Hello?" he asked, dizzy with adrenaline. "Hello? Hello?"

Looking at his screen, he saw the call had disconnected. Furious, he tried the number again. A busy signal purled in his ear. He slammed his fist into his thigh. Rain started to fall from the clouds.

"That son of a bitch," he said, returning the phone to his pocket.

He leaned over, collected his breath, and wiped his eyes. Calm again, he stepped down into the party. At the bar, Leslie ordered a gin and tonic and asked Ava if she'd like anything. She hastily refused and turned her weary face back to the stage.

Beck swam through the bouncing bodies of the crowd and came toward them. His face wore a sleepy grin, and he winked at Leslie when he spotted them. Leslie swallowed from his drink so quickly he almost choked.

Beck sauntered up with his usual gall and shoved a guy out of the way to keep his steps uninterrupted. Beck ignored the man's cry of protest and stopped in front of Ava.

"Too loud for you?"

She didn't acknowledge him but winced as the tempo and roar of the music reached another peak. Leslie ignored Beck until he started poking him with a finger. Leslie batted him off like a child.

"What, man?"

"Just wanted to know if you want some champagne. Bottle service at the table," Beck said.

"Got my own drink," Leslie said, shaking the glass inches from his face. "Besides, I'm clearly busy."

"With what?" Beck looked around and nodded at Ava. "She's hot, but I thought you were gay."

Leslie's shoulders tightened with a heated anger. "I am gay. She's Russell's girlfriend. Unlike you, I don't sleep with anyone who breathes."

Beck cackled. "I'm open. Very open."

"Well, I'm closed," Leslie said quickly.

Beck leaned close to Leslie, his breath tickling his neck. "Too bad."

Ava grimaced at them.

Beck pulled back and held out his hand. "Hello, I'm Beck, and you are?"

"Ava," she said, twisting under his glare.

"Welcome to the party," he said with another short cackle. He strolled back through the crowd toward his table.

18

"Have you drunk the bar dry yet?" Kat asked Leslie as she shouldered her way up to the bar.

He gave a sneer. "I certainly tried."

Kat glanced over at Ava who had somehow slipped into a cardigan and was scanning the room, widening her eyes fearfully. Kat choked back a laugh and then offered a sympathetic look to Leslie. He narrowed an eye in disapproval, then popped his lips at Kat to punctuate his emotions.

A broad black man sauntered through the herd up to

Ava. Through the smoke, he offered her a lusty smile. He stepped in front of her with a brassy audacity and licked his lips. He was handsome, his posture curved with muscles.

"Hey, what's up, ma?" he said to her.

Ava drew back a gasp, her face befuddled in such an exaggerated horror it appeared comical. She stumbled back into Kat and Leslie, the heel of her shoe sinking into Leslie's foot. He yelped and lurched back while Ava pitched forward, arms wheeling in the air as she hurled into the man before her. They collided with a painful slap. The man dropped his beer to catch Ava and the bottle splintered on the rough concrete.

Ava let out a screech, and several people near the bar stopped to stare. People nearby chuckled, while others pointed in disapproving scrutiny. Startled, the man pushed Ava back and backpedaled toward the crowd. "What the fuck is wrong with you?"

Kat and Leslie exchanged looks of annoyance as Ava turned to them, her face flushed.

"Do you know him?" Ava asked Leslie in a shaky voice.

Leslie leaned toward Kat, shielding his face with his hand and hissed at her, "Why do *I* gotta know him?"

"Don't you know all the black people?" Kat countered, trying not laugh.

"I missed him at the monthly meeting," Leslie said. "Oh, you know you're paying for all my drinks, right?"

Kat locked eyes with Russell, as his head and shoulders bobbed a foot above the stirring commotion. Like a scout on watch, he'd seen everything and was soon skimming through the crowd to Ava's side. She quivered like an injured child, verging on hysterics. Russell reached out for her, and Ava jolted back in disgust. "Why are you so sweaty?"

Kat closed her eyes to contain her agitation. There was no justification for why Kat wanted to leave. Likewise, no sensible reason for the heated daggers shooting through her as Russell's wide hands palmed Ava's shoulders and brought her closer in a futile attempt to calm her. There was also no explanation for the lingering gaze they shared and why she was drawn to him tonight. The sheer confusion threaded through Kat, knotting heavily in her lungs.

Her phone chirped with a text from Jacob: *Meet me at my office.* The message was such a relief she nearly forgot to say good-bye. She settled her tab and barreled out of the dark basement club. Once she reached the alley, she gasped for air as if she'd been underwater.

A follow-up text complete with a winking semicolon smiley face expressed his desire to see her. Ordinarily, she would put up a front, pretend she had some other place to be. But the urge for skin-on-skin contact overpowered her sensibilities. Her skin seemed so hot it could sizzle raindrops.

She replied to his message, cradling her phone against the rain. Kat was swiftly on the street, her ears whirring from the loud music. She hurdled puddles, keeping close to the building under the weeping night, until she rushed toward the street, arm outstretched, hoping for a taxi in the secession of cars rushing by. With great satisfaction, she saw a cab stop in front of her.

Rainwater rinsed the debris-covered streets as the cab moved through and below the alpines of Chicago skyscrapers. Glimmering streams flooded into sewage drains to the dirty, bloated innards beneath the city. Kat tipped her driver handsomely, not sure if she rewarding him for being there or giving an offering to the serendipity of the universe.

She stepped into River North and pushed through the

revolving door of an office building, into a brightly lit and warm lobby that seemed an affront to the cool, wet night outside. A droopy security guard sat behind a counter accompanied by Jacob, a handsome, suited sentry leaning on the edge of the counter. At the sight of Kat, a sly half smile surfaced on his unscrupulous features.

"Damn rain," Kat said, walking up to him as small drops of water traced paths along her skin.

"Damn rain," Jacob repeated as they made their way up to the elevators and to a dim floor of offices.

This floor made up the entirety of the advertising company Jacob worked for. They walked along an open section of rounded cubicles, colorful conference rooms, exposed brick, and overhead ductwork. The space was an empty tomb, and this wasn't Kat's first time tiptoeing around its corners.

Jacob placed a hand on Kat's back, sliding along the opening in her clothing. By the time they were in his office, his hand had slipped under her shirt, pinching open her bra.

"Sorry about brushing you off the other day," he said, and closed the door to his office.

"You're always sorry about something."

"Let me make it up to you," he offered. He moved to his desk in the center of the office.

The only light came from the ceiling-to-floor windows that overlooked the dewy cityscape. They illuminated the low-hanging storm clouds with a thousand golden lights from below. In the murky glimmer, Jacob stood a featureless shadow. His face was completely devoured in blackness. He swept papers off his desk and pulled off his suit jacket and tie. No longer Jacob, but a blank figure, he ushered Kat onto the desk and kneeled before her, his warm fingers crawling along her legs, under her skirt, and looping between her panties and nylons. He tugged and Kat lifted herself as her clothes slid off and exposed her damp flesh to the night. Still on his knees, he began to nibble at the flesh of her thighs, drawing his kisses higher and higher until his warm tongue lapped her insides.

Kat drew shaky breaths in the darkness. She heard the jangle of his belt and slip of fabric as he tugged his slacks down. Jacob was no longer Jacob but an empty vessel that allowed her mind's eye to construct walls of flesh, muscle and dark curly hair swirling upon them. She could almost smell a familiar sweetness as he entered her.

She moaned softly, closing her eyes and building this man, cell by cell, follicle by follicle. She exhaled, eyes pinched closed, with her hand digging into the flesh of this man, who slowly revealed himself, as if he were hidden behind a curtain slowly being drawn in her mind.

She saw Russell's face rise inside her like air bubbles to the surface. In that moment, she wished for him. Before his name passed her lips, a piercing telephone ring shot through the night. When she opened her eyes, she was back in the office, suddenly thwarted by desire.

Jacob pulled away and bent down toward his suit jacket, exposing his pale ass to a small amount of light.

"Who's that?"

"No one," he said, squinting at the screen.

"Clearly it's someone," Kat retorted as the ringing replaced the lust in the darkness.

Annoyed, he brought a finger to his lips.

"Who is on the phone?"

"I'm going to need you to be quiet, Kat," Jacob said forcefully.

"It's your wife?"

The ringing phone stopped, followed by one last chirp.

"Dammit, Kat," Jacob said, throwing his hands in the air. "Why do you have to make shit so difficult?"

Kat narrowed her eyes and said, "I'll make things real simple."

She tugged on her panties and nylons, pushed past Jacob and flung the door open. Her rushed feet propelled faster and faster. She heard Jacob stammering behind her. She glanced back at his advance, brazen, pantsless and still clutching his phone. It began to ring and he stopped to look at it. Kat came to a halt and watched him shrug at her and answer the phone.

"Hey, honey," he said. "Yeah, I'm working late—yep, the MacIntyre project."

Kat felt herself sinking beneath the soft words of Jacob and his wife, the possibility of pregnancy and, strangely enough, the image of Russell holding Ava. She retracted into the shadows of the elevators and back into the soggy night.

19

Saturday evening, Russell, Leslie, and Kat gathered in front of a brick storefront. Brilliant light from the window's mouth poured onto the path that led into open doors. Soft acoustic music purred on the temperate air while they drew near.

"Who has a formal art show?" Russell asked with disapproval.

"Let's actually see the art before we start judging," Kat said. "Curtis is kind of a big deal now."

Leslie playfully brushed the shoulder of his grey suit jacket. "Do you know how glad I am to be wearing something besides jeans or scrubs?"

"This is way too pretentious for us," Russell said.

Kat expressed a tut. "We've done a lot worse for free

booze besides getting dressed up."

"Ava's supposed to meet up with us, right?" Leslie asked.

They passed into a wide open space. The building's walls and concrete floor were painted white while rays from pensile lights beamed onto dark canvases scattered along the walls.

"Yeah, I gave Ava the address," Russell said as they ambled through the growing crowd.

The burgeoning rich and pseudo intellectuals composed this group of men in suitcoats and women in bright cocktail dresses. They spoke to one another, hands gesturing between wine glasses. Russell overheard didactic observations of the art suspended on the walls as he probed for the bar. Caterer waiters wove quietly within the group, collecting empty glasses and peddling hors d'oeuvres that appeared more appealing than they tasted.

Russell spotted Isabelle Boldwyn, the gallery owner. She wore a bright pantsuit and a flower in her hair. She locked eyes with Russell and sauntered toward him with a nervous smile. She took a sip of wine before extending her hand.

"Hello again," he said, offering a handshake.

"Hello," she said. "I'm surprised to see you here."

"Well, I'm surprised to be here."

"I'm glad you could make it," she said.

"Are you trying to get Curtis to show at your gallery?"

She dropped her head and chuckled. "Curtis is part-owner of my gallery."

Russell felt his stomach drop. He searched around for the bar. "He owns a gallery."

"Yep," she said. "He never gave up on the dream."

"Ouch," Russell said, crossing his arms over his chest.

"No, I don't mean it like that," she said. "I always put my foot in my mouth around you."

"Yeah, you do."

"It's because I still want your work in my gallery."

Russell located the bar and shook his head. "I'm not an artist, and if you'll excuse me."

He headed toward the bar, not wanting to look back at Isabelle. He nodded to the bartender and ordered a glass of white Zinfandel. Russell scanned the crowd, searching for friends in the vague faces. Leslie and Kat were standing in front of a canvas at a respectful distance. They gazed at it with awe, speaking emphatically. Leslie touched Kat's shoulder and whispered something. They laughed, and he walked in the other direction.

Kat shifted in her heels, still standing before the piece. Her shoulders began to slump, and her smile faded. Kat's face was taut, and a small line parted her brows over her darkening eyes. Russell treaded forward but, instead of walking directly toward her, circled around. He navigated the gaps in the crowd, careful to conceal his advance. Kat wore a crimson sheath dress, her black hair wound in loose curls. With the subtlety that dusk fades into night, a rising sadness began to resonate on her face. The despondency was that of a beautiful stranger—maybe a femme fatale from an old noir film—not the friend he'd been living with. Russell felt he was pooling through warm water, as if the charged air around her took on another quality.

He stood next to her in silence, looking down at Kat's red lips, formed in a doleful pout.

"The art sucks that bad?" Russell asked, pantomiming normalcy.

She rolled her eyes. "No, you ass. I've just been having a really horrible week."

Kat rested her head on his bulk and it barely reached his shoulder. His blood warmed, rushing into his skull.

Wordlessness found him again as his eyes settled back on Kat, then followed her gaze to the artwork.

A wide canvas framed in steel stretched out on the wall. Harsh tones of blue and purple oil paint had been smeared within the frame, causing the surface to rise and fall with divots. At first glance, Russell couldn't perceive anything past the grainy texture. But somewhere, as the static of the party circulating around them faded leaving only the soft sounds of Kat's breathing against him, the violent juxtaposition of colors rearranged into contours. Those contours then diverged into a violet face shadowed in blue trying to press through the canvas and out to them. The face was contorted with grief, eternally fastened to the frame.

"It's called 'Trapped,'" Kat said, reading from the small title card just left of the picture.

Russell couldn't deny the gravity of this moment, unsure if it was triggered by the painting or if it was a symptom of Kat's closeness. Her earthy, floral scent drifted into the air as she adjusted on his shoulder. Russell felt his head swim with a giddy dizziness. The world around them inverted, blooming with sullen shades of indigos and lilacs curling around Kat's feminine lineation.

"I believe you can do this," she said. "I know there's something... boiling in you."

Her voice was a forlorn whisper he wouldn't have heard if she hadn't been so close. Sadness bled through the fragile membrane of Kat's sudden beauty. Maybe she was a dispirited figure in one of these canvases. She seemed as if she, at any moment, could plunge into one of these art pieces, her angst displayed in a volatile composition. He raised his arm to comfort her when the sight of Leslie and Ava's approach halted him.

Ava sauntered toward them, smiling with a wine glass in hand. She reached up to kiss Russell casually. The noise of the party rushed back with jarring clarity. Russell felt as though he were pulled out of a dark room into the searing light of high noon. He blinked and forged a smile for Ava. When Russell turned back to Kat, she was feet away, chuckling with Leslie as he handed her a glass of water.

In seconds, Kat managed to shove away her secret despair and return to being the roommate he lived with.

Ava ensnared his arm, wrenching him away from the crowd. She was muttering about something and her voice threaded itself into another indistinguishable fiber of noise around him. He peered over his shoulder back at Kat. The twinge of what had drawn him to her had all but receded into her face.

"Russell, are you listening to me?"

He gave Ava another false smile. "I'm sorry, what?"

Ava sighed, then said, "I was saying I'm so glad you gave this up. There's no future in spending your time making overpriced wall decorations."

Russell couldn't put together the sequence of Ava's words. He simply nodded and, locked arm in arm, continued to tour the art. Ava spoke blindly about the art and her day, again her voice fading into the distance. All he could hear was *I'm glad you gave this up* pressing its weight into his mind. And when the words finally came together, he scanned the room for Kat. He longed to catch her gaze, but she refused to look in his direction for the rest of the night.

20

Kat drained the last bit of sparkling cider from her glass. She had been afraid to drink, to smoke, to do anything, really. She tried to take a pregnancy test this morning but couldn't. She even thought to tell her roommates, but things with Russell were growing complicated and Leslie had just lost his mother.

She saw Leslie in the middle of the gallery and tiptoed up behind him. He was engaging Curtis Newman, the artist of the show, in exorbitant praise. She smiled listlessly, hoping for the conversation's eventual lull, and surveyed the widening gaps within the crowd as the room slowly emptied.

As the artist left to gather more admiration, Leslie turned to her. "You have the ready-to-leave look."

Kat clasped his hand. "You know me so well. Where did Russell and Ava go?"

"They left twenty minutes ago," he said as they stepped out of the storefront. "Probably to go fuck at her daddy's country club or something."

They walked through the golden columns of streetlight. The petulant screech of grinding metal stretched overhead as the train toiled on vaulted tracks, spitting illuminating static sparks. In the distance, the Sears Tower spires jutted into rumbling black storm clouds, and the surrounding skyscrapers convened into one lit monolith shining like a yellow constellation of glass, metal, and concrete.

Kat felt the night's ripeness stirring in her. "What do you want to do?"

"I've got to see Isaac tonight," Leslie said with hints of lament in his voice. "In fact, I probably should catch this train."

Kat and Leslie hugged and parted for the evening. Leslie headed down the street toward the elevated platform. Kat's shoulders fell as he ascended the stairs, out of sight. She then turned to the street, hailing a cab north through the city to Wicker Park. The cab's silence was measured by the soft click of the meter. The cab yielded onto the Kennedy Expressway, accelerating into a concrete tunnel. Kat imagined her ride as what a bullet felt like—subjugated to the violent, unfaltering forces of physics. She let herself go slack against the momentum. The cars that moved outside the window shined like wet, black stones.

The bullet soon crossed through the barrel and she was off the Kennedy Expressway, breaking through layers, passing into the night's tumult. Agitation prickled the tiny hairs at the base of her neck as she decided how to handle the rest of her night. Bucktown's streets, palpating with glowing restaurants, were stuffed with gleeful couples joining hands on the sidewalk.

Kat's uneasiness doubled and her desire to keep moving struck a familiar pang. It was a ghost reaching back from the past, brushing her with its cold fingers and telling her that if she just kept moving, if she just left, there might be another chance for reprieve. She wouldn't have to deal with the possibility of pregnancy or Jacob and his wife.

She'd spent her childhood migrating from one foster home to the next, most of her childhood belongings designated to an old brown suitcase. Kat, who had spent years on her own and without obstruction, still could feel that underlying instinct that laced her muscles—that irrefutable urge to migrate. Maybe she should instruct the cab driver back to the Kennedy and take it as far as the night stretched.

Because of her upbringing, she was rarely concerned with inhabiting strangers' homes or abiding by arbitrary house rules. One set of parents would let her watch television, another household wouldn't. Some foster parents reigned over her with tyrannical regulations, catapulting her into months of dismay. Others' overt apathy, albeit a welcome interlude, offered little in the way of an actual home. There was no cooked food; those homes were simply places to sleep and checks for those foster parents. Kat often shared rooms with other foster children, who were caustic and resentful. If the foster parent actually had biological children, they would glare at her like some outsider, only to be favored greatly by their real parents.

There were the reproachful eyes of provincial Latinos who almost chastened her for not speaking Spanish. She recalled older women glaring at her in the supermercado and looking down on her with pity as she picked up odds and ends for her foster mom. Her embarrassment left her wordless, not even wanting to speak English. Kat sometimes felt she belonged to nothing, not even her own race.

But the most pronounced memory in the legions of small, lower-class homes that populated her childhood was the reoccurring moment of fear. She would steady herself, say she could endure this, but her body would always betray her. It began with heat in her cheeks and heaviness in her feet. A moment that she was ushered into an alien home by an overworked social worker, to look into the face of strangers. The strange houses with their different smells made Kat a perpetual nomad in Joliet, Illinois.

She would survive that fear and those icy moments of subtle rejection only to move on and endure it again. The social worker and foster parents would sign papers and she would be carried off. She soon learned the act of moving from one place to another was the only true place of freedom. Same thing with making a decision. In the fleeting moments before it's made, you're free. Once the change has been made, you're merely a victim of consequence.

"We're here," the cab driver stated.

Kat shoved a series of bills through the plastic partition and climbed out of the car in front of her apartment. She stepped inside and unzipped the side of her dress. Despite herself, she was going to climb into bed and putter around with some new editing software.

There was no need to head out into this night. She was an adult who'd survived all of that. She was no longer a foster kid. She could possibly be someone's mother.

There was an abrupt dragging underneath Kat's shoe. Startled, she reached for a nearby lamp. The living room's open space was saturated in muted light. Kat lifted her leg and a lace bra dangled from the end of her heel. Kat had to take off her shoe to liberate the straps from her heel. Once in her hand, she knew it didn't belong to her. Disgusted, she flung it across the room where it landed on a bright patterned cocktail dress.

Kat paused, taking in the room. Clothes were strewn along the floor and couch. Pantyhose, stilettos, and a thong trailed into the rear of the apartment. An Oxford shirt lay opened and deflated like the victim of a melee—the same Oxford shirt Russell had been wearing. Kat stood at ground zero taking in the wreckage, her mind constructing the chaos, suddenly seeing Ava slip out of her dress and Russell reach around the bra's clasp.

Maybe they fumbled around in the front room for a while, possibly on the couch with lustful hands exploring their bodies' newly naked spaces. Ava's pale soft skin might have been rubbed tender by Russell's wide, hairy chest. The groping would be followed by Russell hoisting her up with her legs wrapped around his waist, their faces joined in kissing. The imagined phantoms would then lumber into the rear of the apartment, into Russell's bedroom. With the door closed, Kat wrenched back on the reins of her imagination, afraid of what it could conjure.

An arousal quivered in Kat's thighs, followed swiftly by revulsion, as an ascending thump rose over quiet. There was a pronounced crack as a bedpost slammed against a baseboard. Kat clasped her mouth to keep from gasping. She turned off the lamp and stepped back toward the door.

Ava's muffled moan curled around the blackness.

Kat's head swam with an angered panic, and the darkness, combined with the heat behind her eyes, made her blind. She zipped up her dress and reached for the door.

She burst outside and stumbled down the stairs onto the sidewalk. Tonight, she would have to give in to her instincts. Tonight, even if it was merely up the street, deeper into Wicker Park, she had to migrate.

21

The exertion between Russell and Ava ended and dots met in colorful currents underneath his closed eyelids. He heard Ava's tender panting across the bed. He scoured through the knotted network of bed sheets and duvet until his fingertips touched her smooth damp skin. She sighed in approval as he gathered her into the crook of his arm. He opened his eyes and peered down at her, nestled tightly into his side. Amber streaks streamed in through the slightly open blinds and across her naked flesh.

"Are you okay?" Her face, suddenly earnest, was half hidden in shadow.

"Yeah," Russell said quickly.

Ava paused and considered how to proceed. Sometimes

after sex she would fall into a spell, asking him any question that leapt to her mind. Russell wanted to defy her psychological probing, but he was outgunned post orgasm with her slender nude body in his arms.

"Are we okay?"

Russell watched the spheres of her breasts rise and fall as they pressed against him. "Why wouldn't we be?"

"You seemed... distant at the art show," she said.

Her voice quaked, and Russell turned to her face. "What's wrong?"

"I'm just in love with you," she said. "And I'm in love with where this, us, might go."

He should want to start a future with Ava Von Hoffman. Everything about her lent to settling down. She often hinted at marriage, friends' engagements, and her thorough analysis of wedding magazines, from color schemes to tacky flower choices. "Who chooses carnations?" she would say. Across small coffee shop tables, in front of steaming lattes and through a dexterous repartee, she guided conversations about hypothetical children. Sunday mornings after sex, she would stand naked before Russell, newspaper in hand, proposing real estate options. Later, with their stomachs full of a costly brunch from a restaurant Ava's yoga instructor recommended, they would interlock their hands and stalk department store aisles while Ava discussed the merits of their eventual dishware. What astounded Russell was that Ava only looked for his consent as they traversed the perilous minefield of this presumptive future.

As a woman of means, she'd worked out all the particulars and all she needed was for Russell to show up and play his part. The good life—the American dream, a house in the suburbs with a thick green yard, a plush 401(k), kids, and a golden retriever—could all be his despite the grim evening news, the frightening unemployment rates, and the dubious global market. Terrorists plaguing the Middle East with fundamentalist ideals and accruing threats of global warming all wilted in sight of Ava's plan.

Ava, interwoven between Russell's limbs and the sheets, her face swathed between strips of shadows and dim streetlight, would ensure this man would never have to return to the double-wide trailer of his youth. With her, he could permanently sidestep his father's fate, damned to occupy a beaten lounge chair, comatose under the glare of the best TV the pawnshop could offer, swollen with obesity. In Ava's future, there was no place for men who drowned out the senile cries of their live-in mothers with bottom-shelf whiskey. There would be no tolerance for that type of apathy, no room for the trappings of poverty. No failed attempted as an artist.

Together, they could make a practical life. And that is what Russell needed.

"I'm here, Ava, right here with you," he said.

He kissed her, and he slowly opened her legs and mounted her.

22

Club Peppermint pulsed between a docile tattoo shop and darkened boutique, with a line of would-be partiers collected around the building like beads on a necklace. Their chorus of throaty cussing and drunken guffaws met the bass detonating from within the building. Kat put an unlit cigarette in her mouth and treaded past the line. She stopped at the entrance guarded by broad bouncers. One stood with his arms crossed, his face stolid, while the other, in a beanie, sat resolute on a stool.

Kat dropped her voice to a purr. "Boys..."

"Kat!" The bouncer's arms dropped while his face cracked to reveal a smile.

"How's your night?"

"Fucking idiots." He nodded over to the line.

Kat chuckled as she handed him her lipstick-stained cigarette.

"Have a good night, baby," he said as he reached for it.

The bouncer with the beanie pulled open the glass doors. Kat blew him a kiss and immersed into the swirling lights. She heard the irritated groans and protests from the line as the door closed behind her, enveloping her in a neon brilliance the shade of blood. Mirrors blanketed the walls and, from an unknown station, a smoke machine produced a low-hanging fog around her ankles. Perched high on a stage, one could only make out the deejay's face glowing behind the blue eye of a laptop. This floating head of light, this manic composer of hard beats and booming bass, summoned a trance and a torrent of movement surging at the club's center. Bodies rocked and pitched around her in a calculated thrashing. A euphoric tingle moved over Kat's skin as the thumping rattled her ribcage.

She shuffled her way to the bar and ordered soda water. She leaned back on the bar and sipped on it slowly.

"Damn, girl."

A guy in a black skull and bones T-shirt leaned over the bar next to her. He edged toward her with a lopsided grin and slid his arm around her waist. Enraged, she ripped away from him, and his heavy palm lingered on her hip like a handprint.

Kat winced, noting his low sloping forehead and close-set

eyes. The arrangement of his face appeared rushed and poorly constructed.

"Excuse me?"

"What's your name, girl?"

He plodded forward, his muscles bloated to cartoonish exaggerations. Kat wondered if his gym routine was meant to compensate for the weak configuration of his face. This guy was a rare descendant of the Neanderthal, untouched by evolution's softening.

"My name is not one I'm going to share with you," she said, covering her nose against the incursion of excessive cologne.

A scowl lowered the decline of his forehead into a severe V. He opened his mouth to utter a retort, when someone behind her said, "Fuck off, she's with me."

Beck Ashby snarled at the Neanderthal with a stern, bronze face unflinching in a convincing display of dominance. The spectacle played out before Kat like documentaries she'd seen on VHS, looped by a substitute teacher in high school science class, with predators besting one another. There was a brief period of wager; could the hyena actually take down a lion? But the Neanderthal knew his place in the pecking order, and no blood would be spilled. He conceded with a quick and oafish retreat.

"So I'm with you now?" Kat asked, crossing her arms.

"If you want," Beck said with a smirk. "I can get that meathead to come back, but just warning you, he's probably a really bad lay."

Kat frowned at him. "I don't need to be rescued."

"Well, I need to be rescued from this boring night," Beck said, leaning toward and a gallant effort to show innocence.

"I'm not getting rid of you, am I?"

"You owe me," he said. "How about I buy you another drink?"

23

Steam eddied in heavy clouds from the small cubicle bathroom adjoined to Isaac's room. It clung to the rusty pipes underneath a tiny sink and rolled like a phantom over the dirty floor, discarded clothes, spilled lube, and silver condom wrappers. The steam moved along the room and hazed the glass as if to conceal the storm churning outside. Its opaque extremities crawled up the walls, curling the taped picture of the two lovers and collecting in beads on the bottom of fern fronds posted on the windowsill. The lone centurion's branches buckled under the water's weight in its little black pot.

Water sputtered from the calcium-crusted showerhead in a hot spray over Leslie and Isaac's bare forms. Leslie scooped mounds of white suds over Isaac's back. Isaac was limp from Leslie's scrubbing. Leslie could see the muscles beneath Isaac's tan skin adjust and readjust.

"I hurt all over," Isaac said.

"I'm sorry," Leslie replied.

"Are you ever going to talk about your mother?"

"No."

"Are you really going to use all the money to pay for rehab?"

"Yes. If you want, I can get you out of here."

"I don't need you to take care of me."

Remorse lurked in the shower with them. Leslie pictured Isaac arising early that morning to don a shapeless shit-brown jumpsuit with "MARVIN'S CLEANING SPECIALISTS" sewn onto the front pocket. He would then trek downtown through the inky crest of dawn. His route was a lengthy stint on a bus along Chicago's crumbling streets, followed by an even longer train ride. This tremendous test of will taunted Isaac at the start of every workday. He would meet the rest of the cleaning crew, a group of grunting misers with little concern for the new, soft-spoken queer. Leslie could see him dragging a mop along the tiled floors of deserted office buildings.

Isaac's once smooth hands owned a new hardness.

Leslie initially believed Isaac would resume his staff writing position at *Chicago Sun-Times*, but when asked about it, Isaac skirted around the reprehensible behavior that led to his firing. His vagueness left Leslie to speculate the worst. Isaac instead said the janitorial work allowed him the flexibility to attend Narcotics Anonymous meetings whenever he needed to.

The convenient rationale eliminated Isaac's writing career from future conversation, leaving Leslie to ponder Narcotics Anonymous. He didn't know what went on at the meetings Isaac attended with devotion. He didn't know what was disclosed or how bleak the stories were, and he dared not ask. He didn't even know where the group met—a church hall or empty gym, hell, maybe even someone's garage out in the suburbs. No matter what the backdrop, Leslie envisioned a circle of foldup chairs where the wretched, the weeping, and the recovering would flock to recite, in despair, the Serenity Prayer.

Leslie's imagination would be bitten by guilt after his inflated depiction of sadness, with his boyfriend's hollowed face, prostrate with addiction, surrounded by other addicts who mutated into green goblins. He rinsed the last soapy bubbles from Isaac's back and his guilt accelerated to fear.

Isaac turned off the water and reached for two towels. He handed Leslie a towel, and Leslie returned to the mattress. Isaac retrieved a small radio from his closet, where his homely brown janitorial jumpsuit hung like a convicted man at high noon.

"Please let me get you out of here," Leslie said. "Even though I can't get ahold of my dad, I think there is more coming."

"No," Isaac said. "I just want us to go back to normal."

Leslie looked around him. "This is normal?"

"Is that why you're never around?" Isaac asked. "If I meet you out at a bar, you freak out and think I'm going to relapse. And you know I can't go to your place because your roommates think I'm going to steal."

"I'm sorry," Leslie said. "I'll work on them. I need you."

Isaac turned on the radio and the indie station's pretentious yammering masked any noise penetrating the room from the outside. Isaac stole into Leslie's arms and kissed him. Leslie held him tenderly, knowing the odds of a successful recovery were against them. He knew little about the recovery process Isaac had set out on, but Internet searches told him most relationships perish under this kind of stress, and addicts have a sixty percent chance of relapse. He hoped those grim statistics would bring ruin to someone else.

There, harbored in layers of steam and the cadence of cheerful music, Leslie could pretend they were spared.

24

The music endowed Kat with vigor. Her body disjointed, she renounced her limbs to the brutal uproar of music. On the dance floor, tight-knit bodies collided like the cells of a throbbing entity. She felt a delicious loss of self, succumbing to rampant swaying, now connected to this nocturnal beast formed by wayward dancers. Incandescent red lights bloomed around her as the union with this lovely new beast gave off a sweet release through her veins. She was liberated.

Beck stepped in tempo next to her. He was sandwiched between his sordid clique, encouraged by their own reflections in the mirrored walls. Their bony frames, visible ribs, and gnarly joints contorted into sharp angles, beautiful and desperate, seething in their sartorial valor. His friends gave off accomplished imitations of European fashion models.

Beck's stoic lieutenant, tall and Asian, veered on a nearby wall less than a few feet away. In a cutoff shirt, his arms bore a massive nexus of black tattoos that reached under the shirt and to his neck. His ivory face was gorgeous, save the slashes shaved in his eyebrows and the piercings punched through his lips and nose. He scanned the club, prowling the crowd.

Beck advanced on Kat, timing his ups to her downs, and their bodies aligned like cogs in a clock. His pelvis located the nook in her hips, and he began to grind with the beat thundering upon them. Kat, at first, didn't mind. She was rather impressed with his apt dance moves. She noticed Beck's lieutenant drawing back his lips in lust and the women's faces souring with envy. The glimpse she stole in the mirror of their harmonious animation pleased her.

The sudden jab of Beck's stiffening cock caused her to recoil. She blundered back, flustered, feeling immediately out of place. She'd crossed into Beck's world and realized she was ignorant to the customs.

"I'm getting another drink," she said, withdrawing to the bar.

In duress, she flagged down the bartender and ordered another soda water. Beck, undetected at her side, instructed the bartender to place it on his tab and ordered a drink for himself.

"You don't have to do that," Kat said.

"It's fine."

"I'm not sleeping with you."

Beck brayed with laughter. "Me and you? Fuck?"

His face scrunched in amusement, but Kat knew this performance was part of Beck's manipulation. Curiosity forced her ask, "That wasn't your little boner poking me?"

Beck's laughter came to an abrupt stop. "'Little boner?' Do you always hit below the belt?"

"Only when what's underneath is poking me."

The drinks arrived. Beck guzzled his down, leering at Kat in contemplation. Kat, lapping at her drink, engaged in Beck's staring contest.

He finally sighed and said, "Fine, I was trying to sleep with you, okay? To be fair, I try to sleep with everyone."

"We're friends, and it's never going to happen."

"Your goons would probably kill me, anyway."

"Goons?" Kat asked.

"Russell and Leslie," Beck said.

"First of all," said Kat, her neck rolling in assertion, "they're not goons. And have you looked at your friends? Do those ladies even eat?"

Beck laughed and Kat strained, but then joined him. He kneeled down and kissed her hand, and Kat accepted his gentlemanly display of defeat.

"You know," he said, "I always thought you and Russell had something going on, until he started hanging out with that blonde chick. Now she's a nice piece of..."

"Please, shut up now," Kat said, feeling her anger double back.

Beck regressed back into contemplation. He examined Kat, like he could pierce her brain and pull out what she'd been trying to hide all day: Jacob's dismissal, Russell's thumping headboard and a possible pregnancy. Kat grew rigid, afraid the smallest slight would allow him to deduce something.

"I can see why you don't like her," he said after a while. "She's terrible."

She should have defended Ava, but his attack chimed righteously in her ears.

"Come with me," he said, leading her to a remote break in the club, away from the dance floor and behind the deejay booth.

"What is this?" Kat said.

Beck grinned at her, slipping his hand in and out of his jacket pocket. A clear bag filled with beige pills dangled from his fingers. He dumped the pills into his empty palm. They were small and unassuming, imprinted with a tiny "20" on one side and "OC" on the other.

"I dry hump you, I insult your friends, and I get all in your personal business," he said. "I hate to ruin your night, so please accept my condolences."

"Oxy?"

"Take as many as you like."

He forced Kat's hand open and dumped half of his spoils into it. Startled, she frantically shoved them into the pocket of her dress. They moved back to the dance floor and a nausea crashed over Kat. She stumbled back and gripped Beck. A sharpness in her lower belly began to burn and her ankles buckled in her heels.

"You okay?" he asked, placing his arm around her for stability.

She felt like she was being ripped from inside out. She bit back a scream. A cramp tore through her back and tears blurred her vision. For a moment, she thought she was dying. Or that something had been slipped in her drink. The movement around her was no longer inviting. The club blurred and turned vicious, threatening to gnaw at her. An elbow from a nearby dancer nudged her side and she stumbled forward. A foot stamped down on her shoe in the inky red lights. She yelped in her throat and reached back for Beck, digging her nails into his arm. Pain rippled through her stomach and, for a moment, she saw herself dying on the dance floor.

"I need a bathroom," Kat said, clutching her stomach.

Beck part carried, part dragged her toward the women's bathroom. He shoved past the line and kicked open the door. Inside, a few women cried out at the intrusion of a man, but Kat's vision blurred again and a spasm coursed over her body. She had been blind for a moment, with her hand outstretched on the cool surface of the walls. Sweat from her clammy forehead burned her eyes and tickled down her back. Her back felt broken and she gasped for air.

Her guts twisted and she felt an eerie warmth slide down her legs. She glanced down and saw her heels fill with blood. Beck gasped, and she heard a few yelps from the women in the bathroom. Kat's knees buckled and she felt weak, falling into Beck's arms.

Beck glared at the small group of women in the bathroom who stopped to watch the show.

"Get out! Get the fuck out, now!" he said, leaning Kat against the wet sink.

"Gross," a woman in a leather skirt said.

Beck grabbed her arm and shoved her toward the door. The rest of the women filed out quickly as Kat's blood crawled down the length of her leg and past her shoes. She gripped the faucet and peeled off her bloody stockings. Her blood formed a puddle on the floor and ran through the cracks between the tiles. She felt faint and choked on her soft sobs of icy fear.

"What's happening?" Beck asked.

"I don't know," she said. "I need to get to a hospital."

"Should I call an ambulance?"

"God, no," Kat said, pushing herself away from the sink. She gathered brown paper towels. Her hands were jerking so violently she could barely hold onto them as she wiped between her thighs. Her legs gave out and Beck opened his arms to catch her. He slung her arm over his shoulder and they shuffled out of the bar. At the entrance, the doorman smirked at them.

"Too good of a time?" he asked as they stepped into the cool night.

Kat's chin shook as a sickening wave of embarrassment collided into her. Beck nodded to him and gave him a thumbs-up, trying to maintain normalcy. He leaned her against a streetlight and flagged down a cab.

"Move over, I'm coming," he said.

The tears finally broke and Kat gave into her sobs. She shook her head and closed the door. She grabbed her stomach against another attack of cramps. Kat knew the truth. She had been pregnant, and she knew what was going to happen when she arrived at the hospital. She knew what they were going to tell her. She knew it was over now.

"I need to get to Northwestern Hospital," she said.

The cab rolled away from the curb and Beck's stunned face receded into the night.

25

Leslie's watch read 4:32 p.m. The sun's lazy westward descent casting shadows from nearby buildings over Saint Rose Community Living, which skulked into the small room where he stood. He gazed out the window onto the street, four stories below, watching an ambulance make its journey across town. There was no urgency to collect the deceased remains lying prone in the hospital bed nearby.

Up until now, the day's momentum had moved predictably. The nursing staff mobilized, fed and medicated residents all over the building, and Leslie had roamed the facility's wide, white halls with a thick binder under his arm and a stethoscope coiled around his neck. He floated around, burrowed deep in his own reverie, operating on autopilot while taking vitals, assessing the regularity of bowel movements, and preparing insulin syringes for the diabetics. Most days he was left unaffected by what went on inside the hospital walls.

Today, he fell out of the groove, caught in a dance routine that left him one step behind the entire day. Leslie at first attributed this to sleep deprivation, or maybe worry. Whatever it was, he felt like a visitor in the white florescence of Saint Rose Community Living. Sweet industrial cleaner, with the underlying stench of sweat, feces, and stagnation clung in his nostrils as if he was smelling it for the first time.

He was amazed by how successfully the building hid its true nature. The checkered linoleum and pristine walls marked a stark contrast between the sloppy decay of its residents.

Most of the elderly housed in Saint Rose weren't fortunate enough to age gracefully. They were the victims of time. The residents, smashed up like meat for the slaughter, fell into two categories. The first group was full of bodies ravaged by crippling diseases. Arthritic arms and joints grew gnarly and stiff like bare tree branches. Emphysema left lungs fluttering and cannulas shoved up noses, all connected with long, hissing aluminum oxygen tubes. Spotted skin, minced like brutalized leather, crumpled in embittered horror, prisoners of their own bodies. Some patients would lash out at the nursing staff, determined to alert all in their reach of their private ruin, until they received a forced sedation. The second group was segregated to the Alzheimer's ward on the second floor. Instead of bodies falling into wreck, their minds degenerated.

The Saint Rose Community pamphlets lied. The stock photos paraded jovial senior citizens content to accept reality. The glossy prints promised families would be unburdened. The halls held old faces locked in wide smiles with knowledge that this place, with an overworked and underpaid staff, was the best place to decline into death. Omitted from the pamphlet was how quickly Saint Rose would haul out the deceased with unflinching efficiency, clean up the room with a rancid lemon cleaner and prepare it for someone new.

Leslie discovered early in his career that no hospital, clinic, church, or industrial cleaner could sterilize the messiness of death.

Leslie turned to the stiff body next to him. Over the last hours, it had grown increasingly rigid. Sometime after lunch and before dinner, its last bit of life had pulled in rattled breaths, heart toiling with each beat. Then, it stopped. During rounds, Leslie discovered only dense carbon under the sheet. No longer human, the body was ready to be emptied, embalmed, and posed like a mummy. The lifeless face gave off a greyish hue and stared into nothing, eyes and mouth agape thanks to the swift onset of rigor mortis. Leslie had made several attempts to close them, but they merely popped back open.

When life had wavered within, the body had been a kind woman, tranquil as death encircled her hospital bed. During her last week of her life, she'd made no demands of the staff.

She'd outlived her husband and children, and no one was left to cry over her death or hold onto the memory of her existence. Her life would be tossed to the oblivion of a lonely plot and cement slab. Throughout her treatment, Leslie knew her mind wasn't food for Alzheimer's and the woman must have known the solitude of her demise. A soldier with a sober march, she'd come to her end quietly, and with dignity.

Her husk now lay like a snuffed match—the Saint Rose Community Living promise.

With no one to grieve for her, Leslie stayed until the ambulance arrived. This honor wasn't necessarily for her. His vigil had more to do with his own mother. His shift ended forty minutes earlier, but he couldn't move from the room until the ambulance arrived.

The ambulance rounded the drive and moved to the back of the building. The EMTs would soon cart her away, discretely free from the residents' view, down a rear hall affectionately nicknamed "Death Row."

Leslie stroked the corpse's hard hand and muttered a few parting words. In the barren halls, he passed the EMTs with a gurney in tow. Leslie took the elevator to the first floor, aching for fresh air. He opened a locked staff door and cruised through the back halls, past the kitchen, and to the break room. Resident aids with slacked faces slouched in their chairs. Here, among the lockers and vending machines, they openly expressed fatigue.

He walked out in the cool evening where most of the sun had slipped away and stepped down into the train. On his commute home, he drifted outside of himself and was thankful that the apartment was quiet when he stepped inside. He slipped quietly into his room and shook off his scrubs. He pulled his MacBook from his nightstand, opened up a Google search, and typed in his mother's name.

He was ready to know how she died.

Search results pulled up a multitude of women who shared his mother's name. He attempted again and narrowed his search by adding his hometown of Novi, Michigan. He clicked on the second link, a news article from the area, and read in detail about a car accident on February 26. Debris on I-96 popped the tire of semitruck, which rolled out of control and crushed several vehicles in its wake. Leslie's mother had been in the accident, one of eleven casualties. The article stopped there, and he threaded the gaps of information with his imagination—ghastly images of his mother flattened under the semi's tonnage. In his mind's eye, Leslie's mother lay splattered on the cold street with blood pooling underneath her twitching limbs. Leslie felt the sharp burn of bile in his throat.

He hoped she hadn't been in pain and that, given the chance, his mother would have faced death with as much grace as the woman who died today.

Leslie slammed the computer closed and tried to think of that day, tried to recall what he was doing as his mother lay dying. He felt cold. He hoped knowing how she died would give him a chance to say good-bye. A chance to move through all this grief, if only by an inch. But now he knew, and he felt himself sliding deeper into it.

He returned to the search results and clicked a link to her obituary from the same newspaper. He read it through his tears. The obituary was sterile in its mention of her husband, sisters, nieces and nephews, and lastly her faith in a cloying passage of God's goodness and kindness.

Nowhere in the notice was he mentioned.

His chest constricted. He had been the most obedient child he knew, loving and kind. He'd loved his mother and father, but all of that was wiped away. It was as if he belonged to no one. He felt a burn in his chest, like poison. A poison he had to get out of him.

He reached for his phone and called his parents' home. As suspected, the call went to the answering machine. He steeled himself against the recording of his mother's voice and cleared his throat.

"I will never forgive you for this. Never. You want me gone. So be it."

He hung up the phone and waited for the stinging in his chest to fade.

26

Russell hated driving in the city so much he tried to escape it altogether, but there were times when it was unavoidable. On the rare occasion, when a chore fell out of the reach of the trains and the predicted cab fare passed his twenty-dollar threshold, he turned to his Subaru Impreza.

Missing hubcaps and sporting a rearview mirror bandaged by duct tape, the car was wedged in a parallel parking spot two blocks down from his apartment. Rust writhed up the bumper like a flesh-eating virus, a testament to the car's brutal fifteen years. As he made his way down the road, it had seemed possible the concrete had attempted to pull the old sedan into the ground overnight. But the stubborn car sat. Tucked under a chewed wiper on the cracked windshield was a small, orange envelope.

Russell cursed the parking ticket, another souvenir from his ongoing war with Chicago's meter maids. Over the years, his driving pilgrimages had been tormented by parking tickets. The local meter maids undoubtedly sought out his car like easy prey, for the day his city sticker expired, or the minute the parking slip elapsed, they struck. He compiled enough tickets to make a large bonfire and probably paid enough fees to finance a college education.

Like a giant, Russell folded himself into the front seat and extended the seat as far back as it would go to pull his knees out from his chest and operate the vehicle. The car sputtered to life, belching out a grey cloud. The engine, a patchwork of used junkyard parts, groaned as he made his way into the congestion of rush hour traffic. By the time he hit the Kennedy Expressway, traffic slowed to a torturous speed Russell suspected must have defied the Geneva Conventions. His car crawled past fellow inmates, some shaking the surrounding area with thumping music, others on cell phones, but all alone in their little cabins moving at a walking speed.

A man not much older than Russell wheeled next to him in a shiny sports car. The car was too close to devise its exact make but close enough to show off the vehicle's slick interior, wired with GPS guidance and a high-tech sound system. The man noticed Russell's appreciation with a smug chin nod. Russell startled and turned back to his console, embarrassed by the bolts of jealousy shooting through him.

When he acquired the used Subaru at nineteen, gas was remarkably cheaper and he'd been happy for the escape from the trailer park and his father's malignant drunkenness. He would have ridden away on a tractor if necessary. He spent his nights parked outside or cruising the streets until alcohol dragged his father into unconsciousness. Only then it was safe to tiptoe back into the house, free from his father's ridicule. Russell would shut himself in the small alcove of his room, armed with sketchpads and a pencil. Over the years, stacks of sketches became heaped piles of drawings made by his adolescent hands, depicting the world around him. He thirsted for any particle of beauty he could find outside the trailer park's grey borders.

When Russell considered retiring the car at the nearest junkyard, protests from Leslie and Kat won out. At least one of them needed at car, they insisted. "What if a terrorist attack happened?" Leslie would say. Kat chimed in with, "The car's paid off, keep it until it dies." These valid points kept him subject to endless tickets from the city. Silently, he mulled the possibility he'd outgrown this ashtray-smelling, teenaged haven.

The Subaru turned from the Kennedy Expressway toward the lake, still moving at a grueling pace. Russell's endurance dwindled at the unavoidable fact that the car barely contained him. He was a clown, crammed in the toy car at the circus.

Once in River North, he feebly hunted for a parking spot in the city of more than two million and instead parked along the road, boxing in an empty car. Quickly switching on his hazard lights, he wedged his phone free and dialed Ava, who picked up after a brief peal. "Hey, babe. Where are you?"

He saw her across the street, looking out from the glass door of a small, overpriced boutique. The boutique owner—a has-been French stylist according to Ava—enjoyed a short-lived career at a high-end fashion magazine. None of this made any sense to Russell, but for Ava, who didn't need a job, this place had enough allure for part-time employment. "I'm only doing it for the discount," was her defense. "Where else can you get twenty percent off on a Stella McCartney?"

"I'm outside in my car," Russell said, waving to her.

Ava pushed through the doors and stared with her eyes wide and mouth gaping.

"You're not expecting me to ride in that rat trap."

"Ava, come on."

"The fumes alone can be blamed for climate change."

She peered cautiously down the street and looked back into the boutique's glass doors. Deciding she could approach the car unnoticed, she scurried across the street. Her vanity almost ended in tragedy when a passing SUV nearly clipped her. She shrieked and collapsed in the car.

Once inside, hair windblown, eyes livid, she howled. "Go! Go now!"

Rattled from the hysterics, Russell floored the gas pedal. The engine wheezed and shuttered while they shot down the street, undetected by the French stylist and her lavish dresses.

"Are we in the middle of a heist?" Russell asked, looking back to determine if they were being pursued.

Ava glared back at him, smoothing her hair. "You know I hate being seen in this car. Why would you pick me up in it?"

Russell's muscles constricted in his chest, and his face pulled into a frown. "You wanted to meet up after work. Here I am. But I get it—I'm not good enough to pick you up."

Unflinching at Russell's anger, Ava said, "You're perfect, Russell. This car, on the other hand, is awful. I'm surprised you let yourself be seen in it."

"Enough."

"Okay," she said. "But if it's a money thing, there's an assistant manager position opening up and I can have my father put in a good word for you."

"How quickly we make the jump to nepotism."

Ava turned to him, her face softened. "I'm sorry."

Tension fell from Russell. "Me, too."

"I love you," she said. "And I know you love this car, but it's okay to let it go. It's okay to grow up and have things that aren't hand-me-downs. I mean, you can't drive it forever, just like you can't live with your roommates in a crappy apartment forever."

He knew she might be right. Things at home hadn't felt good for a week. Leslie was in a dark place and Kat had suddenly shut down. He couldn't hold on to who they used to be. At times, it was as if he didn't know them at all. How could they fit in with the life he wanted with Ava? Would he have to toss them aside like he did with his paintings? They had been like his family, giving him so much. But no one was giving anyone anything lately, except sad, unfocused stares. The apartment was beginning to feel like his father's trailer.

At a red light, Russell turned to Ava. She sat tensely in the passenger seat as if his car interior would attack her. He sighed in defeat.

"I know. I can't stay with them forever."

"The sooner you leave, the better," she said, giving his leg a squeeze.

27

One of Belle Journee's two studio locations was an expensive downtown office that overlooked Chicago's skyscraper morass from dizzying heights. The small, sleek office space was trimmed in chrome and ergonomic furnishings that hugged bodies and supported lumbar vertebrae. The smoky glass desks were topped with high-end iMacs. This beautiful spectacle could service a science fiction movie better than the studio, since little to almost no production came to the office. Instead, the prime real estate acted primarily as a showpiece, a place to gather prospective clients and woo them into signing contracts. Sometimes it served as the backdrop for elite parties.

The second office was banished into the nether regions of Rogers Park, a forty-minute train ride up north—on a good day. Unlike its prettier sister, this wide office building was constructed from ugly brick. Belle Journee could generate productivity within four immense studio spaces and save one to store all the equipment. The building shared its jammed-packed block with a tall apartment building and a fenced-off lot that harbored bulldozers, cranes, and excavators all working over crumbled concrete piles, digging holes and flattening black expanses of asphalt. Most employees spent their studio days ignoring the clamor of construction. Offices shuttered and unnecessary reshoots were forced. No one knew what the men in hardhats next door had been toiling over during the last months, but whatever it was, the cacophony produced no structure—only a deepening hole in the ground.

Kat suffered through the train ride from the downtown office to Rogers Park. She jostled into a crowded train car and found standing room, while her nostrils were invaded by piss drifting from an anonymous source. The stench was full-bodied and everyone in her view was suspect. At Loyola, she liberated herself from the car and onto the street, grateful for a cleansing breeze rolling in from Lake Michigan.

There was comfort in her trip up north. An abled sense of business as usual. As she journeyed the few blocks to the office, she started to believe her life could be about her again. It had been a week since her miscarriage. A kind doctor at Northwestern Hospital assured Kat she would be fine, but since then, her body felt alien. Her skin was different to her touch. Her face unfamiliar. She was spinning without anything to hold onto, unable to laugh or to speak. The doctor warned her of a hormone flux, and she was sure it was related, but until then, she had work to do.

At the door to the studio, her phone pulsed in her purse. She fished it out, peering down at the screen to see an unread message from Jacob. She snarled and shoved the phone away. The text messages had been sparse at first, but due to her indifference, they now buzzed every hour.

She pretended she was too busy to respond, but truthfully, she was too drained to deal with Jacob. He knew nothing about the short-lived pregnancy, and she had been angry with him before the miscarriage. Kat knew what would follow if she responded to him: sweet words, empty promises, eventual forgiveness, and sex. She would avoid this as long as possible, even though the thought of him was comforting. She needed to collect herself before she gave in to him, just a bit longer.

Kat stepped into the building, greeted the receptionist, and moved through the drab industrial rooms to the office she shared with three photographers and a handful of interns. She popped in a zip drive and put the finishing touches on a series of portraits featuring a neurotic pastry chef planning for a Lincoln Park bakery relaunch. She'd spent days drudging through proofs, Photoshopping the mania out of this nervous man and his decorative cake platters. Just as she was preparing the photos for print, the phone rang.

An intern picked up and placed the caller on hold.

"There's a Jacob on the phone for you."

Kat sighed heavily. "Tell him I'll call him later."

The intern relayed the message and hung up. He then said, "That dude seemed rather insistent."

Jacob was upping the ante on their little game, and Kat could feel the tension closing in. But she held out, curious to see his next play. On the rare occasion she could assert power over him, she stirred with a debased titillation. It felt delicious, twisting his desire for her against him with mere silence.

Stroking this new source of pleasure, she missed the deliveryman strolling into the office, armed with a clipboard and a vase packed with roses and Peruvian lilies. All work halted while the office members' faces scanned one another with anxious and hopeful glances. The gift-bearer paused, holding the suspense longer than appropriate, and consulted his clipboard.

"Katherine Davalos?"

The room exhaled a rush of disenchanted sighs as the deliveryman deposited the vase on Kat's workstation, accepted her signature, and vanished. A bomb may as well have gone off with the way the flowers captured her co-workers' attention. Kat flushed, grabbed her purse, and excused herself out the back door.

She pulled out her cigarettes and phone and drew in several puffs, grateful to be smoking again. She called Jacob.

"Must've gotten the flowers?"

"You know I'm immune to clichés, right?"

"It got you to call me."

This truth made Kat frown and deserved some sort of counter. "Is your wife around? She might hear us."

"No, she's not. She's out of town most of the week."

"Okay."

"I want you to come over."

Irritation dissipated from Kat and she felt hollow. She hadn't anticipated this maneuver and had long ago resigned herself to meeting him in hotel rooms. She'd been thrilled when one of their trysts ended on the desk in his office. Kat had often wondered what Jacob's home was like, where he placed his things, and what it would feel like to lie in bed with him for the entirety of the night. A strange longing warmed her as she turned over this new dimension of intimacy.

"Just think about it," she heard him say, "then call me."

"Sure," she replied and hung up.

She finished the last of her cigarette, staring at the abandoned cranes and bulldozers in the neighboring construction site. The lone machinery, yellow and beginning to rust, bowed before the audience of Kat, rubble, and a gaping cavity in the earth.

28

Leslie stepped into Stratosphere with his head swimming in anger. A good shower and an outfit change hadn't calmed his nerves, and the last bit of weed went up in smoke the other day. His rattled nerves carried him to a barstool in search of Kat, but a pudgy, curt mixologist had taken her place behind the bar. He managed his disappointment when the bartender recognized him as a regular and dropped a stiff gin and tonic in front of him.

Leslie took swift gulps and rubbed his temples.

"You look like someone took a piss in your favorite shoes."

Leslie's stomach tensed as Beck appeared on the stool next to him, drinking a red cocktail from a tall glass.

"Don't you have a home?"

Beck snorted. "I have a home. You're welcome to join me."

"No." Leslie forced down the rest of his drink.

Beck pointed to the bartender. "Get him another, on me."

Leslie reluctantly accepted. "What are you doing here? Isn't there a coke den missing its leader?"

Beck smiled, unaffected. "My friend is gonna do a set tonight, I had to support."

Down the bar, past the mulling patronage, Leslie saw Beck's pin-cushioned lieutenant toiling over a laptop and a pile of sound system cords.

"It's going to be awesome. He's also doing Marcie's party tomorrow," Beck continued. "You're welcome to join us. Or maybe it can be just the two of us..."

"I'm not planning on overdosing this week, but I'll check my schedule."

"Come on."

Leslie opened his mouth to retort but felt malice rise in his chest. He decided to sip his drink instead.

"You blaming me for something?" Beck asked, laughing. He turned listlessly in his stool, looking into the crowd for something more interesting.

"I blame you for a lot of shit," Leslie said flatly.

Beck spun back, face taut and eyes narrowed, the air suddenly charged. Leslie's adrenaline spiked as he realized he'd stepped out of Beck's grace and was nowhere near prepared for the brawl of wits that would follow.

"What the fuck does that mean?" Beck asked in a harsh whisper. "Is this about your little boyfriend?"

Leslie clenched his jaw, scrambling for his fading conviction. "He thinks you're his best friend. He practically loves you, man, and you've been nowhere in sight."

Beck smirked coldly. "You know I've been throwing the best parties here for years. Epic shit. Shit you're ashamed to tell people about afterward. Shit where you wake up wondering where you are the next morning."

Beck edged closer, an icy grin laced on his copper face. Liquored breath tickled his ear canal while Leslie heard nothing but Beck's harsh whispers. "Parties where you rage all night and feel alive, man. Where you push yourself to the limit. And you've been at most of them, drinking my booze, fucking my crew, and smoking my shit. That's why I like you and your friends. You guys get it. At least, you *did*."

"We're not twenty-one anymore," Leslie said. "What happened to Isaac?"

"It was just as much your fault as mine. You brought him into this. You invited him to hang with us. Blame yourself."

Leslie felt the air yanked from his chest. Beck pulled back and nodded to the bartender.

"Hey, man, another one for me and my friend here."

Beck's taunting smile was unyielding. The drinks were refreshed and Beck's reverberating whispers submitted to the rising thump of music. His lieutenant swayed with ecstasy, and his laptop filled the room with the mechanical drone of dubstep. The overhead lights faded into the haunting blue glow of black lights, and the crowd slowly convened at the deejay station.

"I remember Isaac when he first started dating you. This beautiful, small-town fuck excited to be in the city with his first Chicago boyfriend. I love a grown man with childlike innocence."

The image of Isaac in the gritty halfway house hadn't left Leslie's mind, and tears threatened his composure. What if Beck was right? What if all the suffering had been his fault? Leslie lost himself in the melting ice of his glass. Everything felt unrecognizable.

"You blame me for some lightweight bitch losing his shit?"

At Leslie's hard look, Beck wavered slightly. Something akin to remorse seemed to grip him, and the sharp edge of his attack dulled.

Leslie clutched his drink and lapped the first tides of drunkenness.

"He was beautiful," Beck said. "He was one of us."

Beck's words formed bricks in Leslie's stomach, and he glanced up to see that any remorse had evaporated quickly. Leslie wondered if he'd actually seen any at all. If he was hoping to share the weight Isaac placed on him with someone, he shouldn't have turned to Beck. He watched Beck smile without authenticity, sucked in a shaky breath, and rested his gaze on the deejay station. That was easier than readjusting his view on Beck.

If Beck truly wanted to help him, he would allow Leslie to hate him.

"Let me know if need another drink."

"Sure," Leslie said.

"Maybe I'll see you at Marcie's," Beck said, stepping off his stool and into the growing crowd.

Leslie wished he could melt completely into a glass of gin. He thought about going home but knew he shouldn't be left alone with this anger. The voicemails to his father had gone unanswered, and Leslie felt a heavy poison festering deep in his chest. Being alone with that tonight would kill him. He stood up and stepped into the crowd.

Beck's head rocked to the lieutenant's feeble attempts at spinning. Leslie crept up behind him and placed his hands on his lower back.

"You're right," Leslie said. "Tonight I want to feel like it used to."

Sobering concern worked its way across Beck's face, and he looked strangely warm, almost amicable, like Leslie could tell him anything. The softness encouraged Leslie to unburden himself. It was as if Beck had said, "Tell me all those things you have no words for. Let me comfort you." The desire to help was so unflinching Leslie felt repelled. He didn't want the balms of friendship, he wanted Beck's fistful of pills and tightly cut lines of coke. How could he express that he needed to hate Beck? That he needed Beck to share culpability for the state of things? He couldn't, so he simply said, "Let's party."

29

No one was home to greet Kat when she returned from Belle Journee, and the quiet in the empty apartment was cruel. Without a distraction from her roommates, Jacob's invitation rang in her head. A few laps around the apartment didn't stop her desire to see him, so she showered, shaved, and outfitted herself in skinny jeans and a black leather jacket. She paused before the open mouth of her jewelry box and allowed minutes to pass, hoping some act of providence would stop her. But nothing came. No diversion, no phone call, only the silent certainty that she would push forward. She sighed and slipped on a pile of thin silver bangles before following this pull out the door. Out on the streets, she transferred from bus to subway and headed toward Lincoln Park. On the train, she was another stone-faced commuter, arms folded and weary in her seat as the train ran through dark, underground tunnels.

The train emerged onto elevated tracks, her heartbeat matching the pulse of metal gears that pushed her forward. The train itself trudged through the night as if forcing a path through the darkness and rooftops.

Kat exited the train and headed into the dim streets. Nausea drenched her as she followed the blue dot of the GPS. When she'd accepted Jacob's invite, he replied with his address. On the map, the route seemed simple enough, but navigating the streets of Lincoln Park at night would have been difficult even if she had been clearheaded. Thick trees obstructed the streetlights and created swathes of blackness along the residential streets. Kat paced a block several times when her frustration had nearly tempted a journey back home. She stopped to orient herself with her surroundings, looking for some sort of landmark, when movement across the street caught her eye.

The chains from a swing groaned in an abandoned playground. Kat paused for a moment, trying to find the source, when closer examination revealed that the entire playground was alive with movement. The hanging monkey bars swayed softly, random debris moved up into the air in circles, and above, leaves from the surrounding trees glimmered like a dark liquid. The fenced in park that had been closed for hours only housed wind moving through the castle constructs made of up bars, chains, and Astroturf like invisible children. The playground was illuminated like a stage throwing light and shadows in odd corners on the street. Kat stared at it a little longer, as if she waited for shapes of children to appear in some haunting.

Her phone rattled in her hand, and she yelped, her voice bouncing off across the street turning the playground from supernatural to empty and ordinary.

"Hello?"

"Where are you?" Jacob asked.

"Across from the park."

"Good, I'm up two blocks," he said, "I'll meet you outside."

She paced forward, straining to see Jacob's figure a few blocks ahead folded in shadowy sheaths of darkness. Her hammering heartbeat overpowered the clamor of unsure footsteps. Kat slowed before a few yards away from him, allowing one last moment before she crossed this line into the home this married man shared with his wife. And before she could conclude what type of woman this made her, Jacob was moving toward her, calling her name stepping into streetlight. In that golden hemisphere of light, he was fraught with desire. He stood, hands and arms open, and Kat left her convictions behind.

He swept her into his arms, back into the blackness. Kat's blind feet stumbled upward onto the few steps that lead into a narrow courtyard shared by four condominiums. The condominiums were lit from within, and through tiny spaces in blinds and gaps in the curtains, yellow light escaped to be trapped in overhanging branches. The courtyard somehow took on the unearthly quality, and Kat was certain she wasn't in Chicago anymore. Instead, she was in this nebulous domestication moving through the night. The street was clean and the stray cigarette butts would be certain to find the nearest receptacle. Homes were furbished urban spreads in Home and Garden with Pottery Barn, antiques, and Crate and Barrel, and the crime rates were low by any modern metropolis standards. Yet somewhere in those rooted shadows festered a quiet dystopia and Kat wondered how many other husbands were bold enough to creep like spies with their mistresses trailing steps behind.

Jacob slipped the keys into the front lock. The lock tumblers popped like gunshots and Kat felt her heart outright stop. He pushed the door open and Kat followed him into a house blacker than outside. After a moment, Kat's eyes adjusted and she made out Jacob's figure tugging off clothes in the murkiness. They stood in a wide room, and Kat perceived the shapes of large furniture and the glass from mounted picture frames reflecting the dim light. A noxious sweet stench burned the lining of Kat's nose and throat. In the dark haze, she made out a decorative bowl filled with potpourri dried twigs and petals.

Her heart stopped again. No man would ever place a bowl with potpourri or choose such a sickeningly sweet fragrance, but his wife would.

Jacob stood with an erection peeking through the slot in his boxers. His hand ran along the wall for a light switch.

"Don't," Kat said.

"Huh?"

"Don't turn on the light."

If she faced the house's interior details, she was certain she'd clutch her head and run away in terror.

Jacob's hand moved from the wall and rested on his crotch. "Want the tour?"

"No," Kat said, disrobing. "Let's just go to bed."

Jacob chuckled, drawing her through the dark halls and upstairs. Long rugs muted their footsteps and the night graciously hid their stripping down. Kat's naked body dipped guardedly onto the bed and she sank into a heap of decorative pillows and a soft duvet. The bedroom's massive cathedral ceiling hung far above them. Long French doors opened up to a patio, and dim light waned from an adjoining bathroom.

Jacob's silhouette stalked forward with the ease of a man in his home. Wondering how many times his wife had seen this exact same image, from this very spot, Kat leapt from the bed, rocked by a hot nausea.

"You okay?"

"Yeah, I'll be back," Kat said, and with four wide strides entered the bathroom and locked the door behind her.

She leaned back on the door, her eyes settling on his-and-her sinks and a pair of toothbrushes settled in their holders. Two beige towels hung over a matching rug, and the walls' soft yellow trim sectioned the space and complemented the shower curtain. Another bowl of potpourri, much smaller than the other, expelled sugar into the air from the top of the toilet tank.

She'd never felt like such an invader.

Her ragged breath tore through the silence. A pale reflection gaped fearfully back at her from the mirrored medicine cabinet. She stepped forward and opened the door to reveal a varied collection of soaps, lotions, and perfumes, all arranged by size. Pink razors and a pink, flower-covered tampon box dominated the bottom shelf. Jacob's wife's femininity was an overblown presence around her, aggressively closing in for the kill.

Kat quickly shut the cabinet, her breathing more desperate than before. She felt provoked, and in some way, no matter how small, she had to combat this presence. She stilled her breathing, remembering she had been the one hidden like a terrible secret. She was barely holding onto herself. She was not his wife. She was not the woman with the horrible potpourri. She was the one who had suffered the miscarriage.

"Kat, you okay in there?" Jacob called.

"Yeah," she said, and slowly pulled the silver bangles from her wrist. She gently placed them by the potpourri bowl. She wouldn't return for them. She would leave them there.

She left the bathroom aroused by her quiet retaliation.

30

The lieutenant's hawkish attempts at playing deejay were over, and the more qualified DJ Heavyrox took his spot. Leslie gritted through it, allowing Beck to buy him drink after drink. Leslie veered into a warm drunkenness and followed Beck and his crew out of Stratosphere into a cab. The lieutenant sat up front while Leslie and Beck squeezed into the back with the two ever-present women. They headed westward into Logan Square and got out in front of Broken Jaw.

Leslie trailed Beck and his group as they moved through the densely packed space, where the air rattled with screeching rock music from a Detroit garage band playing in the rear. Another round of drinks was ordered and everyone raised their glasses for an empty toast. The cheap gin was sharp on Leslie's tongue and burned going down his throat.

His phone rang, and Isaac's number scrolled over the screen. Leslie quickly silenced it. He didn't want to see Isaac or try to explain hanging out with Beck and his friends. He couldn't even explain it to himself. So much had slipped away. A pang of guilt struck and flooded over him. For a moment, he felt helpless. All he wanted was another drink. He leaned over and locked eyes with the bartender. He ordered a shot of whiskey and upturned it as soon as it arrived.

Beck and his crew cheered valiantly at his recklessness. One of the women reached over and kissed him on the cheek. Her lips left a wet spot, and when the group turned toward the band, Leslie wiped hard with his sleeve to erase the sensation.

He couldn't get drunk enough. His chest pounded in acrid anger, louder than the uproar of music. He couldn't escape it. He couldn't shake free. He pushed through the crowd, passed the band, went through a set of graffiti-covered doors, and stepped onto an open back patio. Strings of multicolored Christmas lights formed a canopy overhead, casting a sickly glow on the patio's stone-faced smokers. Leslie, on cue, reached in his pocket for a pack of cigarettes. His phone rang again, and he didn't have to look to know it was Isaac. He pulled out his phone and toyed with the idea of calling him.

The door squeaked open and Beck emerged from the bar, reaching for a cigarette, relieving Leslie of having to make a decision about Isaac.

He handed the cigarette to Beck and they shared it in silence.

Beck finally said, "Shit must be really bad if you're out here with me."

Leslie snorted and nodded. "Yeah." He smoked the last of his cigarette and stamped it into the cobblestone beneath them.

"How's Kat?"

Leslie raised an eyebrow. "What do mean?"

Beck narrowed his eyes and shook his head. "Nothing." He glanced around uncomfortably. "We're not friends, are we?"

"I don't know, really," Leslie said. "Maybe if you weren't

trying to sleep with me and everyone I know."

"You should be flattered," Beck said, lighting another cigarette for them to share.

Leslie stared up at the prismatic glow cast by the lights. "Do you believe in God?"

"Wow, this got deep."

"Seriously, I want to know," Leslie said. "I was raised in the church. It's all I remember. All I know. My parents made me go every Wednesday and every Sunday. It's where I grew up, where I laughed and cried, where I met my friends. It was what we were and who we were. And I came out and lost everything and everyone... Funny thing is, I thought I was over it."

"Well, we didn't do that in my house. We did Mass once in a while on the holidays," Beck said with a long drag of his cigarette. He joined Leslie in gazing up at the lights. "But look around you, Leslie. This is your church now."

He held out his glass and cigarette. "This is your sacrament. Each night is your confession. You and I are members of this church. This is where we grow and cry. This is where we worship. You've lost nothing."

Leslie took his cigarette and pulled from it. He smiled at Beck. "You're fucking sick."

"I think you like it," Beck said, moving close to Leslie.

Beck stared deeply at Leslie. He smiled softly and placed his hand on Leslie's shoulder. Leslie didn't move and felt himself grow slack. Beck's hand followed Leslie's shoulder, grazing his neck and moving up his cheek. Leslie shivered underneath his touch and pressed his face into his warm hand. Leslie closed his eyes and felt his hard anger give, just a little. Muscles uncoiled in his chest, and he wanted to stand there with Beck, close to him, with his hand on his face. But

Isaac drifted into his mind, rising up like a sharp spike. Leslie pulled back and adjusted his shirt.

"My mother died," he said, turning away from Beck. "And I couldn't even go to her funeral."

"Shit. How do you feel?"

"There are no words."

"Then let's get you fucked up, man," Beck said, tossing his cigarette over his shoulder.

Beck took Leslie's hand and they bucked into the crowd. Beck nodded at his lieutenant and the three of them convened in the men's bathroom. Inside the graffiti-covered walls, the air was rancid with vomit. Leslie swallowed to keep from gagging. The lieutenant pulled a small glass cocaine bullet from his pocket and unscrewed the lid.

"Wait," Beck said, and turned to Leslie. "Are you ready for communion?"

The lieutenant passed the bullet to Leslie, and a surge of guilt crested over him. He ignored Isaac's phone call. He missed his mother's funeral. The anger and dismay felt crushing, and he didn't want to feel anything anymore. He looked past Beck's eager face and into the mirror, where he saw his mother's saintly ghost reflected at him.

"Thank you," he said to Beck as he brought the coke to his nostril.

31

Kat lay breathless in the bed, her mouth coated with Jacob's sweat and spit. Her thighs were raw, and she could still feel his cock like a vacancy inside her. She'd wanted him in that moment—that wild thrashing, his deep plundering. She wanted to be in his bed, coming in the sheets his wife probably bought from a catalog. Spitting at this woman she never met had become delicious. The anger sweltered between her legs. But the orgasm left her. The moaning broke to the awkward silence of strangers.

She didn't know where she was or who she was with.

Kat eyed an overturned picture frame on the nightstand. The frame likely held a picture of Jacob and his happy wife. Suddenly, Kat was up and groping in the dark for her panties and then her clothes. Jacob didn't try to stop her, because certainly he was feeling it, too. A shame pervaded the room like an icy high tide, and before Kat could drown, she was tripping down the stairs. She heard Jacob follow her, his footsteps just as frantic.

"Kat, stop!"

"What did we do?" she said.

"I'm going to leave her."

Kat tried to make out his face in the inky darkness, hoping to find truth in his eyes or at least some absolution to make her feel better—feel human—about how much she'd deeply enjoyed their sins.

In the darkness, a small question came to her. Would he leave his wife for Kat?

He leaned forward to kiss her and asked her to stay, encircling her in his arm. She grew slack in his grasp, leaned against him, and felt his cock grow stiff. She gave him an empty smile and departed quickly, before he could initiate round two. Kat was sluggish as her rubbery limbs carried her out of his home and toward a main street. A cab came to her like a lifeboat at sea and she gratefully let it carry her back home.

Only Russell was in the apartment, staring blankly at the TV. Without acknowledging him, she shot straight to the bathroom. She ripped off her clothes and let her momentum pull her into the shower. The hot water washed away Jacob's smell and burned away his touch, but the guilt lingered like a stain underneath her skin. When she was out of the shower, wrapped in a towel and moving toward her room, Russell met her in the hall.

"You okay?"

"I'm fine."

"Yeah, well, you look like you're lying."

"I'm fine."

"You've been weird all week."

"It's Jacob," she admitted, tears burning in her eyes.

Russell hooked her in his long arms. The wall of his wide body and bouncing drum of his voice comforted her.

"Whatever happened, he's stupid," he said. "Any man can see how good you are."

Kat put her arms around him and buried her face in his chest. "Why are you being so nice?"

"Well, you are acting like a girl," Russell said.

Kat snorted, then shoved him. She headed to her room to put on an oversized T-shirt and sweatpants. Back in the living room, she sat on the couch and drew her legs up to her body. Russell stood up and reached for the record player.

"Want to dance?" he asked.

"Dance?"

"Go in my room and get my Cure album before I get bored with your mopey attitude about your boyfriend."

Kat pretended to be annoyed while she trekked into his room. After a quick scan, she found his records packed neatly in a short box next to his unkempt bed. She scaled piles of dirty clothes to fish through the vinyl. She yanked out The Cure, wedged tightly in the box, and lost her balance in the struggle, tumbling backward. She yelped as she smashed into canvases stacked against the wall and scrambled to her feet while the stack fell forward onto the floor.

The rumble brought Russell into the room, and he almost stepped on her, scooping up the canvases. His face flushed with embarrassment.

"Please don't look at these," he said in a small voice.

"Russell, I've seen your work before," she said. "You don't have to hide it from me."

"You haven't seen these."

Kat advanced to see, but he was quick to place them in his closet. He blocked the closet with his body, a gesture of finality on the matter. Kat shrugged as Russell led her back to the living room, and soon The Cure was crooning "Lovesong" from the spinning record player.

"Come on, Kat. If you're going to be a girl tonight, let's go all out."

"I'm going to ignore your misogyny," she said.

He scooped Kat into his arms, and she laughed as they stumbled over each other with awkward steps. Her feet on his socks, his hands on her shoulders, then slipping down to her hips, they worked like kinks unwinding from a thread until they moved in full accord. They were synchronized. They were friends who laughed at the same jokes, ate each other's leftovers, endured each other's TV shows, breathed the same air, and shared the same space. Kat felt her head slope into the gravity of his chest. With her feet on top of his, he carried her with his swagger to the music.

32

The Detroit rock band had stopped playing hours ago, but

the bar continued to thrive. Outside, the temperature had dropped and the air smelled of storm clouds, cigarettes, and liquor. Leslie was perched on a stool next to a small table in the rear of the bar. He nursed another gin and tonic, held the drink in front of his face, and tried to recall exactly how it ended up in his hand. Beck stood across the bar, arms slung around his women, smiling wildly. He turned his grin toward Leslie and waved. The women followed suit, blowing kisses.

Leslie chuckled and brought his drink to his lips. Everything in the past few hours had been extremely funny, so much so his sides were tender from laughing. The world existed exclusively within the dark walls of this bar, in this moment. He swayed to an alternative rock song from his youth, unhinged by a delicious chill in the cooling air.

Leslie was adrift in the dark corner of the bar. He could dance. He could sit. He could think great thoughts and nothing all at once. He never wanted to leave this stool. He took one of his feet off the stool's rungs and planted it on the sticky floor. Around him, conversations babbled and he felt like he was connected to every word, every gesture, in the darkness.

He swallowed his gin and clenched up as it slammed into his stomach. He closed his eyes and tried to shake it off. Tiny sweat beads stung his forehead and the back of his neck. A jarring panic tugged at him. His mouth dampened and a harsh burp parted his lips. The contents of his stomach blundered inside him. He shot up from the stool and charged to the bathroom, locking the door behind him. He lurched forward and vomit blasted from him. He aimed himself over the toilet. Tears clouded his vision.

He tried to account for how many drinks he'd consumed since snorting coke with Beck. He couldn't be sure of the number.

He emptied his stomach and sat in a corner of the bathroom, too beaten to care. He smacked his lips and wiped his mouth with the back of his wrist. The world outside the bar, the one that had momentarily faded away, barreled back, and he wailed, sniffing back tears, the funk of urine, and his own vomit.

He pulled out his phone and called Isaac. The call went to voicemail, so Leslie tried him again.

"H-hello?" Isaac's voice was thick from sleep.

"Please come get me," Leslie said.

"Are you okay?"

"No," Leslie said, bringing his knees up to his chest. Isaac bristled with irritation when he heard Leslie was at Broken Jaw but promised to come. Leslie hung up and looked over at the smeared bathroom mirror, afraid of who he would see if stood before it. He was certain the ghost of his mother was in this bathroom with him, staring back through the mirror at the mess he had become. Her face would be tight in anger, eyes soft with disappointment. He couldn't bear that thought so he placed his head on his knees and screwed his eyes closed. Many unknown minutes later, a sharp knock jarred him back to life.

"Hey, open up the door, man," Leslie heard Beck say.

Leslie placed his hand on the slick floor and pushed himself to his feet. He opened the door and Beck rushed in, mildly panicked.

"What is with you and your friends in bathrooms?" Beck muttered. "Are you okay?"

"No, I need to go home."

"Yeah, clearly," Beck said. "Isaac's outside looking for you."

Leslie straightened his T-shirt and brushed off his jeans,

careful to avoid the mirror as he stepped out of the bathroom. Isaac stood at the bar next to Beck's threesome, staring darkly at a drink set in front of him.

Leslie stopped and pulled on Beck's wrist. "Did he do anything while I was in the bathroom?"

Beck blinked at him. "I don't know."

Leslie's heart hammered in his chest as he approached. Isaac turned to him, and Leslie's eyes dropped to the drink on the bar. Isaac sighed and pushed it away. He stood and turned to the rest of the group.

"I've got to take him home," he said, coolly jabbing his thumb at Leslie.

Leslie waved at them halfheartedly and trailed Isaac out, close enough to step on his heels. They walked silently through the smokers on the street. Leslie wrapped his arms around himself against the cold and turned down the block toward the train.

"Did you do anything?" Leslie asked.

Isaac spun around. "Are you fucking serious?"

Leslie nodded.

Isaac stepped closer to Leslie until he was inches from his face. "What are you on right now?"

Leslie backstepped and rubbed his face with his hand.

Isaac smacked his lips. "Exactly. You're so worried about me, but look at yourself. Your mother is dead and we're..." Isaac pulled back a sharp breath. "We are hanging on by a thread."

"I'm sorry," Leslie said. "Cut me some slack."

"That's the only reason I'm here."

Leslie slammed his fist into his leg. "She's been dead for two months. I missed the funeral. I never got a chance to say good-bye. What do you want from me? I'm trying."

"How? By pulling me out of bed in the middle of the night?" Isaac turned toward the train and marched forward. "Do you want to know what I was thinking the whole time I was in rehab?"

Leslie stumbled behind him to keep pace.

"I was thinking I didn't belong there. I was thinking that I was *normal*. It was a waste of my time. You went on without me. The whole world went on without me. The party went on without me."

"I just wanted to help you," Leslie said in a small voice.

"How can you help me when you can't even help yourself?"

Leslie didn't speak anymore, and he strung along behind Isaac, careful to avoid his own reflection in the dark storefront windows.

33

Friday had all the makings of a good day. Russell didn't have to be at work until ten o'clock. He rolled in bed at the pleasure of more sleep. After too many beers the night before, at a bar down the street from his branch of Midwest Regional Bank, he'd been left with no choice but to crash at Ava's Gold Coast apartment. He hoped for a leisurely morning, just the two of them in bed. Ideally, he'd wake up to fool around with her and fall back to sleep until he had to get up for work. Instead, Ava took his company as a test-drive of her domestic prowess.

Around seven-thirty she left bed, and the sounds of tussling challenged Russell's determination to sleep. He squeezed his eyes shut. He placed a stray pillow over his face as the last warm slivers of sleep shattered against slamming kitchen cupboards. The TV murmured with morning news announcements over the sound of running water.

Russell lay in bed wondering if he had been thrown into the future, seeing how the mornings would be spent with Ava. This wasn't the first time he had spent the night at her place, and her perpetual early rising forced him up earlier than he wanted. Her mattress was suddenly too soft, her duvet too dense, and her footsteps too heavy.

He wished he could recede back to his apartment. But he was here with Ava.

Defeated, Russell flung himself from bed, through the bedroom, and into the open living space. Her apartment, much like Ava, was refined but not at the sacrifice of taste. Everything lent itself to minimalism and straight lines. The couch and a few well-placed lamps were square. The walls held little artwork, for Ava regarded the large dominating windows as enough visual interest for the room. Being on the eighteenth floor, her apartment windows framed an ever-changing cityscape.

Ava stood in her robe, jabbing her finger at the coffeemaker. She smiled at Russell with an aggressive cheeriness. Russell nodded, fumbling toward the couch. He collapsed onto it and felt plastic slide underneath him.

"You're sitting on your dry cleaning!"

Russell slumped forward, pulling the navy suit from underneath him. The suit hung from a wire hanger and was covered in thin, clear plastic. He groaned while Ava ripped the suit from his hand, scanning it for damage. She then placed it like an injured child on a kitchen stool, safely away from Russell.

"Why are you up so early?" Russell asked.

Ava placed her hands on her hips. "I was trying to make you breakfast and be a good girlfriend."

Russell heaved with a sigh. "Thank you."

Unconvinced, Ava made her way to the bathroom. She turned on the shower and popped her frowning face out from the doorframe. "Sorry for trying."

A sharp panic rose in him. "Baby, mornings make me stupid."

"No arguing there," Ava said, and her face withdrew into the bathroom. He heard her pull back the shower door and step inside.

Russell followed her into the bathroom. If he didn't make an attempt at atonement, he would have to endure Ava's passive-aggressive lashings all morning. He wasn't awake enough to withstand that. He grabbed the spare toothbrush and watched her through the glass.

"No, seriously, sorry," Russell said, straining to sound amicable.

Ava, lathering up her loofah, gave him a considering gaze. Appeased, she began to scrub her body.

"Saturday is my father's friend's wedding," she began. "I say we meet up with my father for lunch and then ride with him."

"Sounds cool," Russell said, between spitting out toothpaste.

"Tonight, I was thinking we could meet up for dinner."

Russell stopped with the toothbrush in his mouth. His shoulders slumped with the realization he wouldn't be able to avoid conflict this morning. "Um, I have plans tonight."

"Plans?"

"Yeah, a friend named Marcie is having a rent party. Everyone's showing up to support her. There's going to be a deejay and everything," Russell said, suddenly feeling like a twelve-year-old pleading a curfew case.

"Well, if there's a deejay, you *have* to go," Ava said, her voice cold. Then she added angrily, "Isn't she the stripper with a child and stretchmarks you were talking about a few weeks ago?"

"She does have a kid, but I was joking about the stretchmarks. She doesn't have stretchmarks."

Ava cracked open the shower door so she could narrow her eyes at him. "How the hell do you know?"

Russell looked around for reinforcements that would never come. Ava glared at him. Russell snapped the bear trap he'd unknowingly stepped into—it was common knowledge he'd gotten drunk and slept with Marcie a few years back.

"It's not like that! She's just a friend of a friend, and she's going through a tough time."

"Well, maybe she shouldn't be a stripper with stretchmarks."

"The economy is tough."

Ava laughed. "What does the economy have to do with you going to a stripper's apartment?"

"Leslie and Kat are coming to this and you're welcome to join us," he said desperately.

"Why would a gay guy and another woman go to a stripper's party?" Ava asked. "Why can't your friends do nice things? I would go to another art show—that was okay—but this is a bit much."

"I know, but come on. It's a group thing," Russell pleaded.

"A group thing? There are strippers! You can count me out of that," Ava said.

Russell continued to brush his teeth as she scrubbed herself in his periphery.

"Look, I'm going to the wedding," Russell said, words

barely intelligible through his mouth of toothpaste. "But I told my friends I'd be at this party."

Russell's defense was halted by Beethoven's Ninth Symphony, serenading them from Ava's phone on the kitchen counter.

"Could you get that?"

"Can I go to the party without you getting pissed?"

"Russell, get it before it goes to voicemail, please."

Russell, toothbrush bobbing out of his mouth, lumbered with heavy footsteps, expressing his grievance. He brought the phone back into the bathroom and pressed the screen to the glass.

Ava dropped the loofah and clutched her breasts tightly. Her fingers dug so deeply into the skin her fingertips disappeared. Her gaze was far away and fraught with terror.

"Ava? Are you okay?"

She stayed silent. Under the shower's warmth, she quivered. The water ran over her pale face, overtaken with wild, fearful eyes. Russell placed the phone on the lip of the bathroom sink.

"Ava, what's wrong?" Russell demanded. "Is it the stripper?"

This fear, whatever the source, had now gripped Russell. He banged his fist sharply on the glass. Ava jumped and her hands dropped to her sides.

"What is it?" Russell asked. "Who was on the phone?"

"No one," Ava said, struggling to gain composure, her face still holding panic.

"I don't have to go to this party if it's a problem."

"No, it's nothing," she said. "Go to the party, whatever, but can you please leave the bathroom?"

"Okay," Russell said.

Dismayed, he backed out of the bathroom, staring at Ava.

"Closed the door please," she said, her eyes still gaping back at him with a strange horror.

He did as she asked and returned to the couch, where he noticed his dry-cleaned suit had slid off the kitchen stool and lay crumpled on the floor.

34

Daylight stretched out longer and longer with each passing week, but this spring day had resigned itself to night. Warmth that descended during the day lingered, and soil, no longer stiff, gave easily to the weight of footsteps. Tiny buds awoke on dry branches from trees anchored in the concrete where people, liberated from the cold, walked with unbuttoned coats.

Kat justified skipping her Friday night shift at Stratosphere with a series of prudent calculations and an assessment of her checking account. Seniority allowed her to manipulate a newer bartender into taking her shift. She wished to feel like herself again with her roommates, but Jacob called and she told him about Marcie's party. With no convincing, Jacob agreed to join them. He was insistent on taking advantage of his wife's absence.

Jacob had been attentive and thoughtful to Kat all week. The initial guilt she felt about sleeping with him in his home had been cumbersome, and now it was a small needling in the back of her mind.

Tonight, Kat and Jacob shared a colorful sushi spread in a tight Japanese restaurant. Struggling for room, hunched over the table so small it could scarcely contain their entrees, they stared at each other with amorous gazes. Kat felt heat prickle over her face in a blush.

"This has been amazing," Kat said, wedging raw fish between her chopsticks.

Jacob nodded, his face somber. "I'm going to leave her."

Kat nearly choked, her fish suddenly a sticky mass in her throat. Tears filled her eyes as she contained an eruption of coughing. "What? I didn't think you were being serious."

"I'm not happy," Jacob said. "I haven't been for a long time. I thought this was the way it had to be."

He reached over the table and brushed fine strands of her hair from her face.

"But then you, this beautiful woman behind her camera, reminded me it could be different."

His motives appeared genuine. Kat dispelled her screaming voice of reason. He was a liar—a gifted liar. She saw him lie effortlessly and without hesitation. But his sweet words, coming from his handsome mouth, were lovely.

She cradled his unbelievable words like a fragile new gem. Despite how unlikely they were, she chose to believe them, if only for that night. She refused to prod past the surface. In this public restaurant—away from hidden hotel rooms, dark bedroom corners, and closed office doors—she would simply accept that she was wanted, no matter how temporarily. She survived so much to be here with him, and she could endure a bit more.

The check came, and Jacob put his arm around Kat's waist. They shuffled through the narrow restaurant and out onto the street.

After a westbound cab ride to Ukrainian Village, they emerged in front of a five-story brick apartment building with a clandestine entry hidden behind a thicket of old trees. Kat followed the rising babble of partygoers to the entrance, where they walked past a fog of cigarette smoke and drunken guffaws and up the five stories of groaning wooden stairs. A short woman was posted at the door's entrance, her lips traced with a severe lip liner. She stood in six-inch platform heels with a cigarette in one hand and her phone in the other. Her ample breasts were crammed so forcefully into her tiny tank top that it seemed the slightest change in air pressure would cause the straps to pop and her breasts to spill out.

"Hey, Marcie!" Kat said, meeting her in a quick embrace.

"The best bartender in Wicker Park," Marcie said. "Glad you came!"

"What are you doing out here? It's your party."

"It's stuffy in there and a lot of people showed up. I had a few jugs of vodka and some jungle juice, so you better get in there," Marcie said. With a predatory sneer, she turned to Jacob. "Who's this?"

Kat instinctively grabbed his arm and said, "My friend, Jacob."

Jacob's eyes lingered on Marcie's breasts, and before he could greet her, Kat hauled him into the apartment.

"It's ten dollars a head!" Marcie called back to them, and rejoined her cigarette and phone in silent contemplation.

Jacob shoved a twenty-dollar bill into an overflowing coffee can on a nearby table. The coffee can looked full enough to cover Marcie's rent for at least two months and was guarded by a densely muscled man. His grimace held a diagonal slash that had been long healed over but still caused his skin to rise and a ragged beard to grow around it. Kat couldn't help but stare at the scar as he frisked Jacob and peered into her purse.

Deeper inside, struggling through the compact flux of people, Jacob turned to her with a weary expression.

"What the fuck do you have me into?"

Kat smiled. "A girl can't have a regular night on the town?"

Jacob smirked and said something, but it was swallowed by an explosion of bass. In front of the living room's rumbling speaker, Kat saw Beck and his ladies dancing while the lieutenant stood nearby, his skull encased in headphones. The lieutenant rocked his body and fussed with the dials of a wide console he'd plugged into his laptop.

Kat quickly veered out of sight. She hadn't seen Beck since her miscarriage and wanted to avoid him as long as she could. She'd have to tell him something, or at least she owed him some gratitude, but she wanted Jacob to be out of earshot when they spoke.

She headed toward the rear of the apartment, past a room comingled with hookah and bong smoke. The lamps had been draped with burgundy scarves, and under the lamps' red overflow, calloused men cloaked in leather and baggy jeans gathered on a twin bed and a rocking chair. They lit a hookah and grumbled like cavemen around a fire. A few women were scattered in and around their laps, aiding in the rotation of pipes and blunts. As Kat passed, she realized Marcie's child's room had been repurposed for the smoke lounge. Thankfully, the kid was nowhere in sight.

Kat then moved toward the porch where Leslie and Russell perched, drinking jungle juice from Styrofoam cups.

"Kat!" they both exclaimed, and gathered around her with silly grins, nearly shoving Jacob aside.

"Are you two drunk?" she asked, crossing her arms in mimicked condemnation.

"I had a few of these," Russell said, bringing the cup to his face in playful scrutiny.

Leslie rolled his eyes and turned to Kat and Jacob to

excuse Russell's behavior, only he was just as intoxicated. "Don't pay him any attention—he's trying to forget that he's going to a wedding tomorrow."

"You guys should all come with me," Russell said, his face lighting up at the epiphany.

"Please. You know they aren't letting black people into that event unless they're serving the food," Leslie retorted.

Kat giggled, eager to join them. She turned to Jacob, who had glanced around the room with a bored, slack face.

"Do you want me to get some drinks?"

"Jungle juice?" he asked skeptically.

"It does the trick," she said, pointing to Leslie and Russell.

Jacob reluctantly agreed, watching in mild disgust as Russell began to lumber into a hapless dance to the bass and Leslie's strained fortitude crumbled as he burned his fingertips lighting a cigarette.

Kat wedged her way through the crowd toward the kitchen. On the counter, two fifty-four-quart metal coolers had been transformed into containers for a mysterious pink cloudy bath. A few ladles bobbed above the surface, destroying any hope of the drink remaining sanitary.

"You okay?" Beck said, stepping up to the coolers. His manic eyes held wide pupils and, quickly sniffing, he wiped white powder from his nose with a jerky hand.

"Yeah, thanks for that."

Beck sneered at the jungle juice. "Gross, huh?"

"I've put worse things in my body," Kat said, gingerly fishing out a ladle and filling her Styrofoam cups.

"Including your boyfriend over there?" Beck asked, reclining into the counter. "A little too clean-cut for this crowd, don't you think?"

Kat followed Beck's wild gaze across the thrashing bodies to Jacob. He stood stiffly, staring at her roommates like they were zoo animals. She grabbed her drink, ready to charge over, but Beck grabbed her arm and held her in place.

"Wait," Beck said. "Watch him."

Kat wrenched back from his grasp, nearly spilling her drinks. "What the fuck?"

Beck ignored Kat, not taking his rabid eyes from Jacob. "I know his type. He's going to do something terrible."

"This is stupid," Kat sighed, but Beck had baited her curiosity. She leaned next to him.

"Just give it five minutes," Beck said. "That's all it takes with his type."

35

Leslie scrunched his face to hold a cigarette between his lips and thumbed a lighter shooting nothing but sparks. Russell, tired from too many failed attempts, grabbed the lighter and ignited the flame. He brought it up to his friend's cigarette.

"Thank you," Leslie said with an indulgent puff. When they first arrived at Marcie's, they'd roamed to the porch, putting a well-intended distance between themselves and the inside fray. The party and its attendants held a certain level of menace, nothing to outright deter them, but enough for them to yield to the social order at play. Scantly clothed women turned to each other to grind to the backfire of music, their drunken cackles rising in the maelstrom. Marcie's friends wore next to nothing, grazing on impossibly tall shoes. Russell attempted not to stare as breasts shuddered around him and nearly bare asses and thongs were displayed in cutoffs and miniskirts.

The scarred man who guarded the door looked like he'd been out of prison just a few weeks. Some similarly brusque guys joined him in conversation, swaggering violently through the cramped space. The men never subscribed to the same uniform. Some were armored in oversized jeans, sweatshirts, and knit caps while others were dressed in sleek black suits. They came in different variations and races but shared a bravado that demanded respect and the recklessness to fight for it. They were a clan made up of drug dealers and con men. They could always be depended on to produce good weed or coke for the masses. Hundred-dollar bills passed through their hard hands in back alleys, parked cars, and bathrooms, exchanged for vials of coke, baggies of decorative pills, and compact lumps of marijuana and dried mushrooms. These harsh-faced rebels were likely foot soldiers for larger organizations, but their impetuous lives were revered as they pumped the lifeblood into artists and these types of parties.

Russell had a fearful love of drug dealers, and this party, populated by familiar faces, was crawling with them. Russell turned his attention to Jacob, bored and clueless, standing just far enough to separate himself from the group. Russell suddenly felt oafish next to his slender and polished presence.

"So Kat brought him here," Russell said in a hushed voice to Leslie.

"He wasn't going to stand her up forever," Leslie said, again inhaling his cigarette with vigor. "Why does it matter?"

Russell was suddenly aware of his own inebriation. He pulled his shoulders back and raked his hand through his curls. He turned to Leslie. "How do I look?"

"Like a jackass," Leslie said, his face twisting in speculation. "What's wrong with you?"

"Nothing," Russell said, watching Jacob abscond deeper into the party. Leslie drew back his gaze, sized up Russell, and raised a dissenting eyebrow.

"Are you jealous?"

"No, I just don't like that guy," Russell said. "Something about him isn't right."

"That doesn't change that she's with him."

"What?"

Leslie breathed in his cigarette with long intervals, punctuating Russell's alleged foolishness. "Yep, you don't know what I'm talking about."

Leslie stepped further out on the porch, kicking a crushed beer can over the edge. Russell joined him, and they drooped over the railing and stared off into the night. Over the smoking chimneys, rusted gutters, and patchwork of tarred roofs, Chicago's downtown towers radiated with light, vivid in their nocturnal magnificence, a psalm to the ceaseless night. The buildings were so far away Russell could see the very northern tip all the way to the south, where the massive silver citadel stopped, leaving blackness.

"It's beautiful, isn't it?" Russell said as Leslie offered him the other half of his cigarette.

"It is," Leslie agreed. "Absolutely."

36

"Coke makes you psychic?" Kat asked, sipping her syrupy jungle juice.

Beck drummed his fingers against the countertop. "No, I just read people."

"Read me, then," Kat said, as Jacob parted from Russell and Leslie in their joint view.

Beck grinned and shifted his eyes to her. He licked his lips and adjusted his stance to aid in his efforts.

"You know how I get away with all the shit that I do?"

Kat crossed her arms and took a few steps toward the party. Beck's drugged ramblings flattened her curiosity. Any nugget of truth she heard would be too clouded to decipher.

"Don't leave, Kat," Beck pleaded. "That guy doesn't care about you and you know that."

Anger rippled through Kat, and she spun to face Beck, spraying the floor with jungle juice.

"He hasn't looked at you once since you got here. At least, not in the way people who care about each other do. And what's even worse is you haven't looked at him either. So the real question is, why are you two fucking each other?"

The weight of Beck's accusation forced her to look down as jungle juice puddled around their feet. "You don't know what you're talking about."

"Bullshit," Beck said. "What is it that keeps you with this guy? He's good-looking, sure, with all the trappings of a good fuck, but not a guy you keep around. He's weak and pedestrian. You don't love him. Hell, do you even like him?"

The pink juice formed a thin stream and coiled away from the kitchen under a stampede of heels, boots, and sneakers. Kat followed its path with her eyes and thought about chasing it out of this conversation.

"So what happened?" Beck asked.

"It was nothing," Kat said. "No one knows."

"Not even Leslie and Russell?"

Kat looked up at Beck, suddenly finding her resolve. "Enough."

Beck smiled, his eyes more manic than before. "That's how I get away with things, Kat. I can see what people are trying to hide." He moved closer. "Whatever it is, you should deal with it. That guy is standing in the way of a guy who really wants you."

"Who?"

He gently caressed her hand and ran his fingers over the grooves of her knuckles. A chill prickled her neck, and she yanked her hand from the heat of his touch. She stared at him for a moment, undecided at this advance. But he was looking past her, almost through her. Kat turned to see him staring at Russell, and she blushed, her heart quickening. Beck smiled, and she shook her head, stepping back to allow air between them.

Beck tilted his head and looked past her into the party. He laughed to himself and pointed. Kat followed his finger to Jacob and Marcie, affectionately isolated in a corner. Jacob smiled and gestured coolly, placing his hand on Marcie's shoulder. She giggled at something, and Kat watched in horror as she arched her back and vaulted her breasts forward. Jacob's eyes stole a lustful glance at the perky spheres.

"I know his type," Beck said proudly.

"That doesn't mean anything," Kat objected.

Jacob bent down and whispered in Marcie's ear. She smiled and brushed back her hair, leaving her ear unobstructed from his mouth. Kat recoiled in revulsion as Marcie's breasts crammed against his chest.

"Still think so?" Beck countered.

"That bitch!" Kat seethed, charging forward to Marcie and Jacob.

Beck stammered a few steps behind her. "Let me handle this. You don't want to piss off the hostess and her scary friends."

Kat jerked her head back at Beck, who openly enjoyed

the drama playing out before him. He placed his hand on the small of her back, stepping in front of her to greet Jacob and Marcie.

"Hello, guys," he said gallantly. "Look who I found."

Jacob lunged back from Marcie, his eyes gaping in horror.

"Marcie," Beck said, rescuing her, "I didn't get the tour. Show me around."

Marcie shifted her glance from Jacob to Kat, then took Beck's arm and said, "Kat I didn't know, certainly not by what Jacob told me."

Kat gave her a brief and forgiving smile.

"I can have his ass kicked for you," she offered.

"No," Kat said. "He has a wife to get back to."

Beck bucked with laughter, catching berating glowers from the group. He raised his hands in penance, shuffling off with Marcie through the party and toward the rear of the apartment.

"Kat..."

"Don't say anything," Kat said. "We need to go."

"I'm sorry," Jacob said, like a child bracing for reprimand.

Kat's mouth tasted sour, a mix of jungle juice and loathing. "I have to say good-bye to my friends, I'll meet you downstairs. Try not to stick your dick in anyone on your way out."

She pummeled past him and he stumbled back. On the patio, she gave Leslie and Russell a quick farewell, ignoring their wounded faces. When asked why she was leaving, she blamed it on a queasy stomach. Kat turned on her heel, jostling through the walls of people. Pressure swelled behind her eyes and tears veiled her vision. Sucking back breaths, she managed to keep the tears at bay until she was descending the stairwell.

"Kat?"

Russell was above her on the stairs, following with uncertain steps. His forehead was wrinkled with concern, which forced the tears to rush out beneath Kat's eyelids. She was overwhelmed with embarrassment as he grabbed her shoulders and led her off the stairs into a quiet hallway. His hands cupped her face, and he wiped back her tears with his thumb. He offered her a sympathetic smile.

"What's wrong?" he asked.

"Nothing," she said. "I'm fine."

Russell probed her with his eyes, smile unwavering. Kat, unguarded, leaned into his chest and churned with sobs. He stroked her head and cradled her gently. She pressed her face completely into his chest. Russell's tall body crouched and curved around her as if to cover her entirely. Kat looked up through his beard's dense stubble and into his eyes.

"Does Ava really love you?"

Russell's focus drifted past Kat, his contemplation nearly audible on his face.

"Yes," he finally said. "She does."

A calmness settled over Kat. Something in her detached, and her tears stopped falling. Russell's features sharpened with clarity. Light from the stairwell faded in its reach, leaving heavy shadows over the curvature of his face. The sound of their breath played over the calamity resounding through the creaking floorboards. Faded cigarette smoke with the sweet musk of Russell's body odor seeped through his waning deodorant as Kat stayed in the assured warmth of his arms. He wasn't her roommate anymore. He wasn't her brother anymore. He became very much a man who was holding her. She closed her eyes and tried to take in every sensation of it.

"Well, then, marry her," she said, drawing back from Russell, watching his hands fall to his sides.

She cleared her throat and rubbed away the wetness from her face. Russell's head dropped, completely immersing his face in shadows. His shoulders slumped, and his tall frame seemed to sink into the blackness. He reached out to Kat, but then hesitated and returned his hands to his sides.

"So you and Jacob?" he asked quietly.

"If it wasn't him, it'd be someone else," she told him, then backstepped toward the stairs. "See you later."

Russell's despondent silhouette fell out of view as she descended the stairs. She skirted through the foyer, past a couple lapping at each other's faces, hands writhing beyond clothes. Outside, Jacob paced fearfully between the trees. He spotted Kat and dashed to her side, his arms open. Kat swatted them away and moved past him toward the street.

"Really?" he said, his voice ascending in anger.

"I don't know why I'm surprised," she said. "You fucked me in the same bed you share with your wife."

Jacob snorted with a chuckle. "It didn't stop you from coming all night."

Every muscle in Kat's body tightened sharply. "After all I went through with you..."

"You knew I was married before we even started."

"I was pregnant! I was pregnant with your baby," she whispered, breathless.

Tears returned as Kat reeled her fists back and released them at Jacob. He jumped back, unsuccessful at missing her blows. Her savage fists pelted Jacob's chest and face. His head jerked back with the blows, and he pinned Kat's arms to her sides. She squirmed and twisted, even hopped and kicked, but his grasp remained fixed. He glared back at her and his eyes, more silver than she remembered, flashed in cold rage. She almost feared he would throw her. All of his muscles were contracted and his fingertips pinched down into her. Her anger was gone now, and there, in the briefest moment, was the physical threat of him. A fleeting but real possibility that he would hit her. Kat found herself bracing for it.

He closed his eyes. His arms rattled around her as if he had to mount his strength not to move. He took in a deep sigh.

"You're pregnant?" Jacob asked, locking her in his grip.

She could barely take in air. Would he hit her?

"I lost it," she said, and his grasp softened into a tender embrace.

Barely able to stand, she leaned into him. She was the one who hit him. She felt foolish and tired. Blinded by tears, her mind wound back to Russell's face. Her swollen fists gripped Jacob's shirt, but Jacob's embrace didn't cover her in the way Russell had.

Kat and Jacob blundered into the night like wounded soldiers.

"Let's go to back to my place," Jacob said.

"Okay," Kat agreed, too tired to fight anyone else.

37

Russell unfolded himself from the back of Von Hoffman's German sedan. He stood in the smooth paved drive of White Oaks Country Club. He offered his hand to Ava as she stepped out after him, her face shielded by her sunhat's wide brim. Von Hoffman, who was out of the car and handing the keys to a balding valet, took the arm of an aging beauty queen, her face strained from too many injections, tucks, and peels. She rounded a sinewy arm around Von Hoffman, her surgically tightened chin held high, proud to be Mrs. Von Hoffman number three.

When Mrs. Von Hoffman III wasn't looking or emptying her fourth large glass of imported Chardonnay, Ava, balanced effortlessly on the tightrope of passive aggression, would find every way to disparage her. She muttered about her stepmother's simple intellect and tallied her string of social missteps. Ava shared her shrewd observations with Russell, where she would angle herself as the poor princess to her evil stepmother, a desperate woman who offered nothing but diminishing beauty.

Russell was as much of an outsider as Mrs. Von Hoffman III. He felt sympathy for the woman, trampled on by Ava's sharp condemnation and by the inhabitants of their social echelons. Russell knew he'd meet Mrs. Von Hoffman III on a shared mission to find some alcohol to cut the edge of the day. By the cool expression of her modified face, she was far from sober.

The valet drove off and the group ascended the pristine stone steps. Artificiality castrated nature on the surrounding grounds. The vibrant green courtyard grass was pampered and trimmed, and the tree branches were groomed. Stray branches were mercilessly chopped off in the name of beauty. Out to the west, a shimmering circular pond showcased a fountain sputtering in three perfect tiers. The smells of soil and cut grass made Russell very aware of his distance from the city. Without concrete underneath his feet or the ceaseless drone of traffic, he felt dizzy.

The path led them to the main clubhouse doors, bordered by smooth white pillars. Once inside, they moved along shiny marble floors through a great hallway with burnished wood doors, echoing with antiquity. The hall ended with a set of arching glass doors that opened to the rear courtyard. A smooth cobblestone path reached out to a gazebo made of the same white pillars that populated the country club. Its roof was made entirely of copper ornamentation turned sea green from oxidization. In a mawkishly romantic presentation, a series of white fold-up chairs were set up in rows, divided by the cobblestone path and outfitted with pink ribbons and roses.

Friends and family paired off and settled in reverent conversation as a violin and cello swooned in a classical rendition of a sappy pop song.

Russell was indifferent toward this, merely grateful he had been able to compile his aching body into his suit and meet Ava at her building on time. At Leslie's insistence, Russell had inhaled four vitamin B pills with two large glasses of water before going to sleep. His comprehension had been strained under the lingering effects of the poisonous jungle juice, and when he woke up, he heard Kat's words replay in his mind.

"Marry her."

His shirt remained tear-soaked long after Kat left. He'd stood in the hall, wobbling with drunkenness and confusion. Her face had been so soft from her deep sadness he couldn't help but hold her. Even now as he breathed in warm spring air, her scent haunted his nostrils. Like an unreachable itch, he felt her body in his arms and his chin on her head. He still felt the hairs on her head detangling from his beard's coarse fibers.

Kat's words had been clear and definitive. He would propose to Ava and it was a good thing. It had to be. Kat was always right.

Next to him, Ava flowed in a beautiful patterned frock. He expected an analytical commentary about flower arrangements or for her to frown upon the gift table clichés, but she said nothing. In fact, she had been silent most of the afternoon. Russell was at first grateful for the freedom to suffer quietly in his hangover, but as intense pain gave way to dull aches, he became more suspicious of her demeanor, to the point of fear.

Ava was never a woman to hold back criticism, and her pronounced silence at a wedding—a place where her judgment flowed in easy quips and witty assessments—was jarring.

As the ushers led their group to be seated, Russell decided to stir her.

"Nice chairs," he said. "It's like we're at a picnic."

This comment would normally spark a frenzy of disapproval, but she simply stared ahead, stone-faced.

Soon, the wedding party began to make its way down the cobblestone path toward the gazebo. Men in tuxedos and women in pink gowns ambled slowly to pop music rehashed by the ill-equipped cry of the violin. The group stopped in formation along the gazebo.

"The pink flowers are nice, too, in a Barbie's Dreamhouse sort of way," Russell continued.

Her eyes were blank and her gaze set ahead, as if Russell had said nothing. A sudden twinge of panic popped through him.

"Ava?"

She startled and gave him a weak smile, then returned to the stillness of her reverie.

The music shifted as the tiny orchestra set made a spirited attempt at Felix Mendelssohn's Wedding March. A bride and her father stepped along the path, locked arm in arm. Her wide, white skirt swelled with taffeta and lace, and she moved like a menacing storm cloud over the cobblestone. Her face, ghostly underneath the chalky layers of pale makeup, was taut with an emotional smile. In response, the crowd rose to its feet issuing in obligatory awe at a woman so labored down in the massive dress she was monstrous.

Russell knew the production was to illustrate the everlasting beauty of love, but it seemed grotesque. He felt as though he was watching something he shouldn't—something too intimate. Like watching someone defecate in an alley. He felt embarrassed for the slaphappy groom, the bride, and everyone watching, including himself. He fought the urge to turn away.

He grabbed Ava's limp hand as she stared off into space. A vision of her in a white dress snared itself into Russell's mind.

38

Leslie had the apartment to himself for most of the day. Kat had dropped by for a shower and a change of clothes for her shift at Stratosphere. She had been morose, her eyes carefully averting Leslie's. Her words weren't unpleasant, but they had been flat and brief.

Alone, Leslie assessed the smell rising from the overflowing kitchen garbage, the dust collecting on wooden surfaces, and the debris that could only be detected by a bare foot making its way along the wood floors. Determined to keep at least the illusion of civility, Leslie ran a broom and mop across the floors.

He would stop momentarily to complain to himself

about the signs of disorder, making a game out of pinpointing the offending party. The chalky nail file and stained purple cotton balls were clearly the work of Kat, while Russell's negligence came to bear in an empty toilet paper roll still in the holder, its shredded ends caught in the air. Due to the frequency of this inaction, Leslie was certain Russell got off on dooming people in the bathroom without toilet paper. However, the true mystery was who left the crumby plate on the couch behind the throw pillows. Even Leslie was suspect.

When Leslie got the rare chance to be alone in the apartment, he would usually turn a blind eye to the collective mess and enjoy the solitude. But today required preparation. Leslie wanted the shitty apartment to be as pretty as two hours of dusting and wiping down every possible surface with Lysol could get it.

Tonight, Isaac would be in the apartment for the first time since rehab. More importantly, for the first time since stealing Kat's tip money. He'd mentioned Isaac's visit to his roommates, and they had been quick to offer their support. Leslie was grateful, of course, but also concerned that their encouragement was more sympathy for his desperate set of circumstances than generosity on their parts.

After his fight with Isaac, much remained unresolved. Isaac said they were just barely holding on and Leslie began to wonder if that was true. As he wiped down the end tables in the living room, he wondered what his life would be like without Isaac. Leslie had lost his father emotionally and his mother was gone forever. Leslie shivered at the possibility of losing someone else.

He ordered delivery from a nearby Italian restaurant and sat on the couch, shifting from cushion to cushion in a sad bid to be casual for an audience of no one. His anxiety eventually forced him out the front door, the squeal of the screen door slamming behind him. He fumbled for his pack of cigarettes, crushed in his back pocket, and breathed smoke into the tepid night. According to the clock on his phone, Isaac was moments away and they could commence the parody of normalcy. The agenda was set: dinner and a senseless action movie.

Leslie should've been happy about this. He desperately needed to be happy about this, but his frayed nerves acted otherwise. No amount of self-delusion could mask Leslie's fear that when Isaac arrived, all he'd be able to see was Isaac's distressed face and the prospect of a breakup.

Leslie suppressed his thoughts by focusing on the glowing end of his cigarette. Grunting gears and labored metal indicated a train stopping on the tracks above the neighborhood, its mechanical sounds breaking over the traffic, footfalls, and clamor of Wicker Park. A moment passed and the gears cried out again, carrying the train off to the northwest. Somehow, Leslie knew Isaac had been on that train, and his stomach rolled in confirmation. He wasn't surprised when he saw Isaac's figure moving down the sidewalk.

Lambent under the streetlights, Isaac held an even gait and carried a DVD in his right hand. He seemed so wonderfully average, even handsome. His was no longer arresting, as he had been before his addiction, but his image was still there, like a snowy picture on an analog TV. Shadows pronounced his cheekbones, and the cut of his jacket showed off shoulders that were broad and strong. His face held a smile acknowledging Leslie on the steps.

A hot surge washed across Leslie's insides. He fought the urge to weep. Maybe it was being away from the oppression of Isaac's halfway house or finally doing something conventional, but Isaac finally appeared to be his. The threat of what could happen suddenly seemed abstract and Leslie gave in to the moment. Isaac ascended the stoop and, sensing vindication, kissed Leslie.

Leslie sighed and reached for the door. The doorknob was fixed in position, and after several turns and yanks, Leslie released it.

"We're locked out," he confessed.

"Call your roommates."

"Russell is out of town and Kat's at Stratosphere."

"Well, Stratosphere is in the neighborhood. Let's go get the key from Kat."

"No," Leslie yelped. "We're not going to a bar."

Isaac jerked back as if he had been dealt a blow. His face darkened slightly. "I won't relapse if we go to Stratosphere to get Kat's keys."

"I didn't mean it like that," Leslie said, beads of sweat dotting his forehead.

"Let's just go get the keys."

"I don't want you to go to another bar."

"You were the one with a problem, last time I checked."

"We have food coming, and I don't want us to miss it."

Isaac face was stern in his skepticism.

"Look, I'm prepared for emergencies like this," Leslie said, trying to keep his voice light.

Leslie leapt down the stairs into the narrow alley along the duplex. Isaac reluctantly followed him as they crossed trashcans and potholes. Movement darted through Leslie's peripheral vision, and when he looked over, he caught a small rat fleeing into the shadows of the neighboring building. He stopped in front of his apartment's small bathroom window and looked up to the crisscrossed telephone wires to pinpoint a pair of gym shoes gnarled by the elements. Below the shoes and near the garbage bins sat a small pile of broken concrete blocks—inconspicuous as any other rubble in the alley. Leslie confirmed they were alone, held his breath against the stench of garbage, and knelt down to pick through the rocks.

"What the hell is this?" Isaac asked. "Why am I watching you dig in the street?"

Leslie moved heavy pieces of concrete to expose a tiny brass key. He picked it up and headed back to his front door, unlocking it and letting Isaac into the apartment. He returned the key to its hiding spot and joined Isaac inside.

"This is Chicago," Isaac said. "You shouldn't have a spare key out in the open."

"Russell locks himself out all the time," Leslie said, patting the couch next to him and smiling at Isaac.

"Why did you react like that when I suggested getting the key from Kat?" Isaac asked, arms crossed.

"I just wanted it to be us having a quiet night in," Leslie said.

"Bullshit."

"Come on, let's just enjoy the evening."

"I don't need you to judge me," Isaac said. "I have enough people doing that."

"I don't judge you—I support you. I used my mother's money to pay off your rehab bill," Leslie said, rising to his feet. "Are you serious?"

Isaac stalked toward the door. "You going to throw that in my face every time we fight?"

"Oh, come on!" Leslie screamed. "I've been sacrificing everything for you. I used all my money."

"I'm trying here, and then you look at me like... like I'm still some stupid pill head."

Leslie sighed, wishing his hammering heart would stay in his chest. "Look, I want to explain what happened the other day. I know it may lead to you relapsing..."

"You can't be serious."

"No! It's not like that," Leslie said. "I'm worried."

"Fuck this," Isaac said, and flung open the door.

"No, please stay."

Isaac narrowed his eyes in a cruel grimace. All the beauty Leslie had seen was gone in an instant. The illusion was broken. Isaac was broken, just a skeletal man from the halfway house.

Isaac charged out the door the moment the deliveryman rang the buzzer. He held the paper bag, dumbfounded as Isaac blasted down the street, then smiled awkwardly and held the food out for Leslie.

"Hold on a minute," Leslie said as he pushed past him and headed in Isaac's direction.

He rushed down the sidewalk, his feet quickly carrying him to the end of his block. He looked around for Isaac, who had been quick enough to slip out of sight on Damen Avenue. A steady crowd churned upon the street, and he knew he'd lost Isaac in the mill.

"You gotta sign for this!"

He turned back to see the deliveryman waving at him near the apartment's open door. His head shrank into his slumped shoulders as he dragged himself back to the apartment. He relieved the deliveryman and, defeated and alone, opened the bag and placed the heavy containers of food on the kitchen counter.

Leslie piled spinach lasagna and chicken Parmesan on a plate and decided to eat until he couldn't feel or until there wasn't any more food. He felt too foolish to cry.

39

Beck's couch, a lone survivor of his apartment furniture, had become the centerpiece in a fort made of empty cardboard boxes. After assessing his belongings, he called a cab and shamefully collected his forty-three-inch television. The cab driver cried out in protest when he saw Beck's precarious walk to the vehicle, but before anything could be done, Beck angled the TV in the backseat and gave his best front of indifference to the cab driver's scowl. Beck led the miffed driver and the dusty TV to a pawnshop in Ukrainian Village, where a puckered old man of an indeterminate Eastern European origin squinted over the TV and two platinum chains Beck unearthed from his pocket. Beck spent a painful half hour bartering with the man whose English was as broken as Beck was feeling. Over a weeping radio stream from the old country, they agreed on $325 for the booty.

Beck's trip to the pawnshop meant his email and phone pleas to the esteemed Ashby clan had gone unheard. Eviction was no longer a possibility but an inevitability. He hoped the years spent picking up the tab on his now dwindling trust fund and maxed out credit cards would buy him a few weeks on a friend's couch, but truthfully, he wasn't sure what his next steps should be. His exile from Boston was cemented, and in all his twenty-six years on earth, he had never worked a job or finished his bachelor's degree.

He figured the best option was to sell everything, so he spent the week negotiating with pawnshops, auctioning things on eBay, and posting furniture on Craigslist. For his efforts, he'd pooled together $961.47. Between that and the two thousand dollars left on his last good American Express card, he'd be able to survive for a few months—if he did nothing at all. But his phone bill was past due and there were minimum payments to make on his other credit cards, and now the matter of eviction. His negotiations with the landlord had failed thanks to his lack of payment and the frequent noise complaints his parties tallied.

Beck sat, legs crossed, on his couch looking down on an upside down moving box he'd fashioned into a coffee table. On top of the grungy sheet he'd laid over it was a travel magazine, the happy faces of tropical vacationers covered by crushed Oxy pills. Beck divided the pills into three white mounds as the tourists' faces looked out onto a Photoshopped beach.

Even though his current living situation remained dire, he'd conservatively stockpiled enough pain pills and coke to prevent him from feeling anything for at least three weeks. He kept his white pills and tiny baggies of powder rolled up in pairs of gym socks, held in a small traveler suitcase. He placed the suitcase on the far wall of his apartment, in view wherever he walked. He found himself emptying his guts on the toilet, wondering if this batch of coke was cut with too much laxative, watching the suitcase. He would look at his reflection in the dark windows of his apartment with one eye noticing red roots coming in at his scalp and his skin going from tan to sallow and the other eye on the suitcase.

It was only a matter of time before the rolled up white socks would no longer produce white highs and he would be faced with loneliness. With his apartment empty, the loneliness and quiet mutated into something hostile. Ricocheting off the empty walls, even his footsteps were brutal. Something in the vacancy bit into Beck, flooding him with venom.

Beck felt relieved when his evening meal of Oxy pills was interrupted by the buzzer. He buzzed the unknown visitor in just to break the silence. The steady pound of footsteps ascending the staircase soothed him, and Beck was swift to the door. He flung it open, hoping to greet his lieutenant or Marcie, but instead, Isaac stood in the doorframe like a haunting photograph from a violent crime. Isaac, an alarming preview to a movie Beck never wanted to see, was rung out like a dirty towel. His face was all cheekbones and dark circles.

"Beck!" Isaac said, reaching out to hug him.

Beck stiffened as Isaac wrapped his thin arms around him. He felt the bend of each rib and slowly liberated himself from the unexpected embrace. Before he could object, Isaac stepped into the apartment and puzzled over the empty boxes.

"What's going on here?"

"I'm moving," Beck said, grateful that this was partially true.

Isaac walked around the room restlessly and nearly completed a full circle while searching for a place to sit.

"What do you want?" Beck asked, feeling unsteady and growing irritated.

Isaac snapped his head in Beck's direction. His face, no longer friendly, grew dark. His eyes narrowed and his mouth tightened. Beck almost jumped back from the immediacy of the change.

"What do I want?" he said. "I want my old job back. I don't want to scrub fucking toilets. I want to go out and have a good time. I want my boyfriend to quit thinking I'm an addict."

"You shouldn't be here."

"Oh, come on," Isaac said. "Let's have a good time like we used to."

Isaac started a trek through the apartment, peering into the empty bedroom and going back to the kitchen, opening empty cupboards and finding nothing. Beck drew back a breath when Isaac absently looked at the drug-filled suitcase and moved on.

"Something's wrong here," Isaac finally said.

"You should leave."

Isaac's face mellowed and his posture collapsed. There was a fleeting second, hardly measurable, where Isaac became the striking man who had initially seized Beck's attention. When they first met, Beck would intentionally slip Isaac and Leslie small hits of coke in Chicago's back alleys, only to watch the two beautiful men giggle. His mind was etched with images of them nabbing secret gropes when they thought no one was looking and defiant kisses when people were. Their love was reckless, something Beck had always wanted, so he collected them in a way. He invited them out, injected himself into their lives. Beck, stoned himself, perilously craved something beautiful around him. As the world dazzled from the shine of snorting shit up his nose, nothing was more splendid than watching Isaac's slender hands on Leslie's dark skin. Sometimes, when he'd wrangled a random woman or man into his bed, he'd act out the way Isaac and Leslie touched each other. In the blackness of night, kissing that nameless warm body, he'd perversely contemplate Leslie's brown skin. Pretending to be Isaac's friend was the closest he could ever get to Leslie's skin, and maybe Leslie knew that. Maybe that's why Leslie never trusted him.

"Beck, I thought you were my friend," Isaac said, stepping closer.

"Does Leslie know you're here?"

"Leslie doesn't..."

Isaac stopped talking. A wild mania grabbed Isaac's face as he caught sight of the pills, divided into perfect piles over the Photoshopped beach. The pills on the magazine appeared to open the tiny boats' sails and fill the spaces of palm trees over the glossy magazine cover.

No one moved for a moment. Isaac barely blinked and Beck grew lightheaded from holding his breath. He didn't know what Isaac was going to do.

Beck had seen Isaac party a little too hard in the past. Isaac danced close to the fire and went off the tracks long before rehab. He'd lost everything in almost the same manner Beck was losing everything now. Beck gaped at Isaac and wondered if they shared this fate. Was he just a few months away from this?

Isaac looked at him and then at the pills, his eyes expanding into wide spheres.

"Can I?"

All of Isaac's muscles condensed on his protruding bones until there wasn't a round edge on his body. Beck's stomach dropped and he was fearful of what he had let in, something far worse than loneliness. This wasn't like before. This wasn't a party favor or a friend trying to get stoned. Something spectral and menacing permeated the room.

"Get out of here," Beck said.

Isaac backed away, not taking his eyes off the Oxy until his back was pressed flat against the door. Beck moved to obstruct Isaac's view of white powder, and the two them stayed suspended until Isaac eventually came back to himself and reached for the door handle. "Leslie blames me for what happened to you," Beck said as Isaac opened the door.

Isaac barked a bitter chuckle and curved around the door and into the hallway. Beck scuffled over to lock to the door behind him, and then flopped on the couch with his hands quivering in his lap.

40

Ava was exhausted from trying to maintain social etiquette. The wedding ceremony had ended and the guests moved in slow egress back to the clubhouse while the bridal party posed for photos.

Ava stood and smiled at her acquaintances, some she hadn't seen in years. Tightly knit brows questioned her from afar, but up close, people rushed to ask about her life and the man she'd brought along. When she looked at people directly, confused glances shifted to strained smiles of feigned warmth.

Russell, who had been trailing so close he crushed her heels a few times, offered a friendly handshake to anyone he met. As always, Ava noted, he was blissfully unaware that the second they were out of earshot, whispers would certainly follow.

Ava glared at her father, edging through the white chairs with Mrs. Von Hoffman III, for putting her in this situation, for making her part of a business deal.

Some business deals were all calculated risks made with crossed fingers, and two years ago, one of her father's bets paid off. Over a series of months, Von Hoffman spoke in dozens of cool conference rooms atop Midwest Bank headquarters. Up in the clouds, surrounded by men in suits, like knights of the roundtable, Von Hoffman converted sellers and buyers alike into believers, performing for them in a righteous clarity. His fervent voice couldn't be disputed. He spoke of the rise in projected profit margins and the benefits to shareholders. He underwent a brief spell of insomnia, nearly sweating through his suits, until he'd spearheaded Midwest Bank's purchase of Floyd & Tharp Investments.

During that time, Ava watched her father become more alive than she had ever seen him. His movements were usually contained, but during those months, he was stirring like a man half his age. He was thrilled and blinded with victory when the sale went through, knowing when he added the struggling investment firm's clients to his own books, he'd be virtually untouchable. This undeniable apex was what he'd angled toward all these years, crushing friends and pillaging wives.

Blinded by his victory, he let Tharp's sliver-tongued son take Ava on a series of dates. They came together like cars yielding to traffic, at a party celebrating the merger. In the soft light of the elegant party, the young man was respectful and confident and thoroughbred, poured into a designer tuxedo. He glowed from within, a fact Von Hoffman was convinced of after a golf game in which Tharp's son demonstrated his superior handicap. Tharp helped Von Hoffman secure the ringing high note of this career, and the Tharp family was full of people he needed to know. If the Tharp family could do this for Von Hoffman, who knew what their son could do for Ava?

A low-risk chance with the possibility of a favorable outcome.

Ava protested her father's suggestion that they date, but Tharp had a reckless handsomeness designed for glossy magazines. He captivated Ava on their first adventures through the city, where he strutted like a peacock as he entered exclusive clubs and chic restaurants with her on his arm. The couple constantly fielded invitations to formal parties and casual gatherings, but Tharp's charm curdled and his beauty twisted quickly, exposing a wild temper underneath. Familiarity became a force that cracked his demeanor and what bled through was a barrage of vile curses, shattered windows, holes in the walls, and finally, fists in Ava's face.

Von Hoffman fell from his sky-high apex of victory like a missile dropped from plane. In the burnt wreckage, facing Ava's eyes full of tears, he did nothing. No charges were pressed, no lawyers consulted. He warned Ava to do the same. She realized she was fallout from the deal, the bankrupted purse of a lost gamble. If any charges were pursued, they would fundamentally jeopardize her father's career.

When he did nothing, Ava all but disappeared. She bore the brunt of this and became a social leper. Tharp continued unscathed and dated a new woman less than a month later. Ava fell under the scrutiny of gossip. She showed up less and less until she could count her friends on one hand. This wedding was the first time since then that she'd seen many of these people.

When she stood in the shower days before and saw his number blinking across her phone, she wondered how much more she'd have to pay. She wondered if she had anything left to give. For an instant, she felt the crack of his fist. She felt the soreness of her throat from crying and screaming. She'd ousted Russell from the bathroom before he saw her cry. Since then, the memories had hung around her in a soupy fog, and she hadn't been able to see or think or sleep.

Ava excused herself from Russell and tried not to think about how she'd been on Tharp's arm the last time she'd rubbed elbows with this crowd. She tried not to think about his phone call or his voicemail. If he hadn't reached out, she would be here as the bold, poised Ava Von Hoffman she normally was. If she hadn't known his words were floating out there, waiting for her to hear them, she wouldn't be this feeble woman walking toward the bathroom with her trailer park boyfriend.

41

Night swept over the grounds and the endless sky above the country club was saturated with glimmering pinpoints of stars. Russell upturned his gaze and a giddy vertigo shifted his insides. He hadn't seen this many stars in years. He'd spent too many nights under the harsh glare of light pollution. His mind jumped back to the time when he could spend his evenings safely tucked off a country road, outstretched on the hood of his rusty Subaru. He would lace his fingers over the back of his head and wonder if the night, with its multitude of stars, stretched out infinitely.

He suddenly felt young and silly, his mood helped along by the wedding reception's open bar. The party meandered from the courtyard to the clubhouse, through those heavy antique doors and into a banquet hall. To Russell's relief, the intrepid yet failed three-piece orchestra had finally retired, replaced by a sound system and wedding deejay. What sent Russell back outside and away from the heavy-handed bartender was the playful screeching of the Chicken Dance. Russell was surprised that the guests—moments ago a group of tight-lipped stiffs—eagerly amassed on the dance floor to partake in the synchronized hilarity. He gulped down his drink and scurried out to the gazebo.

He tried to spot Ava as he made his retreat, but he couldn't see her through the crowd. He was certain she wouldn't be dancing and felt a pang of guilt as he left her in the carnage. He turned away from the stars and toward the building. Through the wide arched windows, beneath shimmering chandeliers, the wedding guests bounced, stumbled, and pranced. Inside the clubhouse, the air was electric with celebration. The groom's suited figure was interlocked with the bride, and her large mound of white fabric swarmed the hall.

Their faces were wound in set grins. The couple gazed at each other in love's drunkenness.

Russell tilted his head and wondered if it was supposed to feel that way. He wondered if love was supposed to leave him in a slacked stupor. What he felt for Ava didn't leave him in that condition. He knew Ava wouldn't have respected him even if it did. They were one of cool heads, of simple resolution. They were the settling of inevitability. They were results of the conclusion that Russell would never have the life his father had and Ava, in return, would continue to have a man who would never tell her "no." Russell would carry on her father's two-plus decades of trying to please her.

Russell had surrendered to Ava the night he met her.

It was a little over a year ago when he stood outside a pub, sucking on a cigarette and grimacing between breaths of icy winter air. Midstate Regional Bank had reserved a pub in the financial district for its annual holiday party, a time for employees and their families to crowd the space and enjoy dinner and drinks on the bank's dime. Camaraderie was the goal. Most of the evening, Russell suppressed his disgust at the excessive flattery issued to the managers. Employees with fabricated interests laughed and shared topical conversations, careful not to skim into anything too personal.

Russell drank cautiously and counted the hours to freedom from this social obligation. He kept conversations brief and sought out quiet harbor in the room. Finding none, he took his coat and cigarettes and pushed through the door.

Outside, his toes tingled as the cold drained feeling from their tips. His chin shivered violently, but he couldn't be the businessman any longer. He planned to finish the cigarette and take a cab home.

The pub's revolving doors spun and ejected Ava's slender frame, encased in a long wool coat. She wrapped her arms around herself as the breeze caught her. A police car wailed by, flooding her in trembling red lights. She stepped back from the street as if all the sedans on it would be pressed onto the sidewalk by passing police cars. She blundered back into Russell and then turned to him with a small, embarrassed smile. He held her gaze and returned the smile as the siren's savage cries faded with their red glow into the cold.

"Here for the party?" she finally asked.

"Yeah," he said, tending to his cigarette and feeling suddenly timid. "I'm an employee."

"I'm the family of an employee," she said back.

Frigid air whipped between them and dragged an icy chill across Russell. Instinctively, they drew closer for warmth.

"I'm Russell," he said, holding out his hand.

"Ava," she said, taking it. With a smile nodding toward his cigarettes, she added, "Those cause cancer."

"I'm trying to quit," he lied.

"Want to have a drink somewhere else?" she said.

He stamped out his cigarette and nodded, beginning his long concession to Ava. The way she held his gaze made it an easy resignation. That night, before he knew her last name or who her father was, he knew that she carried a possibility. This woman could be the fork in the road he needed to carry him away from the disappointment of his art and the images he etched in canvas. As simply as she'd extended her invitation for a drink, Ava could easily lead him far away from his own "acts of contrivance."

They stepped in a cab and drove farther into the city, toward a smaller, more intimate bar. Over elegant stemware, he felt a certain relief. That defeated trailer park boy, whose hands were covered in muddy acrylic paints, withdrew into Ava's shadow.

At the wedding reception, Russell sighed and gave the stars one last glance, hoping to draw strength from them. He ambled along the path toward the clubhouse and pulled at his tie as he wove through crowd back into the banquet hall toward the bar. He ordered a whiskey and spotted Ava laughing casually with a small group of women. Similarly, Von Hoffman and Mrs. Von Hoffman III talked with friends at their own dining table.

Russell downed his whiskey and made his way toward the table. His legs and feet felt like they were dismantling underneath his weight. The whiskey burned in his throat and left a heavy mass in his gut. He approached Von Hoffman with a shaky smile.

He cleared his throat, uncertain of the etiquette for this moment.

"Sir," he began, "can I have a moment to talk to you?"

Von Hoffman turned away from Mrs. Von Hoffman III and nodded.

His wife stood and smiled. "Excuse me, I'm going to get another drink."

She glanced at Von Hoffman and then at Russell as if she knew what would happen in her absence and receded into the party.

"Sir, I love your daughter very much and with your permission, of course, I'd like to marry her."

42

Leslie awoke with a start as a fist rapped on his bedroom door. He stood on jittery legs and opened the door, the bright noon light searing his eyes. Leslie squinted against a moment of white blindness until Russell's tepid smile came into view through a crack in the door.

"Dude, Shakes is here," Russell said.

Leslie grumbled and searched the surfaces of room. "How much?"

"Give me fifty," Russell said in a low voice, "and you're coming out there with me if you want to smoke it."

He scrambled through the mess on his nightstand, shook his dirty jeans empty, and finally uncovered his wallet on an oak dresser. Leslie plucked out the loose cash and turned to Russell with his hand on his hip. "Isn't it enough that I'm paying for my cut?"

"No," Russell said, his eyes narrowing in severity. "You know I can't get him out of the house alone."

"Kat can help," Leslie said, looking at his tussled bed longingly.

"She told me to get you," he said. "You want to piss her off?"

"Are you serious?" Leslie demanded, throwing his arms up and shoving the money in Russell hands. "Fine!"

Leslie wiped the sleep out of his eyes and treaded into the living room, where Kat turned to him with humor on her face. She sensed his irritation and didn't hide her amusement.

A man slumped on the armchair next to their couch. His face was flushed, the redness concentrated on his porous nose like a circus clown, and an angled, toothy smile eased over his face. He slicked back his long, dark hair and wiped the excess grease on his jeans. In his other hand, between his thumb and index finger, he pinched a blunt so tightly his knuckles turned white.

Several dollar bills lay neatly piled on the brass coffee table next to a Mason jar filled with dried weed. From where Leslie stood, the round THC crystals sparkled in the noonday light. They glimmered like frozen drops of water atop tiny curled leaves. Russell added Leslie's money to the pile and joined Kat on the couch, followed by Leslie, who sat between them.

The man in the armchair sucked on his blunt and huffed out spinning donuts of smoke. The condensed smell of weed masked the funk of the man's dirty hair and acute body odor. Leslie made a mental note to douse the chair with Febreze.

A quaking hand passed the joint to Leslie.

To appear polite, Leslie took the joint and, with all the self-restraint he could manage, tried not to recoil as his lips closed around the end of its soggy surface. He could feel his roommates' eyes on him and knew they, minutes ago, had been victims of the same blunt. The smoke was sharp in his throat.

"Thanks, Shakes," Leslie said, handing it back with a cough.

Shakes chuckled and stared back, his eyes as bloodshot as his gin-blossomed nose.

"You're going to like this shit," Shakes began. "Hindu Kush, man. Not grown here."

Shakes placed the joint back in his mouth, reaching for the pile of cash. His face grew tight and serious as he thumbed over the bills and placed them in his jacket's inner pocket. His smile returned, and Leslie noticed the convulsions that moved throughout Shakes were now concentrated in his left leg.

The weed she'd inhaled brought a slow tempo to Kat's voice. "Thanks for coming by today," Kat said. "It would've been a rough week without you."

Shakes was remarkably benign for a neighborhood drug dealer. At times he was an average door-to-door salesman, but when a strange or a particularly potent strain of weed came into his possession, he spoke like a religious evangelical. His hands and legs would shudder with zeal and his face would wince in tics from the neurological damage caused by his legendary heroin overdose all those years ago. Shakes wasn't much older than the roommates, but his occupation had worn on him. The guy had dealt every kind of street drug over the years and liked to get high on his own supply, which explained why he never expanded his business model.

Since Russell found the twitchy dealer, his services were steady. He'd been dry only a few times in all the years they called on him, and the only issue they had was he always wanted to stick around and smoke with them, regaling his latest adventures. At first, Leslie found this aspect of the transaction amusing. He would place his head in his hands, enjoy the sample blunt, and get whisked away with pothead story time. The storytelling was now an unfortunate tax that left him drained.

Russell always had what Leslie regarded as a perverse admiration for drug dealers. He sat transfixed, laughing in the appropriate pauses. After every meeting, Russell would suggest they call up Shakes, and Leslie and Kat would scowl at him, united against it.

The pot's fuzzy warmth swept under Leslie, dulling the edges on his vision to the point where he barely saw that Kat and Russell were sitting on opposite sides of the couch. He leaned over, and Kat was slack-faced, bowed back on her side of the couch, nodding absently. Her small form clung tightly to the arm of the couch and Russell's rear edged off on his side, as if at any moment he'd explode into a sprint. They were as far as they could possibly be from each other without being across the room.

It was unlike them to be so far away from each other. He licked his lips and tried to think of the last time he saw them talk to each other. Sure, there was an attraction between them, but had something grown sour?

Leslie opened his mouth to comment about this but noticed a newfound irregularity in Shakes' face. The rough skin, the dark flesh heavy underneath his hollowed eyes, the medley of jerks and involuntary shivers all amassed into something familiar. Something tried to pass undetected in their company but left the smallest odor, the faintest noise.

Leslie took another hit of the wet blunt and handed it to Kat, weary not to offset the rotation. He was startled slightly at the pluck of revulsion stirring in him—a simmering, quiet anger. He wanted to spit or cuss. He watched Shakes carefully. He no longer listened to the words being said and only saw the urgency of the synthetic normalcy behind them.

For a fraction of a second, he saw Isaac in the armchair sucking on the blunt, dirty and twitching. He saw Isaac desperate to connect but separated by the impregnable wall of addiction. It was as if Isaac pulled off a rubber mask and he had been the one sitting there all this time.

Leslie's heart leapt into his throat, and the moment passed as he blinked his eyes. Isaac was gone, and Shakes and his jagged smile sat in his place.

Leslie let go into the coaxing lull of the blunt as it came around to him again.

43

Beck was already seated at the bar when Kat's shift started at Stratosphere. He was staring with a blank face into a long glass full of ice. He shared the bar with a few other people, a woman with mismatched roots at one end and a plump guy wearing a too-small T-shirt that attempted to strangle his torso. Kat suspected Beck had been there for hours and wondered what she could do to get him out of the half-empty Sunday bar. Then she thought better of it. Clientele coming this early in the evening were true alcoholics, uninterested in ambiance or the upcoming deejay. If Kat served them without judgment, she would be rewarded with heavy tips. Beck was no exception.

She placed a glass of water in front him, and he nodded in appreciation.

"So, have you told anyone that my boyfriend's a married man?"

He jolted backward and chuckled humorlessly. "No."

"What are you drinking?"

"The usual," he said as she replaced his empty glass with a full one.

"Well, you have ammunition on me," she said, scanning the other patrons to determine how much time she could devote to Beck.

"Believe it or not, I'm human," he said, sipping from his glass. "And I'm sure you have a reason for doing what you're doing."

"That's generous of you," Kat said, rinsing his glass in a tub of soapy, sanitized water.

"I'm charitable," he said with a half-smile. "What I don't get is how Russell and Leslie don't know."

"It's complicated."

"I'm being kicked out of my apartment in a week, and I'm broke until the first of next month. I might be homeless," Beck said. "*That's* complicated."

"Since when have you been broke?"

"You'd be surprised by how much money I go through," Beck said, "but don't worry, I'll call my lawyer."

"Beck, I won't lose any sleep worrying about you," she said. "That drink's on me."

She went to either side of the bar, refilling drinks and exchanging empty pleasantries with customers. Kat noticed Beck's probing glare and knew he was siphoning through her words to reach his own conclusions. Her curiosity drew her back to him as the overhead lights slowly began to dim and the glow of black light saturated the still air in a dreamy blue. The whites of his eyes and teeth glowed like he was lit from within.

"We're all messed up," he said when she got close enough. "You should be honest with them."

"Are you trying to be a friend?"

"I don't have that many *real* friends," Beck said. "If you won't let me sleep with you, I can at least be your friend. And whatever happened can't be as bad as what happens to me every Saturday night."

Kat crossed her arms, rolling over his offer in her head. Before she could find a reason to stop, she said, "I was pregnant."

Beck's mouth fell open.

"I told him I was pregnant. No one knew about it, and I told Jacob at Marcie's party," she said casually, like they were talking about the weather. "I had a miscarriage. The doctor said I had an 'insufficient tolerance' to the pregnancy. Some immune system disorder where my body attacked the fetus. Chances are I might never get pregnant. And funny thing is, I'm not ready for a kid, but it's all I can fucking think about. All the time. And I almost had one with him."

Beck finished his drink and reached over the bar. His glowing face, swathed in orange and blue, softened, and he squeezed her hand.

"I'll get you another drink," she said. "If you tell anyone..."

"Come on," Beck said. "You're the only person stupid enough to really talk to me."

The regulars started to mill in. The meathead sauntered to a corner, beginning his choreographed posturing, the woman with knock-off designer shoes stepped in to order her cosmo, and the horny new lovers waited for the deejay so they could spend the evening thrusting onto each other. Thumping trance music rolled through the dark bar.

Kat returned to Beck with two shots of tequila, limes perfectly balanced on the rims.

"This is going on your tab, poor rich boy," she said as they touched shot glasses and upturned them. They sucked on the limes afterward, trying not to wince.

They shared illuminating grins while newcomers started to use elbows and force to get to the bar. Kat focused on the heat of the tequila in her stomach and the crowd growing before her. She tried to keep her thoughts from traveling to the familiar memory of cramps and dull backaches warring deep inside her body. The memory of scrambling from the dance floor to the bathroom with Beck. She turned to him and realized how grateful she was that he'd been there to help.

Rather than think about it, she focused on the level of beer in the glasses along the bar and purposefully ignored a woman who shoved her way forward, disregarding people now in line behind her. Kat would make sure she served that woman last, or maybe not at all. She took notice of the humanity swarming through blue light and dark shadows, grouping and laughing and filling the air with words. She noticed the foreign state of Beck's genuine smile.

She wouldn't think about how she and Russell barely talked anymore or how any physical closeness they'd had was now unbearably awkward. Since Marcie's party, she'd been hiding in her room because if she stared at him for too long, she would want to be back in his arms. Unbelievably, she felt more comfortable confiding in Beck now than in Russell. She couldn't think about how safe and whole it felt to be wrapped in Russell, surrounded by his warmth and smells. She didn't want to start another affair with another unavailable man. No, she couldn't think about that.

Tonight was just another shift at Stratosphere. Her tears and childless arms and occasional hotel romps with a married man were far away.

Kat raised herself up on her toes, passed the woman who had cut in line, and addressed the group behind her. She flashed a charming smile and asked, "What can I get you guys?"

44

Russell and Leslie shuffled past the bodies gathering at the narrow entrance to Stratosphere. Russell gave the doorman a nod as he and Leslie stepped through. Russell scanned the bar for stools, finding a few open but none together.

"Damn, we should've have gotten here earlier," he said to Leslie.

"Look, man, I think we should go home," Leslie said, his brow wound into a tight frown. "It's Sunday night, and I have to work tomorrow."

"Old people are going to die whether you're hungover or not," Russell said.

"You're an asshole."

"An asshole with permission to marry Ava."

"When?" Leslie asked. "And why are you just telling me this now?"

"Hindu Kush," Russell said.

Leslie grinned in agreement. "Yeah, that shit makes everyone stupid."

Movement caught Russell's eye as a woman stood from the bar and moved toward the bathroom. With unwarranted urgency, Russell darted toward the stool and nearly collided into another patron. Russell gave him an apologetic smile as he and Leslie took their rightful stations at the bar. Russell stuck his head past the growing crowd and searched for Kat.

His heart fluttered when he saw her. She hadn't seen him yet, so he let himself stare at her. Her dark hair swinging in the air, her hand forceful and elegant with the liquor bottles and glasses. She glowed from the light around her like some forgotten deity. She leaned over the bar in front of Beck and laughed casually. Beck locked eyes with Kat and smiled. He then placed his hand on her shoulder, bringing her closer to say something. Russell's hands tightened into fists, and he felt his jaw clench.

"Beck's here," he said between his teeth.

"Damn, doesn't he have some other shit he could be doing?" Leslie asked, following Russell's gaze down the bar and back. "Why do you look like you're about to kill him?"

"What?" Russell asked, distracted as Beck reached for

Kat's hair as she playfully batted his hand back. He felt his diaphragm tighten as sharp breaths pulled past his lips. When did she get close to Beck? Did they become friends when Russell wasn't looking? He and Kat weren't talking, but now she was dealing with Beck?

Leslie placed his hand an inch from Russell's nose and snapped. Russell nearly fell off the stool into woman next to him.

"Dude!"

Leslie pursed his lips and crossed his arms.

"Don't do that," Russell said. "You look like someone's mother."

Leslie flinched and Russell instinctively cringed.

"I'm sick of your bullshit," Leslie said.

"What are you talking about?"

Leslie grabbed his arm and pulled him off the stool. This time Russell did collide with the woman next to him, spilling her drink and causing her to cry out in anger. As Leslie pulled him toward the door, Russell readied himself to protest, but the sight of Beck and Kat laughing took the words out of his mouth. He held his gaze on them as he was pulled through the crowd and out into the street.

Leslie tapped out a cigarette and offered one to Russell.

"We just lost a prime spot," Russell said, pulling out his lighter for both of their cigarettes. "Are you going to lecture me about something that isn't a real issue?"

"Fuck you," Leslie said calmly. "I should bash your head in because you're about to ruin everything."

"What?"

"First of all, you woke me up this morning so you wouldn't have to be alone with Kat," he said. "You could've gotten Shakes out of the apartment without me."

"It's not like that."

"Then what is it like?" Leslie asked, catching a few stares from people entering Stratosphere. "It's the same reason you're dragging me out on Sunday night when you know all I want to do is sleep."

"Then go home," Russell said, his anger now shifting to Leslie.

"Not before I say my piece," Leslie said. "You're going to propose to Ava, right?"

"Yes," Russell said, throwing his hands in the air. "Of course."

Leslie sucked on his cigarette and shook his head. "I've tried to play along, hoping you'd get it, but you're absolutely blind, Russell."

"Oh my god," Russell said, stamping out his cigarette and moving toward the door.

"You're not in love with Ava," Leslie called back. "I think you're in love with Kat."

Russell stopped and stumbled as if he had been shot. His feet faltered on the cracked concrete, and cigarette smoke parted his lips in a slow moving fog. He turned to Leslie and shoved him backward into the wall. His cigarette flew over his head into the crowd of people moving along the street.

Leslie glared back at him, his face wide with shock.

"Fuck you," Russell said. "You don't know what you're talking about."

Leslie spat his words in hisses. "You're a damn coward. You run away from everything. Your feelings, your artwork, *everything*. And you think you can put on that suit every day and be someone else? You think marrying Ava is right? She can't even *see* you! And the one who has been there, who fucking *believes* in your stupid, big, clumsy ass, believes in your art, loves your life, and doesn't care that you can't do a dish to save yourself, is right here! She doesn't care that you're a nasty straight man who laughs at fart jokes like they're the funniest thing in the world."

Rage chastened the muscles in Russell's body and crackled the air between them.

"All we have is each other, Russell. And you're going to ruin everything because you're a coward."

"I'm a coward?" Russell said. "Leslie, look at yourself before you judge me. You forced Isaac into rehab and wasted all of your mother's money on the bill. He only went to rehab because he had no other place to go."

"Shut up!" Leslie said, stepping up to glare in Russell's face.

"He's going to relapse. We all know it."

"Shut up!" Leslie growled.

"Trying to fix him won't bring your mother back," Russell said, just before a thud rocked his face. It was followed by sharp pain in his jaw. The earth tilted in and onto itself, sweeping Russell completely off his feet. For a second he was suspended midair, then his shoulder smacked onto the ground. Gasping for breath, he looked up at Leslie, watery-eyed and clutching his wounded fist.

People gathered around them in a wall of bemusement and horror. They stopped midstride, nudging each other to look. Russell heard snickers and howls. Flashes from camera phones captured the moment. Some people assessed the commotion and scurried in the other direction.

"Damn, did you see that guy knock him out?"

"Shit, son!"

Russell hustled to his feet, and the sudden elevation change brought a new wave of pain to his jaw. He flexed and rolled his shoulders. He extended his hands and balled his fists.

"Don't do it," someone called from the crowd.

"Come on, man," Leslie said.

"Fuck you," Russell said, his stomach quaking with rage.

Leslie cleared his throat and mirrored Russell's stance. Russell lunged at Leslie, his fist quickly popping Leslie's cheek. Leslie cried out as he drove his fist into Russell's kidneys. They both stumbled back, Russell grasping his side and Leslie holding his face.

"Fight!" rang out like a gunshot from the crowd, igniting them, and in the drunken haze of adrenaline, Russell and Leslie dove at each other. Russell used his height to his advantage and threw a wave of fists at Leslie's head. Leslie blocked a few of them in between his sharp assaults to Russell's side. They filled the air with grunts and cries until stronger arms ripped them away from each other. Russell swung his arms until Leslie was out of reach. He connected one more time with Leslie's head, and Leslie reacted with a kick to Russell's shin.

Russell bellowed as the bouncer's arms clenched him, and he tried to wrench himself free. He nearly succeeded but a punch to the back of the neck zapped his strength. His knees gave out, leaving his captors to support his weight. He saw Beck holding Leslie, screaming and jerking around, his face rabid with angry tears. Russell wanted to turn away but Stratosphere's doormen had him locked forward in a loose chokehold. Russell's heart dropped when he realized his friend's voice and face were unrecognizable.

Kat shoved her way through the crowd, which had ballooned around them, yelling at people to move. Her face went quickly from shock to anger, and her eyes shimmered with tears.

Bile burned Russell's throat and his asshole puckered. He had never seen his friends look at him with malice this way. Everything had escalated so quickly.

She spun to Beck. "Get Leslie out of here before the cops come!"

Beck pulled back on Leslie's arm, allowing him to twist and free himself. Leslie leapt over the few feet that separated them. Kat caught his arm and Beck was back on him in seconds, lugging him into the crowd. She turned to Russell.

"What is *wrong* with you?" Kat screamed. "Why are you guys trying to kill each other? And why outside the place I work?"

"I don't... I mean, he called me a coward..."

"Are you serious?" She looked up to the sky for help as tears fell from her eyes.

The doormen looked at Kat for direction, and she nodded for them to let Russell go. He stumbled but kept on his feet. Now that the show was over, onlookers returned to their original destinations and the sidewalk quickly emptied.

"You could've killed him." Kat's voice was shrill with anger.

"He's not that much smaller than me," Russell said in a small voice.

"What did you do to him?" Kat asked.

Kat turned away and enclosed herself in her arms while a familiar and peculiar sadness stretched over her. With her face upturned, she caught the golden glow of the streetlight. Russell, still shaking with adrenaline, reached out for her. The desire was great as his trembling fingers, with their busted, bleeding knuckles, moved along the air, over the drone of traffic, the rumble of trains, and the tumult of night. His fingertips touched her and he pulled in a breath.

He felt the tension leave her shoulders, and he tugged her closer to him. She resisted for a moment, and he felt her pull away, but soon she was in his arms with her face buried in his neck. His chin rested on her head and the bristle of his beard picked up a few strands of her hair. He inhaled her scent and his knees began to steady.

Kat tilted her head upward to look in his face, her eyes brilliant with tears.

"Look, I'm sorry..."

She pushed away from him and toward the door. She wiped her eyes carefully with the length of her index finger, trying not to smudge her mascara. Her face hardened in front of Russell. His knees started to weaken again, and he stepped back to keep upright.

"You shouldn't come home tonight."

She rushed back into Stratosphere, leaving him alone with the glaring doormen, daring him to follow. Russell's breath went shallow as Kat was absorbed into the blue light and churning crowd.

45

"Get away from me!" Leslie barked as Beck ushered him back to his neighborhood.

"Man, I'm just here to help," Beck said.

Leslie snorted and sped up. Rage rippled through him, churning in his stomach and weighing on his limbs. He took labored steps, fighting gravity that seemed to have tripled in the passing minutes. The path home seemed marred by distress. City trees in their shallow sidewalk pits pointed accusingly at him with their brittle and starved branches. Each shadow that crossed his weak feet was deeper tonight, the concrete more cracked, and the streets held more litter than before. The street he lived on didn't belong to him.

Russell's face, narrowed in fury, plagued Leslie's mind. The impressions of his fists still stung. He squeezed his eyes closed over and over again, hoping he'd wake up in bed. He was confused, unsure of what led to him to attack his best friend like a feral animal. Russell, a friend and ally, had turned so quickly into a stranger, and Leslie hit him with everything he had, determined to draw blood.

The trauma and the very violation laced everything he saw. His chest ached from the familiar poison of grief. He was saturated in it, from thoughts of his mother to his last encounter with Isaac. He still didn't know exactly where they stood, and now his grief and sorrow were creating a division between him and his best friend.

"I thought we were friends," Beck said, not losing step alongside Leslie.

"You have no friends," Leslie said.

"Give it a rest," Beck said. "You want to fight me now? I don't think you have it in you."

Leslie stopped, his body ragged and throbbing in pain. Leslie scowled at Beck, who remained smug and smiling. Beck offered his arm, which Leslie took with a grumble, grateful for the support.

"I still hate you," Leslie said as they shuffled.

"You're so sweet when you're swelling up," Beck said.

"Why are you helping me?"

"Because even though you think you're better than me," he said, "we're the same."

Beck's words burned like curses, and Leslie fought back angry tears. Maybe his parents had been right all this time. He had changed so much from that young, skinny, suburban kid. His Sundays had been spent in their company in the second row of pews at New Calvary Life Church, listening to the elated swoon of the choir. He sat next to his mother, bound tightly in a beautiful dress made of pale pink or an elegant print. She sat poised, ankles crossed, hands folded gently in her lap, appearing regal. She was a beautiful woman, with kind features that softened with her age. His father sat stoic and strong in a crisp suit, a battered Bible in his lap. His face was assembled so similarly to Leslie's that he could often see himself when he looked at his father, some kind of preview for the future. During the course of her life, his mother, along with his father, had become a well-known fixture in the church. They managed and governed their social positions with fairness and decency. He recalled endless events they'd organized—food drives, picnics, prayer groups—with an unearthly amount of civility. Leslie always respected that, and there amongst his parents, under the admiration of the church, they would all sit.

Years later, that church, and the people who had inhabited it, seemed far away. Their faces had lost detail. Memories were now blurry and misplaced and felt to Leslie like the plotline of an old TV show. The congregation who glared at him for years with expectations of virtue and warmth had regressed into one giant entity of disappointment, disapproval, and repulsion. He remembered the storefront church, nestled in the apex of suburbia, more clearly than his childhood home. Without looking, he could have accounted for all the surrounding oak trees that shadowed the parking lot. He recalled growing up protected by the tall brick walls of the church and peering out at the world through sea-colored stained-glass windows. He would stare fearfully at the six-foot cross looming in the sanctuary, casting a shadow on the thin red carpet. Long after the crowds left, he would stay, a kid breathing in the smell of old Bibles and listening to the tick of the air conditioning. On Sunday afternoons, when the sun was bright and high, light would part the heavy shadows cast by the encircling oaks and shine directly above the church, as if God himself was looking down. No other place he had ever been felt so certain.

But now his father sat alone, not as stoic as he once was, unable to utter Leslie's abhorrent name in the holy New Calvary Life Church. Leslie, still stumbling down the street, body wracked with pain, could see his father's face, now older with deep lines gathering between his brows. Leslie could picture the strained expression on the face his father shared with his son. His jaw clenched as he focused hard on the sermon before him, struggling to evade the rumors. Those rumors, hissed stealthily out of earshot, began with alleged sightings of Leslie in seedy gay bars and blossomed into false tales of stripping and prostitution to foster a drug habit in the city. Someone even invented a story of him stalking the streets at night in four-inch heels and a long blonde wig, a story that trickled down to Leslie through a series of gossip channels. That story in particular wedged him thoroughly between despondency and rage. He could only imagine his father in the pew, shoulders sunken, heart broken.

Up ahead, lit by streetlight, Leslie finally saw his apartment steps. Beck helped him up the stairs and inside.

"Thanks," he said, pushing through the door.

"Sure," Beck said as he joined Leslie in the living room. Glancing around he added, "Is it supposed to be decorated like this?"

Leslie tenderly lowered himself on the couch and grimaced at Beck. "What are you talking about?"

"Are those purple curtains?" Beck asked with a sneer, moving to the windows.

"Get out." Leslie leaned over and held his head, letting the full force of pain drop onto him.

Beck paused for a moment, his face offering sympathy. "Shit happens," he said finally, and walked out the front door.

"Yeah," Leslie said, and sank into the couch.

46

Russell aimlessly walked on the sidewalk. Pain left him limping past crowds gathering in the doorways of bars, passing dark alleys, and walking unevenly over crosswalks. Paranoia itched at the nape of his neck as he collected a few stares from passing drivers. A weary, lone dog walker spotted him and hurried to a quick trot. He caught a glimpse of himself in the blackened windows and grated doors of the closed shops. He couldn't hide his circumstances; his clothes and hair were tussled and his gait was slow, injured and dragging.

He had to get off the street, even for a moment. He veered quickly into a much darker patch of night. He walked through a dormant, condensed residential area and spotted a neon light up ahead, glowing like a beacon. The sign marked a neighborhood bar with a generic name.

Russell had been there a few times, first bated by curiosity and then disappointed enough to walk back out. The poorly lit interior appeared to be more of a hole than a bar, a subterranean cave hidden in plain sight. Tonight, though, he could hide amid the peeling paint, the cracked walls, and the dirty linoleum scarred by the sharp legs of barstools. The people in the bar had rigid, lined faces that told of too much alcohol, too many bad decisions, and heavy loneliness. They came here to commiserate their pain, to drink to agony.

Russell limped toward the bar and smelled the air, sweetened by liquor and sweat. He ordered a whiskey from the old, round bartender who shared the same harsh look as his patrons. Russell settled into a booth where his forearms stuck to the table's gummy surface. He peeled back his arm and filled his mouth with cheap well whiskey.

He had to figure out where he was going tonight. He wasn't sure if Kat meant what she said, but he was too battle worn to test her. He couldn't look at her or Leslie right now. He couldn't see his friend's face damaged by his fists.

The space between them would crackle from the accusations made earlier on the street. The thought of Russell's supposed cowardice left small embers burning with anger.

He told his best friend he was one step closer to marrying the woman he loves and fists were thrown. Weren't congratulations in order, as opposed to street fights? The world seemed to be against everything he was trying to do, to being pursued twice by Isabelle Boldwyn and her gallery, to Ava wanting him to be a manager at Midstate Regional Bank.

Russell sipped slowly from the whiskey. His empty eyes gaped at basketball clips from the dirty TV posted above the bar.

A dread he hadn't felt in years wormed its way into him. He was lost in that hole of a bar. He was back in the trailer park, counting the hours until it was safe to return home. He wondered if he would have to sneak back into his apartment, like those cartoon exaggerations of cat burglars balanced on their tiptoes, a mask knotted over his eyes. Would he have to creep past his roommates as if they were his father? If he was discovered, would they hurl empty liquor bottles and curse at him?

He finished the last of the whiskey. Heat built behind his eyes. He swallowed down those knots of emotion and stepped back into the dark streets, moving with a new determination. He was back on his street, peeking at the low glow of light from his apartment windows. He felt like a stranger watching the slow-moving silhouettes behind the curtains.

Emotion climbed back up this throat, and he rushed down the street into his car. He slammed the keys into the ignition and, with a sputtering choke, moved the car quickly down the street. He stopped at red lights with jolts. His Subaru shot forward along the highway, deeper into the city.

Could Leslie be right? Was he in love with Kat?

Russell could still feel the tickle of Kat's skin close to his.

He pressed on the gas pedal and his car threatened to explode as it rolled over a pothole. The car squealed as he turned left, driving into Gold Coast.

He was drowning in the urgency to see Ava. If he could see her, she could wipe all this away. Her touch would mute the sting of Leslie's fist. Ava's voice would silence Leslie's claims. Her kiss would sap away the knots of emotion he was coughing up like vomit.

In her presence, he wouldn't wonder how Kat's lips tasted. In her presence, he wouldn't be burdened by the awkward guilt of wanting to taste Kat's lips.

He pulled into a large parking garage a block from Ava's building. This time of night, nearly all the spaces were filled and he was forced to drive to the highest level. He found parking on the rooftop and pulled out his phone to call Ava. After a few rings, the voicemail chirped her prerecorded voice. Russell let out a rattled sigh and tried again. Then again. Each time the ringtone would end with the voicemail message.

Russell bashed his fists into the steering wheel, letting out a guttural cry.

He was out of breath, gasping, and very tired. Part of him was glad Ava didn't answer. She would see him this way and ask questions. He couldn't hide the fact that he'd fought with Leslie, and she would tell him to grow up. She would look at him and lecture, and he felt small already. He was too drained to be probed by her.

Tonight, he'd hide from all of them.

He reclined and leaned his head against the window, staring out into the cityscape. He wished he could look past the wicked glow of the city and see the stars.

47

Beck wanted to drink, move his body, and have some ceremonial act to offer to his dread. He hadn't yet sold his laptop and spent all day looking at the screen. He searched aimlessly for unimaginable employment he was in no way qualified for. He couldn't pass a drug test and had no experience to list on a resume. At the peak of his frustration, his sad pursuit was punctuated by porn and crushed pills. His recent days were also regularly interrupted by bill collectors. His phone would rattle and buzz, crawling off the couch— that loyal couch now serving as a bed—and onto the floor. Beck's voicemail had reached capacity in a matter of days and now refused to record the threats.

This was to be the last night he allowed himself to stay in the apartment. Tomorrow he would angle himself into someone's bed. He would woe or charm, beg if he had to. Even though his tan had all but faded and he could no longer spike his hair due to the sickly calamity where red roots met bleached-blond, he was still Beck Ashby, gleaming party boy. Although he had missed out on three nights of partying, he'd kept up with everyone's Facebook and Instagram accounts.

After a very conservative bump of coke, Beck journeyed out into the night. He was surprised when no one had called him or invited him out. He knew a few parties that were set to happen, but etiquette dictated everyone gathered at a bar first. Beck sent out a few text messages but got no response. He was no guest star or recurring character. Hadn't he bought himself onto the opening credits as a series regular?

This abnormality hurried Beck along the sidewalks, and he was in a full panic by the time he pushed through Club Peppermint's doors. His heart sped up to the droning dubstep as he looked through the hazy red luminance for a familiar face. In the scarlet neon, beneath the far-reaching rumble of bass, the weak-kneed, cokehead prophet collided with the truth. Beck wished he'd chosen painkillers instead.

His minions were gathered in a tight circle near the dance floor. Marcie slithered rhythmically, bound in a lewd miniskirt, against her disfigured and brutish boyfriend. His female duet moved with feigned disinterest to the beat. Holding sovereign command in the center of the circle stood Beck's lieutenant. Their ranks were closed, the circle impenetrable. This gathering shouldn't have happened without Beck and yet it did.

Beck had suspected his overthrow would be gradual enough to be managed, but this coup d'état was as swift as a mob-led hooding, kidnapping, and beheading. He gathered himself on a barstool, straining to breathe. He ordered a shot of tequila to ease the sting.

Once he choked down the shot, Isaac slipped into view. He danced on lurching feet, staggering too far left, then too far right. His eyes were closed, his head upturned, and the pulsing red light stained his face the color of blood. Isaac's arms were stretched out in worship to nothing in particular. He was wonderfully hysterical and made beautiful by the crushed pills.

He blinked at Isaac several times. He wondered if Isaac had called Leslie—if Leslie knew what he was doing. Should Leslie even know after the bad trip he had in the bathroom of Broken Jaw? Beck had seen people fall apart around him, but something about watching Isaac spinning, lost within himself, stung. Something about it echoed his own crippling loneliness.

He knew it now—that no one left these nights unscathed. Now it was Beck's turn. All he had done to other people in the name of his own loneliness, his own boredom, was coming around to claim him.

Beck stared at Isaac until the lieutenant blocked him. Their eyes met. Neither of them blinked.

Beck narrowed his gaze in fury despite his impotence. The lieutenant smiled with the deep knowing of someone who had finally overpowered an old opponent.

The lieutenant excused himself from the circle, which parted to let the newfound king step away from his throne. The lieutenant was suddenly terrifying and beautiful, swaggering through the ruby light in his uniform of a cutoff black shirt to display his aggregation of black ink. Those detailed tattoos were a testament to his patience and endurance. His wide smile exposed his handsome, sharp canines—a predator. It was likely the coke causing Beck's clairvoyance, but maybe the lieutenant had been duping him all this time. Beck had been a host for this dangerous parasite and now that he was emptied out, it was time for the herd to move on.

"What's going on here?" Beck asked with his chin up, putting on a thin show of hostility.

"Isaac said he stopped by," the lieutenant said, leaning in to be heard over the music. "For a little bit of blow he told me what he saw. I know about your apartment. I know about your money problems. Wasn't hard to figure out."

Beck's bluff wavered and crumbled. He was exposed and desperate. He grabbed the lieutenant's shoulders. "Dude, I'm going through a tough time."

"Yeah."

Beck sucked in breath and tried to smile. "You think I could hang at your place for a few days?"

The lieutenant shook free from Beck. He didn't speak as he returned to his haughty state. He placed his finger on his chin, turning his consideration to a cartoonish pantomime. The lieutenant elbowed past Beck and nodded to the bartender.

"You can't stay with me or any of us really," he said finally, handing Beck a glass. "But here's a drink for old time's sake."

"Fuck you."

"The only one fucked here is you."

The lieutenant clinked his glass against Beck's and flashed his saw-tooth smile before returning to the circle.

Beck dropped his head and crept out unseen, saving what dignity he could.

Out into the night and without any other option, he pushed into the nearly vacant Stratosphere. He swallowed bile and stood in front of the bar until Kat appeared before him with a soft smile.

"Hey, ass. What are you doing here on a slow night?"

His shoulders quaked as the loneliness finally crushed him. What regard he had for appearance, for the mythos of the wild Beck Ashby, was gone.

"It's over."

Kat stepped back self-consciously as warm tears filled Beck's manic eyes. She glanced around and crossed the bar, pulling Beck away from the few customers and toward the bathrooms.

"Are you having a bad trip?" she asked.

"It's all over."

"What the hell are you talking about?"

"I'm going to be homeless *for real*. I'm broke. I've spent it all."

"Okay," she said, shaking her head as though trying to convince herself of the offer she was about to make. "Stay with me."

48

Leslie called in to work for a few days to allow his swollen face a chance to heal. He didn't want explain his bruises to his coworkers and confused patients, and he couldn't construct a lie believable enough to avoid becoming fodder of gossip. In his self-induced banishment to his bedroom, he walked to the bathroom only to relieve himself and the kitchen only to eat.

He spent his first day of isolation comforted by burning bowls of weed, Chinese takeout, and a pack of frozen peas he used to reduce the lumps on his head and face. At some point, Kat pelted his door with soft knocks, but he refused to answer, undeterred by her insistence. He knew she would want to talk about the fight, but Leslie couldn't stand to have that conversation. He hadn't come to any conclusion about himself and Russell, drifting from extreme guilt to a strong sense of justification for their clash.

The next afternoon, as the haze of weed parted like heavy curtain panels, he smelled himself. In the comatose state, his filth had flourished. Now that the bruising had gone down, he decided to run a few errands. Maybe he would call Isaac. He could go over to the halfway house and make an attempt at reconciliation. In his weed anesthesia, his argument with Isaac dangled over him. Unlike what took place with Russell, he believed their relationship could be salvaged with a reasonable conversation and a few kisses.

Certain Kat would be at work this late in the afternoon, he stripped down and strolled toward the bathroom. Halfway there, the creak of floorboards froze him in place.

"Nice ass."

Instinctively, Leslie spun around to face the voice. Beck stared back, and a devilish smile played across his face. Leslie glared as Beck's eyes dropped to his crotch.

"Wow, you do have a big—"

Leslie let out a bellow and dove back into his room, away from Beck's hot glare. He slammed the door behind him and pulled on sweatpants. He opened the door and charged at Beck, pushing him back into the wall.

"What the fuck are you doing here?"

"Whoa," Beck said. "Why all the violence? Too much rap music?"

Leslie backstepped and sighed. In a shaky, slightly calmer tone, he asked, "Why are you here?"

Beck stepped from the wall and headed to the couch with a frown. He sat on the fitted sheet that had been stretched over the cushions and pulled one of Kat's flowery comforters into a bundle.

"I was evicted."

"And you couldn't have stayed with someone else?"

"No."

"I heard the street corners are real nice. There are also highway underpasses."

To Leslie's disappointment, this elicited no response. Beck meekly picked at the frayed end of Kat's comforter and gazed at his feet.

"Seriously, you have no one you could stay with?"

"No."

"Can you get another place?"

"I'm broke."

Leslie's face screwed with confusion at the squatter before him. Fatigued, Beck sat on the couch like the start of a cautionary tale about the inevitable fall of the mighty. In the course of his sad parable, Beck found himself at the mercy of his rivals.

His tan had faded, exposing a soft dusting of freckles along his neck and face. Red roots had gained footing over his greasy blond mane and looked like moss slowly growing up a wall. At the other end of the couch were a few suitcases. Leslie wondered if that was all Beck had left.

"Can't your friends help you?"

Beck laughed sharply. "You guys are the closet thing I have to friends. Kat is letting me stay here until I figure shit out. I thought she told you."

"Well, I haven't really been in a talking mood," Leslie said, recalling Kat at his door. "And I guess after what happened with Russell we have the space."

Beck tried to smile. "You guys will be back to normal sooner than you think."

Leslie shrugged and turned to the bathroom.

ll help you figure this out, but don't get too
…able," Leslie called back. "And please don't tell anyone
…me naked."

…ait," Beck said. "I need to tell you something."

…eslie continued toward the bathroom. "Look, I'm
…g you stay here—don't push it."

"It's about Isaac."

Leslie swallowed and faced Beck. He'd seen him many
…nes—laughing, stoned, angry—but for the first time he
…emed so fallible, almost human. In this grand unmasking,
…hese unfortunate circumstances had rubbed and scored away
his face into something soft, pink and vulnerable.

There was a prickling start of numbness in Leslie limbs.
He knew what Beck was going to say, or some version of it.
He sat on the chair next to the couch out of politeness.

"Last night," Beck began, "Isaac was at Peppermint with
my friends—or ex-friends, I guess."

Leslie bit back a sob and stared up at the ceiling. Beck's
report tumbled over him in an avalanche. The desire to pray,
which Leslie hadn't felt in years, rolled and stretched in him
like a slumbering animal shaking itself from hibernation.
Pieces from old sermons surfaced in his mind. They were
little earworms working their way up through black earth,
pushing through roots, finding cracks in the concrete. Those
hopeful and sometimes cryptic little sermons, those beautiful
orations of God's almighty grace and indomitable love, were
little maggots ready to be crushed by feet or plucked up by the
nimble bird. Leslie, the lost little lamb, was the blaspheming
sodomite, the fucker of innumerable men, the wayward
son. He'd discarded God like an adult shedding the fear of
monsters that growled under the bed. As a drunken, self-
important cleric, he'd loudly expressed his feelings at parties,

waxing on the great disservice of organized religion. He'd boasted about his ascension to the world of the pragmatic, the agnostic, the level-headed. But at this moment, the image of joining hands with his mother and father, bowing their heads in holy reverence—or in the steadfast arrogance of the modern Christian—to pray for the poor or thank God for their unshakable family, rounded his mind. He could still tap his feet to that singsong rhythm of prayer constructed from a humbly spoken play of words. The same fervent prayers that couldn't cure his homosexuality or stop the semitruck from flattening his mother.

Yet still he found himself looking up at his apartment's watermarked ceiling and wondering if heaven was above it and if monsters were rolling around underneath his bed. He found himself praying that God would take it away.

Beck grabbed Leslie's hand and gave it a soft squeeze. "Your boyfriend was out there dancing, and your boyfriend was high out of his mind."

49

Kat stared into the mirror before her shower and took notice of the flawed reflection in front of her: the unevenness of her skin, the puckering of a clogged pore, and the wild mess of hair tossed by the wind and flattened by her tight commute on the subway. Then she showered and stepped out, ready to arm herself with sexuality, which sharpened to a razor's double-edge as she zipped up her black dress, painted her lips red, and balanced into black leather heels. She transformed herself into a witty, deliberate woman who stalked the well-traveled path through the city's night streets to the hazy bar of the Grant Park Hotel.

The bar, like the hotel itself, was a faulty Midwest satire of European chic, burdened with too many ornate trimmings and refurbished art deco paintings. Kat slinked quietly to a table that overlooked a gilded Victorian mirror. A martini named after the hotel was on special, so she sipped from an over-sweetened drink that coated her mouth in film and smacked her lips.

Lately, she hadn't felt much like that vixen looking back at her through the gold-framed mirror. In fact, the beautiful costume of the woman in the mirror clung to her like tight binds. If she squinted hard enough, after coughing down her offending drink, she could see the irregular tones in her skin and the start of a breakout below her foundation. She could see her right foot quivering underneath the table. She could see the woman who just wanted to go home and dance to albums played on a record player she found in the garbage with her roommate, the roommate she'd recently kicked out of the apartment.

Soon Jacob walked up behind the woman in the frame. He exposed his toothy grin and, with a smooth gait, made his way to her. He carried another martini and joined her at the table.

"How have you been?" Jacob asked in the fluid, purring voice he reserved for their rendezvous.

At this moment, Kat realized he, too, was playing a role. It was a necessity in their commerce, maybe to protect themselves from one another or to distance themselves from adultery. He needed these little customs shared between them over the passing nights.

Kat emptied her drink, and she struggled to smile.

"Fine," she said.

"You look amazing."

His statement was customary, in part a justification for how badly he wanted her. She did look amazing—so amazing that how could anyone blame him for wanting to take her upstairs in one of the cheaper rooms to fuck?

"You look pretty good, too."

And he did, as always, thanks to his polished bespoke suit, slicked-back hair and square jaw, darkened slightly from stubble. Jacob was always true to his character. They finished their drinks in a lingering silence. Jacob placed a fifty-dollar bill underneath his glass, and they walked through the restaurant to the hotel's hallways. He played with the key card to the room, tapping it eagerly against his leg as they headed into the elevator.

Kat eyed them in the mirrored walls of the elevator, a beautiful couple appearing devoted to one another. Familiar smiles drifted on their faces. Jacob bent forward and Kat demurely threw her hair back. Their practice was starting to feel familiar, though when she drove through her own feelings, it was like plodding through ankle-deep mud. Each step was labored. Each smile was hard. Each word was a struggle. Maybe she should have allowed him to make her feel good, to kiss her, to screw her until there was nothing left to feel.

He reached over with his left hand and playfully squeezed her arm. She felt his wedding ring pinch her skin and knew she was not just trapped in the mud—she was drowning in it. She submerged into the sludge and ran her tongue around a membrane left from the sickly sweet martini. They stepped off the elevator and into the room, like they always had. Across from the bed was another golden baroque mirror like the one in the lobby. Kat would be forced to watch herself and wanted to turn away but felt herself stealing glances.

"What do you say to your wife when we meet up?"

Jacob's smile shrank. He moved over to the bed and pulled off his suitcoat. He cleared his throat and returned to his role. In that moment, in that small quiver, he exposed himself. Kat knew she had seen who Jacob was and it was coming through now. He wasn't the frustrated husband trapped in a loveless marriage, enclosed in that beautiful golden mirror and poised on the bed like some tragic figure worthy of her affection. He was a meek man with violence in his eyes, flirting shamelessly with a stripper when she wasn't around. He was a man who had seemingly wanted to punch her at the time. He was the man who fucked her in the home he shared with his wife. He'd betrayed both Kat *and* his wife.

"When are you leaving her?" Kat asked.

Jacob opened his mouth and floundered in a series of stutters. He glanced at her helplessly, almost pleading her to go back on book. Why had she left their script? Why had she strayed from their boundaries into this murky place?

"I'm working up to it," he said, trying to draw her back. "Let's not worry about that tonight."

Kat, somehow roused by his hesitance, continued with tepid steps.

"It's been nearly a month since I miscarried," she said.

"Please, Kat," Jacob said. "Let's not do this."

Kat lurched over the bed and all but hissed at him, "Let me talk!"

Jacob's face cemented into a frown. "Fine, if this is how you want to play it."

"*Play?*" Kat asked angrily. "We never talk about this—I'm haunted, Jacob. Do you know that? I'm haunted every day. I could've been a mother. Being pregnant... it did something to me. I never really had a family. No one wanted me but this baby... maybe, I don't know, maybe it could've been different."

"I'm married," he said. "You wanted to have the baby and we live happily ever after? You wanted us to be a family? You, me, and our baby? I didn't think you were that type of girl, Kat."

She felt like he had pressed her face down into the mud. She could see his hand, on the back of her head, forcing her into the dark, wet muck. The quiver in Kat's foot grew rapid and her heel strained under the shock.

"You were relieved when I miscarried."

Kat's face was delirious in the revelation. She resisted the urge to point at the woman in the mirror and throw her head back in laughter. This whole affair had been a lie. She had been so stupid.

"No, I wasn't relieved."

Jacob was crumbling now and just as muddy as she was.

"You're lying," Kat said.

She took a breath and stilled her foot. With a sudden gravity, she said, "Please tell me the truth. Just once, Jacob. I haven't asked you for much, you can tell me the truth just one time."

He was snared deep in the dirt with her. He adjusted his suit jacket. His expression deflated and turned cold, and he stepped completely out of his role. They were too soiled for their customs now. Violence reappeared in his cold, silver eyes. His hands were tight fists at his sides. His body was strained, and she was certain he wanted to hit her. She glared back defiantly, daring him to lash out.

"I never wanted to you to be pregnant," he said. "It... I mean, the baby would have ruined all our lives. Personally, I'm surprised you still continued to sleep with me after you lost it."

He tilted his head and tapered his mouth into a thin line. "Wait, is that the *reason* you kept sleeping with me?"

The air around Kat was too heavy to breathe.

"Don't leave your wife for me."

Jacob winced. Maybe he was surprised that she was starting to see through him. He had been a manipulative bully. A knock-off of the love she'd always wanted.

Wounded, he said in a low voice, "Kat, let's not fight, please?"

"I can't sleep with you tonight," Kat said. "Or ever again."

This was the end of her role. She couldn't exalt his poor ego any longer. She stood on certain feet, and the woman in the golden mirror walked until she was out of its borders and out of the room.

50

When Russell showed up at her apartment bruised and battered, Ava was certain he'd had a confrontation with Tharp.

She was breathless, and the tide of blood rushing to her ears made her deaf. Russell repeated his story several times until she finally believed him. The fear of the Tharp boy dug in deep after he'd called, and when Russell said he was without a place, she quickly suggested he move in with her.

Once her panic subsided, she was unsurprised that the black homosexual and Latin tramp had turned on him. It was bound to happen, she thought, with the manner in which they all carried on. As he sat on her couch that morning, leaning over on his elbows and almost in tears, she stifled her own cheers of relief. For months she'd been scheming up ways to cauterize Russell from his friends.

Ava saw Russell enjoyed a certain social upheaval, a sort of juvenile rebellion from being seen with them, but she was sure that in the long-term nothing good could come from them. The black homosexual, despite his moments of kindness, was egregious. Ava had no objection to him being gay, she just didn't want to see it. She didn't want to share the same space where men slept with one another, and she certainly didn't want to hear it.

The Latin woman, on the other hand, was clearly in love with Russell. She was only pretending to be friends with him until she could get him. Ava worried one night the woman would creep into Russell's bed when she wasn't there.

The best part, the part that made her want to jump for joy, was that she wouldn't have to attend their dangerous parties anymore. He sat before her, ready to be spruced up into the handsome man she saw beneath his beard and cheap suits.

Soon, an entire week had passed. Russell plundered in and out of her doors leaving behind a dense man musk, a growing flock of dirty socks, and a shower full of tiny, curly hairs. Ava hadn't realized how hairy he was or how dramatically his stench choked the atmosphere in her apartment. No amount of open window breeze could exorcise the whiskey, cigarette smoke, farts, and man sweat. He dwelled in her apartment like a mythical giant, leaving slimy food chunks in the kitchen sink and used dishes in the dishwasher, too lazy to turn the dial. She began to suspect that when she wasn't home, he smoked in her apartment.

His swarthiness overtook her mattress. The bed began to slump on the side where he lay, rattling each night with deep snoring. In his sleep, his mouth slack-jawed, he spewed bad breath. Ava found herself losing sleep.

How could she have imagined Tharp standing a chance

against Russell? Russell could have simply stepped on him. Tharp was muscular, but short and soft like a fox. Russell, on the other hand, was a fortress of hard, hairy muscle, as if he'd swung into her life on a vine. She knew Russell would never physically harm her. Despite his mostly inferior upbringing, he lived by a code regarding women. He had a near sense of honor, even chivalry, as he opened doors and gave up seats for Ava. He gathered her close when they walked on the streets at night. Despite his good manners, Ava wondered how much she could take of his presence in her apartment.

If he made no effort to change, or at least take one of her suggestions, she would have to let him go. His honor was great, but it came up short when he didn't know which fork was the salad fork. They had wonderfully numbing sex, but his warm embrace was losing its allure.

The only benefit to his presence was that it gave her something to focus on. He became her living, breathing project. She had Russell measured for suits and spent two days shopping for him. This was an effective distraction from Tharp's call and his still unheard voicemail. In the long minutes she spent lighting candles to burn out Russell's stench, she didn't have to wonder what words he had said or what effect the purring growl of his voice would have on her.

She didn't have to picture that foxlike man, with his handsome, sharp-toothed grin, silver eyes, and hard fist standing next to her. She could instead contend with a grandiose Italian suit maker. When she was busy, she didn't have to recall the way Tharp made her crumble into a blubbering, fearful mess. She had an appointment to get to and simply no time for his voicemail.

Storm clouds brought darkness swiftly tonight. The smell of low-hanging moisture from outside mingled with the funk inside the apartment. Ava stepped into her nightgown, eyeing the growing slope in her bed frame.

Russell came late in from work somber, with whiskey on his breath. He forced the window open as much as it would go and lit a cigarette.

Ava stuck her head out of the bedroom.

"Please don't smoke in here."

Russell blew smoke out through the screen.

"Your doorman won't let me smoke outside the building."

"So what makes you think you can smoke *inside* the building?"

Russell sighed. He strolled into the kitchen, dropped his cigarette into the sink, and ran water over it.

Ava crossed her arms and stamped her foot. "Russell, you aren't going to do this here. I know you're hurting over your friends, but you're not going to take it out on me."

Russell's stench wasn't the only thing he'd packed. He also brought skulking, infested grief, and even more whiskey. He was a glum specter of the man who wooed her, who had collected hours upon hours making love to her, as if mastering a skill that left her nerve endings raw. Now he was lost underneath an unkempt beard, free falling curls, and rumpled suits. He spoke in shallow pleasantries and only touched her when they passed through doorways. The man she'd very recently been convinced she wanted to marry was gone—lost like a set of misplaced keys that she spent hours checking the same places for.

"Don't tell me how I feel, Ava."

"Well, then, what is it?"

"Just a shitty day at work."

Ava sucked her teeth in disbelief. "How long is this shitty day going to last?"

Russell took a small glass from the cupboard and began a lazy search of the cabinets.

"You drank all the whiskey yesterday."

"Do you always have to bust my balls?"

"Don't bother coming to bed tonight," Ava said, marching into her room and shutting the door.

She crawled into bed, sliding toward the dip Russell left, and wondered if she should let him into her room—not for his company, but out of fear of what his mass would do to her couch.

51

Beck's shirt was damp and he shivered in the dark alley behind Stratosphere. His wrinkled fingers reached for his cigarettes while he squatted down in the shadows against the graffiti-covered brick, hoping to stay outside a few minutes longer. The cigarette smoke flooded his nose and concealed the smell of cheap lemon detergent coming from the soaked apron around his waist. He shifted his weight forward to relieve his suffering heels.

The back door to Stratosphere opened and then closed with a sharp slam, and Beck caught himself with his hands to keep from landing on his face. He peered up at Kat, frowning down at him with her hands on her hips. She yanked the cigarette from his mouth and pulled a drag from it.

"You better get back in there," she said, exhaling smoke into his face.

"Just a few more minutes," Beck begged, dropping to his knees in an overdramatic show of angst.

Kat reached down and tugged him to his feet, her frown unchanged.

"I put my ass on the line to get you this job," she said.

"I know," he said, "and I'm forever in your debt."

Beck stared back, pleading. Kat sucked once more on his cigarette, handed it back to him, and relented.

"Hurry up. And when you get back, I'm going to need more clean glasses."

Beck watched her return inside the building and thought, in theory, about his need for employment. He'd been grateful to Kat for using her clout to get him the job. Beck had been to Stratosphere enough times to believe he'd seen all there was to see, but as a member of the staff, Stratosphere transformed into a place completely unrecognizable to him. He was rounding his first week as a barback and had already been yelled at by everyone at Stratosphere and made the reeling discovery of a hidden passageway in a room he thought he always knew.

The surly manager scoffed at him and formed a scowl made up of more tattoo ink than skin. He told Beck he was only there as a favor to Kat. The staff members dismissed his questions like he was a child interfering with grown-up talk. Their frustration asserted itself in an outbreak of hazing. He was delegated to clean bathrooms, vomit, and any other suspicious fluids. At the end of his shift, pushing brown water across the floor with a mop tight in his hands, he heard their low whispers.

"Is he really living with Kat?"

"He's a charity case now."

Those hushed mutterings slammed into Beck and his faltering social status. He was crushed in absolution and, for the first time he could remember, unable to retort.

The nights spun in a dizzying pace. He towed an endless accumulation of glasses back and forth between the rear of the bar into the deep, soapy sinks in the back. The job required muscles he'd long left dormant, setting his body ablaze with pain. As he hauled heavy kegs from the rear of the bar, he silently calculated the lengthy inventory of sins that brought him to this place. He tallied the thousands upon thousands of dollars spent on the greedy desire to free himself from loneliness. He counted his laundry list of shallow friends. His mind stretched over numerous nights made of vacant intimacy with any woman or man willing to join him in bed.

As he swiftly evaded swinging limbs and compressed bodies to wipe tables and collect empty glasses, he realized he'd met a fate worse than loneliness. He wasn't the wild Beck Ashby who could silence a guy with his stare. He wasn't Beck Ashby who had literally pissed on another person. He was wet, sweaty, greasy, and on the low end of a week-long cocaine comedown. Arms loaded with glasses, he returned to the sink through the swinging doors.

As he looked back at his tribe, those avowed to remain beautiful and cool, he felt invisible. From this vantage point, they appeared different, too. Maybe this is where the hidden passage led to: a place where his entire world seemed inverted, where the regulars' oafishness radiated in the black light. The young woman in the faux-designer heels was no longer attractive. All he could see was her spilling a drink and leaving a sticky residue to mop up. The exaggeratedly muscular guy who was too concerned with posing had already broken a glass. The forever horny lovers in their drunken hubris thought they'd gone unseen when they snuck into the bathroom to engage in a crazed sex act. Beck could only hope that whatever they had done wouldn't result in anything he'd have to gather strength to clean up after.

In Stratosphere's cloud of blue neon and piercing

music that grew into an indiscriminate roar, the crowd's drunkenness reached a fever pitch. Empty glasses became an endless legion rising up from every table, nook, and corner. Finally, the night that felt like it would sweep Beck into infinity came to an end. The bouncer shooed out the last few patrons who drank away their dignity as if they were flies on a dinner plate. Beck was left gathering up glasses to take back to the sink. Another half hour passed, tips were split and Stratosphere prepared for slumber.

Kat tugged Beck's aching body down the loud street back to her apartment. He moaned about his feet in between cigarettes as they made their way off Damen and into the apartment. It had been enough to convince Kat to let him have the first shower—contingent on him shutting up.

"I'm not made for labor," he said, limping onto the couch, which was now his bed. "You can have the shower first, Kat."

This week reminded Beck of his exile in Boston, where his indistinguishable exploits had forced those around him to look away. And while everyone else was looking in another direction, the Ashby's had discretely disposed of him. He could imagine the smug revulsion on their faces if they saw him now. It would be a wonderful affirmation of their disgust.

He was woefully certain no one would care if the now-invisible Beck Ashby went to sleep without a shower.

52

Russell swallowed back his dark mood and powered through his morning. He hunched over his desk, glaring at emails. He responded to a few customer calls. Afternoon approached and he settled into his day, the burn of Ava's ceaseless nagging replaced by office responsibilities. A mound of work stretched out in front of him and today it was a reassuring barrier between him and home. Around afternoon, a teller came to his office.

"A customer says she has a meeting with you."

"Bring her in," Russell said, clearing his desk.

The teller rushed away and Isabelle Boldwyn appeared, dressed in business attire. A good-natured smile played on her face, and she stepped forward and sat in the small chair in front of his desk. Russell winced and shuffled papers. He struggled to remain nonchalant. He peered over her shoulder to see if the manager or any bank staff was looking into his office. He couldn't think of any real reason she was here and sweat began to itch the back of his neck.

"How can I help you?" he said. "Interested in setting up a checking account?"

Isabelle's eyes widened and she giggled. She pulled her lips into a pucker and glanced around the office. "Hmmm," she said, folding her hands in her lap.

She was judging him. Russell saw it in her face, and pricks of anger shot down his back. He'd been judged enough. It was why he chose to step away from the art world and into this office. He wondered if he had the grounds to have her thrown out by security.

"What do you want?" he asked in a harsh whisper.

"This what you gave up your art career for?" she asked. "I pictured a bigger office. This room looks smaller than the average prison cell."

Russell clenched his teeth. "Did you come here to piss on me?"

Isabelle's scrutiny was replaced by a warm, genuine smile. "You know I co-own an art gallery with Curtis Newman?"

"Yes," Russell said flatly.

"You guys were rivals during college and let me just say I was always more a fan of your work. It was always more honest, more vulnerable. You opened your heart on canvas. And don't let me start on your technique. It was so advanced. Selling work like yours would be effortless. I have never pursued anyone like this for my gallery. Normally, they come to me. But I had to try one last time—sober. Please, Mr. Cowell, would you consider allowing me the honor of selling your artwork at my gallery?"

Russell sucked his teeth and shook his head.

Isabelle sighed and stood. "Well, then, thank you for your time." She walked to his door and turned around. "Please be true to yourself."

Russell fought the urge to throw something. The rest of the day his mind was scattered and his nerves twisted into knots. Near the end of his day, when the last of the staff left and he was working on a call block, his phone rang. It was Von Hoffman with an address and clandestine instructions to meet him. He wondered if Von Hoffman knew he and Ava had been fighting every night.

Following the instructions, Russell walked to a dim alley under the steady rainfall, triple checking the address on his phone. Cool raindrops fell golden in the streetlight between the skyscrapers of the inert financial district. Russell tiptoed toward a thick steel door with the faded words "BLUE JAY" inscribed on it. He looked over his shoulder one last time, surveying the alley, unsettling in its emptiness.

Russell forced the door open and found himself in a small galley club, lit softly from an unknown source hidden somewhere in the wood paneled walls. The bar and the booths lining the walls were carved from shiny mahogany.

The atmosphere was dank and the air carried gentle notes of wine and a lingering ambrosial cigar. The bartender was an older, weary man dressed in a formal white dress shirt fastened with a black bowtie. He wiped a wine glass with a towel and eyed Russell suspiciously.

Russell nodded at the bartender who glowered back. A stirring from the rear caught Russell's attention, and he saw Von Hoffman curled in a leather booth like a lazy cat after a meal. He waved at Russell with a half-full wine glass and a stony expression. Russell walked toward Von Hoffman and wondered if this bar had ever seen a smiling face.

"Hello," Russell said, trying to ease himself into the tiny booth. His knees knocked against the table, shaking Von Hoffman's wine glass. He contorted himself to fit, knowing if he stayed like this for long his back would begin to ache.

Russell imagined the meetup like a gangster movie. Von Hoffman was channeling Al Capone during the days of prohibition and this conversation would end in blood. The bar certainly felt like it had been a speakeasy at some point.

"How are things?" Von Hoffman asked.

Russell rolled the question around in his mind like one deciding at which angle was best to untangle a knot. Communication with Ava had been reduced to a few words. They had quickly become strangers struggling to share the same space. They were like flustered commuters, frowning and cursing, jostling along in the same subway train. Ava resisted giving up any more of her precious space. Most of Russell's belongings remained at his old apartment, but when he decided to retrieve them, a horrible heaviness stopped him. He didn't know what he would be stepping into. He'd spent the first few days at Ava's waiting by the phone. The few times it rang, the voice on the line wasn't Kat's or Leslie's.

The desire to call them, to reach out to them, grew like a deep-seated itch that left him with only one way to process: drinking.

Russell had been drunk, high, and hungover so often he was beginning to outright fear sobriety. He couldn't predict how his emotions would express themselves. In his few clearheaded moments, he heard the rumbling of a natural disaster, a slow landside, a rising tsunami overtaking him.

Ava's regard for him contained a newfound disgust, and he could only image her reaction if she woke to a grown man weeping all over her couch like a child upset by a playground tiff.

"Things are fine," Russell lied as a server materialized with an expensive bottle of wine. As he drank, Russell tried not to wince from its bitterness, but a twitching eye betrayed his resolve.

"Well, Russell," Von Hoffman said, "I'd like to make it better."

Von Hoffman smiled briefly, and Russell was puzzled, his mind drifting back to Isabelle. The last words she'd said rang out in his head.

"I was speaking with a few of my colleagues at Midwest," Von Hoffman continued, "and I was made aware of an assistant branch manager vacancy in one of our River North branches."

Russell nodded slowly and felt Ava's mighty hand of manipulation at work. Even when they were at odds, she charged ahead.

"I put in a good word for you and, as you know, my words have a lot of weight," Von Hoffman said, pausing to give Russell an opportunity to cherish this gift. "If you'd like, I could set up an interview for my future son-in-law."

Russell cleared his throat and smiled. "Yes, that would be excellent."

Heaviness rose from his feet and settled into his back as he lied.

"Speaking of which, when are you going to propose to Ava?"

"Soon. Very soon."

Von Hoffman smiled graciously and a chill tickled Russell's spine. As Von Hoffman emptied another glass of wine and opened up about his early years in the banking industry, Russell fell silent and felt all his lies pierce down on his back. Von Hoffman softened under the glow of nostalgia and spoke with tenderness about money, as if he was describing a love who managed to get away. Russell anesthetized himself with more wine and understood that Von Hoffman loved banking, loved it deeply and more passionately than Russell ever would.

Both men were buzzed as their desire for conversation waned. They politely departed the Blue Jay, looking this way and that as if to guard the secret clubhouse from interlopers. In a synchronized arc, they unfurled their umbrellas and headed north—Von Hoffman toward the nearby parking garage and Russell toward the subway. The two men ambled forward in harmonized steps as if they shared the same load. Their feet rose and fell on wet cement in tune with one another, creating a calming percussion. Even after Von Hoffman waved and turned into the parking garage, Russell kept up the rhythm they'd created. He was lulled by it as he stepped into the subway. As he saw the pinhole of light coming from the approaching train, he realized the horror of what had happened. The horror of walking in step with this man who was so foreign to him, walking in step with someone else when so recently he'd moved in step like this with Kat and Leslie.

53

Leslie surely deserved a bit of sympathy—or maybe an award—for spending the week on the phone trying to track down Isaac. Once Beck relayed the news, Leslie spent the rest of the night calling Isaac. But he still had to work and produce at least some facsimile of life. The whole week had been like trying to navigate a landmine. His worry would ebb and flow and occasionally immobilize him. At any moment, Leslie would clutch his chest like one of his patients at Saint Rose Community Living and dive into a supply closet to dial Isaac. He filled Isaac's voicemail in one night and the next morning began to call with the same frequency until he was certain Isaac had turned off his phone. He paced the apartment and swung between fury and despondency that ached in his body. Kat tried to comfort him but seemed distant and too ensnared in her own unspoken issues to really help. Beck said nothing and could be found in three positions: sitting on the couch, lying on the couch, or pulling a shift at Stratosphere.

Leslie's emotional state eventually got him sent home by a supervisor, and he threw a Hail Mary by contacting Beck for help. They wound up sharing strained silence in a cab headed south along those cracked streets that led to the derelict halfway house. As he entered the lobby, Leslie's heart jackhammered so loudly in his ears that he didn't even hear the attendant behind the glass angrily telling him to check in. Beck grabbed his arm while the attendant spoke again.

"Have you seen Isaac Ortiz?" Beck asked.

"The faggot left," the man seethed behind the glass. "You betta too."

Leslie was too stunned by Isaac's disappearance to care about the slur.

The volume of the world dropped out around him, replaced with the toneless hiss of white noise. He barely noticed Beck, furrowed in embarrassment and flapping his mouth with nothing to offer. Wide-eyed and stumbling, Leslie worked to put one foot in front of the other as they ducked back into the cab. Thanks to Beck's foresight, it was still there waiting for them.

The ride back carried a dread worse than when they had left. Beck stared back at Leslie with a dotty expression, and Leslie knew he was out of his depth. As they entered the apartment, Beck again made an attempt to say something but no words came out.

Leslie entered his room and, with one last unraveling strand of hope, dialed Isaac's phone.

This time it rang and clicked as someone picked up. Leslie felt a flux of dizziness.

"Isaac? Isaac, is that you?"

"No."

Leslie recognized the voice as Beck's former right-hand man, the lieutenant.

"Let me speak to him," Leslie demanded, then realizing he had no advantage, added kindly, "please."

A long silence ballooned between them.

"Look, I like you," the lieutenant said. "I really, really do. I heard what you were doing for Beck, and I appreciate you looking out for him. And I hope we can still be cool after this, but Isaac doesn't want to see you anymore."

Leslie shook his head, unable to grasp the words.

"He says it's over," the lieutenant said. As if he could see Leslie's face, the call ended.

Leslie was dislocated by the finality of it. It was over.

Isaac was truly gone.

Leslie sat on his bed and hung up the phone. He felt like the spray out of the back end of a wood chipper. He took to his room and stayed there for the remainder of the week, auditing the fragments left of himself. He cashed in his remaining personal days and expanded his chest with skunky marijuana to study and rearrange the shape of his life like a puzzle—the same thing he'd seen residents of Saint Rose do just before they were swallowed into the sink of senility.

The day after his call with the lieutenant, Leslie grabbed his pipe and emerged from the bedroom, dislocated. Beck was lacing up his boots for another shift at Stratosphere.

"Your hair looks fucking horrible," Leslie said, burning weed in a bowl and heaving off the smoke.

Beck, a witness to yesterday, stared back him with kind eyes. "I'm too busy trying to keep from being homeless to worry about it."

"You just look so sad," Leslie said, passing the bowl and a lighter to Beck.

Leslie wasn't sure if Beck understood how awful he looked or if he was being sympathetic because he'd been in the first seat on Leslie's recent trip to hell. Beck—who strangely enough was a considerate houseguest under the circumstances—started to help out with the household chores and when he returned from a late night shift at Stratosphere did it soundlessly.

Leslie, overtaken by a wave of inspiration, stood over Beck. He raised his hand and placed it onto the greasy, compounded mess. Beck closed his eyes and let out a soft sigh underneath his touch. Leslie worked his fingers deeper into his scalp and Beck's shoulders slumped.

"We need to do something about this," Leslie said, threading his fingers in Beck's hair.

"What?"

"Cut it off."

Leslie couldn't mend what had happened between him and Isaac, and he should have seen it coming. He thought about Russell's words during their fight outside the bar. A part of him wanted to call Russell and tell him he was right. But instead he turned his attention back to Beck.

Considering a haircut, Beck's eyes widened in horror and he pulled back from Leslie. He reached up to cradle his follicles, but once he did, he nodded in consent. The two moved like executioners as Beck brought a stool into the bathroom, pulled off his shirt, and dropped down. Leslie met him armed with scissors and his electric trimmer. Leslie's first snip made every muscle in Beck's upper body swell, too tense to submit. Leslie continued to cut, hair piling at their feet, trying to exhume something from the broken and bleached mop. He smoothed out the final mess with the trimmer and underneath the mechanical growl emerged a buzz cut the color of hot cinder and autumn leaves.

Leslie clicked off his device and stood back, adjusting to the stranger before him. Beck touched his head uncertainly and looked back at Leslie with fear. Snipped hair fell from his shoulders as he stood and turned to the mirror. In silence, they examined this exposed and hairless Samson. He brushed off his broad shoulders and translucent freckled skin, breathing in this startling vulnerability and frail humanness.

Moved by Beck's kindness, Leslie felt more pieces of himself reassemble. As he gazed at the beauty of the frightened Irish man touching his face as if it were new, Leslie gained clarity. The white noise finally let up and he started to process. In that brief stillness, he recognized a familiar feeling. A simple if-this-is-true-then-so-is-this equation. It was a coldness in his fingertips and toes that defied logic and rooted itself to the remnants of Leslie's spirituality, still banging around inside him. This tickling feeling of darkness was the same thing he felt as the old woman took her last breath at Saint Rose. It was the same sense of nausea he felt when he woke up from nightmares of the semitruck tire exploding and tilting to roll with the force of a wrecking ball over his mother's car.

It was death. It felt close.

He knew Isaac was going to die.

Beck turned back to Leslie and smiled.

Leslie couldn't smile back.

He knew soon this clarity would end. And he would have to find some logical explanation for this feeling. Maybe it was his broken heart with the pieces put together wrong. It could have been that Beck was so handsome—bare chest, muscles and flesh—and Isaac had stopped looking like that long ago.

54

Someone had picked and pulled the tiny thread that unwound the world around Kat. Despite his nature, Kat was uncomfortable with Beck on the couch for so long. She knew his stay would be temporary but still found herself drowning in her own well of sympathy. Beck was unanchored and without a home, which echoed her childhood, so she forced her mouth closed as he turned the couch into his station.

Leslie, on the other hand, walked around shell-shocked about Isaac, useless to anyone including himself. He attempted to appear normal and to have conversations with Kat, but his words twanged out like notes from an instrument wound too tightly.

No one spoke about the gaping cavern left by Russell. The kitchen sink didn't hold his dirty dishes, the bathroom was free from his smell, and the apartment overall was less cluttered, even with Beck posted on the couch. Russell's bedroom door remained closed as if it were a quarantined area. His PlayStation gathered dust while his mail piled up on the kitchen counter. His leftovers sprouted hair and green fuzz. Kat thought about throwing out the rotting food but determined the act would confirm Russell wasn't coming back. Before work, she walked up to his door as if he was behind it. She heard a phantom noise in his room that caused her heart to jolt but quickly realized it was her imagination and grief slammed her off her feet.

He wouldn't be coming out of that room, lumbering around in his oafish way, album in hand to play on her garbage record player. He wouldn't provide any distraction from the outpouring sadness she had over Jacob or her growing concern for Leslie. His ghost commuted with her that afternoon, through the underground tunnels of trains. Emotionally sedated, she shuffled memories of Russell like a deck of cards. Kat considered what he would say if she told him about Jacob and the miscarriage. She wondered why she hadn't told him when it happened.

The crackling speaker pulled her out of her daydreams and she realized she'd missed the stop for Belle Journee. Cursing herself, she rushed out of the train at the following stop, shifted her camera equipment to her other arm, and pushed through the compact stairway and onto the street. She glanced at her phone's clock and realized she could make it if she hurried. She plowed through a red light and ignored the cars that responded with punitive honks.

She was on her way to photograph a small Lincoln Park imports store. A woman from the store had called the Belle Journee offices a few days prior, explaining the photos would be used for advertising in a Chicago-based art magazine. Kat hadn't heard of the imports store, but someone there had heard of—and specifically requested—her. Searching online, Kat determined the business was pretentious, the kind of store that priced its items three times more than their worth. The website, in need of a severe overhaul, featured beaded jewelry, Buddha statues, and artisanal, organic potpourri.

Today's shoot included test shots and getting a feel for the owner's artistic direction. This customarily took place at the company's sleek downtown location, surround by shinier equipment and a dazzling view of the city. Even after all this time, Kat still snuck a whimsical glance off into the distance over the roofs of nearby skyscrapers.

She rushed through the oscillating doors, gripped her camera to keep it from banging against the glass, and hurried up to a series of elevators. Her stomach flipped as the elevator shot through the building to Belle Journee's offices. Once there, she checked the clock to know she'd made it on time and exchange brief smiles with the receptionist. Photographers and art directors manned computers like they were crewmembers at battle stations, and Kat pushed into the studio at the rear of the office to turn on umbrella lights, computers, and to gather up memory cards.

"Hello?"

Kat turned from her work toward the door to see a

beautiful Indian woman, hiding behind a guarded smile.

"Hey, I'm Kat."

"I'm Nita."

"Cool, I'm one of the photographers you'll be working with today."

The woman was weighed down by a few bags from her store, so Kat hurried to help her set them on a nearby table. The woman's beauty compounded with proximity. Jet black hair rounded her shoulders in thick curls and her skin was the color of a new penny. Her shrewd hazel eyes scanned the set before focusing on Kat.

"Today I'm going to do some test shots of you and some of the merchandise you brought," Kat began. "The photographer who will be handling it should be in shortly."

Nita shared another reserved smile and began sorting through her bags, pulling out organic candles and tribal brass jewelry.

"Don't worry about that," Kat said. "We'll have one of our interns help. If you could, I'd like to take some pictures of you."

Nita grimaced with uncertainty as Kat directed her in front of her camera and the white backdrop. Nita stood in a sleek grey wrap dress adorned with the jewelry from her store. Her soft brown skin was luminous underneath the umbrella lights. She hunched her shoulders and pulled a fearful smile over her face.

"Nice dress," Kat said, trying to loosen her up before she began a flickering round of shots.

"Calvin Klein," Nita said back.

"A successful, smart, businesswoman with a good eye," Kat said, watching Nita's shoulders recline.

Kat pulled the camera back from her face and scanned

over the pictures on the tiny Nokia screen. She knew they were as stunning as the woman in front of her. They would need little editing.

"Hope you don't mind me saying this," Kat said, "but you're a knockout, Nita."

Nita nodded appreciatively and asked, "Am I done?"

"Uh, yeah," Kat said, and watched Nita return to her bag of merchandise.

An intern emerged from the offices and into the studio to help organize the fair-trade beaded jewelry into decorative bowls.

"Your store just reopened?" Kat asked, joining them at the sorting table.

"I'm getting more serious about it," Nita said. "Up until now, I've been treating it like a hobby."

"If you don't bet on yourself, no one will."

"Yeah, something like that."

Nita opened a bag of potpourri, which released a burning saccharine stench as she dumped it into a bowl. The familiar smells of stringent perfumes and dried petals collided in Kat's nasal cavity and stung her throat. She gave it another cautious whiff, trying to remember where she'd smelled it before. Realizing where, her eyes widened and she quickly glanced at Nita's discerning face.

"Do you like this smell?" Nita asked as the stinging continued to pinprick Kat's throat.

"Yeah," Kat lied, her heart hammering in her chest cage as if it were trying to be set free.

"I made this batch for myself," Nita said. "It'll be in my store this fall."

Kat's head felt like it was submerged under water.

The intern left the room to retrieve the lead photographer

and Kat stepped in to join him.

Before Kat could escape, Nita called back, "Wait."

Kat smiled through her numb face. Her bladder felt as if it would give out before this elegant, suddenly frightening, woman. The woman seemed older and wiser in a way Kat wondered if she could ever be.

"Yes?" Kat smiled.

The woman walked over, dug deep into one of the bags she brought, and placed several silver bracelets on the table. The bracelets looked cheap and thin next to the other merchandise Nita had brought, simply because the bracelets didn't belong to her. They belonged to Kat. She had left them in the master bathroom of Nita's home.

The smell of potpourri was so dense Kat's eyes began to water. In the blur, she was back in Nita's home. Back in the bed she shared with her husband. Kat's stomach rolled so hard she wondered if she would ever be able to eat again. She looked back in the room, crumbling with her own fear. There was Jacob's wife, staring at her with a sad curiosity.

"I'm going to have to take my store more seriously now," Nita began. "I'm going to have so much free time after leaving my husband."

Kat shook her head and tried to open her mouth to speak.

"Please don't try to deny it," Nita said. "I know you're having an affair with my husband. That, in part, is why I'm here."

All of Kat's muscles locked as Nita stepped closer, a few inches from her face. She was so beautiful and so controlled. Kat had no idea what the woman would do. Kat couldn't look at her and instead turned her gaze to her feet.

"I thought he was done cheating on me," she said. "You

know there was another woman. You weren't the first one. He beat her up."

Kat's jaw tightened, and she stifled a sob.

"Did he hit you?" Nita spat, her voice quivering.

Kat thought about Jacob's fist and the brutality of his eyes. Her mouth was suddenly dry. Jacob had done this before. He hit women. Tears welled up in her eyes.

"I hoped he did hit you," Nita said. "I don't know what type of woman that makes me."

Kat blinked back the tears and opened her mouth to speak. She searched for words, but nothing came up. There was nothing she could say.

"I just had to see you," Nita said softly.

Kat stepped, unsteadied by the burning, volatile glare from Jacob's wife. She rammed into the photographer and the intern in the doorway. She yelped, almost dropping her camera, while her composure shattered. She handed the annoyed photographer her camera and said, "The test shots are great. Excuse me, I'm feeling a little sick."

With one more glance at Nita's hard glare, she fled the room and its smothering fog of potpourri.

55

Russell walked around, disembodied after his surrender to Von Hoffman. Ava had been considerably kinder to him. Once he returned from Blue Jay and told her about the conversation he had with her father, she disrobed, pulled off her blouse, and released her breasts before him. Russell, bewildered and desperate, plunged into her. That night he held her tightly and hoped that soon the world she had constructed around him would feel right.

Days later, in a grey Italian suit Ava had gotten with the enlisted aid of the boutique owner she worked for, Russell sat in a cold, sterile office of Midwest Regional Bank. The office belonged to the friendly yet smug regional manager around Von Hoffman's age who entered ten minutes after their interview was supposed to begin. He spoke briefly about Russell's history with the company but let his golf game with Von Hoffman dominate the conversation. After twenty minutes of this, Russell realized the interview was merely a formality. All it took was Von Hoffman passing Russell's name on the lush golf courses of White Oak Country Club to secure the job. Also, Russell promised the manger a future game of golf.

He did even know how to play golf.

He smiled, facilitated the appropriate pleasantries, and was told the offer letter would be in his inbox later that day. He had everything he wanted. Ava and the permission to marry her. A new job that would allow him to get a new car.

That afternoon he read and reread the offer letter. He was on the verge of that American dream he believed he should have. He was in reach of the promise he had seen in Ava's eyes the first night he met her. She had given him all of it. She hadn't been trying to set up residence in his sordid world amongst the irreverent, drunken, and stoned. Instead, she'd been trying to pull him out of it. A soft few nudges here and there, a few whispers at the right times, and they were positioned to have it. This was what he wanted. This was who he was now. He could have that house, the yard, the good job, maybe even kids in the future.

This was no act of contrivance. This wasn't a sad painting of a stoned artist. He was a businessman, confirmed by the great knight, Hayes Von Hoffman. Despite how silly, how uncomfortably ill-fitting this all seemed on Russell's body, he could walk in it. He could grow into it. He *would* grow into it.

So why did it feel so abnormal? Why did he feel like a monstrous circus attraction waiting to be gawked at? Why did the gravity around his body seem heavier? Why were his muscles burdened?

After work, he changed out of the suit into an equally uncomfortable tuxedo. Ava met him at the office, gleaming with a smile and a new dress from her boutique. Von Hoffman had invited them to take his place at a charity event hosted by Midwest Regional Bank. In the town car on their way to a sleek skyscraper, Russell asked what the charity night was for. Ava shrugged and said the details didn't matter. Of course the details didn't matter. He was yielding to her plan for their lives. He didn't have to ask questions anymore. He could keep his mouth closed and let Ava take care of everything.

They strolled into a massive cultural center at the base of a dazzling lakeside skyscraper. Rows and rows of round tables were draped with white tablecloths overlooking a small stage and podium. High on the arched ceilings, crystal chandeliers dripped with red light and cast the room in the color of dusk. Ava chirped happily about something that Russell didn't have the means to listen to. They walked through the local royalty of capitalists, financiers, industrialists, and B-list celebrities clad in couture gowns and pressed tuxedos. The venue buzzed with a reserved but palpable excitement. A few photographers snapped pictures around the venue.

Russell followed Ava as they searched for their table. Ava walked with ease and he knew this wasn't her first fundraiser. This was her world. Russell felt so alien. Was he a citizen of her world? He had all the trappings now. He kept tight-lipped as they found their table in the middle of the room. He was afraid that someone would see him as he saw himself—a circus freak in a tuxedo.

Ava smirked as she caught him adjusting his bowtie.

"You look fantastic," she said. "Now all we have to do is shave your beard."

Russell had grown a beard most of his life. These days he groomed it, but his beard had always been a matted tribute to his puberty. Hadn't Ava called it handsome? He recalled the pleasure of putting his chin on her head and strands of her hair getting tangled in his beard. No, that wasn't quite right. Then who was that? Russell wished he had a mirror. If he could see himself, maybe he could get a grip on tonight.

A shiver moved through him when he realized it had been Kat who liked his beard. A waiter in a white tuxedo came by and Russell quickly ordered a whiskey on the rocks. His mind drifted on holding Kat's tiny frame and how her sweet smell sustained itself through his own musk.

"Please don't get drunk," Ava whispered with a tight smile.

Russell fought not to roll his eyes and simply nodded. He sipped from his whiskey through clenched teeth. A young fair-haired woman and another tuxedoed man joined them at the table. The woman's eyes gleamed with recognition as she locked eyes with Russell and then Ava.

"Hello," Ava said, getting up to embrace her friend. They hugged quickly and then parted to inspect each other affectionately.

"You've lost weight?" Ava asked, her voice an octave too high.

"Hot yoga," the woman said, matching Ava's shrill. "Your haircut is *so* chic."

"Thanks," Ava said, touching her hair, feigning modesty.

"You can always pull off edgy looks." Realizing they weren't alone, she pulled the man who had been behind her to her side.

"Good to see you again, Ava," he said with a hug.

Ava turned to Russell and all their gazes fell upon him. He felt the first drops of sweat brush along the arch of his back.

Ava slipped into formality and introduced them to Russell. He was so nervous he didn't hear their names when Ava said them and stood up from the table to shake their hands with sweaty palms. They all sat at the table and another waiter came by to get the couple's drink order. Russell emptied his whiskey as if it were a well of strength. The waiter returned with a bottle of champagne and quickly filled the glasses.

The couple, married a little over a year ago, were old friends of the Von Hoffman family. They had recently relocated to New York. They were the same ages as Ava and Russell, and Russell began to wonder if this was purposely set up by Von Hoffman. Young, beautiful, and successful, the couple seemed set out in front of them like a measure for his future. He turned to Ava, and she glowed with a bright smile. Russell hadn't seen her this happy in weeks.

"We should raise a toast," the man offered.

"Sounds great," his wife agreed, lifting her flute to the air.

"To a good cause and good food," the man said as the glasses joined in cheerful chime.

"It better be good food at nine hundred dollars a plate," the woman said, as her husband and Ava laughed.

Ava and the woman led the small conversation as the waiter came to gather more orders.

"What is the charity for?" Russell asked again.

He felt the daggers of Ava's embarrassed glower between sips of champagne. There was an exchange of critical glances between the husband and wife. They smiled at him in sympathy before the conversation picked up its pace again. The woman spoke of her last years of residency in the oncology department of a Manhattan hospital while the husband made a failed attempt to temper his arrogance by recanting his most compelling cases as a corporate lawyer. Russell spent most of the conversation trying to ignore the hubris spilling across the table.

"So what do you do?"

"I'm a personal banker at Midwest," Russell said.

"He's about to become assistant branch manager," Ava said quickly. "My father's mentoring him."

"Yeah," Russell said meekly.

No one said anything. The couple nodded as if this was an acceptable vocation—an easy gesture of their acceptance and an induction into their world.

Russell felt a pang of fear at this and found himself saying proudly, "I used to be an artist. A painter."

This left the couple puzzled in silence and Ava flinched.

"Thank God you stopped that," Ava said with a nervous laugh.

This prompted the couple to burst in haughty guffaws.

Sweat trickled along Russell's back, and he was certain underneath the room's judgmental gaze his fear was visible through his tuxedo.

56

Beck opened the window to let in the temperate spring breeze just as Leslie made his way back to the apartment after work. Beck turned to him, still cheery from the novelty of his haircut.

"Hey," Beck said. "There's dinner in the microwave."

Leslie snorted in disbelief as he passed through the apartment, observing the new gleam of the hardwood floors and the trim along the walls. The air within the apartment had the light scent of lemon wood polish and the sweetness of surface cleaner. Leslie stepped onto the kitchen's vinyl floor, which had been scrubbed with a zeal never before seen from a roommate. The organized cupboards and counters were also benefactors of this eagerness.

Despite Leslie's past exasperation, this gesture left him with a strange gratitude for Beck, who joined him in the kitchen. "You'd be surprised what you can pick up watching cleaning ladies."

"You did this?"

"It's my day off," Beck said, "and I just wanted to thank you for letting me stay."

"You're creeping me out acting like a human being."

"I ordered pizza," Beck said. "Leave some for Kat when she gets back from work."

They ate pizza in the living room accompanied by the TV and a formless spring breeze. This breeze was heavy with the smells of wet earth, Northern Catalpas, and huckleberry blossoms erupting along the cutouts in the sidewalk. Stark white and soft pink flowers subdued the harsh breath of the city caught in sewage drains, exhaled from rooftop ducts, perspiring within dumpsters, and coughed from exhaust pipes.

Leslie tried to meet the buoyancy of warm weather and Beck's kindness, but at home, forcing down pizza and away from the predictable, measured demands of work, grief found him.

Beck noticed Leslie's sour face and said, "Let's do something tonight."

"Drinks at Stratosphere?"

"No," Beck said at once. "It's my day off and I can't believe I'm saying this, but Stratosphere is the last place I want to be."

"Peppermint?"

"And risk running into my old friends and Isaac?"

Leslie slumped into the couch at the thought of this and swallowed a wad of pizza.

"You're single now," Beck said, "and we're going to celebrate that."

"By finding a building to dive off?"

"By going to Boystown."

Leslie wasn't quite sure what made him eventually relent to Beck, but he was soon dressed and in a cab headed east through the city. Anxious stillness detained the two of them on the ride toward the Lakeview neighborhood. Leslie alternated between truly enjoying Beck's company and questioning its authenticity. After Isaac's breakup and Russell's exit, had he gone from bad to worse with Beck? Could he even trust him, with his boundless disregard for people and his unapologetic narcissism? A few weeks ago, he'd blamed Beck for Isaac's feckless dismount into addiction.

Beck was climbing out of the pit dug by his own making and would probably say or do anything to win favor until he was in the position to regain his social throne. He would clean the house and be attentive—ultimately, what choice did he have?

The cab dropped them onto the dense streets of

Boystown, known locally as a village within a neighborhood. Lakeview and Boystown fell upon each other like puzzle pieces with Boystown heralded by prominent rainbow pylons. Within these few blocks, surrounded by businesses and compact, overpriced apartments, the various delegates of the LGBT community heaped upon each other. They drank and mingled with audacity along a strip of palpitating bars that had survived years of police raids and both righteous and political scorn. In direct contradiction to the far right, these bars and, consequently, the surrounding neighborhood became a reflection, chic and trendy, drawing bug-eyed tourists and dreaded bachelorette parties. Beneath the surface, a fervid sexual frustration asserted itself in the dark bars, this time from men who spent their days concealing their desires to accommodate the heteronormative world.

For Leslie, this scene lost its shimmer a while ago. He'd rather stay in his neighborhood, having fun with his drunken social circle. To the queer native of Lakeview, Leslie may have come off as self-hating, but he found his enclave within his friends. Quite frankly, he'd rather save the cab fare and the trip across the river.

Leslie's insides mangled at the soft, easy smile swelling on Beck's face. He remained as beautiful as he'd been when Leslie took the clippers to his head. Had the shears excised the source of his hostility, like Delilah taking her razor to Samson's mane?

Leslie concluded he was lonelier than he thought as he followed Beck toward the booming cadence of the nearest bar. Beck glanced back and grinned, helping Leslie's skepticism find its ire and froth over in a fever pitch.

A few yards away from the bar, Leslie asked, "Why are you doing this?"

"What are you talking about?" Beck replied, moving toward Leslie, who stepped back and kept the distance between them. They drew away from foot traffic and closer to a nearby restaurant.

"All this," Leslie said, gesturing rashly only to have Beck gape at him with an open mouth. "I'm not like Kat. I haven't forgotten how much of an asshole you are."

Beck grunted. "*I'm* an asshole? What about you? You've done nothing but judge me and all I ever tried to do was be your friend."

The heat of Leslie's indignation started to taper off and plummet. There was a numbness in his limbs, and his vision hazed behind a veil of tears. Beck had been nothing but fair to him. He had journeyed with him to Isaac's apartment. Beck had even tried to take care of him when he found out his mother died. Leslie was so broken he couldn't see what was in front of him.

Beck was in front of him again. Like he had been many nights, offering up a joke, comfort, even a target to hate if need be.

"What's wrong with you?" Beck asked.

"Everything," Leslie said as the straps of his composure popped one by one.

"Isaac doesn't care about you and he hasn't for a long time. He never wanted to go to rehab, and I'm so sorry. And I, fuck... I feel responsible about it, too. On top of that, I know you miss Russell. He'll come back; you guys are like brothers. I know, I watched you guys for years. You are real friends to each other. That why I'm always hanging around and following you guys." Beck hesitated at his own words. "Sound creepy?"

"Yes, it does," Leslie said, sniffing.

"I see things in people," Beck continued. "I see how you guys are with each other. And I see you. I see how badly you're hurting. Hurting all the time. I just want to make it stop."

Beck stepped closer. His was so earnest that Leslie didn't step back. Beck smiled and his face softened, still moving closer. They stood nose to nose, encompassing one another's vision.

Stripped from his fake orange tan and bleached hair, Leslie saw Beck for the first time in startling brilliance. And when Beck kissed him gently, underneath the lambent streetlight, he forgot why he'd felt anxious.

57

Kat felt quite near death when she made it through the door and was relieved to find the apartment empty and clean. Having nothing more to give, she dragged her bags into her room and crumbled onto the bed.

Her body rang from Nita's scorn. The face of this beautiful and shrewd woman seared deeply into Kat's memory. It was a gash on Kat's flesh that would heal into a grotesque scar, another unseemly keepsake of the affair.

Kat's counterfeit sickness helped her retreat from Belle Journee, and in her departure from the building, she expected Nita to follow and demand an explanation. This fear was bottomless in Kat, as her feet blurred underneath her and the people along the sidewalk ogled the panicked woman surging forward. Their eyes needled her as if they knew she had been sleeping with a married man. The accusatory faces blowing past her forged one admonishing glower, shaking its collective head and clucking in united tongues at Kat.

She ran, ignited for blocks, her bag thrashing against pedestrians and her body walloping into shoulders. She was assaulted by a roar of swears. Her muscles wrenched in sharp protest. She kneeled over, rasping for air. Her legs, no longer sturdy, trembled like sprigs. Her weak stems almost brought her face-forward on the pavement. She wanted desperately to migrate, to keep running, but her muscles hindered her.

Everything she had been trying to escape from hit her in a brutal force. She tripped back into the nearby alley, finding brief asylum, while Jacob's misbegotten kisses began to haunt her. The memory of cramps and the thick slime of dark blood oozing down her leg found her. Phantom children moved along dark playgrounds and cried out at her.

No child would ever be hers.

The certainty of that was numbing. No longer panicked, merely shell-shocked, she pushed herself away from the wall. Blank and slack-jawed, she wandered the uneven sidewalks for miles. Kat milled behind an unremitting flock of people, whose bobbing heads rippled like wavelets on Lake Michigan. She shuffled forward, forming trails between buildings and city blocks as if seeking the exit to a maze. She walked until the numbness waned and her feet ached, until the sun rolled over and its shadows repositioned themselves from west to east.

In her bedroom, Kat lay flat-faced on the bed and slipped her shoes off. Dangling over the edge of the bed, her feet pulsed. She closed her eyes, but the pain in her feet kept her lucid. She listened to the susurration of an empty apartment—a refrigerator's low strum, the hum of her laptop on the nightstand, the evening's exhalation along the window, and the perpetual undertone of traffic. Kat nearly induced sleep when the jangle of keys on the front door's handle flipped her eyes open. She grumbled in protest, as tepid, yet heavy footsteps traversed over the floorboards. Beck or Leslie must have come home.

"Anyone here?"

It was Russell's voice calling out in the living room.

Kat's heart darted into her throat, and the numbness that had distressed her was crushed. She stepped out and moved past the hallway where Russell froze in front of the door to his bedroom.

In a crisp tuxedo, he tensed, startled like a thief exposed in the middle of a heist. Upon seeing her, his body allayed. Beneath his beard his lips cautiously upturned into a smile.

The apartment's hush, the same that had almost lulled Kat to sleep, unfolded between them. Russell stared back at her, his smile unflinching.

He held up one finger to excuse himself and reappeared from his room with something Kat couldn't quite see. He silently shuffled toward the living room, as if afraid to spoil the sanctity of this encounter.

Kat joined him in the living room to see him standing in front of her record player. The subdued crackle of vinyl abolished the silence, followed by the twang of a guitar and the haunted cry of a keyboard. With his back to her, it was almost as if The Cure's "Lovesong" opened up from within Russell's looming body. He turned to face her with that wary, radiant smile.

He stretched out his hand. In the tuxedo, he looked handsome enough to be the topper of a wedding cake. Kat felt like she'd conjured him, ready to comfort her, his face soft and reassuring. She reached out for him, but when their fingertips touched, she pulled back like she'd been burned.

She choked up.

"What are you doing?" she asked.

"What do you mean?"

Kat rushed to the record player. She ripped the needle from the vinyl and the speakers screeched in a piercing death cry before returning to rest.

"I just came from some dumb fundraiser with Ava," Russell said. "I needed some things."

"You can't just come in here and dance with me."

"You looked... sad."

"Do you want to know why I'm sad?" she asked, tapping her foot to fuel her anger.

Russell was dumbstruck.

"I was pregnant with Jacob's baby and he's a married man."

"What?"

"Then I miscarried because apparently my womb isn't fit for habitation."

Russell tried to comfort her, and Kat pushed him back.

"And I stayed with him..."

"Why?" Russell asked, making another attempt to enclose Kat in a hug.

She shoved him back harder. "Because I didn't hurt when I was with him."

Russell, with his knees bent, absorbed Kat's blows and heaped her into his arms.

"It hurts when you're with me," Kat said. "You shouldn't be here."

"I wanted to see you," Russell said, his words strangled and fragile.

Kat curled and wrenched until she dislodged from him. Russell stumbled back slowly, wilting in front of her.

"You tell that to Ava."

Russell glanced away, his face flushed. His head shook rapidly, as if he was convulsing.

"Before you give her that ugly ring, you tell her about *this*. About us. About how you look at me and hold me. Because I'll be damned before I have another woman look at me like I'm a whore."

"We haven't done anything."

Kat charged into her bedroom and collected her purse. With a manic pace, she headed toward the door. At the threshold, she turned around and faced him.

"I'm broken. Completely. And I love you. You are my family. I loved you when you were the contrived artist. When you were at your best. But now look at you. Who are you? Leslie was right when he called you a coward."

Kat swallowed hard and raised her chin. She opened the door and the breeze almost forced her back in.

"I can't speak for Leslie, but I don't want you here," she said. "Pack up your shit and leave the keys."

She stepped back onto the street, her feet still crippled with ache.

58

Russell was being watched as he left the apartment, but he was too mournful to notice. In the canopy of shadows, a pair of eyes watched him lock the door while counterbalancing a box and a tied-off garbage bag. Twitching in eagerness, these eyes lurked in the gloom across the street between buildings. Russell didn't notice the still breath from across the street as he moved down the stairs and to his car. His glum shuffle was enough to bring an impatient man to a state of madness. The apartment had already been under surveillance for at least four days. Tonight it demanded the patience of three hours now, standing in the cool darkness and pacing the block casually to avert suspicion. With the coming and going of four people, entering the apartment undetected had proven nearly impossible.

Russell opened his Subaru's creaking rear door and chucked the box and bag inside. He leaned against the door and gazed down, then reached inside his tuxedo jacket for a cigarette.

How long was he going to wait out there? How much longer before someone else comes back to the apartment? Leslie and Beck had left earlier, dressed for a night out. It would be hours before they returned. Kat, on the other hand, seemed as though she could return any moment.

Reexamination of the apartment proved that all the lights were off and it was indeed empty—if only Russell would just get in his car and drive away.

Russell lit the cigarette and from the same pocket collected his phone. He took one long drag before he dialed. His body appeared tense with reluctance.

"Hey," he said, his voice carrying over the street into stretches of darkness.

"Yeah, I know, just dealing with some things at the apartment... I couldn't get everything, but I managed to pack it all... Yeah, yeah, I know... The movers are going to come by tomorrow, I just need you to supervise. It's not a good idea for me to be at the apartment... Thank you, Ava. See you at home."

Finally, he was done. After one last puff of his cigarette, his flick sent it sailing into the air, arching across the street, and falling into the shadows below. The cigarette butt rolled further into the darkness and its orange speck of light was compressed under an anonymous foot.

Russell paused for a moment, like he could sense it, and peered into blackness between apartment buildings. He shrugged to himself and descended into his car without much struggle, in spite of looking like a giant squeezing into a shoebox. The car coughed in agony, burped smoke, and reeled down the street.

Isaac vented a sigh.

In the tedium spent prowling outside this apartment, his sanity suffered. If he didn't make the most out this chance, he wouldn't endure waiting for another.

He darted across the street and behind the apartment, examining the bisecting knotted telephone wirework overhead. Strung up by their laces, like dead hunting game, was a bloated pair of gym shoes. Using them as a marker, he kneeled down along the trashcans. The swell of funk met him and, to prevent gagging, he covered his nose and mouth with his shirtsleeve.

Isaac knew Beck's presence in the apartment meant his coke and pills were there. Isaac had casually reported this to the lieutenant, who suggested Isaac obtain the stash as compensation. Since leaving the halfway house, Isaac found himself curled up on the floor of the lieutenant's tiny apartment.

By all accounts, Isaac hadn't been bothered by this move. He felt almost normal living on the lieutenant's floor and freewheeling the wild highs of whatever leftover pills were passed his way. He felt rapturous.

The lieutenant, of course, didn't mind. He was more preoccupied with his sudden social ascension. But in a span of days, the coke ran out and then the pills. The group deteriorated into a pack of rabid, feral dogs snapping at each other and using barbed insults to draw blood. In a cryptic tone, as if entrusting him with a matter of national security, the lieutenant sent Isaac on this pursuit.

Isaac suspected Beck wouldn't be doing too much coke now that he had finally maneuvered his way into Leslie, Kat, and Russell's apartment. It was common knowledge that they were an easier breed of partiers.

Seated on a cracked leather recliner, the new king on his throne, the lieutenant recounted the many times Beck stared at Leslie, Kat, and Russell. He talked about how Beck longed to be friends with them and mentioned his attraction to Leslie. The lieutenant made lines with the edge of a straight razor and smiled wildly, his teeth almost as sharp as the blade. He snorted the last grams of coke and delighted in Isaac's squirming.

After vigorous digging, Isaac unearthed the key to the apartment from under a cement block. He rounded the house and struggled with the lock, twisting it forcefully. He finally took a breath and tried a gentle turn, and the door swung open. Isaac quickly slipped through the door and, rather than dare to turn on a light, lit his way with his phone's flashlight. At the end of the couch sat Beck's small traveler's suitcase.

Isaac quickly turned the suitcase down on the floor and unzipped it. He pillaged through balled up T-shirts, underwear, and jeans. Coming up empty, he growled in frustration and searched through the smaller pockets in the front of the suitcase to discover a handful of tightly rolled white socks. Unlike the rest of the suitcase's belongings, the socks were placed within the pocket neatly and in ordered rows. He angled the light of his phone over the socks and noticed something protruding from them.

He nearly cried out in victory as he pulled out tiny baggies from the necks of the socks. He giggled at his find and wished he could brag about his sleuthing skills. He knew if he was seen on the street hugging an armload of socks he'd raise eyebrows, so he tiptoed into the kitchen and peered under the sink. As always, there were grocery bags waiting to be reused.

Dating Leslie, he'd spent many days and nights in the apartment, dealing with the constant and ultimately tiresome drama between its roommates. In their endless bickering, yelling, and laughing, Isaac felt he needed to be high in order to tolerate them. He didn't grasp Beck's desire to want to be in this apartment with them.

But his experience did help him locate things. He knew where to find their collective weed: in the Mason jar behind the pasta in the kitchen cupboard. He stepped into Kat's room and saw the coffee can where she placed her tip money. He hesitated. No one would call the police over stolen drugs, but a person would call over stolen money.

He looked into the can and saw a Ziploc bag filled with tiny yellow Oxy pills.

He smiled and placed the bag in his pocket. He would share the rest of the drugs with everyone else, but he would keep the pills to himself.

59

The night of the gala had been awkward at best—Russell had been cagey during the entire fundraiser, twisting his napkin in his lap all night. When he and Ava made it back to her apartment, she'd been relieved when he left to retrieve some belongings from his old apartment. The tension between them had reached a peak. Something at the gala had penetrated Russell's aloofness.

The next morning, Ava received a call from Mrs. Von Hoffman III.

"Ava, sweetie," Mrs. Von Hoffman III began, "I'd like us to have lunch."

Ava paced her apartment, unsure of why she'd answered in the first place. "I have plans for lunch," she lied, convinced by the following silence that Mrs. Von Hoffman III could detect the fabrication. Ava, so busy with distracting herself, couldn't be bothered by Mrs. Von Hoffman III's seasonal attempts at bonding.

Every three months the woman would call and try to force herself on Ava. Most times Ava could elude her, but the woman's persistence never wavered, and Ava had suffered through meals at all times of the day. She'd even withstood live theater. Mrs. Von Hoffman III was impervious to Ava's excuses, scowls, and sighs.

"If you're up, let's do breakfast," she said, undeterred. "I'm shopping in the neighborhood, so it'll be nothing to drop by."

Ava's mouth pinched into a snarl. "Sure. Why not?"

"Wonderful, darling. See you in fifteen minutes."

A quarter of an hour later, Mrs. Von Hoffman III met Ava in the lobby of her apartment. They met in a limp hug, pretending they were happy to see each other. Mrs. Von Hoffman linked her arm with Ava's and escorted her out the door into the early golden light. They walked easily along the sidewalk, veering here and there to avoid the frenzied commuters, on their way to an organic café a few blocks down the street. They departed the rumble outside and, to the cheerful chime of the doorbell, entered the café.

The open café faced east and took in all the brightness of the morning. The women circled the café until agreeing on a table near the windows. The swinging shadows of commuters danced on their faces while a kind waiter greeted them with menus.

Mrs. Von Hoffman III planned to stay in the city until later in the afternoon, when Ava's father would conclude his work downtown and return with her to the suburbs.

Ava knew by her stepmother's rheumy eyes that she'd taken the first of her many painkillers for the day. There was a reckless easiness about her, a mood Ava particularly hated. Her stepmother could say anything like this, and most likely she would.

"Russell is interesting," Mrs. Von Hoffman III began in a detached tone.

Ava clutched her knees under the table and peered out the window at the commuters, wishing she could be anywhere but here. She knew what Mrs. Von Hoffman was going to say. She traveled the predictable path of this conversation and knew better than to fight the woman. To confront her audacity would cause more trouble than it was worth. She could endure one meal.

"Frankly, he's better than your last boyfriend," Mrs. Von Hoffman III continued, "but under the circumstances, any man would be."

Ava swallowed in relief as the waiter approached the table, coffee in hand, and took an order for an egg-white omelet from free-range chickens and gluten-free pancakes topped with local, farm-grown fruit. Mrs. Von Hoffman III also ordered a mimosa, because nothing tastes better with painkillers than a glass of champagne.

"Russell is really caring," Ava said.

"He seems..." Mrs. Von Hoffman III paused and furrowed her brow in rumination, "...*tolerant.*"

"What do you mean?" Ava grabbed the coffee to give her nervous hands a task.

"Tolerance and love are two different things," Mrs. Von Hoffman III said as the waiter arrived with her mimosa. With one hand she reached for the glass, the other for Ava's hand.

"We're good together," Ava said, swallowing her annoyance.

"I'm not your mother and will never try to be. I know we aren't friends. But I know you, Ava," Mrs. Von Hoffman III said. "A relationship isn't hiring a person to fill a position at a company. It's about love. And although you make it clear you don't like me, I believe you deserve to be loved."

Mrs. Von Hoffman III's face suddenly lost its objectivity. Her contemplation gave way to concern, lit by the dazzling morning light and intensified by the rolling shadows. Ava remembered that expression from a year ago, when Mrs. Von Hoffman III caught wind of the incident with the Tharp boy.

On that day, Ava had arrived in Winnetka with her face tight with fear and her hair frazzled in a cloud over her head. Mrs. Von Hoffman III opened the door, one hand extended with a full glass of chardonnay and her face slack with drunkenness. She wrapped her arms around Ava and together they heavily ascended the stairs to Ava's bedroom.

Ava, seated at her bureau, failed to cover her wounds with makeup. She had been suspended in front of the bureau for days now, studying the violence. Staring in the mirror at her unfamiliar and monstrous contortions, she blinked back at herself from swollen eye sockets. Black and blue welts stained her face like an inkblot test. Every stroke from her makeup brush, no matter how gentle, burned her tender skin.

Mrs. Von Hoffman III had entered the room tenderly, as one would advance toward an injured predator. She knew at any moment she could draw back a stump. Doing her due diligence, she collected all the information she could and brought in a first-aid kit.

Ava watched her from the mirror, knowing there was no way she could get her stepmother to leave. Now was not the time to uphold restraint, and anyway, her decorum had been completely abandoned thanks to her puffy face.

Mrs. Von Hoffman III took Ava's hand and brought her to the bed. Ava's chin quivered as the pressure of tears gathered in her eyes.

"It's okay," Mrs. Von Hoffman III had said. "Cry."

Ava had wept loudly, with a fury that almost split her insides. Mrs. Von Hoffman III held her for a long time before looking over the wounds to her face.

Those same comforting hands now met Ava in the morning glow of the café.

"He's been calling me," Ava said with dread that could only be reserved for the Tharp boy.

Mrs. Von Hoffman III's eyes widened. "What does he want?"

"Who knows."

"Have you told anybody?"

"No," Ava said.

"You should go to the police," Mrs. Von Hoffman III said, lowering her voice as if the Tharp boy's dangerous temper and hard fists would appear next to them in the café.

"But my father..." Ava said.

Of course she thought Ava should go to the police and bring even more embarrassment to their family. She was a third wife. She was familiar with the whispers and endless ridicule. As long as she kept up her Botox, painkiller, and Chardonnay routine, why would she care?

Mrs. Von Hoffman III drew in breath to speak as the waiter returned with their plates. Once he left, she leaned over the food and talked in a hushed tone that forced Ava to lean in to hear her.

"At some point you're going to have to quit playing games," Mrs. Von Hoffman III said. "Since all that happened, things haven't been right between you two. I know your father, and if you truly want to be happy, you're going to have to stand up to him."

Ava sat back too hard, jolting her chair. "I'm not playing games."

Mrs. Von Hoffman III sipped her drink as a smile of resolve appeared on her face. "If you're not playing games, what are you doing with Russell?"

60

A silk stream of dawn spilled between the cracks in the blinds directly onto Beck's eyelids. The light felt as if it would sear the thin skin over his eyes before he opened them. His mouth felt like it was filled with sand and his head like it had been used for target practice. Beck pitched back and forth between alcohol-induced sickness and exhaustion.

The mattress underneath him felt warm and encompassing until he realized with overwhelming alarm he didn't have a mattress anymore. The warmth from the mattress was coming from a body lying close to him.

The body belonged to Leslie.

Memories from the previous night emerged in clouded images. He remembered spans of time when the two of them threw their elbows on a dark bar and ordered tequila. Liquor altered the trepidation between them, and soon they were cavorting on the dance floor, laughing at and with each other. Leslie opened up like Beck always wanted him to. He knew he shouldn't have risked the fragile start of this friendship. He knew he shouldn't have entered his bedroom last night. He shouldn't have eagerly, feverishly disrobed.

But there, looking at his brown skin against the darkness of last night, stood the inverse of every frightened, lonely thought that held him captive for so long. He'd become unhinged in his drunkenness—they both had.

Battered and beaten, they stood naked before each other, aroused and breathless with the capacity to take all that away.

The dim spots in his recollection ebbed back to a full picture of the night. They had been surprisingly easy with each other, falling in a certain uniformity like the components of machinery but with the tenderness of longtime companions. Leslie's touch had been proficient and Beck, now pulling the condom off himself, could spend all day trying to recount the times he had been that satisfied.

He turned over to Leslie and smiled. Leslie stirred and opened his eyes. Seeing Beck, his face slowly grew stark with terror.

Leslie popped up from the bed and crumbled onto the floor. His hand, a quivering claw, reached for the blankets and wound his body in them. He stood, panicked, and turned to Beck, naked on the bed, grinning from the slapstick.

"Oh, god!" Leslie cried out, tossing him a pillow. "No!"

"Hey," Beck said. "Calm down, you don't want Kat to hear. Although I'm sure she did. We weren't exactly quiet."

"Shut up!" Leslie said. "This isn't a joke."

"No, it was actually good."

"Oh, my god," Leslie said, starting to pace. "You did this to me."

Beck sighed as he tried to manage his frustration and the sudden arousal spiking up in him. He grabbed the pillow to cover himself.

"I didn't do anything to you."

"Sure you did," Leslie said, grabbing sweatpants from his dresser and putting them on. "You knew I was upset and said those nice things…"

Beck's stomach shifted and he crawled over the bed. He grabbed the waistband of Leslie's sweatpants and wrenched him closer. They stood face to face, and he saw Leslie trembling.

"I meant those things."

Leslie sucked his teeth and his eyes shot over Beck's naked body.

"Sure you did," Leslie said. "Now, please get out. I have to go to work and explain why I'm late."

Foiled again, Beck moaned and stepped into his underwear. He shuffled through the door into the hallway. Kat, on her way to the kitchen from her room, stopped in horror and peered into the open door. She looked at Beck, then Leslie, and then back to Beck. For a beat, no one moved.

Then Kat exploded into cartoonish hilarity, leaning forward and slapping her thighs.

Leslie yelped in humiliation and smacked the door closed.

"I needed that!" Kat said between tears, throwing her head up in laughter and continuing toward the kitchen.

Shamed and frantic, Beck followed her.

"So, you never really wanted to sleep with me," she teased.

"I would've," Beck said defensively. Quieter, he followed with, "I think Leslie hates me."

"It doesn't look like hate to me," Kat said, starting the coffeemaker.

"What did I do?"

Kat shifted her attention from the coffeemaker to Beck. "Do you like Leslie?"

Beck coughed and laughed. "No, I just don't want to get kicked out."

"Russell is moving out," Kat said. "You're about to have your own room."

"Yeah, I knew that."

Kat, as if angling it for accuracy, tilted her head. "You really do like Leslie."

Her words sank into his head like stones. Upon impact, he realized he was standing in his underwear. Without thinking, he'd followed Kat into the kitchen for benediction or, at the very least, absolution. He backstepped from the kitchen and into Leslie, who was donning his scrubs.

Leslie shrugged him back with mild disgust, now as icy as he'd always been.

"Can you put on some clothes?" Leslie asked, pushing into the kitchen.

Beck went to his suitcase, fortifying his shaken ego with memories of social glory. He had many women and men who had been elated to wake up with him. They, of course, had all been high beyond cognition, and Beck couldn't have cared less if the one-night stand led to a second occurrence. Leslie was different, though, and in the quiet of Beck's mind he had always wanted it. Things were ruined again *and* he had to live with Leslie.

He hauled a pair of jeans and a T-shirt from his suitcase and then looked up in the top pocket for a pair of socks. The neat rows were disheveled and turned inside out. Where were the drugs? Where was the coke? The pills? Heat threatened to knock Beck on his back. His heart blasted within the walls of his chest. Blinded by panic, he ripped the socks from the pocket, flinging them into the air. He knew he hadn't moved them, and everything should have been where he left it. He'd checked his suitcase every day. The drugs had been there last night.

"What the hell is your problem?" Leslie said, ducking to avoid an airborne sock.

Beck spun to him, his face white in fear. "Where's the coke?"

"Coke?" Leslie said. "You had coke here?"

Kat stepped into the living room with a coffee mug in her hand.

"It's coke," Beck said. "No one throws away coke, even if they don't plan on using it."

"He had coke here," Leslie said.

"I was *broke* and *homeless*," Beck said. "I wasn't in a position to hold any moral high ground. Where's the coke?"

"I don't know," Kat said. "I never knew about it."

"We don't steal," Leslie said with his arms crossed.

Kat looked at him and then at Beck. "Has anyone let Isaac in the house?"

Leslie's face went stark as he sprinted into the kitchen. Kat ran to her room and in moments they returned.

"The weed is gone."

"So are my pills." She looked at Beck. "The pills you gave me at Peppermint."

Leslie darted out of the apartment, leaving the door swinging open. Beck heard his frantic footsteps round the building toward the alley. Beck jumped into his pants and approached the door as Leslie returned, out of breath and brandishing a pair of brass keys.

"How does he know about the spare set?" Kat asked.

Leslie gave her a remorseful shrug and his gaze fell to his feet. Beck placed his hand on his shoulder.

"I'm sorry," Beck said.

Leslie pulled back and glanced at him, then at Kat. "How could we have this many drugs in the house? What kind of people are we? Isaac never had a chance."

"Leslie..." Beck wanted to say more, to say anything.

"You can stay here," Leslie said, walking back to his room, "but don't ever touch me."

61

Russell had agreed to put the rest of his belongings in storage, a unit Ava found in an effort to mitigate his fallout on her apartment. As a peace offering, she sent the movers to pick up his things and agreed to supervise the move from his old apartment.

Ava glanced at her watch and rushed down to her lobby. Her doorman swiftly called her a cab, and within minutes, she was rolling through the city to Wicker Park. The afternoon was bright and the sun hung high overhead. The cab windows magnified the heat, its warmth a preface to summer temperatures. Sweat stung the back of Ava's neck. Over her fresh perfume, she detected the tiniest malodor. She closed her eyes to find its origin in the cab's musty cell of a cabin, but it was there, like a small drop of dye released in a glass of water. Cheap whiskey and cigarette smoke rose from her clothing fibers. Lately, Russell's stench penetrated everything in her apartment.

Her mind drifted back to her stepmother's reduction of

her relationship to a game. If it *was* a game, Ava felt determined to win. Her next coup would eliminate Russell's beard.

Her ears popped from the change in pressure as she cracked the window. The breezed hissed in and ripped away Russell's stink, so she rode this way until she arrived at the apartment. She asked the driver to wait and climbed out of the car.

A gruff mover with a company's logo stamped on his sweatshirt stepped through the open door. He carried boxes of records to the small moving truck. Ava smiled at him and apologized for being late.

"Who let you in?" Ava asked.

"The lady who lives there," the mover said. "Is she paying us?"

"No," Ava said flatly, sidestepping movers coming from inside the apartment.

She walked in hesitantly and came upon Kat in the living room, sneering back with an icy glower.

"Good to see you again," Ava deadpanned.

"I'm sure it is," said Kat, whose voice was as cold as her stare. "They're almost done."

"I'll go have a look," Ava said, walking swiftly past Kat into Russell's room.

His room was almost empty, causing her footsteps to echo off the bare walls. Next to his closet were two full bags of garbage and a stack of ten thin canvases, their painted fronts facing the wall. When the moving men entered the room, Ava pointed to the bags and canvases.

"Throw those away and I think you're done."

The movers collected the room's remaining contents and left Ava alone. She smiled, happy to be liberated at last from this apartment and its deplorable drama.

"What are you doing?" she heard Kat cry from the living room. "Don't you fucking throw those away!"

Ava sighed and followed the screams into the living room. Kat yanked the canvases from the mover, her body positioned to do physical harm to a man twice her size. Startled, the mover relinquished the paintings.

"It's okay," Ava said to Kat.

"You can't seriously think this is okay," Kat said, cradling the canvases under her arm.

Ava turned to the movers. "That's it guys. You can leave if you want."

Ava pulled out several twenty-dollar bills and handed them to the movers, rattled by Kat's attack.

"Are you sure you're going to be all right?" one of the movers asked in a low voice.

Kat clucked her tongue and said, "She'll be fine."

The mover reluctantly left with instructions to place Russell's belongings in storage. The women stared at each other, reminding Ava of pay-per-view commercials featuring sweaty boxers glowering at each other before a match.

"Are you going to fight me?" Ava asked.

"No," Kat said. "Even though I should kick your ass, I'll refrain."

Ava grunted. "You want to fight about my boyfriend? You know, I watch you with him. I know you have feelings."

Kat said nothing, but Ava saw her face waver. Kat's eyes flickered and her outrage moved to something sadder. Her grasp on the paintings tightened.

"It must really bother you that he chose me."

Kat flinched as she placed the canvases on the ugly glass coffee table. She gingerly, almost reverently, stacked the paintings on top of each other. She sat back on the couch

Ava had always found hideous. All the anger in Kat's face had abandoned her, leaving a mournful smile instead. Ava looked into her dark eyes, glimmering with tears, and found her almost beautiful.

"Russell is an artist," Kat said. "He's a great artist and he'll always be one."

"Russell has grown out of that. I've never seen him paint a day in my life."

"He's the kindest man I know," Kat continued in dreamy sadness. "He's also the softest. That critic broke him, but one day I hope he'll paint again."

"He's fine."

"No, he's not. You should see him when he's painting. That's when he's happy," Kat said.

She sniffed and blinked quickly, drawing back sadness to no effect. She was unmasked, beautiful and tender.

"Sometimes you can forget how..." Kat paused, glancing up at the ceiling as if she could seize the word from the air thickening around them. "You can forget how inspiring it is to see someone truly happy. I miss seeing him like that."

Her smile was gone and only tears remained, swelling in her eyes. She collected the canvases and handed them to Ava, scraping her bare forearms.

"I know you don't like me," Kat said. "I don't like you either, but take these, please. Give them to Russell. Encourage him to paint again."

"Do you love him?" Ava asked impulsively.

Ava shouldn't have asked but she had to know. It was one thing to want Russell and another to love him.

Kat pulled back a large breath that shook her body. Ava's voice was a whimper. The space between the women ossified. All their defenses expired. The biting wit, the backhanded compliments, and the smoldering contempt all crumbled in the heat of candor.

They were cracked, insides raw and ripped. Both felt open wounds.

"Yes."

Ava reeled back and turned away from Kat, her insides liquefied. They sloshed inside her as she pitched left and right, stumbling down the front steps and waking the cab driver, who was nodding off in the front seat. He came to and ran out of the car, grabbing the heavy collection of paintings. Ava swayed from shock and anger, suddenly unsure of herself. She tumbled into the cab and heard the slam of the trunk as the cabbie placed the last relics of Russell's art in the back.

Ava glanced back at the house and saw Kat standing in the doorway, holding herself in her arms. She felt Kat's melancholy ushering her into this other world, some place where she mourned the death of art and the death of love. A breeze caught Kat's hair and it spread out behind her in the wind like a long dark cloak. Like the black cape of a magician and the vanishing objects behind it, she disappeared into the house, but not before Ava saw tears flow from her eyes.

Inside the car, Ava was hounded by whiskey, cigarettes, and the image of Kat's tears. She wondered if she would ever get away from Russell's apartment. Worse yet, she wondered if Kat was right, if the man she had been dragging around was nothing more than an unhappy corpse. If that was true, how long could Ava do this?

Did she love him enough to bring him back to life? Could he be happy?

The cab deposited her at home, and her doorman rushed out to open the door. Her arms were again loaded with canvases, and he offered to help, but she refused. As she shimmied into the elevator, the paintings' wooden backs bit into her skin. She checked for wounds as she set them down, finally, on her kitchen counter.

The paintings engulfed her, as if the floor had tipped and she would fall forever into them. In all her time with Russell, she'd never truly seen his art. It was abstract conception, like the jokes she shared with a friend, shadows of the past, a childish naiveté. His artwork couldn't have been substantial enough to invoke such grief.

It wasn't as if he had been beaten in the face like she had. He hadn't tasted blood in his mouth.

Russell had to grow up, just like she had.

She held out the first canvas. It was an unfinished patchwork, a blending of blues and whites, maybe the start of a sky. The work showed skill in its depiction of fluffy clouds. There was a light, airy ease in his brushstrokes. In the center of the canvas was an empty space, a cutout in the shape of a person. Ava wasn't sure if this was deliberate or incomplete, as she suspected. She dropped the painting next to the pile and browsed the next piece. This canvas was filled with a brick background of a city alley, complete with graffiti. Like the prior painting this, too, was done with jarring photo-like accuracy and featured another empty person vacancy in its center.

Confused, Ava frowned and went to the next one, wondering if this was the fabled greatness of Russell's art career. Her hands rushed over his canvases, frantic, suddenly hoping to find why he bathed in whiskey, was content with a rusted car, and delighted in the darkest parts of the city. Maybe this pile could explain why he befriended that black homosexual and the crass Latina.

The next one was of a green lush forest with another

person hole. The canvas beneath that was one of a subway terminal, again with the same missing person.

Ava's heart milled and hammered in her chest. She savagely flipped through the canvases, and the sound of smacking wood and tarp pinged through the apartment.

Who was missing from this painting?

She pulled back the last canvas. Color drained from her face. Air vacated her lungs.

In the last painting, amongst the dark, almost stormy, backdrop of a bar, underneath blue lights and glowing liquor bottles with that deft photo veracity, was Katherine Davalos. Her face was tilted down, framed by black hair painted so exquisitely Ava could make out the strands. Her red lips were depicted with such care they looked like they would open up and speak, and her eyes were interpreted as dark soulful pools. She was wearing a simple tank top, like the one she often wore to Stratosphere, but in this portrayal, there was something devout in her smooth skin and round breasts. The brush seemed to caress her skin and neck, drawn by the hand of an admirer. Kat's image was presented too lovingly, too carefully.

Through the eyes of Russell, Kat appeared in divinity, fixed in acrylics and oils.

62

A hazy heat rose from the concrete and obscured Chicago's skyline like dirty film as Russell rode the train high above the street. The train pulled further in, treading between the buildings, and the evening sunset poured a burnt orange glow onto the surrounding steel and glass into the train. Russell's weary reflection flickered in the window like a dying flame.

He should've driven, but he couldn't risk losing his spot in the garage down the street from Ava's apartment. Instead, he stood with the working population, packed elbow to elbow like overstocked cattle, his muscles bundled in the train car. Strange breaths infected his own. Russell knew the core of his frustration wasn't the commute, or even the first day of manager training—a forced explanation of the new and innumerable demands of his new position. All day in the frigid conference room, amongst other managers in training, so eager and willing, he'd strained and smiled. He nodded and agreed with the profit margins. He endorsed the company's ethos, when asked.

He had been knighted into this commerce and was no different from the men and women in suits, the proud commandos of capitalism. Jarred by his participation in this, Russell had to mock even himself. During the lunch break, he separated from the guild and fled into the dark bathrooms, enclosing himself in a stall and closing his eyes. He suddenly wondered what missteps had sent him here.

He held out his hands. Years ago, those hands were marked with acrylics and oils. Years ago, small calluses had formed where his hand met the brush. His face had been streaked with dried paints like a tribal warrior. Russell had been untamed and liberated.

It had been those damned words. It had been that damned critic.

Years ago, Russell—under his greasy hair and beneath the unkempt beard of a madman—beamed with a sense of pride. It was like nothing he had ever felt. In front of the series of colorful portraits he had spent the better part of three months producing, an absolution had struck iron along his spine.

The paintings were lined in a row. Hours before, he'd watched the officious art curator instruct a few volunteers on proper positioning. His heart fluttered rapidly in his chest. He palms were slick sponges of his sweat. He'd considered that he might be dying, or at least in the throes of a panic attack. But this was joy he was feeling. It was pure and electric, gumming up his mouth, igniting his stomach. At that time, it had been too much for his body to hold.

He hoped the faces in his canvases could hold the excess.

The portraits were softened and sweetened with the benevolence he found for each subject. Random people, handpicked along his treks through the city. The friendly Indian bodega owner, who sometimes discounted Russell's cigarettes, became a subject. Russell's affection overlooked the man's acne-riddled complexion. Instead, he'd used his brushes to emphasize the regality of his chin and nose.

Another one of his favorite portraits illustrated Shakes, a destitute figure by any definition, but in Russell's translation, a lighthearted, humorous man who brought stories forth with every shady exchange of drugs.

The entire collection read like an optimistic appreciation for those around him, a love song to all of them. His hope for all of them. Set in a modest new art gallery in Wicker Park, that night had easily been the happiest of his life. It was a moment of his truth.

That moment had been like the toll of a heavy brass church bell, a wonderful gong reverberating deep within him long after the initial strike.

The following week, a critic from one of Chicago's highly regarded art gazettes denounced his art as "an exercise in contrivance... a skilled but saccharine and sentimental collection..."

The art gallery hadn't been established long enough to withstand the slight. Soon the owner, who had previously been proud to take Russell by the arm to meet his clientele, was on the phone flatly explaining that due to the economy the portraits had to be dropped. The portraits were given to their subjects, and Russell's only restitution was three dime bags of weed, courtesy of Shakes.

In the train, now, he looked again at his hands. Gilded in the brassy sunset, they were clean and smooth. The calluses formed by his paintbrushes had disappeared.

The words of the critic were far, remote mumblings of the past. Those words, set in a tiny font and arranged in the tight columns of the monthly paper, finally meant nothing. He knew with absolution he was free from them.

Yet this gave him nothing. He was still subjugated by words, and one in particular anchored his emotional state. It rang within him, resounding deep like his joy once had. It chased him into the conference room and penned itself on the faces and suits of his fellow capitalists.

This word had even taken root on the train and stood next to him, struggling for room among the rest of the commuters.

"Coward."

The word needled him when Leslie said it, but when Kat had made the claim, its devastation was monumental. Her love had suddenly come flooding at him and receded so quickly he wondered if she had professed it at all.

His world had crumbled around him once again. And she was adrift in the rubble.

Kat had always been his fixed point.

She had always been true.

She had always been right.

And she had been suffering all this time. He sensed

it, just as she sensed his struggle. Somehow, even in her indignation, she'd used her last act to free him from the critic who'd crushed him.

The train intercom announced his stop and he poured onto the platform with his fellow passengers, the breaks hissing like a pipe releasing pressure. His footsteps were slow as Kat's words and face tore at the inside walls of his mind. The urban topography lost its design, and everything outside the path to Ava's building dwindled into darkness. He walked through the front door and to the elevator inside the tunnel vision of his conviction.

He stood at her door for a minute before unlocking it and eventually opened it at a grim speed. Through the smoky glass inside a psychic's crystal ball, he saw a gaudy engagement ring, a woman in a frothy wedding dress, and the archetypal American dream. Through the long black corridor of the future—past the streaming faces of capitalistic cannibals and mobsters making deals in hidden bars, beyond stoic aristocrats eating off overpriced fundraiser plates, and into the myopic depths of suburbia—lay Russell's future. At core of this darkness sat Russell, drunk like his father, but in a two-car Victorian home instead of a trailer, in a designer suit instead of a spotted undershirt, and scrolling through profit and loss margins at a mahogany desk instead of sleeping in a broke down recliner in front of a flickering tube TV.

This couldn't be his life.

He stepped into the apartment and went immediately to the kitchen for whiskey. He found the bottle of Jack Daniel's half-emptied on the counter and turned to see Ava with a tumbler in hand, her strident mood torrid from sour mash. In her other hand, she held out one of his canvases. Heat rose from his stomach to the back of his neck.

"Where did you get that?"

"From her," Ava said, holding up the portrait of Kat.

Ava gulped the last of her whiskey and tossed the tumbler over her shoulder, stumbling as she did. Glass erupted behind her and she raised the canvas overhead, manic with intoxication. She laughed sadly and hurled it to the floor. On impact, the wood frame fractured with a loud crack. The fabric of the canvas split under the pressure. In a finishing blow, Ava stomped the portrait, successfully shredding Kat's face.

Florid, her breath ragged, she pushed back a few strands of blonde hair.

"I'm Ava Von Hoffman. I'm a victim to no man. It's time I remind you and everyone else of that."

"Ava..."

"Have a seat, dear. We need to talk," she said, heading to the living room. Directing him to accompany her, she added, "Please mind the mess, will you?"

63

With the shreds of Kat's portrait on Ava's floor and Russell on her couch, she said, "You have to go."

"I understand," Russell replied, his intonation flat.

Within fifteen minutes, he'd shoved everything he'd brought to her apartment into two gym bags. Russell took her keys off his ring and set them on the counter with a click. He threw the heavy bags over his shoulder and staggered toward the door. He turned and stood in the opening, giving her a small smile, gentle and regretful.

"I'm sorry, Ava. I'll leave," he said. "I just can't be the guy you need me to be."

Most of the effects of Ava's intoxication had been reduced by her fit. She walked up to him, no longer angry. Her breath quivered and tears fell from her face.

"You really did try," she said, "didn't you?"

"Yeah."

She wiped away the tears. "That's more than any man has done for me in a while."

"You deserve to be happy, Ava."

"Thanks," she said as he headed into the hallway. "Don't change."

He nodded and closed the door behind him. When Ava went back to her bedroom to assess the space in her closet, she noticed he'd left the grey Italian suit behind. She touched its smooth wool and shut the closet door.

That night she finally listened to Tharp's voicemail and texted him to meet her. The town car dropped her off a block from Cibo e Amore so she could walk. It seemed like a good idea, to have the warmth envelope her and soothe her nerves, but soon she started to sweat in her Bottega Veneta cocktail dress, and she wished she'd gotten door-to-door service. She pulled a handkerchief from her clutch and dabbed her forehead. She was determined to appear perfect, to look like the Ava Von Hoffman she was before a series of men came blundering, stinking, and punching themselves into her life.

She gathered herself one last time and pushed open the glass door. The air was lush with spicy foods, and the city cast a glow through the windows. Her heart fluttered in the hollow of her chest as the maître'd escorted her to the table. She was grateful to finally sit in a chair.

A slender man stared back at her with silver eyes. From under the table, he produced a small bouquet of Peruvian lilies and white roses. His dark hair was slicked black and he wore a polished suit. His squared jaw bore a slight stubble. He smiled with a toothy grin, as if trying to disarm Ava.

"Hello, Tharp," she said.

He smiled at her as if he hadn't been the one to hit her, as if he hadn't forced her and her father to feel so much shame. Did he believe they were old friends? That those bruises left on her face were nothing more than careless insults?

"I told you not to call me by my last name."

"Fine, *Jacob*," she spat. "Is that better?"

Jacob pushed the flowers to her. Ava sucked her teeth as she swatted the flowers off the table.

He winced and Ava braced herself.

"Well, that wasn't fair," he said, his silver eyes flashing.

"What are you going to do about it this time?"

Jacob adjusted himself in his seat. "I've come here to apologize."

"For assaulting me or for lying about your wife? Or maybe for making me a social outcast among everyone I know."

Jacob Tharp was the rebellious heir to Floyd & Tharp but rejected it all to work for an advertising firm he'd seeded with his own funds. He had been industrious and fairly successful. The cocktail of his pedigree, family name, and his own success extended his social influence. It had been so far-reaching that he and Ava spent months being seen at social events. She remembered the glee she felt spotting her picture in one of Chicago's high-end gazettes, the caption reading "socialite." She'd received so many shocked looks from it she thought people were envious of her. She relished in the attention until Mrs. Von Hoffman III pulled her aside and informed her Jacob Tharp was someone's husband. In another act of insurrection toward his father, Jacob Tharp married an Indian woman. From the harsh whispers Mrs. Von Hoffman III overheard in the country club bathroom, this wife didn't have the stomach for the level of fraternizing it took to be the wife of a Tharp.

When Ava confronted him in the tacky rooms of the Grant Park Hotel, he descended upon her with fists. She had been shocked when the staff, obscenely tipped by Jacob, gathered her from the surrounding mess of the room and led her through the back and into a ramshackle freight elevator. She remembered the apathetic slack on the concierge's face while he ushered her into the alleyway and into a waiting cab.

She remembered all of this while staring at Jacob across the table. She had to remind him of who she was and free herself, at last, from this burning scandal of being paraded around as the other woman. Her father was embarrassed by his participation in the affair. The ordeal crippled him, and he muttered to himself with watery, sad eyes, "Von Hoffmans don't do this."

"My wife is divorcing me. It has me thinking about everything. About the past and all the things I've done," Jacob started. "I'm sorry for what I did to you. I was drunk, even though that is no excuse."

The heat of Ava's anger caused pinpricks to dance over her vision. Was this an apology or a bid for her? She cleared her throat.

"I'm sorry, too, Jacob," she began. "Sorry I didn't press charges from the beginning. But that's something I can rectify. Your phone call reminded me."

Jacob's face darkened, and his Adam's apple bobbed as he swallowed.

"You *should* look worried," she said. "I sure a man like you has a prenuptial agreement in place. And I'm certain if you're still the coward I remember your wife will barely be able to afford a decent lawyer."

Jacob said nothing, but a familiar brutality rose in his face.

"I've decided to right the wrong I committed against that poor woman. Adultery is such a nasty thing, isn't it? 'Adultery'—such at dated term these days..."

"Your point?"

"My point is I'm going to pay for your wife's divorce lawyer. A lawyer so bloodthirsty, so damn vile that he eats glass. The assault charge I'm going to file against you isn't going to help. Did you know you can press charges on assault for up to two years in Illinois? One way or another, I'm going to bleed you dry. I'm going to find every woman you screwed over and we're going to ruin you. I don't care what my father says, or anyone else for that matter."

He seethed back at her, his jaw tight, tendons popping along his neck from within the collar of his suit.

"You wouldn't want to hit me in front of all these people," Ava said. "That's certainly not going to help you."

She smiled as adrenaline flowed through her body. She held up her menu and then looked back at Jacob Tharp.

"What will you be having? I'm starving," she said, tilting her head to find the waiter. "Dinner's on me."

64

The next morning Ava swayed in the back of the black town car like she was adrift at sea. She sat as close to the door as possible and fixed her gaze on the morning light spearing through the gaps and alleyways between buildings. She tried not to focus on her father's voice, rumbling around her in circles. Through his network of friends—most likely from Tharp's father himself—he'd heard of Ava's plan to press charges against Jacob and now peered at her, his brow mended into compacted lines. His voice trembled like a drum as he spoke.

"Ava," he began as they traveled north through the city. He's eyes were dark. There was so much shame he could barely face her.

"Please," she said, "don't..."

She looked up through the window at the expanding angles of light. From the east, they shimmered across the glassy surface of buildings.

"Ava," Von Hoffman tried again.

She turned quickly toward him. "Don't ask me to stop!"

"This family doesn't need any more scandal."

Ava's cheeks flamed and tears burned in her eyes. The rocking of the town car made her dizzy, and she turned back to the window and watched the sun between the buildings to steady herself.

"You didn't protect me, *Father*," she said. "When I needed you most, you chose your reputation."

"Dammit!" Von Hoffman slammed his hand into the side of the door.

Startled, she turned to him. The clarity of that morning light betrayed Von Hoffman: His suit remained sharp and pressed, and his shoes gleamed with polish, but the grand façade, the great imposing image he sold all over town, wasn't protecting him in the car. Ava saw growing age spots on his worn skin and hollowness under his eyes. Sunken in their sockets, his eyes were cruel and desperate, the eyes of a man who had been clawing at profit from everyone for far too long. Small hairs were out of place along his head, illuminated in that light. His breathing was shallow and the lines of his expression were as deep as that of a wind-torn mountain. For the first time she could recall, he looked old.

"Ava, for the love of God! Do you know your stepmother is filing for divorce if I don't let you press charges? I don't need this."

Ava realized Mrs. Von Hoffman III must have sobered up and reached a clearheaded epiphany. Maybe she, too, had seen the old man for who he was, like Ava was realizing now. Ava wondered if there was any coast left in the country where his third ex-wife could flee.

"I understand now why everyone leaves you," Ava said. "When this is over, I'm going to San Francisco to be with my mother."

"How long are you going to make me pay for what happened to you?" he asked.

"What I'm doing has nothing to do with you," Ava said. "When he hit me, I shouldn't have looked to *you* for anything. I should've protected myself."

The car stopped in front of a Nita Tharp's small imports store in Lincoln Park. Ava looked back at her father. Von Hoffman opened his mouth to speak, but there was nothing to say. There was no deal to strike. Nothing to be gained or won or bought, merely an old man watching as all his relationships vanished before him. He had bartered them all away.

She reached over and gave him a consolatory hug.

Ava climbed out of the car and advanced to the closed storefront. Nita, waiting behind the glass, unlocked the door to grant her entry. Shiny, beaded jewelry hung around them like exotic fruit between an assortment of Hindu and Buddha statues. Rich tapestries hung along the walls accenting racks populated by hemp- and jute-woven clothing. A cloud of potpourri sweetened the air.

"Thank you for meeting with me," Nita said.

"Of course," Ava replied. "Thanks for accepting my offer to pay for your divorce lawyer. You said there was someone else willing to help us in court?"

There, underneath the brass, reverent gazes of Hindu gods and laughing Buddha statues, Ava felt a presence hidden in the shadows.

From the back of the store, Kat moved into the morning light before Ava and Nita.

65

For Nita's sake, Kat and Ava pretended they didn't know each other. Kat braced for impact and wanted to dive behind the racks of hemp clothing. The strained horror on Ava's face brought heat to Kat's skin. Kat stared down and shuffled her feet. She ordered them to stay planted on the floor.

Nita had left a notice for her at Belle Journee, to which Kat considered not responding. The only way to deal with Jacob was to leave him firmly in the past. But with all that had happened to her with Jacob, she wanted vengeance. Nita explained her role: write out a short testimony to present to the judge and the lawyers. She explained that another woman who had slept with Jacob discovered his marriage and wanted to right the wrong. If Kat agreed to do this, they would be even. Hearing the tinkling of silver bangles on her arm, she knew she owed Nita this, at least. Even more, she owed this to herself.

How could Ava be mixed up in this? How could Jacob have attacked her, too? Even without his fists, Kat was knocked back by Jacob, grappling through his world of half-truths.

Kat looked up at Ava, who was staring back at her. Her face had grown pallid but her eyes were wide with shock. Nita talked to both of them, her gestures rapid and her mouth turned in a grin of vindication. She asked if Kat could have her testimony ready by the end of the week. Over and over again, she thanked Ava for the lawyer. Kat nodded and smiled sheepishly, and Ava accepted her thanks. The two of them exchanged contact information with Nita and left.

Kat raced Ava to the door to escape the thick aroma of potpourri. She lunged down the sidewalk despite the questioning glances from a man and his dog. She found herself navigating the same sidewalks she'd taken to Jacob's house. She passed the narrow row of familiar townhouses, fearing he would come out and draw her in. Her stomach curdled at the sensation of his touch. His hands had not only touched Ava, they had beaten her. Kat recalled Marcie's party and the Grant Park Hotel, two places she'd seen violence surge in his eyes.

Her feet kicked underneath her, ready to dive into a full run, when she heard Ava rushing up behind her.

"Wait!"

Kat came to a stop, and her stomach crashed at her feet. She sucked in a breath and shoved her fear in the hole her stomach had left behind. She turned to Ava, left nearly out of breath trying to trail her.

"You were sleeping with Jacob Tharp?"

"No, I was there to buy incense," she said.

Ava grimaced. "You have a talent for seeking out other women's men, don't you?"

"He was married when he fucked you, too."

The women glared at each other, panting and out of breath. Kat turned to walk away when she heard the laughter of children from the playground across the street. When she first saw it, the area had been a black netherworld swirling with shadows, but now the terrain was completely alive.

The flurry of scattering children gave off laughter and cries, which danced in a light measure in her ears. They chased one another in childish bedlam along a metal castle and monkey bars. Children leapt off the slide and hit the Astroturf.

Kat lingered outside the playground, made impenetrable by an encircling chain-link fence. Her familiar longing, now a solid mass of sorrow, entombed her and weighed itself against the whole truth of Jacob Tharp.

"Nita told me you were pregnant," Ava said, her voice drained of animosity.

"Yeah," Kat said. "Is it true he hit you?"

"Yes," Ava said, joining her in the view of the playground.

"That bastard."

Mothers met in a buzzing congregation along the park's edge. Uniformed in yoga pants and gym clothes, they stood ready at any moment to break up the chaos. They commiserated with each other, sipping from lattes and frappes next to an empty corral of strollers and buggies.

"Does this make us friends now?" Kat asked.

"Do you really want to be?"

"I guess not."

"I'm sorry you lost the baby," Ava said.

They stared at each other, silent again. It was as if battle lines were being broken around them. Kat still couldn't believe this. She swallowed.

"How is Russell?"

"I don't know," Ava said. "We broke up. He's gone. Guess he didn't love either one of us."

Kat exhaled, her feet still planted. Nothing felt right. Nothing felt real anymore.

Ava shook her head one last time. "How did this happen to us?"

She turned, shoulders held high, and strode graceful toward her town car.

66

The slow dip of sun released the city from the day and familiar shadows of night inched along the sprawling concrete connecting Wicker Park's bars and apartments. The sun's rays sank deep into the cracks of the pavement, and the ground released heat like a cast iron skillet on the burning eye of a stove. Playnight, hallowed be thy name, would be consecrated this night, one decidedly darker and hotter than most. Social networks lit up like golden lampposts. The rolling eyes of iridescent LCD headlights traveled with them. Text messages and online posts rushed along invisible pathways, beamed into the blackness of space and back, and surged like a pandemic into the pockets of skinny jeans, corduroys, purses, and leather jackets. Phones buzzed on Stratosphere's smooth bar and in Peppermint's back alleys. Some phones pulsed in the quivering palms of drug dealers while others rumbled near piles of coke waiting to be razored into fat lines. The news moved through the complicated webbings of relationships, through the loose tendrils of friendships, along the strangling cords of tourniquet-like love, and between the thick walls of deep rivalries.

The news shouldered room for itself among Wicker Park's readying populous. On Ashland, women puckered and posed in the mirror, rearranging their outfits with a mastery that would purport the most meticulous art curator. On Milwaukee, a meathead squeezed into a pair of Levi's and dropped to the floor like a plank of wood to crunch out fifty push-ups. In the stairwell of a storefront apartment on North Avenue, another woman signed for her UPS package containing knock-off Valentino pumps courtesy of laboring children's hands in Bangladesh. On Damen, one half of the horny new lovers brought his girlfriend to climax using two fingers. He sniffed those same fingers as she left to shower. On Augusta, down in Ukrainian Village, Marcie bullied a friend who owed her money into watching her asthmatic child for the evening. Downstairs, her scar-faced boyfriend sharpened his negotiation tactics in the darkness of a nearby side street, haggling for pills from Shakes, the neighborhood dealer.

In a brick apartment building on Division, Isaac closed one of his nostrils and, with the aid of a five-dollar bill, pulled in coke with the other. Every single light source within and outside the sparse living room began to burst. Nothing mattered except watching the lights and sound move around him. The lieutenant kneeled down next to him and took in the other line. The lieutenant opened up his MacBook and scanned his email invitation.

"This is going to awesome," Isaac said.

The lieutenant was happy to let Isaac stay at his place for a least a couple of days while they shared what was left of Beck's coke. He wiped residue off with his finger and licked it clean.

"No one is going to forget this party," he told Isaac.

In various networks and social constellations, the anticipation was thick. Everyone who knew anyone, had dated anyone, fucked anyone, or even worked with anyone who knew of the party waited around like compressed springs.

This perverse night, a sloppy sacrilege of drunkenness, a lewd parade of lust, and an emphatic cacophony of energy, seduced even the most restrained.

It was a night when one would take a risk. A night when one wouldn't think twice. A night to silence one's conscience. A night when a bit of recklessness felt justifiable.

An empty warehouse in West Town sat next to an abandoned railroad track crushed by layers and layers of hot blackness. It had been an old shoe factory, once upon a time, but now the warehouse was a gutted ghost of Chicago's industrial past. The empty shell was ready to be mounted for taxidermy, like a hunter's game. The building stood four floors tall and looked east at the Kennedy Expressway, at the city that had decades ago left it behind.

Tonight, though, it would awaken from its dusty slumber and show off its sooty floors and cracked windows. The bottom floor had been swept, its glass, metal scraps, and rat feces placed in a neighboring dumpster. A nefarious yet eager member of Playnight's social oligarchy tapped into the power grid. Electricity flowed through a labyrinth of power strips and electrical cords. Miles of decorative lights were lassoed along the walls of the main floor and through the three floors of empty offices above. A brigade of speakers was stationed throughout the building. In a matter of hours, the entire building had been awoken, like men under a covenant preparing a temple for worship.

It was Playnight.

Hollowed be thy name.

67

Kat and Leslie sauntered across the apartment in a

nonsymmetrical cadence. Kat called Leslie into the bathroom to zip up the back of her dress. Her feet faltered in heels and she collided into Leslie. It was a tradition to primp together for the party. They would ready themselves like ancient Roman warriors talking stratagem before the battle. Tonight, the tradition felt incomplete. The two of them lumbered haplessly, unable to compensate for Russell's missing piece. As the night prolonged, dread seeped into the house, into their room, and into their pores. When the hot night began to soar in the sky, drawn over the apartment like black bed linens, Leslie went silent.

An empty numbness knotted Kat's stomach, and she walked into the kitchen, grabbing a bottle of vodka from the freezer. Leslie trailed behind her and extracted three shot glasses. Kat unscrewed the cap and poured the liquor into the two shot glasses, staring at the third. Leslie had been detached, his eyes glazed over in grim thought.

"Who is that for?"

He blinked hard and forced a faulty laugh. "Habit, I guess."

"You miss him, don't you?"

"He made his choice. He left."

Leslie's words dug at Kat as if he'd jabbed a broken bone. Kat tossed back her shot and, with the gut-wrenching spasms of vomiting, confessed everything. She told him about the miscarriage, Jacob's wife, and her love for Russell. Leslie's mouth fell open in horror and his eyes glassed over with tears.

"You should have told me."

"I know," Kat said. "But with your mom and Isaac..."

Leslie sat into the kitchen chair. "Yeah, I guess I wasn't really around much." He stood up and hugged her for a long time.

"So you and Beck?"

Leslie rubbed his hand across his head. "I've never been more scared of anything in my life. And I can't take anything else."

"You still want to go to this party tonight?" she asked.

"We do it every year," Leslie said as he took his shot. "Why should this year be any different?"

"All right," Kat said, slamming her own shot.

The two of them left the kitchen, leaving the third shot glass untouched, standing vigil on the countertop.

68

Stratosphere's staff was restless in the near-empty bar. Most of the bar's regulars were going to attend Playnight. The tattooed manager knew tonight would be slower than most and tried to draw in customers with desperate drink specials. A few customers settled onto the stools in front of the bar. The emptiness was like the mournful evenings in the middle of the week instead of Saturday night.

Beck sanitized the glasses twice in the steel dishwasher. He stocked the bar with liquor and spot-cleaned the bathrooms. His nervous hands wiped down every empty table. With no tasks left, he went through the backdoor into the alley.

He lit and inhaled a cigarette. In his stillness, thoughts snagged him. Playnight pierced into him. He could almost hear it in the distance, recalling the times he had attended. The mighty Bastille of his arrogance rumbled around him. His hubris couldn't withstand the blows of eviction, hard labor, and a shameful ousting. Without this pretense, he saw the very nature of the people around him. He had been surrounded by so many people, under the cover of friendship, who only wanted his drugs, liquor, and his body. He had always been a commodity to be divided and consumed. When he no longer had anything to give, they stole from him.

His old crew—the two skinny women, Marcie, her disfigured boyfriend, the lieutenant—would be at Playnight exhausting his supply, consuming the last evidence of who he had been. Nothing they had ever given him remained either. The parties, the laughter, the sex dried up, giving way to the bitter truth of Beck's identity. This depletion, this self-destruction, was the empirical cause of his exile from Boston and the Ashby clan. This was the root of his crippling loneliness.

Up until now, he'd felt his way around this. He had never truly examined this directly.

Who he had been wasn't who emerged from this.

He thought about Kat who had given him so much when he had nothing. He hadn't even seen her blink before offering him a place on her couch.

His thoughts lingered on Leslie, who challenged him so deeply.

He had kissed him and slept with him. He had felt his warmth all night. Beck's hands were upon his skin. Beck's arms held his resting body. The heaviness of genuine intimacy frightened him and prevented him from eating. Trapped inside were so many things he couldn't say. Even if the air hadn't been soupy in the humid heat, he would have still been covered in sweat at the mention of Leslie.

He knew Leslie didn't want him, but he had waited so long to be his friend and to be close to him.

He could wait longer.

The manager stepped through the backdoor into the alley.

"It's going to be slow night," he said. "You want to leave early?" Without hesitation, Beck walked back into the bar to punch out.

He left the bar and jogged down the street, considering the quickest route to West Town. He waved down a cab and tried to catch his breath. The air inside the cab was condensed in smoggy humidity, and sweat formed on his brow and upper lip.

His heart began to rattle when the cab turned onto a quiet street. Angling his head through the partition, he instructed the driver down the darkening streets. Soon, it felt as though they were moving underground. As they descended deeper into a neighborhood of decrepit buildings, Beck saw crumbling bricks of industrialization, leaning steeples of smokestacks, and barbwire surrounded him. A deep grumble of bass boomed through the night. Soon, Beck felt the low frequency inside the cab.

Cabs, cars, and pedestrians fought for room on the narrow strip of road. Beck paid the cab driver and joined the mass as the pulsing explosion rose to a wild cry. He turned the corner and saw people composed in a knotted clump in front of the door. He edged his way through the tight, condense crowd. The skunk of burning weed and liquor was rancid at the delivery door that served as entry to the party. Some of the people there drank from a flask woefully. From intervals between cigarettes, others complained loudly about the wait. Others danced, determined to party be it inside or out. Some laughed and chatted loudly, clutching to the hope they would get in if their patience withstood.

At the door, a small group of thick muscular men stood waving away and denying people at the door. Beck recognized them from parties he had in the past before. Some subset of a clique that frequented the same places he did.

He went to move forward when a hand held him back.

"They're not letting anyone in," Russell said. "I've tried."

"I know them," Beck said. "I can get in."

Russell grimaced at him, shifting his shoulders forward. Beck glared back at him, moving to challenge the giant back if he had to. He squared his stance and a sharp smile drew on his face. Beck, aware of his demoted social standings within his old group of friends, could still handle Russell. He didn't need Marcie or the lieutenant to ensure that Russell would never see the inside of this party.

"I like your old room," Beck said.

"Well, I'm coming back for it," Russell said.

His eyes were dark and sullen. And Beck knew he had seen that before in Leslie's eyes. Beck's smile quickly faded. He saw the pained displacement of himself in Russell.

"I can't get you your old room back," Beck said. "But I can get you in the party."

Russell jerked back. "You're going to help me?"

"Don't ruin my good deed, okay," Beck said, gesturing Russell to follow him.

"Wait," Russell said, stopping in the crowd. "Are you sleeping with Kat?"

"No, I'm trying to sleep with Leslie," Beck said, still moving toward the door.

Russell blinked, incredulous, and rushed to catch up with Beck as he ran toward the doors.

69

Leslie intended to stay with Kat but, in the savage bombardment of churning bodies, lost her in the bottom level of the warehouse. He called and texted to no avail. He spent a half hour searching, but in the flashing lights, he caught only fragments of faces—the jut of a nose, a wild grin, shining eyes, a swing of hair. None of which belong to Kat.

The music blared like an explosive force, rattling the rusty chains and steel beams above. The deejay spun at the furthest wall from the door, vaulted on stage as if on a pulpit.

Leslie gagged as he passed through a ghost of someone's fetid body odor. At the makeshift bar, he screamed over the music for a plastic cup filled with gin. The liquor didn't ease him, and he knew he would have to leave the frenzy, if only for a moment.

He travelled along the wall next to the bar toward a metal flight of stairs. He followed a couple of women up the stairs and away from the dancing. Above the cacophony of the party, he stepped into a hallway dimly lit by several strings of white lights. Old dust comingled with the heat in a hazy gloom. Soft tempo music played from some unknown source, although the chill rhythm was not strong enough to overpower the music downstairs. He'd entered the darker nucleus of the party. Uncertain and without anyone to accompany him, he walked slowly, hoping to remain unseen.

He moved by open offices, where people convened and laughed. Flaming orange tips of joints and cigarettes swayed in the blackness like the many eyes of an imaginary beast. Shadows upon the night trembled as people danced slowly to the music.

Leslie met another flight of stairs and on the next floor found more music and the low mutter of voices spinning out before him. It was an unnerving quiet that even the thumping party music couldn't mask. In the dark, up here, something felt sinister. He slowed his advance and sipped his gin. The warm charge of intoxication hadn't come yet.

He heard the slap of flesh against flesh.

He peeked into the office door to his left. Leslie couldn't make out much in the darkness but saw a couple with their pants around their ankles. A guy keeled over a woman on some forgotten scrap of office furniture and drove himself manically into her. She sang her response in soft, purring moans. The barking grunts sounded familiar. Squinting into the darkness, Leslie made out a swarm of black tattoos crawling up the guy's arm. The piercings on his face, contorted in pursuit of an orgasm, gleamed. It was the lieutenant.

Realizing this, Leslie rushed quickly along the hall, surging with scorn. If the lieutenant was close, Isaac probably was, too. Leslie stuck his head through each passing door, witnessing an exceptional assortment of insanity. The rooms were filled with the requisite groups of people snorting coke. Playnight's early martyrs were incapacitated in various corners of the next room, crumbling over chairs, folding into corners, bowing in prayer to whatever poisons they'd ingested. He spotted another couple having sex, respectably sticking to oral. The hysteria on the ground floor seemed benign to what swirled in this dark core of Playnight.

Breathless from the heat, Leslie at last felt the drunkenness arrive.

He heard muffled noises from the last room in the hallway and walked in hesitantly. Isaac, leaning against the wall, swayed back and forth like a merchant marine, coasting on the flood of his high.

70

Nervous and nearly crazed laughter churned inside Russell.

Since leaving Ava's apartment, his nerves had been set on a razor's edge. How long had he been away from his world? When did he renounce his citizenship? He was at the very party he and his friends treated like a high holy day, and everything rested on Beck, of all people, to get him inside.

Until Beck admitted to sleeping with Leslie, Russell had been convinced the formerly bleached-blond party boy had commandeered his place among his friends.

What was with Beck's haircut? All Russell wanted to do was giggle. He wanted to let the laughter roar out, bringing forth tears and quakes until everything made sense again, until his friends were his family again.

Russell was out of earshot as Beck nodded and spoke with the two doormen. They convened like members of a delegation appointed to settle the matters of war. Beck looked back at Russell and kept talking. Russell's laughter birthed a cold panic. He recalled Beck's past displays of egotism and wondered if he would be slighted again.

Just as Russell was ready to cry out, the doormen granted entry. He held his breath, waiting for Beck to go without him. This world had entered some strange metamorphosis where anything was possible. He braced himself to wait outside all night.

Beck turned around.

His smile was sly, almost warm. "You coming?"

Russell chuckled despite himself. He stepped through the door with Beck right behind him.

"Let's look for Kat and Leslie," Beck said, straining to be heard over the clamor.

Russell plodded forward, throwing his bulk into the crowd like he was walking against gale-force winds. Inch by inch, they moved toward the center of the whirlpool, drowning in thrashing flesh and bare muscle. Music bayed from all directions. The pervasive thump of bass divided his thoughts into smaller and smaller pieces until they were monosyllabic cries for Kat and Leslie. Like the blinking beam of a lighthouse, he scanned the distant black expanse for a vessel. He spotted Leslie and signaled to Beck with his hands. Beck understood and followed his gaze, and they watched Leslie walk toward the far rear of the room toward the stairs.

Now in the center of the dance floor, they began to force a path through the crowd. Russell pushed and tugged through the masses. Despite the sweltering heat rushing off bodies like matchsticks striking paper, Russell felt a chill of panic.

Beck made it to the stairs before Russell, who was obstructed by blond dreadlocks whipping his face. Russell yelled out as one of the thick ropes momentarily entered his mouth.

"Oh, shit!" Curtis Newman cried, reaching for Russell's face.

Russell nearly growled as he beat the artist's hands away from him. He stepped aside but Curtis moved with him, blocking his path. Curtis was drunk and boozy. Behind him danced Isabelle Boldwyn, plastic cup in hand.

"My friend! My friend!" Curtis placed his arms around Russell's neck and squeezed. Russell coughed and struggled to pull in air. He swatted Curtis away and scanned for Beck, now lost to the flashing lights. He stamped his foot and howled.

"Whoa," Curtis said, his camaraderie unshaken. "What's wrong?"

"Get out of my way," Russell yelled over the music. "I'm looking for my friends."

"Best way to find someone is to stay put," Isabelle said. "Have a drink with us?"

Curtis hooked his arm around Russell's neck, and together they brought him to the bar. He leaned in and screamed his order over the raucous. He handed Russell a plastic cup.

"Whiskey," he said.

Russell drank from the cup and turned his direction toward the stairs, and then to the center of the room. He had to find Kat or Leslie. How long could that take?

"You know, I'm a pretty successful artist," Curtis said, shaking back his dreads.

Russell narrowed his eyes, uninterested in hiding his disgust. "That's only because I don't paint anymore."

"Whatever," Curtis said. "You sure scare easily."

"Shut up," Russell said, clenching his fist.

Curtis balked in drunken laughter, his snorts loud enough to be heard over the music. A nearby woman frowned at them.

"Curtis, please," Isabelle said.

"You think I've come here to brag?" Curtis said. "I mean, I could... All night, really."

Russell slammed back his drink and crossed his arms.

"Look, Russell," Curtis continued, "Isabelle's been trying to get you in the art gallery. We have a few spots open..."

"Just one piece," Isabelle said.

Russell's arms, now dead weight, fell to his sides as he thought about all that had changed in his world. Staying in a cheap hotel after leaving Ava. Turning away from all he thought he wanted. Through the dark he looked at the hands he'd used to smudge paint and thought of the canvases he'd carried with him for so long. Around him there had been small embers, burning, lighting his way, telling him who he was, who he had always been.

71

Leslie shuffled into the office. He kept his movements small, as if Isaac was a skittish animal ready to lunge out in fear. Leslie tipped his head to meet Isaac's glassy gaze.

"Hey," Leslie said with a choked voice.

Isaac's face twisted into a dark smile. His eyes were clouded and cruel.

"Enjoying the party?" Isaac asked, anger laced through his voice.

"No."

Isaac wasn't the person Leslie had known. He was barely any person. Isaac's gentle nature and capturing beauty had been bartered away for drugs. The man standing in the room with him was a caricature of a man. Someone peeled back all the good, all the love Isaac had been and chucked it away. Isaac seemed to gather the darkness around him like a shelter against Leslie. His knotted shoulders slumped and the curve of his ribs stuck out from his V-neck shirt. His face strained to hold onto the pleasure of his high, and he funneled the blackness around him like smoke.

Leslie walked closer in protracted movements, hoping he could find a remnant of Isaac's humanity—a crumb, a granule. Any reason to hope that this wreckage before him was the man he used to love. This man had been at the helm of Leslie's grief for so long. This man had watched him weep for his mother. This man had loved him once. He had to be somewhere in the office.

Leslie would never love him again, even if the flicker of

Isaac *was* knotted and folded underneath this man. He would never seek comfort in his arms. He would steer himself out of this grief alone.

But he needed to see him. He needed to see Isaac in this darkness.

"You stole from my apartment," Leslie whispered.

Isaac blinked and his smile fell away. He retreated a few steps, further into the haven of the night, until he was a faint outline. Leslie feared Isaac would become transparent in the night and never return.

He needed to see Isaac's beauty just one last time.

He needed to see the man who had kissed him and smiled at him. The man who exuded such warmth that Leslie had curled himself around it. He had to find him in the black depths that seemed to stretch beyond this dusty office.

Leslie stepped forward again. His blood quickened in his veins. The heat and the dust in the room pressed back at Leslie as if it had become a corporeal wall around him.

"You stole drugs," Leslie said. "At first, I was mad..."

Leslie crept deeper into the darkness until he could almost make out the structure of Isaac's face.

It had to be here, somewhere among them.

"...but then I realized there shouldn't have been drugs for you to steal."

Leslie was almost an arm's length from Isaac.

"I failed you. I'm so sorry."

Just be the man you used to be, Leslie wanted to say. Just let me see him one more time.

One more time. That's all Leslie needed.

Isaac lunged forward and shoved Leslie back. Air escaped Leslie's lungs, and he found himself gasping in the darkness. He shook, more shocked than hurt. His legs began to quiver, and he wondered if he could stand much longer.

"Fuck you," Isaac said. "I don't need you to be sorry. I didn't need you to save me. And I don't now. This is me."

"Isaac, please..."

"We're over, Leslie," Isaac said, and turned completely away.

Leslie backstepped out of the room, still hoping for one last glimpse. It never came. He glanced once more at the open black mouth of the office door and, defeated, retraced his path down the hallway. He felt like a corpse being rolled through the back halls of Saint Rose Community Living. He was with the dead. He was with the body of the women he'd recently found dead in her room. He was with the body of his mother, crushed on impact.

Heavy footfalls came rushing toward him, and he felt hands on his shoulders.

Leslie looked up into Beck's face and saw his eyes were rounded in concern. He opened his mouth to speak, but no words came out.

"Come with me," Beck finally said, his eyes brimming with desire and worry.

Beck moved too fast for protest. He grabbed Leslie's hand and they trailed through the hallway, down the stairs, and back to the loud dance floor. Beck took him to the bar.

"What are you doing?" Leslie asked.

"You need your best friend," Beck said with a hopeful smile and pointed behind Leslie.

Leslie turned to see Russell's giant girth and hairy round face meekly staring back. The relief was so sudden Leslie nearly lost his footing.

"You were right," Russell said over the music's loud percussive thump.

Leslie nodded, though he wasn't agreeing to anything. He was simply glad to see his friend at last. He reached over and wrapped his arms around Russell's midsection. Forgiveness happened without a thought, like the forces of physics in play.

Why hadn't it happened sooner?

"Are you done being an asshole?" Russell asked.

"Are you?" Leslie countered, and started laughing.

"I *was* a coward," Russell said.

"So there's not going to be a wedding?"

"Not for me," Russell said, then nodded over to Beck.

Leslie glanced back at Beck, who was staring back at them as he always had.

This time, Leslie looked back at him.

The warmth. The tender beauty. The precious humanity. All that Leslie had been trying to see for last time in Isaac, all that he believed was gone, all that he was afraid was dead, was now apparent on Beck's face.

72

Russell had been given a lifeline. Leslie was next to him, and for the first time in recent memory, the landscape of his new world started to make sense.

This thought barely had a chance to root itself when a red beam from the strobe light poured into his face. He stood visionless and blinking. For a moment, the entire room glowed red, the strain so great that ghostly orbs of color floated over the room. He squinted and the colors reeled back slowly.

The room returned to the black, gnashing chaos it had been, but now he saw Kat dancing far off, deeper into the crowd.

Her body flitted wildly, as if she was tethered to the booming rhythm around them. The bass took a physical form in her and silver bangles fell down her wrist as she stretched a slender arm into the party's sticky atmosphere. Her hair was a wild black current flowing and surging around her. Her skin shimmered with sweat and her mouth parted while she took swallows of air.

He allowed himself to acknowledge his desire for her. It was a clumsy, quiet reconciliation of himself. He felt the eyes of Leslie and Beck on him. They had known all along.

Russell followed those hidden places within, the secret caverns buried deep within his thoughts and fears. He ducked into the caverns of himself devoted only to her, those inner shrines that compelled him to dance with her, that toiled when another man touched her. The subconscious urges that languorously painted her. She was still his profane Mary, his Madonna of Sorrow, in a shifting kaleidoscope of strobe light.

She was riotous, and as she spun on the dance floor, something inside Russell gave way. A small buckling perhaps, a splintered crack that seeped until it burst from the unrelenting force behind it. He suffered a rush, a frightful burn in his chest like he wasn't allowed to breathe. It was a quiet alarm that turned into a delirious primal flailing.

Kat was more than his friend; she was more than an artistic inspiration.

Russell's heart out-pounded the rapid boom of the music.

73

As long as man has sought to please the gods, there have been sacrifices and there has been blood. In the lush lands of

Mesoamerica, the Aztecs would slay men and women with the golden rise of the sun. All would gather at the base of a massive temple to witness a dagger puncture a heaving chest. Ancient Greeks would perform *Lustratio*, using a blade to divide dogs into parts and their entrails to feed hungry flames on the altar. Grisly flesh would be chopped away and driven off a steep cliff to the thrashing waters below. The Bible's book of Leviticus details burnt offerings and other creative methods to assuage man's guilt. No matter which god they bowed before, men had given their sons and their daughters, and at times their own bodies, as an offering. Life was snuffed out to pay a penance. Flames were lit. Arms and legs severed. Blood spatter, defacement, and disembodiment rang out millennia after millennia.

Blood was always the cost to worship under the fickle gods of man.

Isaac didn't know this. If he did, he wouldn't have cared.

He was concerned with Leslie and Leslie's continual apologies. Even at the end of the relationship, he still bore the weight of that love. And he hated it. He hated how utterly powerless and invalidated it made him feel. He was never a guy just trying to have a good time. He was an addict in Leslie's presence.

He never wanted to see Leslie again.

Isaac realized was he coming down at almost the same moment he remembered the pills he took from Leslie's apartment. He smirked, proud of his craftiness. He had left the stolen cocaine to the lieutenant and the others, who had snorted it before they arrived at the party. That was hours ago, and now—with Leslie weighing so heavily on his mind, so completely intrusive, and on Playnight, no less—he deserved another high.

He dug the Oxy pills out of his pocket and washed two down with a beer. He hesitated for a moment and took another two for good measure. He wouldn't let anything ruin his night.

Isaac wondered the halls to the highest floor of the warehouse. He did this for a long time, watching the decorative light start to blur into beautiful patterns. He felt horribly hot. His T-shirt clung to his body, and sweat darkened the fabric underneath his armpits. A heavy, yet comforting lethargy deadened his bones.

He waved at a few people, friends of friends, as he meandered through the darkness. He walked into one of the bigger offices in the middle of the hall and stood alone among a few broken beer bottles and empty plastic cups. The office had a wide row of windows on either side, including one that looked out onto the main floor of the warehouse. Must have been the boss's office, Isaac thought. Here, a supervisor could monitor productivity over a functioning warehouse.

He walked up to the window and stared down upon the flux of bodies. They moved below without ceasing, illuminated against the pulsing lights. He no longer saw the individuals of the crowd. The bodies melted into a sheet of beautiful rippling movement. Isaac gazed down into the fluttering membrane in a trancelike state, as if watching a flame dance.

He couldn't have known that this party, while separated by the vast expanse of continents and centuries, emulated the crowds of Mesoamerica before a sacrifice. Cheers rang out like the cities of the Atzec's Tenochtitlán or the Romans' Athens. The deejay was as precise as a holy priest in sacrament with his knife before the lamb.

Playnight was worship.

It demanded a sacrifice.

Sweat dripped off Isaac's forehead in the heat rising to the top floor. Drenched, he walked across the room toward the other set of windows. These windows faced a building over a narrow alleyway.

The heat was too much for him. His knees wobbled and his arms were lead. He needed some air.

He forced his weight onto the face of the window and heard the metal groan. He placed his beer on the ledge, gritted his teeth, and closed his eyes. He leaned into the window harder and he felt it give a bit.

The groan turned sharp and glass shattered. Isaac's stomach flipped forward, and in slow motion, he saw tiny cuts appear along this shoulders, then chest, and heard a ripping along his jeans.

He felt suddenly dizzy but there was a sudden rush of air that cooled him. For a beautiful moment, he felt exuberant. He sensed a liberated thrill he hadn't felt in so long. But when he opened his eyes, the pavement charged toward him.

He reached out his hand and felt it snap along the brick wall rushing beside him. Even though he was hurtling headfirst, he didn't scream. He went slack and yielded to the soft, cool air. There was a quick, hard succession of crunching followed by darkness.

The gods waiting on that hot Chicago night finally received their blood.

74

The familiar itch to migrate stalked Kat down. She wanted to shake free from everything: Jacob's violence, his vengeful wife, Ava's judgement. She wanted to scream, to cry out with as much force as her body could produce on this murky, humid night. All around her, the darkness fragmented with a current of lights. Bodies flashed blue, then red, then black again. She jumped with the crash of the music, her hips, arms, and legs unhinged. She had to keep dancing to keep from slipping into the night. She rolled and swayed in the drunken bevy around her. To keep herself from the dark thoughts of packing her things in her brown suitcase, like she had so many times as an unwanted foster child, she filled her mind with the painfully loud strike of percussion. She had to suppress the nomadic cry, her only true guiding constant, from rearing out of this party and far away.

She stared around her. This was her tribe, her brethren, the intoxicated faces that hung like landmarks over the panorama of Chicago. The woman who freely danced next to Kat was the one with the knock-off designer shoes. She stamped her imitation heels into the floor along with the beat. The horny lovers drowned themselves in lust further down the dance floor. The couple kissed and held one another, a living poem to the craving of flesh and the wanting of love.

The manic spillage of the dance floor held Beck's old friends, the two women gallantly vogue in their beauty, posing more than dancing. Next to them was Marcie, using her stoic boyfriend as a stripper pole, swinging drunkenly off his thick limbs.

Further down the wall was the muscular meathead, his tactics finally successful as he laughed with a paramour, drawing her into his bulky arms. Underneath the exit sign, a small group circled around Shakes, Kat's most gracious drug dealer, passing party favors in a round of illegal commerce.

Kat focused on each and every one them. Maybe she was doing it for the last time. Maybe there was nothing left to do but follow that urge to leave. Nothing left but to abandon everything and everyone. There must've been a certain comfort in anonymity—a certain freedom.

She wanted to put as much distance as possible between herself and her miscarriage, with its haunting thick blood running down her leg, the merciless abdominal pains, and the look of complete relief in Jacob's eyes when she told him. She had to turn away from wanting him only because she had been pregnant for a few weeks. She had to run miles and miles away from her body's inability to produce children—children she never knew she wanted.

She had to run far from the years of moving from house to house as the Puerto Rican girl who never knew her native language, who never knew her parents, who never knew her family.

Family—it seemed as if her own body denied even the possibility of having one.

Kat, now resolved, danced to the music. Her head upturned into the pulsing blue-then-red light.

Leslie would be fine. He had Beck whether he wanted him or not.

And Russell. She loved him despite herself and even he had left.

She would go tonight after this one last party.

She would unearth the brown suitcase from her past, tucked under her bed, and carry it into her future. She would leave all of this behind.

Kat turned her eyes back to the crowd and a figure tumbled forward. The light burst on the figure, and in blood red, then vibrant blue, Russell began moving toward her. Their gazes locked.

Kat's arms dropped to her sides and her joints locked.

The air blazed with a heat that she hadn't noticed until that moment. Her bottom eyelid tickled with tears as the muscles constricted like a fist in her stomach.

Out of the spotlight, Russell was now a black figure treading forward through the mass. Had she really seen him? Had he been looking back at her in the way that she always wanted him to? Was he there for her?

The light flickered again, and it was still him standing a few yards away, weaving through bodies to get to her.

The strobe moved away, and it was darkness again.

Kat was now holding her breath. She couldn't breathe. She couldn't think.

The strobe rotated from above one more time. In the light, Russell was now in front of her. He was panting as if he was breathing not just for her, but for both of them. The music suddenly shifted into new song, and the bass thundered around them. The crowd's energy crested, the dancing more crazed than ever. They stood before each other, inanimate.

"Kat!" Russell cried over the music. "I love you, too."

The bass exploded once more. It shook the earth. The strobe light blinked away. The ground underneath Kat seemed as if it would give way in the darkness. She felt as if she could fall. She felt like she could plunge beneath Chicago and into the earth.

Kat leapt through the darkness and grasped Russell's wide shoulders as hard as she could.

When the reds and blues of the light found her again, he was holding her back, enclosing her in his arms.

75

News of Isaac's death was whispered, gossiped, and slopped

about like a dirty mop. Beck first heard about it while stocking glasses at the bar. His stomach looped and wound itself in knots. When he asked about the facts, he heard incomplete fragments, pieces that couldn't be assembled. He heard the buzzing between women at the end of the bar. One of them, relishing the titillation, claimed Isaac jumped out of the window overcome with a suicidal urge. The other heard it was an overdose. *Did you know he just left rehab?* The other stared back in feigned shock.

Between the smacking of liquor bottles and bubbling of lukewarm water, Beck heard bits and pieces of antidotes, each more fantastic than the last. The only constant in each tale, whispered fervently as if the story was delicious to tell, was that Isaac died of his own doing. The other reoccurring message was that last night would be the final Playnight. The police were looking into the circumstance of Isaac's death and who could be held responsible for the party.

Beck's thoughts bloated with the image of Isaac, standing at the door of his old apartment with an animal hunger in his eyes for crushed pills. Beck scrubbed the bar, pressing harder as if to wipe Isaac from his mind.

Poor Leslie. Always pursued by death. Had he heard yet? Beck hoped the buzz had passed over him, as one would take care to step over a pothole. But that hope was crushed under the realization that if he didn't know, Beck would have to tell him.

The night ended and Beck ached. He shuffled into the apartment and wanted nothing more than to collapse on that lumpy couch, which was better that his air mattress, the lone piece of furniture in Russell's old room. But he stopped at the sight of Leslie stacking luggage.

They stared at each other, and Leslie knew Beck could

read everything on his face, all the sadness billowing around him. The darkness in Leslie's wet eyes, the downturn of his shoulders, the turn of his feet, confessed he had known about the death.

"Where are you going?"

"Home."

Beck walked up to him, as close as when they'd first kissed. Leslie was all Beck could see with the pain so heavy in his eyes. Leslie circled his arms around Beck and wept hard. He shook and strained as Beck held him in return. The pain impaled his tired feet, but he would stand there as long as it took.

He would always stand or hope or wait for Leslie.

As long as it took.

"Will you be back?"

Leslie pulled away and tried to smile. But it seemed as though his wet face was incapable.

"And leave you to cut your own hair?"

The two men gathered the luggage through the apartment and onto the stoop. They waited in silence, surrounded by the night song of Wicker Park, watching the trickle of traffic, the strolling of a couple, and the ever-present rumble of the nearby train.

Beck's hands hung at his sides and his knuckles brushed Leslie's. Leslie turned and stared at Beck. His eyes squinted and roamed Beck's face. Then his face warmed as if he found what he wanted to see.

Affirmed, Leslie slipped his hand off the handle of his luggage and into Beck's grasp.

Soon, a cab diverted from the flow of traffic and to the curb before them. In reverence, they didn't break the silence as Leslie and his luggage were loaded into the cab. They held each other's gaze until the cab turn out of sight, swallow up by the city's quiet ballad.

Beck backstepped onto the stoop and closed his eyes. There, in the absence of the world around him, a soft breeze ran along his neck and he was aware of something that his coked out clairvoyance could have never foreseen.

As he headed into the apartment, he absorbed solitude, an aloneness he'd been afraid of for so long. Fear of it had forced him into the highs of coke, the lows of painkillers, and between the thighs and lips of strangers. Living, maybe even loving, in this apartment, left him broke, tired, dried, and blistered, and isolation was inescapable. He had done everything to elude it, parading himself around empty people and exhausting all of his money. He truly had nothing and no one. But here, with the lumpy couch and ghastly secondhand furniture, he found all the things he hoped to keep.

This aloneness, which had before been so treacherous, clung to him like the warmth of the night and the touch of a friend.

76

The flight from Chicago to Detroit was one hour and fifteen minutes. Leslie put the expensive, last-minute ticket on a credit card he hadn't used since college. Going home was an impulsive, kneejerk, tickled-nosed-then-sneezing reaction to Isaac. He'd read about his death on Facebook early that morning as he curled around his MacBook in bed.

The notice caused Leslie to snap awake. Cold shot up his back and his vision went grainy. His head was flooded with blood and he could only make out every other word on the screen.

Something about too many painkillers, dead on impact, body found the next day, a funeral next week, the body in limbo until relatives could bring it back to Florida, offers of condolences.

Leslie leaned over his bed for a long time, watching grey morning light rise along the wall to reveal his feet. He stared past his toes and into darker thoughts. Thoughts of Isaac folded over himself from impact, lying in the ungodly heat, stewing on the dirty pavement. His image cataloged itself next to the crushed car Leslie's mother was killed in.

Had he been the last person to see him alive? The last image Leslie remembered was a snarling man in the shadows, grasping onto his high.

Getting off the plane, he walked along the crowded glass vestibules toward the competing car rental counters. He passed each one, repelled by the eager cheeriness of sales agents. He found a docile, sallow, middle-aged woman who looked how he felt and trusted her with his credit card. In return, she gave him a humdrum sedan.

The drive from Detroit to Novi was a half-hour journey along I-275 N. Leslie had taken this route so often over the course of his life. Wide stretches of unkempt field spanned out familiarly along the highway for miles on each side, yielding only to sporadic walls of trees. The trees themselves were swallowed up by rambling suburban developments with streets named Honeycomb and Lovers Lane. Leslie drove the car along strip malls, fast food chains, department stores, and supercenters. He was back home, immersed in all that had threatened to stifle him.

He thought it odd that Isaac's death would lead him back here. Maybe it should have been his mother. Maybe he had been too afraid.

The streets he traveled, the stoplights he halted for were saturated with whom he and his family had been. Soon he was on the street of his childhood home, transformed into his skinny nineteen-year-old former self. He removed his foot from the gas and took part of the warm spring day to roll past the beautiful, modest homes. The homes likely found in every well-to-do suburb, below the cloudless blue sky, stood like proud constructs of the working middle class. Green yards appeared kept, dogs barked in the distance, and a lawnmower groaned to life.

Leslie pulled into the driveway of a sandy brown two-story home with brick trimming. A series of steps led to a big bay window next to a door with a stained-glass face. The yard was framed with a white picket fence and held a wide oak tree. Its branches spread a shadow along the recently cut grass, and behind the house sat a crystal blue in-ground pool.

Leslie remembered how proud his parents were of this home. How particular they were about maintaining it as the first black family on the block. His home had all seemed so far away from Leslie and now here it all was. All the memories falling down on him. He hadn't seen this place since he came out. He had been separated by his sexuality and again by his mother's death. He thought he would never come here. But with death visiting him again, there was no other place to be.

He sat for a long while as the heat increased, magnified by the windows of the car. He thought no one was home until movement behind the sheer curtains told him otherwise. Sharp fear jolted within his chest. He opened the car door. He walked along the drive and took the pathway to the door, a pathway he had watched his father cement when Leslie was eleven.

Fear dwindled. His anxiety was snarled by the tree above him and chased off into the distance by the barking dog.

He was home with all the memories, smells, and sensations crashing upon him. His steps became ordered and determined.

He rang the doorbell, and soon a silhouette rippled behind the patterns of stained glass.

The door opened and blinking back at him was a face like his own, just a bit older and puffy with age. Eyes as dark as his own spilt over with such sadness. A jaw rounded, like Leslie's, set tight with tension. Both men were motionless in the standoff. Oceans of unspoken sentiment separated them like nations, and Leslie was certain his father would turn him away. He had braced for it, worked out the harsh words his father would say.

Before the plane, when Beck had held his hand, he had mustered all of his strength. He tapped the well of Beck's beauty and lived in the kisses and embraces they were certain to share on his return.

If his father was going to curse him again, if he was going to deny him grief this time around, it would have to be to his face.

His father slowly reached out and placed a hand on Leslie's shoulder.

Leslie was overcome by this small act of comfort and sucked back hard on his teeth to keep from crumbling to the ground. In his father's face, he saw the same expression, and both men fought off the tears. Leslie's father led him into the house and shut the door behind them.

77

Nearly a month had passed since Isaac's death, which forced them all to examine their lives.

Russell stepped back from the easel and tilted his head. Chills ran in jagged bolts along his skin as he turned to Kat. She laid on the mattress and box spring in the corner of the small studio apartment. She looked at the canvas and narrowed her eyes with skepticism.

"Are you sure?" she asked.

"Yeah," he said.

He went to the small window and let in the balmy air of the summer night. His new place was an efficiency unit. Adjacent to the bed was a small set of counters that held a sink and tiny stovetop. A foot of yellowed linoleum extended from the base of the counter. One wall held his collectable *Star Wars* poster and in the small bathroom, with only a standing shower and toilet, hung his raggedy Chicago Bulls shower curtain. Beck, Leslie, and Kat had helped him move in a week ago. The entire time they joked at how small his place was and Beck mentioned how much he enjoyed Russell's old room. Kat laughed and asked if that was the case, why did he always end up in Leslie's room?

Before they left Russell in his small rental space, Kat presented him with her record player. When they left, he sat the record player next to his easel.

Atop the easel was a wide canvas covered in rich blue oil paints. Russell had spent two weeks working out the sketches for it in an open journal.

Russell returned the ring he never gave Ava to the store. It was surreal to see the illuminated ring from his pocket back behind glass. He used the money to secure his new apartment for a few months and was thinking about picking up a few shifts at Stratosphere, since they could always use more help. That and managing Curtis Newman's art gallery should bring some additional income. He'd have to be frugal for a while. He wouldn't be able to take as many cabs and might finally sell his car, if he could get anything for it.

Now his hands and forearms were marred with dried strips of blue paint, the hue deep in his nailbeds. He turned on the record player and joined Kat on the mattress. He kissed her softly, raking his blue hands through her hair.

She pulled back from him and peered at the canvas again. "It's beautiful."

He kissed her again, tugging at her shirt while she unbuttoned his jeans. They parted, feverishly plucking off their garments. Russell's senses sharpened, and the sight of Kat's tan smooth skin was vivid in his mind. He felt virginal every time he mounted her. What existed between them was profound, carnal, deep reaching. When he was inside her, she caught her breath. He, in the truest adoration he had for anything in his life, looked deeply into her eyes.

Outside his window and into the world, the train clamored overhead. The last light of the sun had receded west, and the breeze kicked up trash in the alleys and in front of the bodegas and their buzzing neon lights. The night elongated across streets and crumbled concrete below the rusted undercarriage of the train tracks. Shadows stretched along opening bars and closing boutiques. The flood of traffic increased its flow, adding cries, honks, and shuddering subwoofers to the rising voices on the streets. Feet carried bodies from the darkest corners of the streets to even darker bars and clubs. Those fellow denizens took the night, stamping out cigarettes and lighting joints. The night was only beginning, ready to be claimed.

Russell heard none of this as the needle scratched along vinyl. There was only Kat's warm breath exhaling in his ear.

SB GAMBLE is an author, playwright, and a semi-retired party boy. He has been telling and writing stories for as long as he can remember. He has written several plays and short stories. His plays have been performed on the stage and over local radio in his hometown of Kalamazoo, Michigan. Over his career he won awards as a playwright with NAACP's ACT-SO competition and Kalamazoo's Black Arts and Cultural Center.

He currently lives and works in Chicago. He is driven to write works that underline his wild belief that people are all equal and have more commonalities than differences.

The Last Party is his first novel.

FROM THE AUTHOR

The Last Party is a work of fiction but I'd be lying if I said it wasn't based off a couple of wild nights I had in Chicago. I'll let you guess which parts were inspired and which parts I made up.

Thank you for reading my novel, I hoped you enjoyed it.

To find out about my upcoming projects, sign up for my newsletter at www.sbgamble.com.